HOLLY, IVY, AND ME

By

Monica Burns
Charlotte Featherstone

Erotic Historical Romance

New Concepts　　　　　　　　　　　Georgia

Be sure to check out our website for the very best in fiction at fantastic prices!

When you visit our webpage, you can:
* Read excerpts of currently available books
* View cover art of upcoming books and current releases
* Find out more about the talented artists who capture the magic of the writer's imagination on the covers
* Order books from our backlist
* Find out the latest NCP and author news--including any upcoming book signings by your favorite NCP author
* Read author bios and reviews of our books
* Get NCP submission guidelines
* And so much more!

We offer a 20% discount on all new Trade Paperback releases ordered from our website!

Be sure to visit our webpage to find the best deals in e-books and paperbacks! To find out about our new releases as soon as they are available, please be sure to sign up for our newsletter (http://www.newconceptspublishing.com/newsletter.htm) or join our reader group (http://groups.yahoo.com/group/new_concepts_pub/join)!

The newsletter is available by double opt in only and our customer information is *never* shared!

Visit our webpage at:
www.newconceptspublishing.com

Holly, Ivy, and Me is an original publication of NCP. This work has never before appeared in book form. This work is a novel. Any similarity to actual persons or events is purely coincidental.

New Concepts Publishing, Inc.
5202 Humphreys Rd.
Lake Park, GA 31636

ISBN 1-58608-886-6
© 2006 Monica Burns & Charlotte Featherstone
Cover art (c) copyright 2006 Eliza Black

All rights reserved, which includes the right to reproduce this book or portions thereof in any form whatsoever except as provided by the U.S. Copyright Law.

If you purchased this book without a cover you should be aware this book is stolen property.

NCP books are available at special quantity discounts for bulk purchases for sales promotions, premiums, fund raising, or educational use. For details, write, email, or phone New Concepts Publishing, Inc., 5202 Humphreys Rd., Lake Park, GA 31636; Ph. 229-257-0367, Fax 229-219-1097; orders@newconceptspublishing.com.

First NCP Trade Paperback Printing: November 2006

Beneath the Mistletoe

Charlotte Featherstone

Chapter One

Harrow Lodge
1797, Christmas Eve

"A..An ... Andrew," Holly stuttered nervously, "whatever are you about?"

"What do you think I'm about?" he drawled, sending her stomach clenching.

"I ... I have no idea." And it was the truth. Whatever had come over Andrew this evening? She'd never seen him quite this way--a constant presence by her side. The sensual aura radiating from him was a side of him she had never been privileged enough to witness--despite years of yearning.

"Come now, Holly," he whispered, taking another predatory step closer to her. "You must know what I want."

She gulped, and took a step back, coming up against the hard, unyielding wood that framed the door. "I'm afraid I don't know," she whispered breathlessly.

She had known Andrew for most of her nineteen years. They'd practically grown up together. His guardian, Lady Mary Montague, was her mother's best friend. Her mother and Lady Mary were inseparable and she and Andrew had become fast friends, entertaining each other while their mothers visited one another. But while they had been very close friends, Andrew had never looked at her with anything more than platonic interest. And how could he, she thought, as her trembling fingers gripped the door jam. She was an unremarkable creature, plain and forgettable. Andrew on the other hand was a living God. No man was more beautiful than Andrew Nightingale. He might not have the noble birth that other gentlemen of the ton could boast, but Andrew had other qualities that made him irresistible.

Oh, there was a part of her, a wistful romantic part, that had harboured dreams of him returning her affection. Even now, as he stood before her, trapping her against the door of the pantry, a part of her hoped that he had done so in order to kiss her. To steal an exciting embrace that would keep her warm the night through.

But that was utterly impossible, for she was Lady Holly Harrington, a lady of breeding and little beauty, and he was Andrew Nightingale, the orphaned child of artist parents--the handsome rake that could and *did* have every eligible and *ineligible* woman clamouring after him.

There was no denying that Andrew had the uncanny ability to charm and entice any woman who possessed a fraction of warm blood, despite his young age of two and twenty. And she was certainly no exception.

He took another step closer and her heart paused in her chest. Only when he stood directly before her did it begin to beat again--a fast, frenzied pace that made her feel lightheaded and dizzy.

His moss green eyes roved lazily along her face. How many times had she looked into those dark green eyes fringed with impossibly thick chestnut brown lashes? How familiar they should be to her. But they were not. There was something in his eyes she had never seen before.

He reached up, and her breathing stilled. His finger brushed her temple before reaching higher. He plucked a creamy white bud from the sprig of mistletoe that hung in the center of the doorway. Her eyes followed his hand and she watched as the sprig swayed on its green velvet ribbon. Carelessly he tossed the pod to the ground. He turned his gaze to hers, then lowered his mouth to her forehead, kissing her softly, reverently.

Then he plucked another bud from the sprig and moved his lips till they rested at her temple. Flicking the seed from his fingers, he kissed her, his lips brushing her skin and hair.

He reached for another, then moved his mouth down to her cheek, kissing her. Another seed was freed and his lips descended to her jaw. Her heart was racing wildly. She felt the pulsation in her throat, felt the tightening of her bodice against her breasts. Her breathing was coming in short, sharp pants, and she could not hide it--she could not hide her response to him.

His gaze travelled lower, to the vein she was certain was throbbing beneath her skin. She knew it was when he reached out to put his fingertip to her neck. He tilted his head, studying his finger as it slowly trailed the bounding vein. He pressed forward and inhaled once, softly, almost imperceptibly, then again, deeper. He moved his head so that his face was pressed against her, so that his lips only grazed her heated flesh. She whimpered and went rigid when he exhaled against her, sending hot breath whispering across her throat. Oh, God, what was he doing to her? Why was he doing this--inflaming her, making her yearn, making her want?

He reached up between them, his face still pressed against her and plucked another pod from the sprig. And then he pressed his lips to the quivering pulse that leapt with his touch. A deep sound resonated in his chest.

His eyes found hers and he reached for the sprig, crushing it in his hand so that all the berries pulled away from the stem and rolled off his hand. "This was the only sprig of mistletoe in the house that had enough berries left to allow me to do everything I want to do to you."

She whimpered and arched her neck, feeling his hands--both hands--stroke either side of her neck. Slowly his hands descended her throat and back up again, his thumbs brushing her wildly beating pulse.

She closed her eyes and tilted her head further back, her lips parting just enough to allow the barest movement of air between them. He groaned and she felt his finger trace her mouth.

"Innocent, perfect lips," he whispered.

Her body was now drawn tight and his words made her lower parts clench, then loosen, emitting a thick wetness on to her thighs. This was arousal. This was consuming need--mind, body, spirit.

"Such perfection," he whispered darkly, stroking his thumb along her lip.

Her eyes slid to his, and she was shocked by his expression. Never had she seen him look at her in such a fashion. There was something dark, almost disturbing in his eyes.

She licked her dry lips, preparing to speak, but his eyes darkened even more as he watched her tongue glide along her bottom lip.

She saw the slow descent of his mouth to hers, saw his lips part, yet the shock of Andrew's mouth against hers made her stiffen. It was wonderful, intimate, and more than a little strange. She had prepared herself for a physical assault, but was pleasingly surprised by his gentle kiss. It was slow, thoughtful, almost as if he were savoring her. One hand left her face and slid along her body until he could thread his long fingers tightly with hers while his other hand stroked the side of her face, down to her chin. His lips pressed once more against hers, then he angled his head and kissed over and over again with his hot open mouth.

What was she to do? She'd never been kissed before. She couldn't think, her mind was a whirlwind of thoughts and emotions, as if she were drugged, disembodied. She was conscious of the moan that escaped her when he slanted his mouth against hers, encouraging her to open for him.

"Your tongue," he said against her lips. "I want to feel it."

She gasped at the same moment she felt his tongue slide along her lower lip. "I don't know how," she admitted, ashamed by her inexperience.

"Let me in. Let me taste you. Let me teach you." He parted her lips and slid his tongue deep into her mouth.

It was strange at first. Holly had to fight the urge to straighten away from the intrusion. But after the immediate shock dissipated, she was left with the feel and taste of him as his tongue boldly swirled inside her, mingling with hers.

He groaned and his hand left her face and cupped her breast. Hungrily he kissed her, his mouth slanting over hers, faster and faster. His tongue drove into her, and she could do nothing but reach for him and wrap her arms around his neck and hold on as he swept her away.

He broke off the kiss and searched her face, then slowly he slid his gaze up to the naked stem of the mistletoe. He pulled it from its spot, the green ribbon dangling from his fingers. He brought the velvet to her mouth and brushed it against her lips.

"Kiss it," he whispered, watching her as she pressed a chaste kiss to the ribbon. He brought it his mouth and peered down into her eyes.

" I couldn't stand to let you go before you had been properly kissed. I couldn't bear to think that anyone had tasted this beautiful mouth before I."

"Andrew, I don't understand--"

"I know," he said, brushing his thumb along her lips. "I know you don't, Holly, but I hope in time you will. Now then, no more words. There is nothing to say. Walk away from me, Holly, and do not look back. Walk away and let me watch you." She started to protest but he placed his finger on her lips. "Ssh," he whispered. "Walk away."

Sliding past him, she took two steps and then stopped. Turning around she saw that he was watching her, the ribbon hanging between his fingers as he brushed the velvet with his thumb.

"Walk away," he murmured.

She did, and when she awoke the next morning--Christmas morning--she discovered that Andrew had done the same. He had walked away. Walked away from her, the Montagues, and England.

Chapter Two

December 23, 1805
Harrow Lodge, Kent, England

"He's come home!" Lady Montague shouted in the foyer.

"Who has come home?"

Holly heard the commotion in the hall. Tossing her needlepoint aside, she rose from the settee and crossed the salon in order to see what the fuss was about.

"Oh, Lucinda," Lady Mary cried, reaching for her mother's hands and grasping them to her chest. "*He* has come home."

Holly felt her lungs burn. She was holding her breath, waiting to hear Lady Mary's words.

"No! After all this time?" her mother gasped, reaching for Lady Mary and hugging her tightly in her arms. "Your fondest wish, Mary. At last. What a wonderful present."

Mary nodded and sniffled into her handkerchief. "My darling boy." She wept elegantly. "I do love him as if he were my own, Lucinda."

Holly felt her heart plummet to her knees. Andrew had come home.

"When will he arrive?" her mother asked, ushering Mary further into the hall.

"Oh, he's already home," Mary said softly as she allowed her mother to steer her to their favorite sitting room. "He returned last night."

"Lovely," her mother said. "You must bring him tonight, Mary. I know everyone will be positively delighted to see him again."

"I shall," Mary replied, then the remainder of her words were muffled by the door closing behind them.

Finally exhaling, Holly let her body go limp against the wall. After eight years of traipsing through India, Andrew was finally home. Eight years, she thought angrily, curling her hands into fists. Eight years without so much as a word from him--without so much as an explanation. Eight years of leaving her wondering *why*.

"Did you hear?" Lizzie cried, rushing into the room panting heavily.

Holly glared at her younger sister. "I did."

"Well?" Lizzie asked. "Aren't you over the moon? He's back, Holly. Lady Montague says he's a rich nabob, as rich as Croesus she says. He's determined to purchase a house here in England and enter into politics."

"How very nice for him," she snapped, folding her arms beneath her breasts and breezing out of the salon. She was headed for the stairs and her chamber when she heard Lizzie's breathless pants behind her.

"Whatever is the matter?" Lizzie asked, falling in step beside her. "I thought you were hopelessly in love with Andrew."

"Was," she huffed, lifting her skirts as she climbed the steps.

"He's coming tonight--here, to Mama and Papa's card party."

"Be sure to keep him entertained, Lizzie. We wouldn't want him running back off to India now, would we?"

"You're in a foul mood," Lizzie proclaimed as she followed her into her chamber and flopped down on the bed. "I thought you would be happy to know that the man you have lusted after for years is back and is intent on settling down. I overheard Lady Mary say that she believed he was entertaining the notion of marriage. He asked about you, you know," Lizzie murmured. "I heard Lady Mary tell Mama."

Her already madly beating heart sped up another notch, but she smothered the flowering thoughts that began to take root in her mind. So, he had kissed her eight years ago--it meant nothing to him. If it had, he would not have bounded off to the ends of the world without so much as a word to her. If the kiss had meant anything to him, he would have written her a blasted letter. But he had not, and she could not forgive him that. She could not forgive him for his thoughtlessness.

How she hated to see Lady Mary arrive with her correspondence. How she despised feeling her heart still in her breast, wondering if this would be the time that Lady Mary would hand her a letter from him and say, 'for you, dear.' But that hadn't happened. Lady Mary had only ever looked up at her, her brown eyes assessing her through her lorgnette. "Andrew says to convey his heartfelt wishes that this letter finds you and your family in good health, dear."

Her and her family, lumped in all together as if they had been nothing but acquaintances. They had been much more than that, even before the kiss. At least she thought they had.

"What are you going to wear this evening?" Lizzie asked, propping her chin in her hands.

"I suddenly feel unwell," she muttered, laying down on the cushion of her window seat. "A sudden headache."

"Headache," her sister asked, "or heartache?"

Holly glared at her before closing her eyes. "Headache, brat."

"I am twenty now, Holly," Lizzie said quietly. "I'm quite grown up. You can talk to me you know. We're sisters. We talk about everything. But not--"

"Andrew Nightingale is not up for discussion, Lizzie."

"I saw you, you know," Lizzie whispered in a tone that made Holly's eyes fly open. "I was in the pantry stealing a piece of plum cake. I saw everything."

"Whatever are you talking about?" she asked, making a great show of arranging her skirts.

"Christmas Eve. The night before he left for India. I saw the two of you."

"Nonsense--"

"He plucked each berry from the mistletoe with every kiss. And then he squeezed the berries and kissed you like I'd never seen before."

Holly nearly flew off the seat. "Impossible!"

"No," Lizzie said with a smile. " I still remember it--*vividly*. I was twelve and thought the whole thing the most passionate, romantic moment I'd ever seen--*will ever see*."

"It was nothing--"

"You see," Lizzie whispered before rising from the bed. "That is where you are wrong. You've always thought it nothing. You've made it something of little consequence, when in fact it was something so magical, so magnificent."

"Lizzie--"

"You didn't see his face, Holly. You didn't see how he looked at you while he kissed you, watching you, watching everything. You didn't see the way he looked at you when you walked away."

"You're letting your overly romantic nature run wild. You're dramatizing a simple little kiss and making it more grand than it was."

Lizzie reached for the latch of the door and opened it. "You didn't see him raise that ribbon to his mouth and brush the spot you'd kissed against his lip. You didn't see the tear that fell from his eye. You didn't see the way he stood staring up at your bedroom window that morning before he left. But I saw it, Holly. I saw it and have never forgotten it."

"Why are you telling me this?" Holly demanded. "Why make me suffer further?"

"If you're suffering it's at your own hands," Lizzie whispered. "It's always been there for you to see, but your pride has gotten in the way. I hope your pride won't keep you away tonight."

"I won't be there," she said bitterly, turning from her sister and staring unseeing out the window. "I am not the person I once was."

"Maybe he'll like this Holly."

"He won't," Holly said in a pained whisper. How could he?

"You'll never know if you don't make an appearance. And besides, he'll be present for Christmas Eve. Mama and Lady Mary always spend Christmas together."

"Perhaps Lady Mary and Lord Montague will wish to entertain Andrew in their own home this year," she said to her sister as she fixed her gaze on the iced branches that waved outside her window.

"Fat chance," Lizzie snorted. "He'll be here. I daresay that you better get used to having him around, for he is intent on staying."

"And finding a wife," she said bitterly. She hadn't a prayer in hell of attracting him in such a way. If she hadn't been successful eight years ago, she most certainly would not be now. She was a spinster and more plump than she had ever been before. No, she was not the sort to attract the rakish attentions of Andrew Nightingale.

"Holly?" Lizzie asked.

"Hmm," she said, looking over her shoulder at her sister. Lizzie had a strange smile on her face that made Holly extremely uneasy. "What are you plotting?"

"Nothing. It's just that I was going to suggest you wear the ruby silk tonight. It's the gown I'd choose if I wanted to make Andrew pay for leaving me all those years ago."

The door closed softly behind Lizzie and Holly could not help but grin. How silly her little sister was. Didn't Lizzie know that she hadn't the ability to make Andrew speechless?

Her gaze drifted to the wardrobe and the deep red silk gown that hung from the hanger. It was daringly low cut. The modiste in London had raved that it was the latest style. Holly had doubted the infamous Madame Lamont and her reputed genius from the minute the lady had suggested she wear such a color. And when Madame had suggested that she flaunt her curves and forgo the traditional square bodice for that of a 'V', Holly had been certain that the lady had bats in her belfry.

But, she mused, walking over to the wardrobe and running an appreciative finger along the expensive silk, the color was stunning and vibrant. It would look magnificent shimmering in the soft candlelight.

"Jane," she called, hearing her lady's maid in the hall outside her room.

"Yes, my lady?" Jane answered as she peered around the door. "You called?"

"Yes," Holly whispered, turning to look at her maid. "I'm ready to start preparing for tonight's party."

"Now?" Jane frowned, "but it's six hours away, Ma'am."

"Enough time do you think to make me into a beauty?"

Jane's eyes widened and began to dance with merriment. How Jane lived for these moments--the crowning achievement of turning a sow's ear into a silk purse.

"You'll be a fairy princess tonight, my lady," Jane cried, rushing in. "I'll see to it. Now first, you must get yourself into the bath. And you must have cream in your water to make your skin even more supple than usual."

Holly smiled, watching as Jane fussed about the room. She'd show him, Holly thought to herself. With Jane's help she'd show Andrew Nightingale what he had left behind when he went scampering off to India and left her without a second thought.

"The red silk," Jane said, suddenly stopping to turn and look at her. "Have you finally decided to wear it?"

"I have," Holly murmured, gazing once more at the gown.

"Oh, Ma'am," Jane whispered, her eyes widening once more. "You'll be the talk of the party in that gown."

"I do hope so, Jane," she whispered as Jane came around and unfastened the tapes of her gown. "I do hope so."

Chapter Three

"Well, my lady, what do you think?"

She was tense, anxious. It had felt like hours waiting to see what Jane had created. Now was the time, and Holly half feared what would greet her in the looking glass.

Inhaling deeply, she lifted her gaze from her folded hands and glanced up in the mirror. A small gasp further exposed a décolletage that was already spilling from her deep bodice.

"A beauty, you are," Jane said triumphantly. "Of course, you always were, but it's been some time since you've allowed me to fuss over you."

"Amazing," Holly muttered, moving her head from side to side and assessing the elaborate hairstyle. "However did you manage to weave the holly through my hair without getting pricked?"

"You like it?" Jane gushed. "I thought it would look magnificent with your blonde curls."

"I adore it," Holly said with a smile as she captured the maid's gaze in the looking glass. "Thank you, Jane."

"It was nothing," she said proudly, fussing with a tendril that had slipped loose from a pin. "Like I said, you're a beauty."

"No, I'm not," Holly whispered. "But it is very kind of you to say so."

"Holly dear--" her mother called as she breezed through the door and stopped dead in her tracks. *"My Heavens!"*

Holly smiled and caught Jane's wink in the mirror. "Good evening, Mama."

"Holly? Is that you?" her mother said, striding slowly across the room. "Why, I've never seen you looking so ... so...."

"Pretty?" Holly supplied, hoping it was the word her mother was valiantly searching for.

"Pretty?" her mother scoffed. "You always look pretty. You're a very lovely girl, my dear. But tonight--tonight you are positively glowing."

"Thank you, mama," she said, feeling a flush creep across her cheeks.

"Jane informed me that you had chosen the red silk for tonight," her mother said, handing her a black velvet box. "I thought you might want to wear these."

Reaching for the box, Holly flicked it open. "Grandmama's necklace," she gasped. "I've *always* coveted this."

"I know, dear," her mother said, reaching for the diamond and ruby necklace and placing it around Holly's neck. "And it shall be all yours for tonight."

Holly studied how the diamonds shone, brilliant and glistening in the firelight. So many diamonds, she mused, like a string of crystals hanging from a chandelier. Rubies were interspersed between the diamonds. At the end of the necklace, nestled in her décolletage, rested a perfect egg shaped ruby of the deepest darkest crimson--blood red, Holly thought, skimming her finger along the gem.

"Lovely," her mother said wistfully. "How your grandmother would have loved to see you in it."

"I miss her," Holly said sadly. "It's the first Christmas without her."

"She's here, dearest," her mother said softly, before kissing her cheek. "She's here, and she's thoroughly pleased to see you wearing her beautiful necklace and that scandalous gown."

"It is scandalous, isn't it?" Holly said, wincing as she scanned her image in the looking glass once again. "I tried to tell Jane that the bodice was too low, but she insisted that it was just perfect."

"Oh, it is," her mother said, laughing lightly. "It is perfect for your needs tonight."

"What do you mean by that?" Holly called after her mother and Jane as they trailed out of the room.

"Never mind, dear," her mother replied, reaching for the door. "And Holly," she said, grinning mischievously, "please make your appearance downstairs at half past eight. I think that should be plenty of time."

"Mother...." she said, a deep warning in the word.

"It will be fine," her mother murmured. "Trust me."

The door closed and Holly glared at the panelled wood. What the devil was her mother up to? Something was definitely askew. Her mother's eyes were far too alight with mischief for there not to be something going on.

Holly looked back at the looking glass and studied her

reflection. Jane had not put any rouge or paint on her lips, nor kohl on her eyes. Holly glanced at the tin of red face paint that sat atop her dressing table. A bit of color, that is what she needed. And something to bring out her eyes and to darken her lashes.

You're an ethereal beauty, dearest. Don't mar it with lotions and paint.

Her fingers stilled on the silver tin. Her eyes flashed to the mirror, expecting to see her mother standing in the doorway. But the door was closed and no one was behind her. And yet she heard a voice, so hauntingly familiar, so much like her beloved grandmama's ... but that could not be. Grandmama was no longer living. She was not here with her.

Wetting her lips she reached for the tin and dabbed her finger into the paint. Just a bit. Just enough to give her a pink glow. Just enough to make her pretty.

"Don't!" Her hand stilled in midair--frozen as her index finger rested a hairbreadth from her top lip. *"You're lovely as you are, Holly. Don't ruin it by making yourself into something you're not."*

"Grandmamma?" she whispered, glancing over her shoulder. There was no one there, yet she heard her voice--so clear in the room with her.

"Yes, Holly," the voice said again and then Holly watched as the figure of her grandmother took shape beside the bed. *"Come to me, dearest, and let see you,"* she urged, motioning her over with a wave of her hands. *"Do not be frightened,"* she commanded when Holly shrank back in her chair. *"Come and let me see you in that stunning gown."*

"This cannot be." Holly said, slowly rising from the chair. "I know that the second I reach for you my hand shall run through you like sunbeams cutting through the fog. You are not real," she murmured, walking toward the vision. "But I so want you to be real."

"I am real, Holly, and I shall be around for as long as you need me to help you through this."

"Through what?" Holly asked standing before the apparition of her grandmother. She looked real enough, Holly could even see the dancing sparkle in her grandmother's blue eyes.

"Look at you," her grandmother said, clapping her hands. *"I daresay you fill that gown extremely well."*

Holly spread her skirts and looked down at her figure.

"Probably too well."

"A woman can never fill out a gown too much for a hot blooded man."

"Things have changed, Grandmother. The fashion in your day was for voluptuous figures. The fashion today is for willowy goddesses."

"Nonsense!" her grandmother scoffed. *"There are very few men out there that do not appreciate a woman who possesses a curvaceous figure."*

Holly dropped her skirts and looked sadly at the floor. "I'm afraid you're living in the past."

"Rubbish!" she said superciliously.

"Why have you come to me?" Holly asked. "How is it I can see you and talk to you and you are...." she swallowed hard, "you are no longer with us."

"Dearest," her grandmother said, smiling wistfully as she reached out and touched Holly's cheek. *"I came because you need me. I came because, like you, I once felt the same way-- unworthy and unremarkable*

"You were always beautiful and strong," Holly said, her voice cracking with wistful memories of her grandmother. "You were so always so confident."

"Not always, dearest. There was a time I stood in this very room and looked in a mirror very much like the one you just did, and saw the same thing as you. There was a time I was just as afraid to reach out and capture what I wanted."

"I am afraid," Holly whispered, her lips trembling. "I'm afraid to see him again. Afraid that I shall want him and that he will turn from me like the last time. I don't want to wear my heart on my sleeve. I don't want him thinking that I've spent the last eight years pining after him."

"And you won't dearest. Together we shall see to that. Now," she said, ushering her to the door, *"you will go downstairs and make the greatest entrance of your life. You will smile and act confident, and you will allow yourself to feel beautiful and womanly in that gown, and I guarantee you that your young man will be chomping at the bit to get at you. And if you have need of me, dearest, stroke the ruby on the necklace and I shall appear. Only you will be able to see me. It will be our secret."*

Holly dug in her heels of red satin slippers. "I do believe I should rest. I think the stress of the day has finally caught up with me. In fact I'm certain I'm much too distressed--heavens, just listen to me, I'm talking to a ghost--I'm seeing ghosts. Yes, definitely, I should lie down."

"Nonsense, it's nerves and anticipation. You're going to see the man you love, and after a long absence. Of course you feel like casting up your accounts--but you shall not. You will not do anything but make a grand entrance, and thus hold the entire room enthralled."

"Entire room?" Holly murmured, swallowing hard, feeling as though her light lunch was going to come up any second.

"The entire room," her grandmother reiterated. *"But most importantly, dearest, there will be one person who won't be able to take his eyes from you."*

"Who?" Holly asked as she felt her grandmother's fingers pressing at the small of her back.

"Why, Andrew Nightingale, dearest," her grandmother chuckled. *"After all, he is the man you've planned to ensnare, is he not? And ensnared he will be, Holly. Be prepared, dearest. Nothing is more demanding than a man who wants what he can't get. And he can't get you, can he, dearest? At least not tonight."* Holly blinked wildly and watched as the vision dissolve into shimmering beads of floating light. *"Make him work hard for you, Holly. Make him earn your love."*

"Oh, God," she groaned, stepping out into the darkened hallway. "What if it doesn't work?"

"It will, dearest," the familiar voice whispered. *"It will."*

Chapter Four

Anticipation coursed heavy through him, sending his fingers tightening around the stem of his wine goblet. Scuffing the toe of his highly polished boots, Andrew kicked at a glowing ember, sending it sizzling into the flaming hearth. Raising his gaze from the glowing log to the clock that sat atop the mantle, he saw that it was nearly forty-five minutes past eight.

Where the devil was she, he muttered to himself before taking a long sip of his claret. He was practically crawling out of his skin with anticipation. Fisting his hand, he forced himself to appear nonchalant. On the outside he appeared to be the controlled man everyone remembered, inside he was as nervous as a beardless boy awaiting a glimpse of his first crush through a crowded ballroom.

Damn her, didn't she know any better than to keep a man waiting--a man who had already been patiently waiting for eight years.

"Lady Holly," the footman announced, swinging open the salon doors. His heart faltered for a beat as he tore his gaze from the clock to the door. For the longest of seconds he waited, hearing nothing but the frenzied beating of his heart, the harsh, quick breaths coming from his chest. And then she sauntered in, a voluptuous goddess that stirred his hunger until it was a gnawing need in his belly. He watched her, her hips swaying in a seductive rhythm, her lips parting in a smile that made his mouth go dry.

This was Holly? The timid little Holly that had never been aware of the stares that men gave her? The shy Holly who hid behind drab gowns and bashful blushes?

"Good evening," she murmured in a soft, husky voice that felt like a caress, a caress that went straight to his straining manhood.

He sat his wine atop the mantle, fearing that if he didn't, the crystal would slide through his suddenly damp fingers. How long had it been seen since he'd seen such a fair woman? How long since his gaze had rested on *her*--her pale blonde curls and cornflower blue eyes?

Blood immediately flowed to his already rampant erection. How he was going to enjoy disrobing her and studying every inch, every recess of her milk-white body that had blossomed into womanhood while he'd been away.

He watched her cut a swath through the crowd gathered in the salon, willing her to find him. But she never looked his way and instead smiled, her eyes alighting when they came to rest upon the Duke of Maitland.

His hungry gaze devoured her as he studied the way she strolled sensuously toward the notorious duke. The predator in him stirred, sensed that someone was eyeing the same prey he was. When he saw the duke extend his hand to her, saw his black rake's brow arch under a perusing eye, he knew it to be true. She had been spotted and marked by another hunter with the same intent.

He should be making his way over to her, but he could not seem to make his feet move, nor could he take his eyes off her, despite being aware of many curious stares his way. Wetting his dry lips, he let his gaze roam over her face--which was glowing pink, down the column of her throat to where a stunning ruby and diamond necklace adorned her alabaster flesh. He felt his cock throb mercilessly when his eyes strayed to the large ruby that was tucked between her pale, ivory breasts.

Nostrils flaring, his breathing coming in short pants, he allowed his gaze to cover the expanse of her magnificent breasts encased in tight crimson silk. Good God, when had she developed such a bosom? Full and firm, they inched provocatively over the deep 'V' of her gown. He counted her breaths, watching the gentle rise and fall of the swells, wondering what it would be like to feel his lips brushing along her splendid décolletage.

He was loath to draw his eyes away from her, away from the tempting mounds that aroused him with numerous possibilities-- the possibilities of tonguing pink nipples, of feeling her soft flesh spilling from his hands, of watching his babe suckle from her perfect breast.

He could not help thinking of her feeding his children when he followed, with his covetous eyes, the pale blue vein that lay just beneath the white surface of her skin. That lovely, erotic vein that snaked from her nipple and aeorole and rose along her breast only to climb up to her neck.

He could not stop staring at it, wondering how it would look, how it would feel, when engorged with milk while she carried his child. He could not stop thinking of how that blue vein truly carried blue blood, and how now, he was actually worthy of it.

Maitland put his arm around her waist, hugging her to his chest, and Andrew watched as the silk shifted and pressed against her hips and her rounded bottom, more than hinting of the pleasurable body beneath the shimmering silk. She was made for loving. Made for a man who wanted to worship her with his body. She was designed for *him*--everything about her was perfect. His ideal. His fantasy.

"Darling," Lady Montague murmured as she came to stand beside him. "You remember Lady Holly, do you not?"

"Not looking quite as she does now," he muttered, hoping his huge erection would subside and he could walk normally and unnoticed through the crowd.

"She's grown up, dear," she said, smiling up at him. "She's seven and twenty now, and filled out nicely."

"Very nicely," he couldn't help but growl. And filled out in all the right spots. Good God, she looked like the Hindu goddess,

Rati. Full and lush, she embodied everything the goddess embodied. Fertility, love, passion, sex. Good Lord, he mused, as he followed Lady Mary through the crowd to where Holly stood beside Maitland, the woman was a goddess. She was made for sex. Her curved body was made for men's pleasures. The fertile contours of full breasts and hips were designed to conceive and create beautiful babies. *His* babies, he added in a silent vow. And he could not wait for the first opportunity to indulge in the activity that would have his child growing deep inside her womb.

This, his brain hissed. This was the moment he had toiled so long and hard for. To have her so close at hand, to be able to touch her and smell her, to anticipate the taste of her on his mouth, the feel of her beneath him was worth every hour spent in the hot, lonely land of India. Everything he had done, everything he had accomplished, had all been in anticipation of this moment. The moment when he would claim her as his. His friend, his lover, his life. The woman who would make passionate love with him. The woman who would be his wife. The woman who would give life to his children. This woman, Holly Harrington, was the reason he had become more than Lord and Lady Montague's ward. He was his own man now, and it was far past time that Holly discovered just how much of a man he truly was.

"You'll have to have to help me," Holly muttered as she pulled the duke of Maitland to the side.

"What's the matter, my dear?" he asked softly before sipping his drink.

"You should know," she said, nearly hissing beneath her breath.

"I confess I do not," he purred beside her. "I don't know a thing, not even my own name. I'm afraid my brain completely shut down the second you entered the room wearing that scandalous gown."

"Oh, *pffi*," she puffed between her lips. "You've seen a thousand beautiful women in your lifetime, pray do not amuse yourself with empty compliments. You forget, I know you too well."

He raised a black brow and peered down at her through thick black lashes. "You look beautiful, Holly, and that dress *is* scandalous."

"All right then, thank you," she said, before hastily checking to see if Andrew was still standing at ease beside the mantle. Her heart fluttered madly in her chest when she saw him bearing down upon her, Lady Mary beside him. "Please, Maitland," she murmured, looking away from the intent green eyes that found her through the crowd. "I need your help."

"I'm all ears," he murmured, sipping his claret.

"Can you...." she wet her lips and looked down at her trembling fingers. "Is it possible that you could pretend ... that is...."

"You want me to play the part of the smitten suitor to make your old friend Nightingale insanely jealous, is that it?" Holly looked up only to see him grinning. "Well, is that it?" he asked expectantly.

"Well..er ... I suppose," she muttered, checking to see how much longer she had before she found herself standing in front of Andrew. "Well, that is ... not jealous, per se. I don't think he's the type. But if you could only make it so that he won't pester me."

"Not the type?" Maitland said, chuckling softly. "My darling, Holly, I can feel the man's burning glare between my shoulder blades even now. He's positively churning with envy."

"Nonsense," she scoffed, looking up to see if the duke was correct. But she could not discern any such emotion in Andrew's green gaze. "Will you?" she asked, her voice almost breathless. They were almost upon them.

"You're playing games, sweeting," he said darkly, "and a man detests games in a woman. I thought you above feminine wiles."

"I'm not playing games. I simply do not want him hanging about."

"Why?"

She looked up, suddenly taken aback by the quiet question.

"Lady Holly, Your Grace," Lady Mary said, smiling brilliantly up at them. "You do remember my ward, Andrew Nightingale."

Before she could speak, Andrew was reaching for her hand and bringing it to his mouth--a mouth she could not stop staring at, recalling how soft and supple it had felt pressed against her lips.

"You are looking more lovely than ever, Lady Holly," he murmured, gazing directly, not to mention deeply, into her eyes.

"Hello, Mr. Nightingale," she said, forcing herself to speak as though she were greeting the vicar or the draper on the street.

"Nightingale," the duke said, removing Holly's hand from

Andrew's grip and placing it on the crook of his arm. "How nice to have you back."

Andrew's emerald gaze darkened as it slid from Holly to the duke. "Your Grace," he nodded with a tight tilt to his head. "May I have this dance, Lady Holly?" Andrew asked as the orchestra began warming up.

"Sorry, old boy, but I've beat you to it."

"What his grace means," Holly said, biting her lip when she saw Andrew's gaze turn mutinous, "is that his grace has already requested the first dance."

"Ah, sweeting," the duke said, raising her hand to his mouth and kissing her fingertips, "we are much too acquainted for all that 'your grace' business, are we not?"

"We are?" and she gasped as he pinched her fingers and looked at her knowingly. "Ah, yes, we are," she said, smiling tremulously.

"Come, sweeting, shall we dance?" he murmured against her hand before leading her to the dance floor. "Say my name," he hissed in her ear before they were out of earshot of Andrew and his mother. "Now," he ordered.

"Oh, yes, Brock," she said, smiling tightly up at him.

He grinned widely and gathered her in his arms. "You, Holly, are the sauciest minx I've ever laid eyes on."

"Come now," she teased, as he turned them into a spin, "you've been squiring Fiona Montgomery about for months. Surely you've realized that she is the sauciest thing you've ever met."

He laughed and squeezed her hand. "It will be a bloody miracle if you avoid getting me murdered in a duel with your Prince Valiant. I swear, you should have seen the way he looked at us when you said my name."

Holly attempted to look over her shoulder and was prevented by the duke's dark command. "Don't, you'll ruin it. You should only have eyes for me."

"Your grace--"

"Brock," he interrupted. "If we're putting on a show, let it be a convincing performance."

"So, you're going to assist me, then?" she asked as he spun her around.

"Oh, indeed. I adore watching hot-blooded males cut to the quick by conniving women they seek to humble themselves in front of."

"You're wrong, you know," she whispered. "I don't mean to make him jealous. I doubt I could, even if I sought to."

"Then what is the purpose of wearing this breathtaking gown and looking so damn gorgeous that you could provoke a saint to sin?"

She flushed, feeling embarrassment creep up her throat and into her cheeks. "It isn't what you think."

"So tell me, and for God's sake quit blushing like that, it makes me want to look at you and to territory that should be forbidden to me and every other gentleman in the room with a pulse."

She flushed further and he groaned. "For Heavens sake, Holly, have a care with those blushes."

"I can't help it," she said mutinously. "You're embarrassing me with all those silly compliments. I know you don't speak the truth."

"Ssh, now," he purred, "or your Lancelot shall think we are having a lover's quarrel. You don't want him thinking that, thinking that he can come over and worm his way into your good graces, now do you?"

"Of course not," she grumbled. "And he's not going to get in my good graces. Not after what he--" she stopped herself in time, before the words betrayed her.

"What did he do, Holly?"

"Nothing," she murmured, looking away from his knowing eyes.

"He made you love him, and he did something that made you think he loved you, too, but then he left for India and forgot all about you." Her eyes went round, and she stumbled over her toes. "It is written on your face, sweeting. We've been friends too long for me to miss the signs."

She looked away, embarrassed. "Come," he said, ushering her to the card room after the music had ended. "Let us give the rogue his just desserts. Let him stew over the treasure he could have had but turned away for the riches of India."

"You're really going to help me?" she asked hopefully.

"Isn't that what friends are for, sweeting?" he asked blandly. "Now then, let us share a game of backgammon."

"No, I prefer whist," she said, allowing him the liberty of his hand at the small of her back as he guided her into the room.

"No, sweeting, backgammon is what you will want to play. You will want a game for only two--me and you. You will want Sir Lancelot snorting and stomping in distemper as he watches us, wishing we would end the game and take a seat for a hand of whist where he could prevail upon some fatiguing dowager to take her place. Then he could sit beside you and watch you from beneath his lashes, he could study you and your delightful bosom, he could smell you."

"Your Grace!" she scolded him. He shrugged and motioned to an empty table.

"It's exactly what I would do if I were as hungry for a woman as your Prince Valiant is for you."

"You're wrong," she said, shaking her head. "We're only friends."

"Is that so?" Brock asked, holding out the chair for her and sliding it in when she was seated. "So why then, sweeting, has he marked me for execution? Why then is he even now standing in the doorway wishing he could wrap his hands around my throat and strangle me for sitting across from you. Don't look," he whispered to her, "just smile."

She flushed and looking down at her lap, she smiled shyly.

"Very nice, sweeting, the blush especially is a lovely touch. He is positively snorting with hatred."

"You're enjoying yourself," she said incredulously.

"Well, one must find *some* way to enjoy themselves at these wholesome house parties."

"You're very wicked."

"And so are you, treating that poor fellow in such a way."

"Just play," she whispered, passing him the cup with the dice.

He smiled, his blue eyes twinkling in the firelight. "Do you know, I almost cannot wait to see how this whole thing plays out. You think you know everything, do you not?"

"Of course," she said, folding her hands in her lap. "I know men."

"But not men who would do anything for the woman they love. You can never underestimate that man."

"Andrew does not love me." She snorted.

"Does he not?" the duke asked, before tossing the dice and starting the game.

Holly spent most of the game trying to decipher the duke of Maitland's cryptic words. How could it be that the duke thought Andrew in love with her? The duke, the man who knew nothing of romantic love. As much as she adored the duke and his friendship, she did not fool herself about him. He was a roué, a libertine. He did not love--he lusted. But then, she thought wistfully, she had glimpsed a softness in him, a vulnerable part of him that yearned for love.

She forgot about the duke and became aware of Andrew as he paced the perimeter of the room, drinking his claret and boldly watching her over the rim of his glass. And every time their eyes met, Holly forgot to breathe, forgot to think. She could only process how handsome Andrew was, how savagely beautiful he was with his tanned skin and thick chestnut hair that shimmered mahogany in the lights.

He walked with a predator-like grace that entranced her, and she found her gaze slipping down from his broad shoulders to his muscular thighs encased in tight breeches. More than once, she was forced to reach for her fan. Never before had the study of the male form left her quite so heated.

"Ladies and gentlemen," the footman announced from the door, "dinner is served in the dining room."

"Oh, good," the duke drawled, rising from his chair. "Now that we've managed to infuriate the poor man by excluding him from our little game, let us see what further damage we can provoke by going in to dinner together."

"Your Grace," she warned. "I'm not trying to incur his wrath, only to make him understand that I have not spent the last years wasting away for him to return."

"But you have, haven't you? You have been wasting away," he murmured, reaching for her hand. "Come close to me," he directed, "and let your bodice skim my waistcoat."

"*Your Grace*," she whispered.

"Brock," he muttered. "Now do it. Brush against me--he's watching."

She did as he asked and then looked up to see Andrew watching them with unconcealed fury. He raised a brow and uncrossed his arms, watching as the duke raised her hand to his lips. She felt a tingling down her spine, and it was not from the duke's touch, but from Andrew's hot gaze as it slid from her face and down her throat to rest upon her breasts.

"Very good," the duke purred. "He'll think that you're trembling for me, but I am not fool enough to think it to be true. Nor am I fool enough to believe that you want nothing but to have that man leave you be. But I am fool enough to make it so that he has to work very hard to win you, Holly. No man should win you so easily. You're too precious not to fight for."

She looked up at him and he winked. "Come, sweeting. Let us

set this wicked plan of ours in motion."

Chapter Five

Dinner was a most uncomfortable affair. Seated at the end of the long table, Holly found herself sitting across from Andrew and to the right of the duke. She was aware of the tension growing at the table, and she worked hard to avoid Andrew's burning gaze. While she was successful in avoiding his watchful green eyes, it did not prevent her from feeling his hot gaze studying her, or from roaming liberally along her.

What did he think of her? She could not help but ask herself the question. When she had kissed him she had been nothing but a girl whose figure only hinted at the woman she would become. She had been plain and nothing out of the ordinary. She was still not beautiful and her figure had become soft and curved, and she found herself wondering how Andrew would ever find her pleasing after years of cavorting with slim, nubile, not to mention exotic, Indian women.

It was no secret that the women in India were small framed and thin with dark skin and eyes. Their breasts were not large and fleshy, nor were their hips overly full and round. Andrew no doubt found her rather unfashionable, now that he had spent so many years surrounded with the sort of exotic beauty the Indian women possessed.

Perhaps he had managed to seduce many of those women. Her eyes darted up to steal a look at him from beneath her pale lashes, only to find him staring intently back at her. He captured and held her gaze, and she found herself flushing and looking away. She could not bear the thought that Andrew had been frolicking about with beautiful women, while she had grown round and more plain and languishing in her misery during the long nights.

Andrew watched as Holly absently pushed around a pile of peas on her plate. What was going on in that mind of hers? He could tell she was contemplating something of great importance--she was biting her lip. She always gnawed at her lips when she was nervous or thinking. What was she, he wondered, stabbing a roasted potato with his fork and chewing thoughtfully, nervous or thinking or both?

"So, Nightingale," Maitland said, sitting back in his chair and tossing his napkin atop the table. "Tell us about India."

Holly's eyes darted to the duke and then settled back on her plate, completely avoiding him.

"It's hot and crowded and the food takes some getting used to."

"But the riches are unparalleled, I've heard."

He nodded and reached for his wine, drinking it down in one swallow. "If a man is enterprising enough and willing to work hard, he can amass a fortune."

The duke smiled. "And were you able to make your fortune?"

"I was," he said, sitting back and willing Holly to look at him. "I have enough to last me and my children a lifetime."

"How nice," the duke said in that condescending tone that made Andrew want to smash his fist against the duke's clean-shaven face. "But alas, no title."

He felt his body go rigid, and he could not help but look at Holly, wondering if he could discern her thoughts. Was a title all that mattered to her? Did she prefer the title duchess to that of his wife and lover? His fingers curled into a fist at the thought.

"Many men are making their way in the world without benefit of a title to hide behind," he muttered, finally addressing the duke. "We're amassing huge fortunes and starting businesses. We're entering politics and we're sharing the same clubs as the aristocrats."

"True," Maitland purred, reached for Holly and stroked his index finger along the top of her hand. "But then there will always be things that are denied you. I, as a duke, will always acquire what is not yours to have, simply because I have the means and the power behind me."

Damn him! Damn her! Didn't Holly see what a pompous ass the duke was? Could she tell that she was nothing but an acquisition for him--a *thing*, he had called her. Damn it, she would not be a wife, only a duchess. She would bear heirs, not children. Didn't she realize it? How wrong the duke was for her?

"What I want," the duke murmured, letting his lascivious gaze wander over Holly's exposed bosom, "I take." His gaze swung back to meet his. "The perks of being titled, I'm afraid," he said, grinning wickedly. "I always get what I want."

He was about to thrash the bastard right there at the table, when Lord Harrington rose and cleared his throat. "Shall we not repair to the study, gentlemen?"

Holly looked expectantly up at him, as if it were her dearest wish to escape him. Not bloody likely, he growled beneath his breath, watching as the duke rose and smoothed his hand down his waistcoat. Titled gentlemen might prefer their cheroots and port, but untitled, hardworking men preferred their evenings spent with beautiful, voluptuous women. And there was no way in hell he was going to be deprived of Holly's company again this night.

"Holly," Lizzie said from down the length of the table. "Did you not say we would go outside this evening and pick the finest evergreen bows for tomorrow night?"

"Er...." Holly stammered, blushing. No one could make a blush as arousing as Holly did. She fairly glowed with warmth and blood, and he delighted in watching her skin pinken along her throat and the tops of her breasts, making him wonder if she would flush like that with sexual arousal.

"That would be a splendid idea," his guardian, Lady Mary, said excitedly. "It's snowing outside and the perfect weather for gathering the greenery for the Christmas Eve celebrations. Andrew, darling, you must assist the girls. It has been a long while been since you've seen snow."

Thank Heavens for Lady Mary and her intrusive instincts. In this, he was more than happy to have her support, and from what he could see of Lizzie and the looks she was shooting her sister, he had her support as well.

"I would be delighted, ladies, to assist you. It has been eight years since I've felt snow on my face."

"Oh, good," Lizzie clapped, smiling brightly. "It's all settled then."

"Indeed," he murmured, finding Holly's gaze once again, "it is."

* * * *

Stepping out into the moonlit night, Holly watched as the glistening crystals fell softly and silent from the black sky to the ground. The stone path was thinly covered with white fluff, just enough to make the stones wet and slippery.

"Have a care," Andrew said, reaching for her elbow and bringing her to his side. "I haven't forgotten how slippery flagstone is when it's newly covered with snow."

His bare fingers burned through the velvet of her cloak, sending her skin tingling. How unfair that he should have this power over her after all these years. That her body should come alive with the most innocent of touches was most telling. She was in grave danger of succumbing to Andrew's rakish charm and handsome good looks.

"Holly," Lizzie said, appearing from the side of the house with a basket in her hands. "I'm going into the garden to snip some holly and mistletoe."

"Of course," she murmured, refusing to acknowledge the frantic beating of her heart. Andrew was pressed against her, and she could feel his muscled chest, hot and hard against her arm.

"And we shall go about cutting some bows for the hearth," Andrew called after Lizzie. She waved as she traveled along the path, and suddenly Holly could not breath. It had been so very long since she'd even seen him, let alone been alone with him.

"Come," he whispered, drawing her along the path. "I recall that you had some very lovely evergreen trees to the east side of the property."

She could do nothing but allow him to drag her along beside him. The small metal blade from the saw he held in his hand glinted in the moonlight, and she kept her gaze on it, finding that it distracted her from thinking other disturbing thoughts.

"Do they offend you?" he asked, stopping her and swinging her around to look up at him.

"Offend me? Whatever do you mean?"

"My hands," he gritted out, his green eyes flashing angrily. "Can you not stand the fact that I've used them to make my way in the world?"

"Not at all," she snapped, offended by his insinuation. "I was looking at them thinking that you must be cold. You've forgotten your gloves."

"No, I didn't," he murmured, stepping closer to her. "I purposely forgot them."

She took a step back and came up against the side of the gardening shed that loomed behind her. "Why?".

"So that I can feel your hot body beneath my cold hands," he replied, dropping the saw to the ground, sending it ringing against the stones. "So that I may have the pleasure of warming them as I reach beneath this cloak and stroke that lovely form beneath that *very* stimulating gown."

"Sir," she said, the word sounding more like a plea for him to continue his scandalous talk than a command for him to stop.

"Just Andrew, love," he said, stepping so close that his boots touched the tips of her boots, and the gray vapor of his mouth caressed her lips. "We were once just Andrew and Holly, not sir and lady."

That was before, her mind screamed. Before you kissed me senseless and left my heart bleeding while you went about your way in India.

His hand snaked through the opening of her velvet cloak, his cold skin seemed to seep through the thin silk, straight to her own skin that absorbed his coldness. She trembled, not from the cold but from the awareness of his large hand that rested beneath the curve of her breast. He seemed to know, to understand her response, for he parted the cloak more, watching her reaction as his hand slid along her waist, curving over her hip and skating over to her belly.

His eyes widened, and slowly his gaze slipped down to where his hand rested against her. What was he thinking? What thoughts about her were going on in his mind?

Lovely warm, soft skin, he thought, staring at his dark hand atop the crimson silk. Despite the layer of her dress and chemise he could feel the suppleness of her skin, could feel her body heat enveloping him, teasing him with the thought of feeling the hotness from the core of her body seeping onto his hand. He could not wait to be wrapped in her heat, in her soft welcoming body, or to feel this gently mounded belly beneath his mouth and hands.

She was breathing hard, and he watched the rapid rise and fall of her breasts that were illuminated in the moonlight. Such beautiful breasts, and the way the rabbit fur lined cloak outlined them was highly arousing--making him desire to see her naked, spread out before him lying on the fur like a pagan goddess. He breathed deep and thrust the cape back along her shoulders, exposing her. She shivered, but he knew she was not cold, she was too damn hot for that. He could almost see it radiating from her body. He could definitely feel it reaching for him and drawing him in.

Her nipples swelled and pressed against the silk and he watched in satisfaction as her flesh seemed to swell, just like the flesh between his legs that had now swelled to an impressive size. How he was going to enjoy giving her that flesh and reveling in her scalding heat.

She whimpered as he slid his hand up the smooth silk, felt her body tremble, heard her teeth begin to chatter as both his hands lightly, teasingly traced the outline of her bodice.

"Such beautiful breasts," he said appreciatively, cupping them. "You've filled out perfectly, love."

She swallowed hard, and he would have liked to have stroked her throat and felt the tremor of anticipation in her heartbeat, but he could not tear himself away from her bodice or the image of her breasts with his throbbing cock captured between them.

"Andrew, please," she whispered, squirming beneath his hands. His cock was now so heavy and engorged that it was painful, trapped as it was beneath his silk breeches.

"Your skin feels like silk--soft, sumptuous, the color of fresh cream."

His eyes left hers to watch his fingers as they traced the moonlit swells of her breasts. His finger traced the pale blue vein and his tongue crept out, his need to taste her almost uncontrollable. "I wonder," his voice rumbled from deep in his chest, "if you taste like cream? Shall I taste you?" he teased, tracing the shape of her breasts.

Holly stood frozen and mute. She had not been prepared for this, nor her reaction to him. She didn't know what to do, her mind screamed *yes*--taste, kiss, lave--but she absolutely refused to plead, which was exactly what he wanted from her.

"Just one lick, love. One glide of my tongue--"

"Please," she whispered, hoping it sounded like an entreaty for him to stop. But then he lowered his head and began nuzzling the valley of her breasts, his hair, soft and silky, teased her throat and shoulders.

"Does this make you burn, Holly? Does it make you ache for me?"

Her teeth chattered, her whole body trembled, but she wasn't cold, indeed she was warm, so very hot.

"I burn. From the moment I glimpsed you, I was consumed, Holly." His tongue traced the cleft of her breasts, while his thumb circled and hardened her nipple. "Consumed by thoughts of seeing these," he pinched her nipple and wetness pooled between her legs. "Consumed by thoughts of me tonguing them, sucking them. This makes you hot, doesn't it, love? I can feel the heat rolling off of you. I can feel the desire building inside you."

"No," she hissed, trying to clear the fog that was making her head heavy.

"Imagine the nights with you in my arms, with me buried deep inside you, moving slowly atop you as I bring you to completion. Think of the long nights of me inside you, the quiet of mornings of loving, watching you, your lush body outlined in the golden morning sun as you sit astride me, taking me deep inside you. The only sounds in the house will be the servants preparing our breakfast downstairs and your deep, panting breaths in the quiet of our room as you find your release. Then, Holly, I will feed you breakfast, nourishing you so that I can make love to you again. In our bed, in the bath, against the wall, atop the chair that sits before your dressing table so that you can watch my hands along your body. So you can see what you do to me, and what I do to you. Now, Holly, give me the lips I've coveted. Kiss me."

"No," she said, finally drawing herself out his sensual haze. "Please, Andrew, I cannot."

"And why is that?" he asked darkly. "You kissed me so eagerly before. I haven't forgotten it, you know."

"That was because of the mistletoe," she said, sliding out from his hold. "A woman is obligated when she is caught beneath it."

"I think not, but if that is the way you wish to proceed, then I shall indulge you. I shall find the largest sprig of it and I shall not stop kissing you until each and every berry is plucked from the stem. I vow to you," he whispered, "I will torture you with mistletoe."

Chapter Six

Holly wrapped her fur-lined cloak tightly around her and ran for the safety of the house. Her fingers shook so severely that she had to try several times to unlatch the door, each time her fingers lacking the strength to turn the latch.

Damn Andrew. He had reduced her to a pile of quivering mush. She didn't want to be so easily swayed by him; she didn't want him thinking that she would fall so easily into his embrace as she did the last time. Didn't he realize that he had broken her heart when he'd left for India? Didn't he see that she was not the naïve little girl he had left behind?

Warmth from the hearths engulfed her as she stepped into the hall that led to the salon. She rubbed her hands together, the leather of her gloves creaking with the cold. She had done the right thing by fleeing Andrew. She had been far too lost in his touches and heated looks. Weak, that is what she had been.

Well, she was not going to be weak any longer. As she sailed down the hall, her half boots tapping on the marble tiles, she surveyed the doorways and hidden alcoves. The Christmas greenery and mistletoe would not be hung until tomorrow afternoon. She was safe, at least for tonight, from Andrew's threats of using mistletoe to gain what he wanted.

Smiling, she let herself into the salon and headed for the table that contained the warm, spicy wassail. A cup of the steaming brew would soon settle her nerves and have her planning the ways she was going to steadfastly avoid Andrew Nightingale.

"You look ravishing with frozen cheeks," a deep voice said behind her.

She turned, seeing that the duke was standing scant inches behind her. "It's devilishly cold outside, and I do believe the snow is falling harder."

"Have you not seen, yet?" he asked, reaching for her hand and strolling with her over to the double-hung window that looked out onto the lawn.

"Oh, Heavens," she whispered when she heard the howl of the wind followed by the white blinding swirl of snow.

"Did you not notice when you were outside?" he drawled, arching his brow in question.

"There's much more protection from the trees in the back of the property than the front," she said coolly, censuring him with her tone. "And I knew perfectly well that it was snowing."

"Hmmm." He grinned, turning his head to gaze out the window with her. "We've sent some footmen to the road to see whether it is really as bad as it seems. No one wishes to be stuck in their carriage at the side of a country road for the night."

She blinked, staring almost mindlessly out at the snow that only seemed to fall harder and thicker the longer she watched. The winds picked up, and she knew that her father's footmen would return saying that it was impossible to travel in such conditions. Her mother would joyously invite everyone to stay for the night, and that invitation would, of course, include Andrew Nightingale. She didn't think she liked the idea of Andrew spending the night under her roof.

"Holly," a commanding voice said quietly behind her. "I must speak with you." She gazed over her shoulder and saw Andrew, looking very determined, standing behind her. He shot the duke a pointed gaze, then turned his eyes back to her. "Alone."

"I ... that is...." She licked her lips nervously and looked up at the duke for assistance. Why was it she could not think straight when Andrew looked at her like that? Why, when she lowered her gaze to the floor, could she not help but think of his hands on her body or the way she felt her body absorb the cold from his fingers. Why did she look at his beautiful tanned hands and long, elegant fingers and wish to feel them sliding along her naked flesh?

"Ladies and gentlemen," her father said, coughing loudly and gaining the attention of the gathered guests. "I'm afraid the roads are treacherous. My coachman has advised that the ice and winds will make any journey too dangerous. I'm afraid this little party shall turn into a country party. You are most welcome to stay for the night. And as most of you were returning tomorrow night anyway, it does not seem so terrible."

Murmurs rippled through the room, and Holly watched as many gentlemen shook her father's hand in gratitude, the women rushing over to extend their thanks to her mother.

"How very interesting," the duke drawled, shielding his eyes with his lashes. "A night spent under your roof. Things are getting better and better."

Holly's mouth dropped open, and she heard Andrew suck in a deep, gasping breath.

"You sir, are a reprobate."

"Ah, sweeting," the duke smiled, lifting her hand to his mouth. "But you did say you wanted the chance to reform me, did you not?"

She shot the duke a look of warning with her narrowed eyes. He was treading very treacherous waters. She knew that people were watching, and she could not afford to have them speculating that there was anything more than friendship between them. And if his words were to be overheard, they would certainly be taken the wrong way.

"I must beg to leave you, gentlemen," she said, expertly sliding her hand from the duke's grip. "I see my sister has arrived and is in need of something to drink."

"Holly--" Andrew bit out, reaching for her arm. "I need to speak with you."

"Perhaps later, Mr. Nightingale," she murmured. "I must see to my sister."

"I will hold you to that, Holly. I will meet you later."

"Very well," she muttered. She was able to shake off his grip, but not stop the remembered feel of his fingers and the warmth of his touch as it snaked its way up her arm.

She must avoid him at all costs.

* * * *

Successful in her avoidance for the remainder of the night, Holly walked up the winding staircase and padded quietly down the hall. Andrew had taken his leave of the guests more than an hour ago. He was probably in bed and she was safe from him. After all, she had tried to stay away as long as she could, hoping to avoid any accidental meetings in the hall.

Turning the corner, she spotted her chamber and was relieved to see that a certain someone was not lingering about. Arriving at the room, she reached for the handle, but was prevented from turning the latch by a dark hand that rested upon hers.

"I have been waiting for you."

The deep voice sent a chill racing down her spine, and she turned, only to be captured by Andrew's arms on either side of her.

"Really, sir, this is highly irregular."

"Is it? Just a few hours ago you and your duke made it seem that it was a very regular occurrence."

She swallowed hard, noticing the strange emotion flickering in his eyes. What did she see there? Anger? Annoyance? Jealousy? No, it couldn't be so. Andrew would not be jealous of the duke and his attentions to her. Attentions that were just a ploy to keep Andrew away from her.

"Is it, Holly? Is your duke meeting you in your chamber a regular occurrence?"

"Of course not," she snapped. "Is that what you think of me, that I am some lightskirt that would do such a thing. Do you think me that desperate that I must resort to entertaining my father's guests when they spend the night?"

"I don't know. How desperate are you for a man's touch?" he whispered, reaching into his waistcoat and withdrawing what appeared to resemble a scrap of velvet.

"I am not desperate enough to stand here and listen to your accusations, sir. And I am not reckless enough to entertain *you*."

She reached behind her for the door latch, but suddenly she was prevented from moving when he raised a dried, brown sprig of mistletoe, one berry, discolored and whizzled, dangling from the end of the stalk.

"One kiss remaining," he whispered, holding the sprig above

her head. He let the ribbon slide between his fingers, and she saw that it was the same sprig he had used to kiss her eight years ago. Her heart did a mad leap, and she felt her breath burning in her lungs.

"Two thousand, eight hundred and forty seven days I have thought of this moment. I have dreamt of it, Holly. And no one is going to deprive me of it. Not you, not me, not your parents or the household staff. Not God and all the demons from hell, and most certainly not your infuriating duke."

She was helpless to resist him. How could she when he said the words with such passion, or when he looked at her with such blatant lust in his eyes. As she watched him, watched his slow descent to her mouth, she realized that she wanted this--this one simple kiss. She had to feel his mouth against hers just one more time.

"Eight years I've carried this with me, Holly. Treasuring, protecting this one little berry. Eight long years and you would deprive me now of the last kiss."

"One kiss," she whispered, her gaze darting up to his eyes. "One."

"Very well," he whispered, "one kiss".

"As soon as your lips lift from my flesh the kiss is over."

"All right," he said, his eyes twinkling in the candlelight from the wall scones. "When my mouth leaves you, it shall end."

She nodded and closed her eyes, pursing her lips, waiting for him to touch her with his mouth. And then he captured her face in his hands and lowered his head so that his breath whispered across her lips and she parted them softly. He captured them slowly and her heart and her mind stopped working as she concentrated on the feel of his mouth, hard yet soft, coaxing her lips wider, and then finally he snaked his tongue inside and tasted her.

She whimpered and her knees gave out. She was forced to reach for him, and he took her mouth hungrily in his, bruising her with his kiss, forcing her to match his deep strokes. She was breathless and dizzy, mindless of what she was doing. But Andrew still had some sense because he reached for the latch and opened the door.

She tried to pull away, but he reached for her head, and wrapping his fingers around her nape, he brought her closer, kissing her harder.

"My maid," she mumbled against his mouth.

"Gone," he said back, his lips never lifting from hers. "Lizzie," he said simply.

Andrew pushed her inside the chamber. Instead of taking her to bed, he closed the door and pressed her against it. His hands were shaking, and his heart was beating a wild tattoo in his chest. He was impatient, thinking of nothing other than tearing the dress from her and ravishing her. He was on fire for her, and watching her with Maitland had only enraged him further, increasing his need for her.

She was going to be his. There was no doubt about it. After tonight, after he sunk himself deep inside her and brought her to completion in his arms, she would belong to no one other than himself.

Holly whimpered with each probe of his tongue, and he rubbed his engorged, throbbing cock against the soft vee of her thighs. This is where he wanted to be, between her thighs, cushioned, welcomed, loved.

She gasped as he pushed against her and he felt the first drops of come seep out of his cock. Careful, he reminded himself. He'd make a hash of things if he thrust against her too many times.

She tried to push away from him, but he followed her, pressing his chest against her, pinning her against he wall. She was panting now and her fingers were tightening in his hair, at times almost painfully clutching, and it drove him wild.

He had one kiss with her. As soon as his lips left her flesh, it would be over. He needed to have his wits about him. He needed control and to summon his will power. He could make this the most unforgettable night with her. He could make it so that she forgot she had promised him only one kiss. He could make it so that she would beg him to thrust into her.

"Andrew," she panted, between brushes of his lips and the plunging of his tongue.

He gave her reprieve and slid his mouth away, only to slide down her jaw to the bounding blue vein that throbbed in her neck. He kissed her, once, twice, a third time, before trailing his tongue down the vein.

"Oh, God," she moaned, her fingers shaking as she stroked the side of his face.

Reaching for the sleeves of her gown, he started to pull them down--slowly, he reminded himself. He didn't want to ruin this exquisite dress. He wanted to see her in it again. He wanted to see her wearing it at his dining table. He wanted to see her pale body in it as he placed her atop the table, taking her hard, watching the red silk shimmer beneath the chandeliers.

Groaning, he reached for the tapes at the back of the gown and opened them, clumsy in his hurry. But he needed her. Needed to feel her, to see her, to taste her. The bodice came free and he pulled it away from her skin as he continued to lick her and kiss her neck. She had pressed herself against the door, arching her neck and thrusting her breasts forward. His hand brushed the hot skin of her breasts, and he groaned before nipping at her neck.

"No chemise?" he asked, his voice rough as he skated his lips along her throat.

"No," she said, her voice a panting breath.

"Completely naked beneath this," he said. "Oh, Holly, you do know how to seduce a man. Had a I known that this silk was caressing your naked flesh, had I known that nothing but silk separated me from these beautiful breasts, I would have gone off right in my breeches."

"Andrew," she gasped, her face turning crimson.

"What?" he said, careful to keep his mouth on her as he talked. He could not afford to take the chance that Holly was waiting for him to lose concentration. He could not stop now, even if she asked him too. "Is it too much to know that I've stared at you all night," he whispered, lowering her bodice and sliding his mouth down her throat. "Does it shame you to know that I've thought of suckling you till your womb clenches and you seep arousal from your body?"

"Andrew," she cried, fisting her fingers in his hair.

He slid his mouth lower, wishing he could pull back and stare at her, wishing he could see her large breasts, but he had to keep his mouth on her, so instead he kissed a wet path down to the full swell. His hand rested beneath her breast, he could feel the delicate ribs beneath her skin, could feel her breast quivering against his thumb in anticipation and escalating desire.

"Ask me," he murmured against her, his mouth coming so close to her nipple. A beautiful pink nipple that was jutting out, waiting for his tongue. He stared at it, while he mouthed her breast. "Ask me, Holly, to suckle you."

She moaned and he was so tempted to brush his thumb along her nipple, to touch her as he had fantasized about for so long. But he wanted his mouth to be the first part of him to touch her there.

"Ask me," he said again, this time more forcefully, and he kissed and sucked at the swell of her breast.

"Suckle me," she gasped, wrapping her fingers even tighter in hair. "Please, take me in your mouth and suck from me."

"Watch me," he commanded, then he went to his knees, his mouth constantly touching her. He met her eyes and he trailed his tongue along the soft tip of her nipple. It curled and budded even tighter. He opened his mouth, curling his tongue along the whole nipple, allowing her to see her pink flesh in his mouth. She was watching him with astonishment and sensual arousal. He slipped the nipple inside and sucked, slowly, rhythmically. She closed her eyes and rested her head against the door. He imagined that her insides were already tightening and she was feeling her honey slide out of her body.

Oh God, Holly chanted over and over in her mind. What was Andrew doing to her, making her feel this way? He looked so wickedly handsome as he'd taken her breast into his mouth. And he was suckling her so deeply, slowly, erotically that her knees felt weak and she could barely keep standing.

"I want to feed from you," he whispered between sucks. "All those long nights in India I dreamt of lying beside you, suckling you. Of being able to awaken in the night and fasten my mouth around you like a babe does a mother. I wanted that contentment. I fantasized about the possibility of making you come with only suckling."

"Yes," she sighed, bringing her nipple and breast further into his mouth and watching as he sucked and caressed her with his long fingers and his beautiful mouth.

It was beautiful what he was doing to her. Never had she been so aware of being a woman. Never had her breasts taken on such pleasure--such simple pleasures as the thoughts of feeding a child and nurturing and pleasuring a man. As she watched him, she became more aroused, needing more. She raised her hand to her other breast and pinched her straining nipple with her fingers. She had done this before, feeling her womb clench as she pinched harder. He watched her, his mouth sucking harder now and she felt her dress glide down her hips and thighs. She was now standing totally naked with the exception of her stockings. She trembled, fearing his scrutiny, yet yearning for it at the same time. He unfastened his mouth from her breast and pulled back, staring at her, reverently brushing his hand along her damp, blonde curls.

"I am on fire for you, Holly," he whispered, skimming his hands along her hips. "I have dreamt of this moment, but none of my dreams have been this perfect. None of them have been able to capture exactly how perfect you are."

She felt a rush of heat engulf her body, turning it crimson. She felt that blush deepen as he fixed his gaze on her sex. He ran his hand along her curls again, and he pressed closer, closing his eyes as he kissed her thighs. "I want to feed here, also. Feed forever, tasting and sucking, discovering the texture of you, the taste of your honey. How much do you need this, Holly? How much do you need my touch?"

He skimmed his finger along her wet cleft, and she whimpered.

"I am going to take very good care of you, Holly. When you are ready--writhing and panting and begging for it, I will take great care of you. I swear it. Now," he said, running his fingers along her thigh. "Part your legs and give me what I want."

And he won't be getting what he wants, will he? Her grandmother's words came floating back to her, and Holly stiffened. She had played too easily into his hands. She was giving him what he wanted without much thought of what would happen after he got it.

"Come, love," he said again, his voice a husky purr. "Just a little look. A little touch. A little lick."

"I'm afraid your one kiss is over, sir," she whispered shakily.

His gaze darted sharply up at her. "Is that what you really want, Holly?" he challenged. "You're wet, soaking in desire. I can see it, smell it." She blushed, but he pressed on. "Do you truly want me to stop and leave you unfilled like this?"

"Yes," she said, but she could not hold his gaze. For she did not wish to go to bed feeling this hunger inside her. She couldn't relieve the ache. Couldn't cool the fire that was burning inside her.

"Fine, then," he said, rising to stand before her. "Just remember that whatever pleasure you find with your hand tonight will be nothing like what I could give you now--right here--in your bed, on the chair before your dressing table, against this bloody door."

And then he walked out of the room, leaving her trembling against the door, fighting with herself not to call him back.

Chapter Seven

"Whatever have you done to the man?" The laughing voice sounded in the black night. *"He is positively snarling and stomping about like a caged lion."*

Holly sat up in bed and pulled the covers tight to her chin. Then, reaching for the bed curtains, she parted them and found the figure of her grandmother sitting in the chair beside the hearth.

"Holly, dearest, come out where I can see you. I want to make certain you're faring well after that ... well ... that encounter."

Smothering a groan, Holly slid from the bed. The last thing she wanted to hear was that her grandmother had been floating about the room, watching Andrew work his lascivious magic on her body.

"Don't be ridiculous, child. As if I would float about spying on people," she said, rolling her eyes. *"I am not gauche, my dear. I know my place, and my place was most certainly not here in this room while Andrew Nightingale was occupying it with you."*

"If you don't go floating about people's rooms," Holly asked, pulling on her wrapper and padding quietly across the carpet, "then how did you know that someone is stomping about like a caged lion?"

"Not just someone, dearest, but your Andrew."

Her grandmother motioned for her to sit by the fire. Holly did as she asked and tucked her feet beneath her. Folding her arms on her grandmother's lap, she rested her chin on her hands and felt her grandmother's fingers brush back her curls.

"This seems so real," Holly whispered. "It must just be my mind replaying all those times I sat like this with you. I can actually feel your legs beneath my arms and your fingers in my hair, and it comforts me just as it did when I was a child."

"This is as real as you want it to be, Holly," she said quietly, brushing her hair. *"And to answer your question, I took the liberty of peeking in on your Andrew, and I can tell you that you've done a perfect job of making him irate. Whatever have you done to the boy?"*

"Nothing," Holly whispered. "I ended a most impertinent

embrace before matters got out of hand, that is all."

Her grandmother looked down at her, her blue eyes twinkling. *"Ah, I see,"* she murmured.

"I'm glad you do, for I cannot understand anything he does. Eight years ago he kissed me senseless and stole my heart. He left the country, never wrote to me, never a word from him, and then he arrives home wishing to carry on where he left off and is perturbed because I won't allow it."

"Hmm, yes, dearest. That is the way men think. Silly creatures the lot of them. They never understand the intricacies of the female mind."

"I'm not even certain I understand it," Holly grumbled.

Her grandmother chuckled and tilted Holly's chin up with one finger. *"It's your heart you don't understand, dearest. And that is perfectly reasonable. A heart is such a fragile thing when it's been broken and mended. The previous cracks are always threatening to come loose again, isn't that so?"*

"Yes," she sighed. " I survived him leaving once before. I don't think I could a second time."

"And what makes you think that he would leave, dearest? What makes you think he hasn't come back because you're the woman he wants above all others?"

"Because that is impossible. I was here eight years ago, and he didn't want me enough to stay, or enough to take me with him, for that matter," she said bitterly. "He didn't want me enough to write me to ask that I wait for him."

"Darling," her grandmother said, sighing heavily. *"Perhaps you should allow the poor boy to explain himself."*

"You mean to talk me into believing him so that he can have his way with me."

"Well, no, dearest. But don't you think you owe it to yourself to find out the reasons Andrew left?"

"It is a question that has burning in my mind for some time."

"Two thousand eight hundred and forty seven days?" she asked slyly.

"You were listening!" Holly cried, rising to her knees.

"Oh, all right, I did hear that snippet, but I vow, I floated away the second after that."

"I suppose you'll be floating in to Mother's room next to tell her that I've been indulging in very unladylike behavior."

"Heavens, no, dearest. You're mother isn't open to such things as ghosts. She would never see me. Besides, I cannot abide your

father's snoring."

Holly smiled and she reached for her grandmother's hand. "I do not understand what has brought you to me, but I am glad I have you. I need you, and most desperately, now that Andrew has arrived."

"Destiny, dearest, is what brought me to you. Your fate awaits you these next two days. I'm only here to help guide you in that. So, my dear--you will allow Andrew his moment of truth tomorrow, will you not? You will listen with an open mind and an open heart."

"If you say so," she murmured.

"I do say so," her grandmother said with a laugh,

* * * *

Pacing along the length of the room, Andrew fumed with frustration and fury. What did she mean by sending him on his way as if he were a lap dog that was panting to do her bidding? What did she mean by denying herself the pleasure he could give her?

Stopping before the window, he stared out at the falling snow, watching as it swirled in the wind. He had not needed this complication. He had not wanted the Duke of Maitland spending the night. He did not want to think about the long night ahead, wondering if Maitland would be visiting Holly's chamber.

His fingers tightened against the chilled wood frame. Is that why Holly had dismissed him? She was meeting Maitland? Was she going to entertain the duke wearing that scandalous gown?

His body tightened when he thought of the body that lay beneath the gown. His mouth went dry as he called forward the image of her standing naked before him, her lovely ivory thighs encased in cream silk hose and matching bows. Good God, how he had been inflamed to see her naked. He'd been speechless as he kneeled before her, his gaze traversing every plane, every indentation and curve. How he wanted to taste her skin--skin he knew would be supple beneath his mouth and sweet on his tongue. He closed his eyes, still able to smell the sweet fragrance of her arousal.

No, Holly would not entertain Maitland the way she had entertained him. He could not bear it--the duke with his hands all over that body, tearing that dress from her.

Mindless, he stalked to the door and threw it open. Stepping into the hall, he barged into a solid figure.

"Sorry about that, old boy," the duke drawled, swinging his

coat over his shoulder.

Andrew scoured the rake from ruffled hair to the tip of his shirt-tails which hung outside his breeches. Bloody hell, was he too late? He looked up and noticed the devilish glint in the duke's eyes. His brow was arched arrogantly and a slow grin parted his mouth.

"I trust you'll be silent," the duke asked. "I'm afraid you've caught me returning from a tryst."

Andrew felt his blood begin to boil and he saw red. God help him, but he was going thrash the living daylights out of the duke.

"Night, old boy," Maitland drawled, whistling as he went on his way.

With a growl, Andrew decided that Maitland's thrashing could wait, he had more important matters to see to. Turning the corner, he entered the hall that led to the family's quarters, the same hall that Maitland had just emerged from. Bloody hell, there could be no other explanation, he had been with Holly, and by the looks of his dishabille, he had been with her intimately as well.

Reaching for the latch, he noticed the light from beneath the door. She was still awake, no doubt still reeling from Maitland's practiced seduction. With a fury he had never known, he opened the door and flung it wide, not caring that the loud crack might wake the household.

And there she was, sitting at her dressing table, brushing her hair--hair that he had never seen down. Hair that made his body tighten and his fingers curl into fists.

She started and met his gaze in her looking gaze. Her brush was frozen midair. Her mouth parted but no words were uttered. In three strides he had reached her, had caged her with his arms on either side of her body. His fingers gripped the rose wood vanity and his eyes captured and held hers in the glass.

"What does he mean to you?" he asked slowly and with an edge that sent her shoulders tensing.

"I ... I..." she stammered, before setting the brush atop the table and reaching for the edges of her wrapper and bringing it tight around her throat. "I don't know what you mean."

"Don't lie," he hissed, tearing the wrapper from her hand and shoving it down her shoulders to reveal the translucent nightgown beneath the robe. Her breasts were heavy against the fine lawn and the candle on the table illuminated the round edges of her breasts. His gaze lowered and his hand involuntarily reached out to stroke the side of her right breast. "Don't lie, and don't hide from me, Holly," he commanded, feeling the edge of his anger evaporate, only to be replaced by a dangerous lust that was coursing unfulfilled in his veins.

She swallowed, and he saw her throat slide up and down and he could not resist following the path with his finger. "What does Maitland mean to you?' he asked again.

"He ... he is a friend," she replied, her gaze finding his. "That is all."

"And what am I, Holly?" he asked as he hooked a finger beneath the collar of her nightrail and began to slide it away from her shoulder. "Am I just a friend as well?"

"You were," she said on a hiss as he bared her breast. He studied the perfect circle, the pert pink nipple that crinkled invitingly beneath his finger. Blood surged to his cock as he stroked the sensitive flesh, then flicked it, watching as her breathing escalated.

"Was?" he whispered in ear.

"You left," she said flatly, looking away from him, but he captured her chin in his free hand and forced her gaze to meet his in the mirror.

"I had to," he said fiercely. "Didn't you see that? Can't you understand?"

"It doesn't matter," she said. "It's over now."

His blood froze in his veins. He did not want to hear those words. He did not want to see that particular expression on her face.

"Why?" he snarled. "Because Maitland is part of your life now? Because you *think* you're in love with him?"

"Please, Andrew, don't do this," she pleaded, but pleas ceased the moment he cupped her breast and skimmed his thumb along her nipple.

"I survived eight years in that hot, unforgiving jungle for you. I suffered, every single day and I told myself it was worth it because I was doing it for you."

"I never asked--"

"You didn't *have* to," he hissed. "I knew what needed to be done and I did it."

"Why?" she asked, "just tell me why you didn't tell me you were leaving? Why didn't you write to me?"

"I was afraid," he whispered, pulling the other sleeve along her arm until the gown rested along her waist and her breasts were bare. "I was afraid that if you begged me to stay that I would not be strong enough to resist your pleas."

He cupped her in both hands and she allowed her back to soften, allowed her head to tilt back to rest against his chest. He went to his knees and began to nuzzle the side of her breast until his lips were scant inches from her nipple.

"I was afraid that I would not be able to continue to stay there once I received your letters. I wanted to do this the night I left. I wanted to see you naked. I wanted to touch you and kiss you, but I was afraid that the memories would prove too much and I would weaken and rush home to you before my plans were ready."

Bringing her back against his chest, he cupped her and brought her nipple to his mouth, licking and sucking, watching in the mirror as he did it. "But I wanted to do this, Holly, never think I didn't. I burned for you, I would have done anything to see you like this."

"Then why did you leave me?" she asked, her voice soft and filled with sensual languor.

"To give you what you want, what you need," he rasped before curling his tongue along the taut bud. "To throw silk gowns at your feet and fit you with jewels. To lavish you with carriages and fancy homes."

Her body went still in his arms, then she reached for her nightgown and covered herself. "Get out," she snapped.

"No," he said, rising to his knees. "I won't leave, not ever again."

"I don't want what you're offering," she said in a cold, distant voice.

"And why not?" he barked. "Because it doesn't come with a title? Because my blood runs hot and red, not blue and cold?"

Her beautiful blue eyes darkened and she reached for her brush, throwing it at him. He moved to the right, barely missing being hit in the shoulder with it.

"Get out," she spat, her eyes blazing.

"Not until I get what I want," he growled, reaching for her. "I suffered every damn day and every damn night in that God forsaken country, and all so I could have you. And have you I will--tonight." He took a step forward and reached for her. "Now, no more talking. The only sounds I want to hear from you are urgent pleas and husky pants."

"You can't do this," she cried, as he picked her up and carried her to the bed.

"I can, and I most certainly will," he said, tossing her down onto the bed. "I'll show you what you're missing, what your blue blooded lover can't show you."

"What?" she gasped as he tore the delicate lawn nightgown from her body.

"What it is like to be taken by a hot-blooded commoner. And I am going to take," he said, his voice gravelly as he sat back on his heels and studied her nakedness. "And you're going to give me what I want."

Chapter Eight

Holly moaned as Andrew fell on top of her. He was hot and hard, and she could not help but take delight in the frantic, almost angry way he tore at his cravat and shirt. When he bared his chest to her, she felt her eyes widen in wonder. How muscular he was, how sculpted his body was beneath his gold skin. Her breath caught in her lungs as he braced his weight on his hands that rested on either side of her head and lowered his chest to hers. He brushed the silky hair of his chest against her breasts, and she stirred restlessly as his hair tickled her straining nipples.

His eyes darkened to the color of moss before he brushed against her again, watching as her breasts softened and molded beneath him. "How perfect you feel beneath me," he murmured, and Holly felt the wetness of arousal dampen her thighs. "I will never get enough of seeing you beneath me. I will always want to see you naked--in my room, in our bed."

This is what she had wanted from him eight years ago. This is what she had needed. She still needed it, yet she could not stop herself from remembering his words, or the ferocious anger she had felt.

"We must talk," she gasped, "there is too much to be said, we can't--"

"No more talking," he growled. "We will talk after we have put our anger to better use. I promise you," he whispered against her mouth, "I will tell you everything as you're laying satisfied in my arms and not a minute before that. Touch me. I burn for your touch."

"No, Andrew--"

But then he was fully atop her, capturing her mouth with his. His kiss turned greedy, frantic. His hands were everywhere. Sliding down her arms, her hips. His fingers cupped her buttocks and then slid up to knead her breasts. He took her nipples between his thumbs and fingers, squeezing, rolling, tweaking until she gasped beneath him, all the while kissing her with unfettered passion.

Holly had never felt anything so sinfully wicked in all her life. She forgot her outrage at his insinuations. Her body was awakening, flickering to life as it responded to his touch, heating her flesh as he made her burn for more. Her breasts ached for his lips, his tongue. The place between her thighs throbbed with a longing she had never felt, that she wasn't able to describe.

He plunged his tongue deep inside her mouth, and her legs slackened, opening for him, as his fingers danced along her thigh. She gasped as he settled his body more intimately over hers. He felt hard and heavy, yet gentle and loving. The throbbing length of his naked arousal rubbed against her thigh, burning her flesh. He groaned deeper and plunged his tongue in and out of her mouth as he pressed his erection rhythmically onto her leg.

"Touch me," he breathed harshly as he rocked his hips against her.

"Where?" she whispered, not really knowing what it was he wanted.

He raised his head then, his lips curving wickedly as he reached for her hand and placed it on his erection. His lashes fluttered closed as she encircled his flesh. She felt his fingers encase hers, moving her hand up and down, showing her how he wanted her to touch him.

"You do not know how many nights I've lain awake imagining this," he groaned, nuzzling a line between her breasts, his hand subtly quickening her strokes. "I've thought of you doing this to me, of seeing your hand stroking me until I'm mindless with need." He shuddered as her finger found the moisture trickling down his shaft. Wetting her thumb, she swirled it along the velvety tip.

Hissing, he let go of her hand, pumping himself against her palm. "You can't know how much I've wanted you. Do you even know that I've had to pleasure myself, pretending it was you loving me, stroking me? When I come, I imagine I'm pouring myself into you, bathing you with it."

Holly was beyond words, so entranced was she by watching the desire in Andrew's face. She didn't even think he knew what he was saying. He could have no understanding what his admission did to her. That he had thought of her in the nights as she had him, that he had been forced to act on his desires, to know that he satisfied his needs while fantasizing about her empowered her.

She clutched him tightly, stroking him quicker, her hand firming as it slid up the hard length. His breath quickened, rasping harshly against her neck as her hand worked up and down his shaft telling her without words that he liked what she was doing to him.

Slipping her nipple into his mouth, Andrew suckled, drawing the sensitive flesh deep in his mouth. His hand cupped her intimately, her thighs immediately parted when his fingers slide inside her. She moaned at the invasion.

"My God," he whispered thickly, his tongue laving her hardened nipple. "I cannot wait to watch you as I sink myself inside you, watching as your body molds to me, taking all of me in. You'll belong to me then. Forever. I'll never let you go. So sweet," he rasped sliding down the length of her, parting her slick sex with both hands, exposing her to his eyes and his mouth. Stubble grazed her thighs as he lowered his head to her flesh, the sensation sending jolts of awareness straight through her.

He licked her then. His hot tongue scorched a path up the length of her, each time using the flat of his tongue to fully cover her sex. "So beautiful," he whispered, nuzzling her with his lips, flicking her with this tongue. "I shall have to feed a very long time to satisfy this hunger."

"No," she whimpered, squirming in his iron grasp.

"Don't be afraid," he murmured, his finger stroking that sensitive part of her. "I will take of you. I'll always take care of you," he said quietly. "Now come for me."

With deliberate strokes, he sucked and teased, and then, when her body tightened and bowed beneath him, he sucked harder and made the world shattered around her.

"Andrew!" she cried, gasping, clawing at his hair.

"Let me take care of you," he whispered. "Let me try, love,"

"Oh, God, please, Andrew," she begged, struggling for air.

"All right, love," he said, slipping his fingers inside her and stroking her, faster and faster. "Give yourself over to me," he encouraged. "Let me give you pleasure."

"Yes," she cried, then began to shake uncontrollably in his arms.

"Next time," he murmured between kisses, "you'll shake like that when I'm deep inside you. Next time you'll beg me to complete you with my cock. Next time I'll give you everything I have, Holly."

* * * *

Holly stirred sleepily beside him. Andrew gazed down at the naked woman lying curled against his body. She was cold. He could feel the heat, that only moments before had engulfed her, evaporate into the drafty winter air. Outside the wind howled, rattling the wood shutters against the limestone walls. Reaching for her quilt, he reluctantly covered her and then wrapped his arms tightly around her, bringing her body against his.

She mumbled something he couldn't really understand, then sighed and nuzzled her face against his chest. Closing his eyes, he savored the feel of her, the smell of her against him. Suddenly, every distasteful minute he had spent in India was replaced by the perfection of this moment, the moment he had worked so hard for, the moment when Holly would be in his arms and would belong to him.

He no longer cared about Maitland and what he meant to her. He knew, as soon as he heard her surprised cry, saw the frightened and confused expression in her eyes that she had never experienced the level of passion that he awakened in her. No, if Maitland had tried to arouse her, then he'd been a miserable failure. Smiling, he took perverse pleasure in knowing it.

"Holly," he whispered, knowing he should be leaving. "Wake up, love."

"Hmm," she mumbled sleepily.

"I must go," he said, kissing her softly.

"I know, you must always go. You always leave me when I need you most. You don't want to be seen with me," she whispered before turning on her side, away from him.

"Not that I don't want to, love," he said, feeling his gut clenching. "It's that I really shouldn't be found here, lying naked in your bed."

"I know," she sighed.

"Holly?" he asked, unable to hide the fear he heard in his voice. "What is it? What is wrong?"

"I knew you'd leave me again after you got what you wanted. I knew it wasn't really me you wanted. You just enjoyed the chase I gave you."

He felt as though he'd been hit in the gut with a hammer. "How can you say that? Wake up," he commanded.

"I don't want to wake up," she mumbled.

"Tomorrow morning I shall be waiting for you outside. Make certain you are there, on the terrace. We need to talk."

"About what?" she asked, bitterness creeping into her voice.

"About everything, love, but most importantly about you becoming my wife and the beautiful babies you're going to give me."

Chapter Nine

Holly looked nervously behind her shoulder when she heard the salon door creak open.

"Holly," Lizzie cried. "Do hold on to me!"

"I am holding on to you," Holly snapped, relieved to see that it was one of the maids carrying in more evergreen bows and not Andrew coming in search of her.

"Will you stop jumping and starting at every sound and pay attention," Lizzie said with a glare as she looked down from her upstretched arms. "Or you may stand on this tippy stool and hang the mistletoe."

Holly glared back at her sister, but tightened her hands around Lizzie's waist, trying to settle her discomposure. Lizzie had been after all her all morning, making veiled insinuations and trying to uncover the source of her discomfort.

"Holly, do you think I've hung the mistletoe too high," Lizzie asked, dropping her arms to her sides. "Do you think the young gentlemen that arrive tonight will see it?"

"Are you asking me if someone will notice you beneath the mistletoe, Lizzie?"

Her young sister blushed before jumping down from the stool onto the floor.

"Lizzie Harrington!" her mother gasped from her spot before

the fireplace. "Do act like a lady."

"Yes, Mama," Lizzie muttered, dusting off her hands.

"Well?" Holly asked. "Do you want to be kissed?"

"A bit, I suppose," Lizzie said, grinning.

"Girls," her mother called. "Come here and help Sarah and me with this bow."

Holly and Lizzie shrugged and strode to where their mother and the housekeeper were struggling to put bows and holly sprigs into evergreen bows.

"We must hurry, girls," her mother commanded. "Cook will have luncheon ready, and we don't have the ballroom fully decorated."

"I'm not hungry," Holly murmured, reaching for a sprig of holly covered with red berries. " I can stay behind and finish the room with Sarah."

"Nonsense. You will do no such thing, Holly. We've guests in the house, if you will remember. I will need yours and Lizzie's assistance at luncheon."

Holly felt her belly churn uncomfortably. Andrew would be at luncheon, and she had no wish to see him. She had successfully avoided him all morning, in the hopes she could use the time to figure out how she was going to face him without thinking of the scandalous things he had done to her last night--not to mention the ease she had allowed him to do such things.

She had no wish to see him and know that he thought her nothing more than a materialistic aristocrat. She didn't want to see him and think how he thought her callous and superficial. She didn't want to look into those green eyes and fall easily into his arms despite the hurt and pain and anger. For that was what truly frightened her--the hold he had upon her. Even when she was angry and hurt by his words, even when he insinuated that she was shallow, he still provoked her desire, her love. For despite his unflattering thoughts last evening, despite what he thought she wanted, despite that those thoughts had hurt her, she had still given him what he wanted.

"Lucinda, dear," Lady Mary called as she breezed into the ballroom. "I've had Andrew carry in more pine branches. Where shall we put them?"

Holly's spine went rigid as she bent to retrieve a red silk bow. Her head snapped to the door and she found him, holding a box overflowing with pine branches. He captured her gaze, staring at her, and it felt as though every person in the room melted away to the periphery, leaving only him and her, standing before each other, staring.

"Holly," Lizzie hissed beside her. "Mother is asking you a question."

She blinked, breaking the spell, and swallowed hard, trying to right her reeling senses and to shove aside the image of Andrew's beautiful mouth capturing her breast.

"Yes, Mama," she said, forcing her voice to sound natural.

"What do you think of putting the wassail bowl and the cups on this table, and then when Sarah carries in the pudding it won't be so far for her to walk?"

Holly glanced around the room, careful to avoid Andrew's shrewd gaze as he set his box down on the floor. "I think it might be too close to the fire," she said, swallowing hard despite her dry, cracking throat. "What if a spark were to land on some poor lady's slipper?"

"Quite right," her mother said. "I never thought of that."

"What about beneath the window?" Holly said, pointing to the beautiful, decorated windows that were swagged in greenery and flowers. "And then one can look out at the twinkling snow in the moonlight."

"You're brilliant, dear," her mother replied, smiling knowingly at Lady Mary. "I vow you will make someone a very good wife and hostess."

Holly cleared her throat and was unable to stop her gaze from travelling to Andrew, who stood against the wall watching her. When he caught her eyes he raised one brow knowingly.

"Now then," her mother said, "shall we not all go in to luncheon?"

"I'm really not hungry," Holly mumbled.

"Nonsense!" Lady Mary scoffed, reaching for her arm and hooking her hand around Holly's elbow. "You've put in a full morning of work getting the ballroom ready for this evening. You must be famished. Come, I will not take 'no' for answer."

Holly followed the countess to the buffet table which was placed in front of a bank of French doors that had been set up in the yellow salon. A line had already formed, and numerous couples were milling about, jockeying for the nearest pile of plates.

"You wouldn't be avoiding me, would you?"

Holly stiffened as Andrew's words caressed her ear. His breath, warm and soft, blew her errant curls against her neck, sending a delicious shiver along her spine.

"Good day, sir."

"My, aren't you being frightfully proper this evening. And here I thought we'd torn down all those awkward barriers." She gasped when she felt his fingers dance along her muslin skirt to cup her buttock. "You haunted my dreams all night. I can't wait to get you alone."

"Sir, please."

"*Please*, is what I intend to do, my sweet Holly."

Holly sucked in her breath as he discreetly rubbed his lower body against hers, shielding the action by reaching for a plate.

Heat infused her cheeks, and mercifully the line began to move, enabling her to extricate herself from his grasp.

"Have a crab cake, sir."

"I'm not hungry for crab at the moment. What else have you to offer me?"

She cast him a disapproving glance and continued to walk the length of the table, taking a few samples of the delicacies being displayed.

"How about some strawberries?" she said hopefully. "They're plump and very likely the sweetest thing you've ever tasted."

"Impossible. I've already tasted the sweetest thing on Earth. It was last night, if you will recall. I, for one, shall never forget it."

"Andrew," Lady Mary said, glancing up from a platter of oysters. "Get yourself something to eat."

"I thank you, but what I'm craving doesn't seem to be available."

"Oh?" Lady Mary asked, her eyes glittering like sparkling topaz. "Perhaps something more to your tastes will become available as the afternoon progresses."

"One can only hope, madam."

Lady Mary searched his face, a wide, mysterious grin unfurling her wrinkled mouth. Refraining from further comment she continued to make her way down the line, far ahead of Holly. Dismayed by the countess' obvious lack of support, Holly continued on, feigning indifference to the towering figure behind her.

"I can still taste you on my lips, my tongue, love--"

"Your Grace," Holly called, waving to get the duke's attention and to distract herself from Andrew's disturbing presence.

"Ah, Lady Holly," he brightened. "Wherever have you've been hiding? I've walked the estate all morning in an attempt to steal a moment of your time."

"Indeed, sir?"

"You seem flushed, Holly. Are you well?"

"I'm well," she gasped breathlessly, feeling Andrew's flingers glide along her hip. "It's just that it is rather hot in here."

"Well, allow me to escort you outside. No doubt you're needing a breath of fresh air."

"Andrew, dear," came Lady Mary's loud voice. "Do take Holly out into the garden for some fresh air, she looks flushed. And don't forget your cape, dear," Mary called. "You wouldn't want to take a chill."

Andrew didn't wait to hear any more. Instead, he reached for her plate and slipped it onto the tray of a passing footman. Grabbing her hand, he promptly began to head for the terrace. Holly had to skip to keep up with him.

She mustn't be alone with him. She mustn't weaken like last night. She had to keep a sensible head about her and not let his green eyes and sculpted lips make a hash out of her thoughts.

Pulling her into a darkened corner, Andrew pressed up against her, his breath hot against her neck; she could feel the satiny softness of his lips as they grazed her wildly bounding pulse.

"Why so skittish?"

"What are you doing? The servants will see us," she hissed, darting furtive glances around them. "We are in full view of the ballroom."

Her legs gave out as his long tapered finger circled her nipple through her gown. Gooseflesh rose on her skin. Her resolve was slipping--she knew it and was helpless to stop it.

"I want you, Holly. Last night was but a small taste of what we could experience together. Come upstairs with me and let me taste you. Let me feel your skin against mine. I'm offering you pleasure beyond your wildest dreams. After tonight," he said thickly, "you will never forget you belong to me."

"Belong to you?" she snapped, irritated with him. "You talk as if I'm an object to be owned or bought," she huffed, pushing him away, her faculties returning with alarming speed. "I will not be bought. No man will ever buy me."

"Holly, you misunderstand."

"Tell me, sir, what facts have I misinterpreted?"

"You're getting this all wrong," he said, reaching for her wrist. "I meant that once I make you mine, I'll never give you up."

"No," she cried, twisting from his grasp. "That is not what you meant. You think that you can purchase my body with meaningless baubles. Do you think that I would actually allow you to bed me simply because you've come back to England a rich and powerful man?"

"What will happen between us will not be a simple bedding--"

"Do you think me that desperate, sir?" Her eyes began to fill with tears she didn't want to show him. "I don't need your sort of false affection and attentions, Andrew."

"Dammit, why must you make everything so difficult?"

"You should never have come back," she countered. "You should have kept your bloody fortune to yourself and attempted to woo some other titled woman who actually wants your filthy money."

"Where are you going?" he roared. "We are by no means finished with this discussion."

"I have a ball to prepare for. Good day, Andrew."

Chapter Ten

What the devil did she think she was about? Andrew watched her stalk away from him, her hips swaying, calling to his rapidly slipping self-control.

She rounded the corner, and no longer in his sight, her words came back, chilling him, warning him that she just might not be willing to give him what he wanted. *A titled woman who actually wants your filthy money.*

What the hell did she want from him? He could provide her with nothing else but his fortune. He had neither a title or a prestigious surname. It could only be said that his fortune was derived from trade--a dirty word in many eyes of the aristocracy. Perhaps Holly was one of those aristocrats who longed for an old title to go along with old money.

What about love?

The soft words reached him with the breeze and he looked over his shoulder, wondering if his guardian had not sought him out. But he was alone, looking out through the terrace windows to the snow-covered path.

What of soft words and odes to her beauty? Why not tell her how you feel about her, how you've always felt?

Is that what Holly wanted? Compliments?

Not wants, but needs, the words whispered in his head.

She should damn well know how he felt. After all, he'd told her last night. Told her that everything he'd acquired in India had been for her sake. For her pleasure. But if she needed to have her desirability confirmed, he'd do it.

And your love, what of that? Will you tell her that?

"If she ever allows me more than five minutes of her time, I'd like to tell her everything," he muttered beneath his breath.

Perhaps you should take her someplace away from here, where you can be alone.

He smiled, thinking how devious his mind was. That was exactly what he needed to do. He needed to be alone with her, where there were no distractions. Where they could be alone to talk and make love.

An excellent notion, he thought, stalking up the carpeted stairs to Holly's chamber. He would take her someplace special, and he would not take no for an answer.

* * * *

"Holly, dearest," the voice came through the sound of her racking sobs. *"Darling, get up and wash your face."*

"No," she cried, covering her eyes with her hand.

"He is coming, dearest. He is coming to take you away. Get up, you cannot wish to have him see you this way."

"Why should he not see how bloody miserable he's made me?"

"Holly, there is no time, dearest. You must listen to me. You must go with him. The future demands it. You must allow him to take you wherever he wishes, and you must listen to what he says."

"I am not going anywhere," she mumbled between hiccups.

"You most certainly are," Andrew snarled, stalking into her room and marching to her bed.

She turned away, but not before she heard her grandmother's voice in her mind. *Everyone's future depends upon this, Holly. Yours, Maitland's, those not yet born--everyone, dearest.*

"Holly," Andrew said, his voice firm and in control. "Fetch your cloak, you're coming with me." And then he picked her up from the bed and placed her on her feet before him. "And I'll carry you through this damn house and put you in the carriage wearing nothing more than that muslin dress if you do not reach for it within a minute."

"The roads," she mumbled, struggling for any excuse she could find to provide her with the means to stay in her room indulging in a fit of melancholy.

"The roads are passable, besides, we are taking a sleigh, and it is not far from here."

"Andrew--"

He reached for her hands and brought them to his lips. "Please, Holly. Say yes. *Please*."

She nodded and reached for her cloak that lay draped on the bench that sat at the end of her bed. "All right, Andrew. But just this one time."

"That is all it will take, love," he said, smiling softly before skimming the pad of his finger along her mouth.

* * * *

The log snapped and sizzled before being engulfed by a huge orange flame that erupted and then flickered wildly. Heat rolled out of the hearth and Holly, chilled to the bones with cold, rubbed her hands vigorously as she stood before the hearth.

It had been a short but cold ride to the estate. The empty house was damp and drafty, without curtains and furnishings to absorb the cold. Another chill reverberated down her spine and she trembled, bringing her hands around her waist.

"Come," Andrew whispered, reaching for her hand. "I have another fire going in the only room with furniture."

She saw that his gaze was pointed on the elaborate staircase that led to the sleeping quarters. She balked, but he soothed her with soft words. Determined, he pulled along behind him.

"What do you think of your house?" he asked quietly as he helped her up the stairs.

"*My* house?" she asked, looking around.

"Yes, your house," he grinned, smiling back at her. "Were you not the one who used to tell me how much you adored this house and its grounds? How one day you would own it?"

She looked up at him, her eyes widening. "You've bought this house?" she asked incredulously, stumbling on a stair.

"I have, love." They reached the top step and were now standing in the upstairs hall. He picked her up and she gasped, but he ignored her protests and continued down the hall. He stopped inside a large room that was dominated by a huge mahogany bed. The bed hangings were done in the most luxurious blue silk she had ever seen. The blankets were pulled back, revealing a fur coverlet and plump, inviting pillows.

"Have I ever told you, Holly, how stunningly beautiful you are?" he asked quietly as he put her down on the bed. "Have I ever told you that when I am near you I can hardly breathe and that I become a nervous fool, afraid I will not be able to speak a word of sense?"

"No," she whispered, feeling her insides begin to heat and twist.

"Then I was a fool," he said, reaching for her half boots and untying them before he let them fall to the floor.

"I was a fool to not have told you that I've dreamt of you for so many years--years before I even left for India." He reached beneath her and undid the fastenings of her gown. "I should have told you I wanted you. That I wanted to see you naked in my bed, naked beneath me."

"Andrew," she moaned, feeling his hot hands skim her flesh as he slowly pulled her gown away from her body.

"And you've only grown more beautiful, Holly. The other night, as you stood before me, naked and aroused, you left me speechless, otherwise I would have told you what you were doing to me. But I couldn't talk. I could only look and feel and think about pushing my way into your body."

Her belly tightened and flickers of awareness tingled along her pores. Her dress was off and his fingers were deftly untying the ribbon of her chemise.

"For eight long years I've dreamt of you, wondering how you would feel. Wondering if I would ever be enough for someone as lovely and perfect as you."

Her chemise fluttered to the floor. She could feel the luxurious fur beneath her, warming her back, and Andrew's hot gaze roaming her body, heating her breasts and belly and thighs.

"Nearly every night since I was seventeen years old, I have dreamt of possessing you, of making you mine. I've seen you round with my children. I've thought of watching you with my babe at your breast." She opened her mouth, but her put his finger on her lips, silencing her. "Every night I've thought of the ways we would make those babies, Holly. I've thought of what I would do when you are round with them, how I would touch you and taste you."

"But you left me," she whispered, feeling his fingers reverently caressing her throat and the swells of her breasts.

"Do you think it was easy?" he asked, eyes gaze flickering up to her face, studying her. "It was the hardest thing I've ever done.

I stood outside your door that night, listening to you prepare for bed, imagining the crisp white lawn nightgown skimming over your body, imagining my hands gathering up the hem and raising it to reveal your blonde thatch and your rounded hips. I nearly burst into your room so many times that night, but I knew if I did, I would have taken you completely, and that was not how I wanted to leave you--defiled and alone."

Her toes curled into the fur and she watched him restlessly, trying to concentrate on what he was saying

"I left because I had to, Holly. I had to make something of myself. I had to show you what sort of man I could be, what sort of provider I could be. I wanted you to be proud of me, proud of the things I could give you. I didn't want to rely on my guardians for everything. I wanted to be my own man--*your* man," he said, thickly. "I wanted to lay riches at your feet, to show you that I was worthy of you, despite the fact that I didn't have a title and my parents were merely artists."

"Andrew," she whispered and suddenly she was feeling tears well in her eyes.

"I don't have a title, Holly. I never shall. But I have an influential position on the board of trustees with the East India Company. I have a seat in the House of Commons. I can dress you in silks and jewels and keep you in the mode you've been raised in. I have a fortune to pass on to my children, and I shall work diligently to make a legacy for them as well."

The tears were now streaming down her cheeks and she reached for his hand that lay on her breast and covered his fingers with hers.

"What does *he* mean to you?" he asked, his eyes darkening.

"Not what you mean to me," she whispered.

"You mean everything to me, Holly. When I was over there, I thought of nothing but how I could make you love me. How if I worked harder and became richer you would love me, and I would have you. I never allowed myself to think or believe that you would marry before I could return home. I prayed every night that you would not find someone to love. I vowed to whatever demon or angel heard me to please let some piece of me reside in your heart." He lowered his head and kissed her fingers, before skimming his mouth along her nipple and breast. "And every Christmas Eve, I would carefully take out that sprig of mistletoe and think of you. I would run the piece of velvet you kissed along my lips and pretend that you were there with me, loving me. You don't know how many times I relived that kiss, how many different endings I envisioned."

He looked up at her, his eyes gleaming. "Say that I have not lost you. Say that there is still a chance for us to be together."

"I never wanted a title, Andrew. I never asked for riches or silks. I only ever wanted you. You didn't have to leave."

"I did, love, because I had nothing to offer you. I loved you too much to confine you to a life of hard work and struggle. I wanted to be a better man, so that I could be happier and make you happy. I was afraid that love was not enough to keep you enthralled with me. Because, Holly, I don't want your love for a year, or five years. I want it forever."

"You have it," she whispered, trailing her finger down his cheek. "You'll always have it, even if you manage to lose your fortune or your seat in parliament. You've always had it."

"I love you, Holly. You've always been the most beautiful creature I've ever seen. I've always wanted you, always desired you. Never doubt that."

"Show me this desire, then," she whispered. "Show me what you've dreamed of doing to me."

"Say you will marry me and love me forever, and I will show you everything. I will tell you everything."

"I will love you forever. For richer or poorer, I will always be yours."

Chapter Twelve

His lips and tongue tasted the sweet skin of her throat and the swells of her breasts. Her hands were fisted in his hair, clutching and tugging, begging him without words for more. He had taken his time, kissing her, stroking her, telling her how her lush figure inflamed him. She was on fire for him and he was hard as iron for her.

"Is this what you want, Holly?"

"Andrew," it was a husky reply that did strange things to his brain, making him think of nothing other than hearing his name on her lips as he slid inside her.

He met her gaze. "I must have you, love."

He didn't wait for her reply, instead he took her lips hungrily in his, kissing her with the need and desire that was swimming in his veins. She felt so soft beneath him, so right. Her breasts were full and high and made for his mouth and hands, and her thighs--good God they hugged and molded his erection as if she had been designed for him. Everything about her was perfect.

With shaking hands, she clasped his head in her hands while he kneaded her belly with his mouth, the masculine scent of him wafting up to heighten her senses. Instinctively her fingers curled in his hair, clenching tightly as he nuzzled her curls.

The feel of his body, the heat, the hardness of him, soothed yet frightened her. His desire was barely leashed, that much she was certain of, and yet she knew he wouldn't hurt her or take her against her will.

"Tell me you want this, Holly. Let me show you what it can be like for us."

"Love me, Andrew."

The words were simple, but true. She wanted this, and she wanted to experience it with Andrew. No man had ever made her feel this way--conscious of her femininity, of her own desires and needs. She felt beautiful and sensual, and this afternoon, in the house and the bed he had bought for her, she was going to give in to temptation.

Straddling her body, Andrew placed her legs over each of his muscled thighs. His hands, a stark contrast against her pale flesh continued to slide up her sides to cup and squeeze her breasts. "You won't ever regret this, Holly," he vowed, trailing his tongue up her belly. His silky hair tickled the undersides of her breasts, making her skin erupt in gooseflesh.

"I could never regret anything I do with you."

His head was atop her breasts, his eyes searching hers through the pale shaft of moonlight. He looked boyish and vulnerable, and infinitely lovable.

"Tonight, I will show you why you were made for me."

She watched him remove his shirt with short, vicious movements, flinging it onto the floor along with his trousers and boots before turning to rest lightly on top of her. The instant his naked body made contact with hers, Holly felt a jolt of awareness. He felt heavy and warm and very male.

"No other man shall ever have you. You're mine, Holly. You have been since the first time I saw you."

His possessive words thrilled her and she moaned, angling her hips so that his fingers would dip lower and part her. "Please."

"Please what?" he teased, his tongue laving her nipple before he captured it between his teeth and bit gently. "Please stop?"

"No."

"Tell me, Holly."

His mouth was pure magic. Just when she thought she couldn't stand it any longer, he turned his attention to her other breast, all the while his fingers continued to tease the flesh of her sex.

"I want to hear the words."

"Make love to me," she panted, her hips arching fiercely in order to feel more of his touch.

And then his mouth was on hers, his lips and tongue demanding as his fingers parted her and stroked her.

"My god, I love the way you respond to me."

She cried out when she felt him insert one, then another finger. *"Please,"* she gasped and begged, not knowing what it was she needed.

He'd never had a woman beg for his touch before. Never had a female made him so aware of his virility. Everything about Holly pulled and tugged at the primitive urges buried deep inside him. The desire to take and plunder was strong, almost impossible to resist. All his senses cried out to take her, to sink himself inside her tight welcoming body and claim her for himself.

But it wasn't enough. He wanted more. He wanted Holly at his mercy, begging him to fill her, to take her as no other man ever had, or ever would. He wanted to hear his name uttered in her husky voice when it was full of passion.

She rocked against his hand. He watched as she learned and responded to the rhythm of his touch, her hips moving seductively in time to his fingers. It would be even more erotic to watch her move when he was inside her, encouraging her to take all of him, watching her lush thighs encase his waist as he stroked her deeper with each thrust.

Oblivious to the warnings in his head, Andrew reached for her hands and pinned them in his, holding them above her head. Her breasts brushed his mouth, teasing him with taut, pink nipples. His erection was riding hard between her soft thighs, driving him forward, urging him to part her. To take her in an act of raw possession.

He gave in, parting her with his shaft, allowing himself to slide along her, feeling the slickness of her desire cover him. Her tongue came out to wet her lips and he captured it with his mouth, imitating what his body would soon be doing inside her.

"I can't wait--please."

"You wanted to know what it was like to be consumed by passion. I assure you the flames of passion are merely smoldering."

"How can you...." she trailed off as he released her hands, only to lightly stroke his fingers down her sides, then circle her hips before cupping her buttocks, kneading in time to his strokes.

"Why are you waiting?"

"Because," he leaned forward, peering into her passion glazed eyes. "You are still thinking. You're not mindless with need."

His touch was light, slow, purposefully not enough to give her release, but enough to make her plead for what she wished.

"Is this what you want?"

"Yes ... *no*!" she twisted beneath him.

"No?" He removed her legs from his waist and resting them against his shoulders. "What about this?"

The minute Andrew set his mouth to that part of her, Holly wished to scream. It was decidedly indecent and wicked and decadent and--<u>ooh</u>, she couldn't think anymore, she didn't want to concentrate on anything but the pleasure his mouth was giving her.

"Ah, this is it," he said between flicks of his tongue. "Yes, this is definitely what you want."

His words were arrogant, assured, and laced with a lethal sensuality that Holly was unable to resist. He was very male, and he made her feel very much like a desirable female.

"Just let it happen," he encouraged, as her body began to shake, splintering her thoughts. And then he was inside her, filling her as she continued to tremble, his strong hands fitting her thighs against his waist as he pushed further and further into her body. Holly moaned his name.

"Say my name again."

"Andrew," she whimpered as he pushed past the last remaining barrier of her virginity.

"You feel like Heaven, Holly. All these years I've dreamed of what it would be like to have you beneath me. I should have known it would feel like nothing I've ever experienced before."

"Is it ... I mean ... am I doing it right?"

"Better than right, my little angel," he grinned, his broad shoulders and arms cocooning her in their strength. "You're perfect, Holly."

And then he was moving on her, the muscles of his shoulders

and arms bunching and tightening with his exertion. His strokes were slow and intentional, forcing her to take all of him, and she did, took everything he had to offer and gave what she could of herself, including her love.

"Move, Holly," he commanded gruffly. "Take all of me inside you."

And she did. She moved with him and gave herself to him completely.

If he didn't get a hold of himself soon, Andrew cursed, the whole damn thing would be over much too soon. God, she felt right. He would never forget the incredible pleasure, the satisfaction of slipping into her tight body, feeling her stretch to mold him. It was a primitive feeling but a powerful one. He had claimed her at last--body and soul.

"My God, it's never been like this," he groaned, feeling his seed start to spill inside her, and then he was fully atop her, whispering into her hair, *I love you, I desire you, I'll never stop wanting you*, as his body tightened and shook, his climax taking over his strength as he gave himself up to her gentle embrace, letting himself sink into her soft body as it cushioned and welcomed him.

His breathing was harsh pants as he rested his head between her breasts, drinking in the scent of jasmine and spice provocatively mixed with his own scent. He had branded her as his own, and he was left wondering just who had done the begging, and which one of them had been left to whose mercy.

* * * *

Holly was awakened by the feel of Andrew's mouth suckling her breast. She was on her side, pushed tight against him and she peered down, watching as his mouth loved her nipple. Slowly he sucked, his fingers drawing tiny circles along her belly and then suddenly they were on her hips, forcing her closer. His hand captured her thigh and flung it over his leg so that she was exposed to the cool air. He suckled her harder and slipped his erection inside her.

"Open your eyes love and let me see you as I make love to you."

Her eyelids fluttered open and she stared into his green eyes. Slowly he stroked her, sliding sensuously and unhurriedly deep inside. "So beautiful," he whispered, his gaze trailing down between their bodies. "There is nothing more powerful than watching your body take me in."

"I want to see," she whispered shyly, a blush creeping into her cheeks.

"All right, love," he said, kissing her, before slowly sliding out of her body. He ignored her moan of protest and began to fluff up the pillows against the headboard and then he placed her against them and hooked her legs over his shoulders so that her hips were angled up and she could see her sex.

"Glistening with desire," he whispered, stroking her with his fingertip. "Beautiful lips swollen with arousal," he said, before parting her and placing a soft kiss at the crest of her. And then he took his engorged erection in his hand and brought it to her, then slid deep inside her. She watched, moaning, as his thick length disappeared inside her and then he pulled back, showing her his length before thrusting it back inside her.

"Beautiful quim loving me," he murmured huskily. "I will never get enough of watching this, of seeing you open for me, of feeling you stretching around me."

"Oh, God," she cried, feeling her legs begin to tremble as he thrust faster. She was so aroused, so hot, watching how he worked her.

"Watch me," he commanded when she closed her eyes. "Watch my cock taking you. Watch as your body takes my cock hungrily inside. It's been waiting, hasn't it, Holly? Waiting for years for this--for me, for my cock."

"Yes," she cried, gripping the fur as her passion escalated.

"That's it, love. Shake for me. Call my name. Tell me when it's time."

"Andrew," she moaned. She lifted her hips and watched as he sunk himself further and harder inside her.

"Come for me, Holly" he said through gritted teeth. "Because I'm coming. I can't wait. I've never seen anything so wondorous and I can't wait for you."

And then he was atop her, thrusting the last few times before collapsing against her.

"I love you, Holly," he murmured. "Forever."

"I love you, Andrew--forever."

"Then I may expect a kiss beneath the mistletoe tonight?"

She smiled and captured his lips between hers. "You may."

"And you will wear that red dress the first night we dine in our home?"

"If you'd like," she smiled.

"I'd like that," he grinned. "I'd like to see you on the table in that red silk. I shall lay you before me and pull up your skirts and feast on you for hours."

"You wicked man," she teased.

He raised his head from her breasts and grinned. "You wanted to know everything I was thinking."

"True," she said, smiling.

"And I'm also thinking that we need to return to the Lodge. I want you well rested for tonight when I come to visit you in your chamber. I won't spend another Christmas Eve alone, Holly. I'm going to wake up with you in my arms on Christmas morning and to hell with what anyone says about it."

"That sounds so very nice. But I'd rather that we spent the night here, so I can wake up in our bed."

"That could be arranged," he said. "right after we announce our engagement, I shall whisk you back here and love you the night through. It will be our secret," he whispered. "And it will get you far away from Maitland."

"And what of the mistletoe?"

"I'll bring plenty of mistletoe," he teased. "Enough to defile you in every room of the house."

"Sir, you are positively the most wicked man I've ever encountered.

"And the last," he said. "Now then, I have a very irritated voice in my head telling me that I cannot indulge myself in another bout of lovemaking. She's quite adamant that I return you to the Lodge. The possibility of scandal, you know."

"Oh, ignore it," Holly giggled, knowing that somehow her grandmother was there with them.

"Very well, love," he said, "then let us indulge again. This time I want you on top of me. Riding me."

Holly, you wicked, wicked, girl. You must get back to the Lodge! Your mother will be in hysterics, the guests shall soon be arriving and you're not even dressed yet.

Holly grinned, and looked down at Andrew. "I love you," she whispered. "Whether you are a prince or a pauper, a Nabob or a duke."

"Good," he said, lowering her onto him and filling her full of him. "Because I love you more than life itself."

Holly, her grandmother protested. *Really child, you must get home. Oh, Lord, you haven't heeded a word I've said. Why, oh why do you have to take after me?*

Grandmama, do float away.

Right dear, she said, but she was laughing. *I shall see you tonight, looking radiantly in love with your Andrew at your side. Your fate is sealed, dearest, and your future set.*

Will I give him children? she asked, suddenly fearing that she might not be able to make Andrew's fondest dream come true.

Yes, dearest, even now your child is taking root inside you. Insist upon an early wedding, darling. Don't listen to his concerns that the house will not be finished and the furniture will not have arrived in time for you to become mistress. Tell him that his daughter will not care as long as he is there to love her.

A daughter, she said, smiling wistfully.

"What's that, love?" he asked, loving her slowly as his hands caressed her body.

"A daughter, Andrew. I'm going to give you one."

"I know, love. And I've seen her and she's the most beautiful babe a man could desire. She's growing inside you even now."

"How did you know?" she whispered, gazing down at him.

"She came to visit me in India. That's how I knew I needed to come home."

"Our daughter?" she asked puzzled.

"Your grandmother," he whispered, drawing her head down to meet his. "I dreamt of her, and she told me the time was right. That you would love me with what I had and that my daughter would be conceived on Christmas Eve. I got on the next boat, thinking of you, hoping that the dream was real."

"It was real," she said, smiling down at him.

"I know love, I'm living it now. It's real. Our love is real. Kiss me, Holly," he commanded. "And pretend we're beneath the mistletoe."

A Bluestocking Christmas

Monica Burns

Chapter One

"I want to know why."

Ivy turned her head away from the stark fury on Simon's face. He'd betrayed her, and he still couldn't see it. In his arrogance, he'd betrayed her trust, just as Carolyn had. Her cousin's betrayal had been difficult enough, but Simon's was far more painful. While their original arrangement hadn't required her trust, she had given it nonetheless. Breaching that confidence, when she had so little to give, was the most brutal of all betrayals.

Even if she tried to explain it to him, she couldn't make him understand that they came from two different worlds, that it would always be a barrier between them. Her cousin had claimed background accounted for nothing, but her actions had revealed her true feelings. When Carolyn had entered the salon a short time ago, the past had rushed up to assault Ivy's senses--the rejection, the humiliation, the constant reminders that she was inferior to those of the peerage.

No. The chasm between herself and Simon was too wide to cross. It was a barrier that would even-- She slammed the door shut on her thoughts. Deliberately, she focused on the Christmas tree in the corner of the salon and the garland on the window. The sight tugged painfully at her heart.

Underneath the tree was the one thing she'd been certain would ensure her happiness, the one possession she owned that she thought would help her win Simon's love. Oh God, how could she give him up? Wouldn't it be worth the price she'd pay in heartache simply to be in his arms, to love him in spite of his betrayal? Could she forgive him that?

She was capable of forgiving him anything, but this afternoon had proven how wide the rift was between them. He'd expected her to forgive Carolyn. If he couldn't understand why her cousin's betrayal cut so deep, he would never understand why his actions had devastated her. Sorrow enveloped her like an icy blanket. Swallowing hard, she inhaled a sharp breath before looking at him again.

"Sometimes there isn't a reason why, Simon. I just know I can't see you anymore."

"Can't or won't?" The clipped words rekindled the fire of her anger residing just beneath the surface. As usual, the man refused to take no for an answer.

"Is there a difference?"

Their conversation was becoming pointless, and if she didn't put some space between them, she would be in his arms, allowing him to kiss her into submission. *But isn't that what you want, Ivy? Don't you want him to fight for you? Don't you want him to say your social standing is of no consequence to him?* The voice in her head taunted her. More importantly, it frightened her that the voice was right. With a shove, she twisted her body out of his grasp. If he were to break through all her barriers, she would be as vulnerable as a newborn babe. Her breath hitched at the thought. She didn't have the strength to risk such a possibility.

Her fingers tightened on the swag of material that hugged her hips and swept around toward the bustle of her dress. "There's nothing more to say. I'd like you to leave."

Ivy turned away, but a strong hand gripped her arm and forced her to a halt. Her gaze dropped to the firm, sturdy fingers holding her in place before flying upward to meet the icy expression glittering in his gray eyes.

"That's where you're wrong, Ivy. I have a lot more to say. But this time I don't intend to use words."

Sweeping her into his arms, his mouth covered hers in a searing kiss. The heat of it stirred her senses into a whirlwind of desire. Dear Lord, with just one kiss he'd managed to drive every sane thought from her head. No matter what he said or did, she always craved his touch.

A strong hand slid up her waist and then over the top of her breasts. She moaned with the need to feel his skin against hers one more time. Just one more moment of passion for her to remember. Without thinking, she melted into his arms, her body controlling her actions, not her mind. Since the first time he'd touched her, she'd always been eager for his touch. Familiar sensations tingled across her skin as his kiss deepened into the seductive caress that had always sent her pulse skittering wildly.

She offered up no protest as he guided her toward the loveseat, his muscular legs pressing into hers. The muted taste of cognac filled her mouth as his tongue mated with hers. Almost instantly, her nether regions exploded as need dampened the area between her legs.

The wanton sensations holding her hostage blinded her to anything but this moment and his touch. Nothing else mattered except for the overwhelming taste, scent and feel of him. Frantic to feel his skin against hers, she clawed at the back of her dress until it fell open and off her shoulders.

Strong fingers brushed hers aside as he undid the lacings of her corset. Brief moments later, his mouth gently clamped down on a stiff nipple. The action pulled a sob of relief from her. God help her, but the man could ask anything of her now and she'd agree to it.

His hot tongue flicked and teased her nipple as they sank down onto the sofa. Eager to touch him, her hand slid down to where his hard length pressed rigidly against his trousers. With one finger, she stroked him through the material. In response to her touch, a deep growl rumbled in his chest. Shifting his body slightly so his erection was out of her reach, his fingers quickly pulled her skirts up to her knee, and he slid his hand beneath the silk to reach her damp curls.

When his fingers dipped into her wetness, another shudder coursed its way through her. Desire drove her body to thrust up against his hand, while the need for him to complete her burrowed its way through every nerve ending in her body.

The abruptness of his sudden withdrawal stunned her. Bewildered, her eyes flew open to watch him as he pushed himself away from her. For a brief moment she thought she saw a flash of pain in his eyes before a closed expression enveloped his features.

"No. No, I don't think so, Ivy. It seems you were right. There really is nothing more to say, is there. "

With a swift move, Simon rose to his feet, his gray eyes dark and cold. Stunned, she watched him straighten his coat and nonchalantly smooth his lapel. The steely frost of his gaze settled on her face and she flinched at the distaste she saw there.

"You'll forgive me, my dear, but if I recall you did ask me to leave. And quite frankly, bedding an embittered spinster who's a mere commoner is the last thing I can stomach at the moment."

Ice sluiced across her skin at the brutality of his words. Shame tightened her throat as she stared up at him. With another look of disdain, he wheeled around sharply and stalked out of the salon.

Stricken by his words and his departure, Ivy gripped the back of the sofa as she pulled herself upright. Fingernails biting into the dark mahogany trim of the velvet couch, she struggled to keep from crying out after him. The cruelty of his words flayed across her heart with the precision of a cat-o'-nine tails. She had barely caught her breath when the sound of the front door crashing closed behind him reverberated through the room.

Reality slowly forced its way into her mind, and a soft sob broke past her lips as she stumbled to her feet. Oh, God, what was she going to do? The cold air on her bare breasts prodded her to straighten her clothing. Numb fingers tied her stays and then fumbled with the buttons of her dress.

She needed to go after him. No. *That* was impossible. What was she thinking? She'd just rejected him. The last thing Simon Carlton, the Viscount Wycombe wanted from her was apologies or explanations. Neither of which he would accept. And why should she apologize? He was the one who'd resurrected her past, brought Carolyn to London.

One hand pressed to her brow, she closed her eyes and sucked in a sharp breath. Fresh and clean, the scent of the decorated fir tree teased her senses. It provoked a mixture of happy and painful memories. She studied the small tree sitting so prettily on the table in the corner of the salon.

Christmas Eve. It was suppose to be a happy time. Even happier than when she was a child, simply because this year was going to be different. Simon was to have been a part of the holiday. But that hope was gone. Now, all she could feel was utter despair. It chilled her far worse than the snowy weather outside.

And his disgust just a few moments ago. His cruel words. He'd deliberately enticed her into his arms just to humiliate her. Blinking back tears, she failed to prevent the escape of one teardrop. Hands clutched in front of her, she moved toward the Christmas tree.

Sweets and several glass ornaments gaily decorated the green branches. Dazed, she lightly touched one of the gingerbread cookies dangling from a red silk ribbon. Simon liked Mrs. Morris' sweets, and the cook had made the ornaments especially for him.

Beneath the tree, she saw the present she'd picked out for Simon. He was fond of quoting Marcus Aurelius, and she'd search the city to find a book of the Roman emperor's sayings. Next to his gift lay the velvet-covered box. Her fingers caressed the square box. The Grand Dame's necklace.

Opening the lid, she stared down at the brilliant diamonds and the large ruby at the heart of the necklace. Simon had once roguishly said he wanted to see her wearing nothing but diamonds. It had been her intent to honor that request tonight.

Fingers trailing over the hard, beautiful stones, she shook her head. The necklace was reputed to bring luck to its owner. Luck in the form of everlasting love. Some of her maternal ancestors had even claimed to have been helped by the Grand Dame's spirit.

Sniffing her disgust at the thought, she slammed the lid closed. Remembering the stories her mother had told her at bedtime as a small girl, she'd pulled the necklace out of her safe hoping it would do for her what family legend said it had done for others. Clearly, the tales were embroidered nonsense. In her wild imaginings, she'd believed that wearing the necklace while she and Simon made love would help ensure her happiness. She should have known better.

If anything, the necklace was a curse. They jewels were as cold as the look in Simon's eyes just a few moments ago. The jewelry had done nothing but bring her pain and sorrow. Like her belief in the necklace's power, her belief that they could close the social gulf between them was nothing more than a figment of her imagination. With another shudder, she wrapped her arms about her waist and bent her head.

"If it meant you could be with him for always, Ivy, would you believe then?" The gentle voice whispered behind her, and she whirled around in surprise.

The room was empty.

Shivering, she shook her head. Her mind was playing tricks on her. The Grand Dame was a myth, an imaginative flight of fantasy thought up by one of her ancestors. She was distraught about Simon, nothing more. Once more, she looked at the

Christmas tree, tears tightening her throat. She couldn't stay here. Not like this. She couldn't bear to remain in this room, this house any longer. Another tear trailed down her cheek. She had to find someplace else to lick her wounds.

The Library. She would go to the Library. It was almost six o'clock and everyone would be gone--gone home to be with their families for Christmas. The thought tugged at her heartstrings.

Blowing out a sharp breath, she grimaced. Enough self-pity. She would go to the Library and work. It would be a source of comfort to her. The warm, musty smell of old books would dim the memory of Simon's rugged scent. In the bookracks, she might find the peace and quiet she'd known before he'd entered her life. Her decision made, she brushed away the dampness on her cheeks as she emerged from the salon and stopped at the hallway mirror. Her appearance was scandalous. Behind her, Morris cleared his throat.

"Your pardon, Miss Ivy, but is there anything I can do for you?" Although his words sounded level and matter-of-fact, she heard the concern behind the butler's question. For all his austere manner, Morris had the quiet habit of looking after her as a father might. He'd obviously been privy to Simon's furious departure.

Dear lord, half the house must have heard as well, given the crash of the front door when Simon had stormed out of the house. All the more reason to flee to the Library. Her staff had been with her for quite some time, and they'd developed an affinity for protecting her. But it was Christmas, and she'd given them time off to spend with their families. If they thought she needed them, they would sacrifice their holiday to stay with her. She wasn't about to let that happen.

She forced a smile to her lips and turned to face him. "Actually you can, Morris. Would you summon a hansom cab for me and then fetch my things? I've decided to work at the Library this evening."

Tall and portly, the butler gave a slight start, but immediately went to the front door to hail the cab as she struggled to repair her appearance. Her fingers trembled as she pulled out the pins holding her hair in place and hastily rearranged her hair in what the Americans were all calling the Gibson Girl look.

Staring at herself in the mirror when she finished, she blinked back another onset of tears. No, she refused to cry. There was no point in it. A moment later, Morris reappeared at her side with her hat and cloak. He waited patiently as she set the hat on her head, before settling the cape on her shoulders. The gentle brush of his hands on her shoulders as he dusted off imaginary flecks of lint gave her a small measure of comfort.

"And will Lord Wycombe fetch you from the Library, Miss Ivy, or shall I make other arrangements for you?"

Forcing a brittle laugh past her lips, Ivy shook her head as she met the butler's eyes in the mirror. "Actually, I won't be seeing Lord Wycombe anymore, so I'll find a hansom cab when I'm ready to leave."

"But it's Christmas Eve, Miss Ivy! It will be exceptionally difficult to find a hackney in St. James Square given the lateness of the hour."

"Thank you for your concern, Morris. But I'll be quite all right." Tugging on her gloves, she stared into the mirror at her reflection. Was that stricken expression really hers? It was the same look she'd seen on her face the day Carolyn had betrayed her so long ago.

It was with relief she heard Morris inform her the hack was at the front door. Not meeting the butler's eyes, she swept past him and climbed into the small vehicle.

As the butler closed the door of the cab, she forced a smile to her lips and touched his hand on the top of the door. "Happy Christmas, Morris. I expect you and Mrs. Morris to enjoy the holiday with your family. Be sure to let the rest of the staff know they're not to return until late tomorrow evening."

Ignoring the deep concern on the butler's face, she looked up at the small window in the vehicle's roof and ordered the cab driver to drive on before she sank back into the cab's leather seat. Despite her warm clothing, the frosty night air bit into her skin. Her sigh blew out a soft cloud of warmth from her lips as she numbly watched last-minute shoppers hurrying out of shops on their way home. Two days ago, she'd been one of those customers, happily calling out season's greetings to strangers as she'd hurried home to wrap Simon's present.

Why on earth did she persist in torturing herself like this? It was over--finished. There was no going back now. One could never go back. Her cousin might have been quite resourceful when it came to Thornton Whitby, but not even Carolyn could turn back the clock.

Whitby. He'd been the first man to pay any attention to her, and she'd fallen quickly for his smooth compliments and false promises. He'd even said he loved her. Although she now recognized what an overbearing boor Thornton had been, it didn't make Carolyn's betrayal any less painful. Her cousin deserved to find herself a penniless widow with three mouths to feed.

Wincing at the memories, she huddled under the cab's warm wool blanket. She didn't want to think about Carolyn or her children. Especially little Ivy. Why would her cousin name her youngest daughter after her? It had to be a ploy of some sort. A way to gain the child money through a possible inheritance. Well, she had someone else to look after now, someone else who would occupy her time and resources.

Carolyn had made her choice a long time ago. If the woman hoped for any redemption from her, then she was sorely mistaken. She could never forgive such a brutal betrayal. But the children. The memory of the three little girls made her wince. They'd looked so thin in their threadbare clothes.

Still their smiles had been sweet and cheerful. Euripides had said that the gods visit the sins of the fathers upon the children. Were Carolyn's children responsible for their mother's sins? Could she abandon them to poverty so easily? No, Simon would take care of them. His sympathy for her cousin had been quite evident. Soon her daughters would be well-dressed and well-fed. Carolyn would see to that. It was only a matter of time. Her stomach lurched as the hack rolled to a stop and interrupted her chaotic thoughts. Paying the driver, she quickly made arrangements for him to return for her at nine o'clock.

Moments later, she was standing in the cold, dark foyer of the London Library. Turning up the gas light on the wall, she shivered at the chill in the air. The head librarian had no doubt allowed the coal to burn out. Moving across the foyer to the circulation desk, she removed her hat and cape. A large stack of returned books rested on the counter. Scooping them up, she examined their labeling and entered the bookshelves to replace them.

She'd returned at least two books to their rightful place when she heard the whisper of a gown against the wood floor. Glancing behind her, the aisle was empty. Blast it, she needed to control her imagination. She resumed the shelving of the books and moved toward another section. Again, the rustle of a gown reached her ears. The remaining books she carried were set down on an empty shelf as she peered through the bookshelves.

"Hello, is someone there?"

When there was no response, she reached for the books only to freeze in shock. Lying on top of the books was the Grand Dame's necklace. Stunned, she could only stare at the glittering jewelry. How had it gotten there? In her dazed state, had she brought the necklace with her? Yes, that's what she'd done. She'd somehow carried it out of the house without realizing it. It was the only explanation.

"Now, Ivy, you know you're far too practical to do something like that."

There it was again, that gentle, yet firm voice she'd heard earlier. She reached for the necklace then jerked her hand back as it suddenly moved to hang suspended in the air. Fear edged its way through her body and she took two steps back. For a long moment, she stared at the suspended necklace before she got angry.

"Who's in here? Show yourself!" The moment she spoke, the necklace dropped back onto the books.

"As you wish." The voice came from the end of the aisle, and Ivy turned to see a swirling mist moving toward her.

Sweet heavens, a ghost. No one had ever mentioned anything about a ghost in the library before. Of course, it wasn't a ghost. Ghosts weren't real. Her mind was playing tricks on her. She was seeing things. This entire affair with Simon had made her so distraught she was becoming delusional.

"No, dearest, you're not delusional." The voice strengthened as a woman stepped out of the mist. Her odd dress was reminiscent of the Georgian era with its wide hooped skirts and her white powdered pompadour. The dress she wore was a rich blue silk with ivory brocade gathered up in a graceful swag on either side of her waist.

Pink lace edged her bodice while a delicate bow of pink nestled at the vee of her gown. The same pink lace trimmed the edges of sleeves that ended just below her elbows. Despite her strange costume, her expression was gentle and sweet. Blue eyes sparkled with laughter as she met Ivy's gaze.

Unable to move, Ivy swallowed hard as the woman halted a few feet away from her. Dear lord, it was the woman in the portrait. The painting that hung in the stairwell at home. The same woman who was wearing the legendary necklace. The

Grand Dame. She blinked and then blinked again. The woman didn't disappear. Nor did the family jewelry that had suddenly appeared around her neck, the large ruby bright and clear in the diamond setting.

"You're not real. You're a figment of my imagination," Ivy muttered as she turned to walk away. A gentle touch on her shoulder stayed her.

"I'm quite real, dearest, but there are only a few short hours left before I must leave you, so we must hurry if I'm to accomplish what I came here to do."

Ivy shuddered. She was mad. Stark, raving mad. It was the only answer. Taking a step backward, she shook her head. "I ... you're not ... real...."

"Give me your hand, Ivy." The Grand Dame stretched out her arm with a look of gentle encouragement. As if in a trance, Ivy took the offered hand. The woman was real and solid to the touch. *"You see, I am real. At least for the moment."*

"I don't understand ... how is this possible?" Ivy shook her head as she stared at the other woman.

"You called me here by touching the necklace. By believing that the magic of the necklace would give you your heart's desire--Simon."

Stiffening, she shook her head. "No. He's not my heart's desire."

"We both know that's not true, Ivy. You're hurting, but hearts are mendable. Come. If after our journey you still wish to forget Simon, I will help you do so."

As the Grand Dame's words echoed in her head, Ivy gasped as a swirling white fog engulfed them and the library shelves disappeared completely.

Chapter Two

The newspaper in Simon's hands was a noisy wind in the quiet of the London Library. He'd already read the daily once today, but the pretense of reading allowed him to observe Miss Ivy Beecham undetected. A soft growl of aggravation rumbled out of him. His task might be an annoying one, but it was necessary.

As Anthony's guardian, he took his duties seriously. The boy routinely protested any interference in his personal affairs, but it was clear his nephew needed supervision, especially where matters of the heart were concerned. In fact, if it were not for Anthony's wayward behavior, he'd most likely be enjoying a sparring match at the club. Instead, he was here in the scholarly setting of the London Library.

He enjoyed reading, but this dry, musty mausoleum was the last place any of his friends would expect to find him. The comforts of his personal library were much preferable to this academic fortress. His gaze swept toward the stacks of books he could see from the main reading area.

Tomes of every shape and size filled the shelves that disappeared into the depths of the building. The pristine marble columns encircling the circulation desk and adjacent reading area only reinforced the austere nature of the library. In truth, this was the last place he'd expected Anthony to encounter an unsuitable woman. It was the primary reason he'd convinced the boy to take up an intellectual activity within this tomb. Of all conceivable possibilities, the thought of Anthony meeting a woman of undesirable character here had been the furthest from his mind. Frowning, he returned his gaze to the woman behind the circulation desk and grunted his displeasure.

Why the devil couldn't the boy find a woman his own age to dally with and preferably of the same social sphere? The woman appeared to be close to his own age, making her at least five to ten years older than Anthony. He growled his displeasure again. Across from him, a library patron rustled the paper he held and shot Simon a glare of irritation. Arching his eyebrow, he returned the man's hard stare. White eyebrows furrowing to form a straight line, the older gentleman uttered a barely audible harrumph before burying his head back in the paper he held.

Soft laughter drew his attention back to the woman behind the circulation desk. A soft pink flushed her cheeks as she handed an elderly man a book. The patron grinned as he took the leather volume, then caught her hand and brushed her fingertips with his lips. The red in her cheeks deepened as she shook her head in reproach. With a laugh, the dapper gentleman shrugged, then walked away.

Something about the scene irritated Simon. It was easy to see how she must have seduced Anthony into thinking he was in love with her. Even from here, she presented an enticing picture.

Sunshine streamed in from one of the windows above her to reveal auburn highlights in the dark brown of her hair. Skin the color of an unripe peach still possessed a rosy hue as she assisted another patron.

Tall and with abundant curves in all the places he liked the most, she was a tempting sight. His jaw clenched at the way his body was reacting to the woman. The high neck of her white shirtwaist was clearly meant to give her the appearance of a serious academician, but all it did was emphasize the voluptuous curve of her full breasts. Unwillingly, his cock stirred in his trousers.

A moment later, she completed another book transaction and smiled at the gentleman in front of her. Simon inhaled sharply. Bloody hell. No wonder Anthony had succumbed to the witch's charms. It was the smile of a siren, and even a well-seasoned gentleman would find her silent entreaty difficult to resist.

She was most definitely trouble. The sooner he disposed of this matter the better. He shifted in his seat as his quarry moved out from behind the circulation desk to head down one of the book aisles. Tossing his paper aside, he stood up and followed her into the depths of the library.

Ahead of him, she turned the corner and disappeared from sight. Determined not to lose her, Simon increased his pace. As he rounded the bookshelf where he'd last seen her, a glimpse of her voluptuous curves vanished into another aisle. Damn, but the vixen was quick.

Lengthening his stride, he charged after her with determination. He made a sharp right only to slide to an abrupt halt as he came face to face with the woman.

"May I ask why you're following me, sir?"

Soft and husky, her voice caressed him with the silky indulgence of a midnight lover. Immediately, his groin tightened in a primal response. The fact irritated him.

"Are you Ivy Beecham?"

"Yes." She frowned with puzzlement. "May I help you in some way?"

"I'm Lord Claiborne's guardian."

"I'm sorry, whose guardian?" This time a frown furrowed her soft brow as she tilted her head to one side. The movement exposed the lovely line of her neck, and he imagined his lips nibbling on her. The faint scent of lilies whiffed its way beneath his nose. She smelled delectable. Would she taste as luscious as she smelled? Aware she was staring at him with just a touch of irritation, he struggled to control the effect she was having on his body.

"Anthony Dardnay, the Earl of Claiborne."

Understanding lit her face as she smiled at him. It was a bewitching smile, and his annoyance grew at his inability to remain unaffected by her.

"Oh! You must be Lord Wycombe." She smiled and extended her hand. "It's a pleasure to meet you. Anthony has spoken of you often."

He glanced down at her outstretched hand, struggling with the tempting thought of touching her. Sensibility won out as he deliberately refrained from raising her fingers to his lips. The snub made her flinch, and the dismay darkening her sapphire eyes sent a twinge of regret through him. He ignored it.

"I'm afraid this is far from a courtesy call, Miss Beecham."

"I don't understand." She gave a slight shake of her head as an expression of wariness crept over her lovely face.

"I came to instruct you to stay away from my nephew. He's young and too easily swayed by a pretty face."

"I beg your pardon?" Despite her sharp, clipped tone, her voice still held the call of a siren. He gritted his teeth to avoid answering its seductive promise.

"I realize you had hopes of a more permanent relationship with my nephew, but that is out of the question."

"Permanent relationship...."

"Forgive me, Miss Beecham, but I'm well acquainted with women of your ilk, and I have no intention of letting Anthony marry you."

"Marry!" The shocked and horrified look on her face made him appreciate the extent of her acting ability.

"While I'm sure it would be a step up for you financially and socially, I cannot allow him to marry a commoner."

He almost missed the swift movement of her hand as she took a swipe at him. Dodging the blow, he captured her wrist in a tight grip and jerked her toward him. The softness of her curved into his body and he drank in the soft, exotic fragrance of lilies. Damnation. Perhaps he'd be better off making her his mistress instead of ordering her not to see Anthony again. Not only would it destroy the boy's affections for the woman, but he was certain it would be a enjoyable pastime to soak himself in her hot honey.

She'd gone still in his embrace, the brilliant blue of her gaze meeting his with an excellent representation of affronted outrage. The emotion was so vivid it gave him pause for a fraction of a second. Could he have been wrong? No, Anthony had been quite clear of his intent toward Miss Beecham. The woman was simply an excellent actress.

"Release me, my lord," she said quietly. The coldness in her voice was enough to freeze the Thames in the spots where it wasn't already bearing a layer of ice. "Now."

The single word was emphatic, and he did as she asked, although his body protested the loss of her warm curves. She took a step back to study him in silence, anger flashing in her vivid gaze. Again, he questioned his assumptions.

"I came here today, to offer you a substantial sum in exchange for your word to stay away from Anthony."

To his surprise, she wheeled away from him and stalked off toward the end of the aisle. Striding after her, he caught her by the elbow to halt her departure. Once more, she jerked away from him.

"If you touch me again, my lord, I'll scream." The ferocity in her voice furrowed his brow in aggravation.

"Name your price, Miss Beecham. I'm sure I can afford it."

"I don't want your money," she hissed.

"If you're holding out for a husband, I can assure you it won't be Anthony."

"You're mad. Anthony is a mere boy." With a snort of disgust, she tried to move past him. Immediately his hand gripped one of the bookshelves to block her path. If she wanted to play games, he was more than willing. In fact, he was certain that playing with Ivy Beecham would be an exceedingly pleasurable diversion.

"Agreed. But *I'm* not a youth," he drawled as he trailed his forefinger across her cheek. She slapped his hand away, but he noticed that her breathing had hitched slightly. That boded well for the future.

"You're despicable."

"Perhaps, but if so, I'm certain I'm in excellent company. After all, you deliberately went out of your way to seduce my nephew."

"I did no such thing." The way her blue eyes widened in horror made him even more appreciative of her acting talent. God, but she would be magnificent on the stage. Once more she tried to dart past him, but this time, he twisted his body so that she had no place to go but back against the shelves, pinned between his outstretched arms.

"Come now, Miss Beecham. I've been watching you all morning, and I can certainly understand what men find so fascinating about you." Lowering his head, he brushed his lips across the lobe of her ear. "Even *I'm* quite willing to be seduced by you."

Delicate pink lips parted in a soft gasp, and he suppressed the urge to kiss her. This was neither the time nor the place to dally with her. Not when he was certain he would want much more when he finally did kiss her. No, Ivy Beecham was going to be his--one way or another. That decision had been made for him the moment he'd heard that siren voice of hers. The question was--how difficult would it be to convince of her of the fact?

"I can assure you, my lord, I have no intention of letting you seduce me. I'd just as soon kiss a toad. Now release me this instant."

He didn't move for a long moment. There was something about the way her pulse was beating wildly at the side of her neck that intrigued him--tempted him. His cock throbbed with need inside his trousers. Damn, but he wanted to bed her.

With great reluctance, he took a step back. She didn't hesitate for an instant as she put several feet between them. The frosty glare she sent him was meant to cut him down to size, but it merely served to amuse him. No doubt, Ivy would be a tigress in his bed. He smiled. If there was one thing he knew, it was women. This one would welcome his attentions as long as he rewarded her well. It was simply a matter of letting her set the pace of their seductive dance, but in the end, the result would be the same. She'd be no different from any of the other women who'd come and gone in his life. She would succumb to him just like all the others.

"You're even lovelier when angry." Folding his arms across his chest, he laughed as she stalked away from him. It was all part of the dance. She had only gone two feet when she whirled back around to face him.

"Exactly how much did you intend to offer me, my lord?" Her features were unreadable, and a flicker of disappointment lashed at him as he pondered her question. His emotional response surprised him.

"Perhaps you had a price in mind?" He narrowed his gaze as he waited for her to name a figure.

A part of him had hoped it would have been more difficult than this to acquire her charms. He was a fool even to have considered it a remote possibility. No matter what their age or station in life, women could always be relied upon to find the highest bidder for whatever it was they had to sell.

"No, I simply wanted to know what price you were willing to put on your nephew's affection for you."

"What the devil!" he snapped. "Threatening me with some misguided belief as to how much control you have over my nephew is something I refuse to tolerate, Miss Beecham."

"It's hardly a threat, my lord." She lifted her chin in a defiant manner. "The truth is, Anthony does listen to me, and I doubt you'll earn his gratitude for insulting me as you've done here today."

Infuriated, Simon glared at her. "By God, woman. If you make the boy more difficult to handle, I'll see to it you're out on the streets without a penny to your name."

"You are most certainly welcome to try, Lord Wycombe." She arched an eyebrow at him. "But that might be more difficult to achieve than you think. After all, as you said, Anthony fancies me, and you've done little of late to endear yourself to the boy. Perhaps all he needs is a wife to support and believe in him."

Without batting an eyelash, she wheeled about and disappeared around the corner of the bookshelves. As she vanished from view, Simon stared after her in disbelief. The witch had as good as said she intended to marry the boy.

"Christ Jesus." His fist slammed into a row of books. Damn the boy for getting himself mixed up with this conniving female.

If she got to Anthony before he did, there was no telling what his nephew would do. The boy had become extremely belligerent of late. Not even his sister had been able to make him see reason. If the boy married this penniless hussy, it would break Abigail's heart.

Knowing there wasn't a moment to lose, Simon stormed out of the book stacks toward the exit. As he passed the circulation desk, he saw Ivy watching him with a cold look on her features. Glaring at her, he bumped into a gentleman in his path.

As he apologized, he glanced back at his nemesis. A confident smile curved her mouth, and for the first time in his life, Simon wondered if he'd met his match. Not about to consider that possibility, he strode out of the library and headed for home.

The walk from St. James Square to Mayfair was a short one, but it would allow him time to formulate a plan to keep Anthony from making a terrible mistake. Marriage to that woman would leave the boy heartbroken and destitute in less than a year. He was certain of it. He was even more certain that he'd move heaven and earth to prevent it.

* * * *

"*Is that when you fell in love with him?*"

Ivy gave a start as Simon's lean, muscular body swirled and vanished in a misty cloud. She couldn't believe this was happening--that she was reliving the past with this woman. The Grand Dame. Her name was a legend in the family, and there were stories about how she'd been instrumental in the love lives of other members of the family.

She glanced at the phantom standing next to her, trying to ascertain what was real and what was a figment of her imagination. With a vehement shake of her head she glared at the apparition.

"*No*. He was an arrogant beast that day."

"*But so attractive and deliciously male.*" The truth in her ancestor's words made Ivy grimace, but she refused to say anything. The woman beside her gave a quiet laugh. "*Surely you can admit that he excited you, no?*"

"Why are you doing this?" Ivy could hear the anguish in her voice as she turned away from the spirit.

"*I believe you know the answer to that, dearest. You think the differences between you and Simon are too great to overcome. I know differently. Like you, I once thought I could turn my back on love, but fortunately I learned I was wrong before it was too late.*"

There was a faint hitch in the woman's tone that made Ivy turn to see a look of nostalgia lighting up the spirit's translucent face. A gentle smile curved the Grand Dame's lips.

"*Come, there is more for us to see before the night is done. We have only until midnight or all is lost.*"

Disoriented, Ivy nodded at her ancestor's urgent tone. Perhaps she had fallen and hit her head. It would explain the phantasmagoric presence of the Grand Dame. Despite her confusion, she didn't refuse to take her ancestor's outstretched hand. As before, the solid warmth of the other woman's hand surprised Ivy. Smiling, the Grand Dame winked at her.

"*Love can overcome many obstacles, dearest, even the distance between your world and mine.*" The Grand Dame touched the necklace at her throat and once again the library disappeared.

* * * *

"Simon!"

Anthony's shout of fury pierced the study's tranquil silence. Rising to his feet, Simon rounded his desk and moved to stand in the center of the room. Patiently, he waited for his nephew. The study door flew open with a crash as it struck the wall.

The force of the angry display caused him to arch an eyebrow as Anthony charged into the room and straight for him. A second later, his jaw was throbbing with pain from the blow his nephew had dealt him. The unexpected assault forced him into a defensive position, and it was only years of discipline and control that kept him from instinctively returning the blow. He'd expected anger, but this physical contact was completely out of character for the boy.

"You *bastard*." Anthony was panting as if he'd run the entire distance from the library. "If it were still legal, I'd call you out for insulting Miss Beecham the way you did."

Flexing his sore jaw, Simon frowned at the young man in front of him. There was a new maturity to his nephew he'd not seen before. "I hardly call it an insult to speak bluntly with a woman of her stature."

"You know nothing about her," his nephew hissed.

"Enough to know she's not suitable for you." Simon glared at the tall youth in front of him. "And I might add that she threatened to blackmail me."

"You're lying."

His anger easing, he turned away from the boy and walked to the fireplace to stare into the fire. He hated to destroy the boy's illusions, but it was time he learned the truth about Ivy Beecham. The thought of her stirred the latent fires inside him, and he cleared his throat. He'd deal with Ivy later. At the moment, he needed to convince Anthony she wasn't worth this emotional outburst. While she would do quite well as a mistress, marriage was completely unacceptable. Turning to face the boy, he shook his head as he met his nephew's furious gaze.

"No, Anthony. I'm not lying. Yes, I offered her money to stay away from you. But she told me she didn't need the money because when she married you, she would be well situated."

"I'm not going to marry her." The young man uttered the statement with quiet, steely precision.

Frowning, Simon studied his nephew's face for any sign of deception. For a man so in love, the boy was giving the woman up far too easily. He couldn't remember the number of times the boy had waxed poetic about Ivy Beecham's charms. The lad had given the woman his highest accolades, calling her lovely, pleasant, amusing and kind. There had been more than a dozen different descriptions of the lovely Ivy's charms. The boy had even stated that he would like to marry someone like the woman.

"Did you hear me, Simon? I said I'm not going to marry Miss Beecham."

Satisfied with this sudden about-face, he nodded. "I'm delighted to see that you've come to your senses."

"I never lost them you arrogant bastard," Anthony snapped. "I was never in love with Miss Beecham. She simply helped me find the means of writing poetry to Olivia."

"I beg your pardon." Simon stared at his nephew in astonishment. "Who the devil is Olivia?"

"The woman I intend to marry. In two months, I'll be out from under your thumb, and we'll be married then."

"Damn it, boy, you're going to break your mother's heart." Simon's muscles tightened into hard knots. He wanted to choke the bloody fool.

"Mother needs to learn her place when it comes to my personal life. As do you, Simon. Would you allow me to meddle so liberally in your own affairs?" Anthony glared at him. Again, the youth demonstrated a maturity Simon hadn't seen before. And the boy was right--*no one* dared to interfere with his personal matters.

"You're right, of course, but that doesn't change the fact that the family hasn't met this Olivia of yours. We know nothing about her, whether she's suitable or not."

"I'll decide what woman is suitable for me to marry, and you won't meet her until I deem it appropriate. I refuse to let you intimidate her the way you did Miss Beecham."

Simon laughed at the comment. Ivy Beecham hadn't been scared of him, she'd been ready to roast him and serve him up for supper. "I can assure you, Anthony, the woman was far from intimidated by me."

"Well the least you can do is offer her an apology."

"An apol--" Simon stared at his nephew. "Why the devil would I apologize, might I ask? I was doing my duty as your guardian. You'd touted the woman's charms so much I could only consider the worst. What was I suppose to think?"

"Don't be a horse's ass, Simon." Anthony gave him an icy look. "You thought the worst and didn't even bother to discuss the matter with me. Now you've insulted my friend, and that's all she is, a friend."

"Somehow I find it difficult to see Miss Beecham as being eager to be only your friend."

"Miss Beecham did nothing more than help me research poetry at the Library so I could impress Olivia." Anthony glared at him. "She was quite helpful."

"I'm certain she was, given the woman's financial and social stature. It gave her the opportunity to try to seduce you." Turning away from his nephew, Simon picked up a stack of invitations from his desk. The woman might have thought to seduce his nephew, but she was about to have the tables turned on her. He would enjoy seducing the avaricious, but tempting, Ivy.

Behind him, Anthony uttered an expletive. "Miss Beecham was right, Simon. Your arrogance will be your downfall."

The comment brought a broad smile to his lips as he glanced over his shoulder. "So the esteemed Miss Beecham found me arrogant. Did she tell you this before or *after* I offered her money to stay clear of you?"

"For your edification, Miss Beecham doesn't need your money. She's wealthier than you and me put together."

"Really?" Simon snorted with disbelief as he turned to face his nephew. "Then explain to me why she's working in the London Library."

"Because she loves books. It's her passion."

Anthony's voice was fierce as he defended the woman. It was difficult to fault his loyalty. He wouldn't have Carlton blood running through him otherwise. As for passion, Ivy was going to realize there were other things besides books to be excited about.

After a cursory glance at the embossed invitation in his hand, he set it aside for later consideration. It was difficult to concentrate on social events when his mind was busy conjuring up the image of Ivy naked before him. The picture in his head wasn't just pleasurable--it was arousing. Soon, quite soon, he'd make that irresistible image a reality. Anticipation nibbling at him, he returned his attention to the conversation at hand.

"And this passion for books, I suppose Miss Beecham told you this." Simon tossed another invitation aside.

"Actually it was Lord Asterly who told me."

"Exactly why would Lord Asterly tell you such a thing?" Surprised by Anthony's response, he dropped the invitations he still held and turned to face his nephew.

"Because I mentioned wanting to supplement her salary with a gratuity. The old man nearly laughed himself into an apoplexy. Said Miss Beecham was Neville Beecham's sole heir."

"Neville Beecham," Simon exclaimed, "the shipping magnate?"

He frowned at this new information. It left him in a decidedly prickly position given his behavior this morning. It would make it damned difficult to bring her to heel. Without the lure of money, he'd need to find something else with which to pique her interest. Damnation, it would have been much easier for him if she'd been poor as a church mouse.

"Apparently she made a sizable donation to the library provided the library board allowed her to volunteer at the circulation desk." The admiration in Anthony's voice was difficult to miss.

"I imagine she caused quite a stir." Simon bit back a smile at the image of Ivy storming the bastion of the London Library.

Given his encounter with her earlier, it didn't surprise him she'd overcome any the board's objections to her presence. His problem was going to be how to overcome her resistance to his advances. Not only did he have his own behavior to overcome, Ivy's substantial financial portfolio was another issue altogether.

An inheritance of such magnitude always attracted fortune hunters. It would make her all the more guarded where he was concerned. In short, she was going to be a challenge. But then he'd never been intimidated by challenges.

Quirking an eyebrow at his nephew, he shook his head. "I'll see to soothing Miss Beecham's ruffled feathers, and you are to consider introducing the family to this Olivia of yours."

"I'll consider it, but don't expect me to change my mind," Anthony said as he headed toward the study door.

"Perhaps, but for your mother's sake, I hope you'll give the matter a great deal of thought." Simon frowned as his nephew sent him a steady look over one shoulder.

"And I suggest you apologize to Miss Beecham, uncle."

"I'll see to it that your Miss Beecham finds me most agreeable when I call on her tomorrow."

As Anthony bobbed his head sharply, Simon glanced down at the ivory envelopes on his desk. He picked up the invitation he'd laid aside moments ago, a plan formulating in the back of his mind. This would do nicely. It was just the thing to entice the lovely Ivy into his arms.

Chapter Three

Curled up in her favorite chair by the fireplace, Ivy jumped nervously as the murmur of voices in the foyer interrupted her reading. With a quick movement, she slid the book she was reading beneath the black lace shawl draped over the arm of her reading chair. A sharp knock preceded Morris' entrance into the salon bearing an extremely large bouquet of flowers. Following in the butler's footsteps was the downstairs housemaid, Mary Rose, carrying a large vase.

"Good heavens, Morris, where on earth did these come from?" she asked as she rose to her feet.

"A young boy delivered them and said there was a card enclosed."

There were yellow chrysanthemums, orange marigolds, red dahlias and rich looking amaryllis of the deepest pink with delicate Queen Anne's lace throughout. Lush and beautiful, the arrangement was a perfect collection of blooms from an autumn garden. The bouquet must have cost a fortune given it was so late in the season. Moving to where Mary Rose was arranging the flowers in the vase, Ivy leaned forward and drank in the fragrant aroma of the blossoms.

Who would have sent her something so lovely? Anthony. She smiled. The poor boy had been beside himself with anger when she'd told him about Lord Wycombe. No doubt he was trying to make amends for his uncle's boorish behavior. The sudden thought of Lord Wycombe caused her stomach to flutter. She'd only met the man once, and he'd done nothing but insult her. Why would the thought of him make her skin tingle?

Frowning, she pushed the troubling thoughts aside. The man was an arrogant boor, even if he was handsome. Gently her fingers parted the blooms in the floral arrangement. With a soft sound of triumph, she withdrew the small envelope from the flowers and opened it. The card inside simply bore one word.

Wycombe.

Stunned, she stared at the card for a long moment. It was the stirring of excitement that made her flinch. What in heavens name was she thinking? The man saw her as a commoner-- beneath him. Indignation swept through her. The man had insulted her, and now he thought to offer her flowers as an apology. Fingers trembling with anger, she shoved the card back into the envelope with a furious movement before stalking to the window. Pulling the sheer curtain back, she saw Anthony's uncle handing a coin to a small boy.

The arrogance of the man. He was insufferable. Whirling away from the window, she moved swiftly back to the flowers and snatched them out of the vase. Water dripped on the ruby silk of her day gown and then on the carpet as she thrust the flowers toward Morris.

"The man who brought this bouquet is waiting outside. Please return these to him."

"Am I to relay a message, Miss Ivy?" Confused, the butler accepted the suddenly bedraggled looking bouquet.

"Tell him ... tell him our deeds determine us, as much as we determine our deeds." She snapped, furious that the man had thought she would welcome him into her home after his insults. Perhaps his lordship might actually glean some small measure of knowledge from George Eliot's words. Impossible. Wycombe was a degenerate member of the nobility who wouldn't know what the inside of a book looked like. Most of the nobility only pretended to be connoisseurs of the arts. Rarely did they attempt to master them.

Morris hurried from the room with Mary Rose on his heels. Her anger still holding her hostage, her foot tapped a rapid beat on the room's Moorish rug. She'd never met such an irritating man before. Why there wasn't even a library board member who was as much of a narrow-minded snob of the first order.

Anger still hummed inside her as she sank down into her chair. Retrieving her book from its hiding place, she glared at the leather-bound volume. Lord Wycombe was a pompous jackass. When he'd cornered her in the book stacks at the library yesterday, she'd thought he was another in a long list of fortune hunters.

In many ways, she wished he had been. It was always easy to deal with men seeking to marry her simply for her wealth. But Lord Wycombe was different. His insults had stung. His callous behavior had recalled the past to her with vivid clarity. Then to suggest that she seduce him--It was ... it was ridiculous. An absurd notion. Her fingers trembled against the leather binding of the book she held. But the man had made the invitation a tantalizing one.

His voice had been a hot, summer breeze as his mouth had grazed her ear. The deep husky sound had literally danced across her skin. Strong and seductive, it had conjured up images that were dangerous, reckless visions of him caressing her more intimately. The pictures fluttering through her head sent a shiver skating along her spine. It teased its way through her body until her skin tingled in the most delicious way.

Struggling to ignore the sensations, she returned to her reading, determined to forget about Lord Wycombe. *The Golden Lotus* was a book she'd found buried in the deep recesses of the library. Certain that Lord Asterly would object to her reading it, she'd brazenly carried it out with several other books she'd borrowed without the Library Board member knowing. She had thought to read the book from an academic point of view, but the book was far from academic. In most circles, she was convinced it would be deemed lascivious and obscene.

While shocking at times, the stories were beautifully written. The words flowed across the page in a lush, lyrical way. Still, it had not kept her from gasping at the erotic writing or drawings. They made her belly tighten and her skin hot. It was the same sensation she had when Lord Wycombe had whispered in her ear. Sweet heaven, why couldn't she get the man out of her head. He was--

The sound of voices in the hall made her glance at the salon door. Tucking the book back under the shawl, she stood up and went to the door. As she stepped into the foyer, she saw Morris holding another bouquet in his hands, this one significantly smaller than the last one. The expression on the butler's face was one of bemused consternation as he stared at the flowers. She smiled. No doubt, *this* one was from Anthony.

"Miss Ivy, I'm--"

"It's all right, Morris, let me read the card before you have Mary Rose put them in water." The white envelope peeked out of the nosegay of chrysanthemums, asters and marigolds. She pulled the card out of the flowers to see familiar handwriting.

Oscar Wilde says always forgive your enemies--nothing annoys them so much--Wycombe

Unable to help herself, she laughed. The fact that Lord Wycombe actually knew the playwright's work was one small point in his favor, especially since she adored the famous man's profound wit. She frowned. Lord Wycombe might be clever, but it didn't make up for his abysmal behavior.

As her butler took a step in the direction of the kitchen, she touched his arm. "I think not, Morris. Just a moment."

Hurrying into the salon, she moved swiftly across the room to the secretaire. Her fingers grasped the warm wood of her Waterman fountain pen as she scratched out a reply on the back of Lord Wycombe's card.

Nevertheless, the esteemed Ralph Waldo Emerson said God may forgive sins, but awkwardness has no forgiveness in heaven or earth.

Her eyes scanned the simple statement and she smiled. That would put an end to the man's blatant attempts to ease his way into her good graces. She had no wish to further her limited acquaintance with the man, even if his voice was warm enough to tighten every one of her nerve endings. The memory of his mouth teasing her earlobe made her straighten upright with a jerk. Sliding the card back into its envelope, she hurried back out to the foyer.

The note tucked back into the arrangement, she sent Morris to return the flowers. As she returned to the salon, a reluctant smile curved her lips. Was the man actually trying to apologize? The first delivery of flowers had been beautiful, but had displayed no humility for his behavior. This last bouquet had been equally lovely, but smaller, almost penitent in nature.

No, she wasn't going to let the man's choice in flowers sway her opinion of him. He was far from penitent. But he was definitely a learned man, and he'd made her laugh. Intelligent and witty. Perhaps she had misjudged him. After all, he'd only been trying to protect Anthony.

Protecting his own, that's what he'd been doing, ensuring that one of the lesser mortals didn't enter the hallowed sanctum of the nobility. As a child, she'd endured the snubs of her aunt and uncle. All she'd wanted was love, and they'd answered with disdain and contempt. Once again, the past threatened to engulf her, and she shuddered. The nobility were far worse than any commoner she'd met. Oh, they had refined manners and the ability to converse intelligently about the arts and other topics, but that didn't stop them from being as conniving and brutal as the most vulgar of commoners.

No, Lord Wycombe wasn't just a scoundrel--he was a nobleman as well. The more distance she put between them, the better. Determined to forget the man, she returned to her chair. Seated once more with her legs curled up beneath her, she flipped open her book and inhaled a sharp breath of shock at the page she'd turned too.

The erotic drawing sent her heart slamming against her chest as she stared at the picture with shocked fascination. The man in the drawing was naked, his body hard, lean and muscular. Strong arms stretched out to caress the hair of the woman in the picture. In contrast to the man's steely strength, the woman in the picture was soft and plump, her derriere pushing upward in the picture as she bent over the man. Intense pleasure tugged at the man's features, as the woman's mouth engulfed his phallus.

Was the act as enjoyable for the woman as it obviously was for the man? Would *he* find such an act pleasurable? Dear Lord, what was she thinking? She suddenly realized her breathing had increased dramatically as she stared at the carnal drawing. Even worse, it was Lord Wycombe's face she saw in the picture.

Slamming the book closed, she leaned back in her chair. Eyes closed, she tried to think of something else, but the illicit thought returned to tease and tempt her. Appalled, she shook her head. She'd lost her mind.

How could she possibly even have such a thought? And with *him* of all men? It was the book. There was no other explanation for why she would even think such thing--and especially with Lord Wycombe. Frantic with the need to dispel the carnal image in her mind, she dropped the book into the chair as she sprang to her feet.

Pacing the floor, she reminded herself of his arrogant assumption that she was a common strumpet hell-bent on seducing his nephew. But of course it was perfectly appropriate for him to audaciously proposition her. Heat curled its way over her skin at the memory of how close he'd been to her. Close enough that if she'd turned her head even the slightest his mouth would have--

She came to an abrupt halt, fingertips pressing against her forehead. Oh, dear lord, how had she gone from thinking about his arrogance to recalling the scent of bergamot that had flooded her senses when he'd hemmed her in at the bookshelf? She needed to think of something completely unrelated. The supper party. Yes, the supper party she was giving before the Library's annual ball this Saturday was an excellent way to forget all about Lord Wycombe.

Although she preferred not to socialize with the aristocracy, it was a necessary sacrifice to ensure the continued welfare of the Library. There were some members of the nobility she'd come to like and respect, but they were rare individuals. Still, she couldn't let her views on the nobility keep her from the Library annual fundraising event. Despite the significant and generous contribution of its members, it was always in need of funds to improve the building and acquire new books.

Rarely one to give parties, she knew this special occasion demanded she do something special for the writers and scholars she'd come to know well through her work at the Library. Whenever she had a question or asked for a book recommendation, they'd freely given their time to help her.

She'd even found herself admitting that there were one or two members of the nobility she liked well enough to invite to her small gathering. But what had started out as a select group of five or six people had swelled to a group of twenty. There was still much to do beforehand. Just one more reason why she shouldn't have been reading that blasted book.

She tried desperately to focus on the party, but despite her most determined efforts, the image of Lord Wycombe's face insistently pushed its way into her thoughts. Teeth clenched with determination, she walked back and forth across the carpet, the deep red of her gown swishing fiercely against the rug. Firm in her resolve to drive any thought of the man from her head, she mentally ticked off her household task list.

The sharp knock on the salon door drew her up short. Wheeling to face the door, she tried to school her features into a serene expression as Morris entered the room bearing a single white rose and another card. Intrigued, she eagerly stretched out her hand. What had the rogue written now? An apology? Well she wouldn't forgive him. He was wasting his time.

The card slid easily out of the envelope, the bold handwriting already familiar.

Wycombe ... 'T was whisper'd in heaven, 't was mutter'd in hell,
And echo caught faintly the sound as it fell.

It was a useless effort to avoid laughing. So the devil wanted to make her think he was a condemned man by quoting Catherine Fanshawe. And the white flower was an excellent touch. How often did Lord Wycombe ever wave a white flag? A reluctant smile pulled at her mouth, and she glanced at Morris. The butler was frowning. Not a good sign.

"I'm sorry Miss Ivy, but the man insisted that he speak with you, and he refused to take no for an answer. He did nothing short of force his way into the foyer."

It was evident the man wouldn't leave her alone until she'd received him. Smoothing the wrinkles in her silk dress, she nodded at her butler.

"Very well, Morris. Show him in."

The frown on the butler's face deepened, his protective nature making him hesitate briefly as if to object. With another laugh, she touched the man's arm. "It's all right, Morris, really. I'll allow him to pay his respects and then I'll send him on his way."

Uncertainty still shadowed the butler's features, but he nodded and went back out into the foyer. A moment later, the door opened again, and her nemesis entered the room. Even if her back had been turned, she would have known the exact moment he crossed the threshold. There was something about his mere presence that sent a frisson sliding over her skin.

Today he was dressed in a blue wool suit. Despite his civil appearance, there was something ancient and primal in the way he moved, the way he looked at her. His dark hair fell casually over his brow and there was the faintest hint of a smile on his lips. The possibilities that lay behind that expression released butterflies in her stomach. He was like the black panthers she'd seen on display at Regent's Park--sleek, dangerous and beautiful.

Even from across the room, his gray eyes devoured her as if she were an afternoon snack. Swallowing the disquieting lump of nerves in her throat, she arched her eyebrows as she met his steady gaze without flinching.

There was no hesitation in his stride as he crossed the room. Reaching her side, he bowed slightly and waited. Lord, the man actually expected her to offer him her hand. After the way he'd snubbed her yesterday. Worse yet, she hated to admit that his actions still stung. She might have found his calling cards amusing, but being magnanimous about his behavior was not something she was willing to do at the moment. *At least not yet.* She ignored the traitorous thought. Beyond that, there was the annoying issue of her damp palms.

One hand grasping her skirt, she swept around him and put several feet between them. Satisfied that he was far enough away from her, she turned to watch him straighten slowly and face her. The charming smile on his face made her pull in a sharp breath. It said he knew why she'd not offered him her hand. Impossible. The man wasn't a mind reader. A skilled ladies man perhaps, but not one capable of knowing her innermost thoughts. Thoughts that were best left buried deep in her head.

"My lord, is there some reason why you called on me today?"

To her relief, her voice was cool and serene. But it was the response his presence created in her body that alarmed her. Any man who could make every nerve in her body scream with a tension that was far too pleasurable was a man to be avoided. He was far too dangerous.

"I thought we might make a fresh start between the two of us." He placed his hands behind his back as he studied her.

"Forgive me, my lord, but I see little point in doing so."

"Don't you, Ivy?"

The way he said her name sent her heartbeat skittering along at an accelerated pace. He moved toward her with a predatory grace that alarmed and thrilled her. Merciful heaven, the man was a sorcerer. In a second, he was standing so close her nose could drink in the male essence of him. The spicy scent stirred the butterflies in her stomach.

"I see no point in our becoming better acquainted since our paths are not likely to cross in the near future." She sniffed indignantly, and turned her head away from his amused gaze.

"Ah, but that's where you're wrong, Ivy. I intend to see you quite a bit. In fact, I even plan on taking you to the Library ball this Saturday."

"Me! To the Library fundraiser?" She snapped. "What on earth makes you think I would go anywhere with you?"

"Because I have something *you* want." As he spoke, he leaned forward and brushed his lips lightly against her ear. In an instant, a wave of fire washed over her as he nibbled at her earlobe. "Has anyone ever told you how lovely your ears are?"

All too aware of her body's susceptibility to the man, she quickly took a step back from him. "I can't think of *anything* you have that I might possibly want, my lord."

He quirked an eyebrow at her and smiled. "Not even the Voltaire papers?"

Stunned, she stared at him. The Voltaire papers were the original documents of the great French writer and satirist himself. Several years ago, an anonymous buyer had bought them at auction in France. They were reputed to be in the hands of a private collector, but no one had ever discovered the buyer's name.

Impossible. It was a trick. The man thought to trick her somehow.

"I don't believe you."

"As you wish, but I assure you, I do have them," he said nonchalantly as he moved to the fireplace and stretched his hands out at the heat coming from the flames.

She raised her hand as he turned his head toward her. "If I were to believe you--*if*, mind you--what do the Voltaire Papers have to do with me?"

"I'll agree to give the Library the papers, providing you agree to let me escort you to the Library's social function this weekend."

"You can't be serious."

"Quite." He chuckled as he turned to face her again. "I admit, it's unusual for me to resort to bribery to obtain the pleasure of a lady's company, but I'm certain it will be a worthy sacrifice."

"But why? Why would you do such a thing?" Completely befuddled, she watched his lips curve in a smile filled with enticement.

"Because I'm intrigued by you, Ivy."

Bemused, she stared at him. The man had her turned upside down. Was she actually considering his proposal? It seemed a harmless proposition. An evening in the man's company in exchange for the Voltaire Papers becoming the property of the Library. They'd be a wonderful addition to the institution's collection.

Her hesitation must have shown in her face because he smiled. "So we're agreed then.

"Aren't the Voltaire Papers rather a steep price for the privilege of escorting a mere commoner to the Library benefit? What would your nephew say?"

His steely gaze narrowed on her at the wry note in her voice. "I suppose I deserve that, but I won't apologize for keeping my nephew's best interests at heart."

With an arrogant tilt of his head, he waited for her reply. Despite her reservations, she nodded her agreement. The sudden expression of satisfaction sweeping across his features made her frown. He was looking far too pleased with himself. About to chastise him for his overly confident manner, she froze as he glanced down at her chair. Oh, lord. She'd forgotten to hide the book.

In an instant, she rushed forward to steal the book out of his reach. As she nestled the rescued volume against her chest, her eyes met his steady gaze.

"How much of the book have you read, Ivy?" The soft seduction in his voice encircled her, teased her, and set off every alarm bell in her body. Stiffening her back, she glared at him.

"What do you mean?"

"*The Golden Lotus*--how much have you read?"

Unable to answer him, she shook her head. Heat filled her cheeks as she met his riveting gaze. He moved closer, his hand reaching out to caress her face. The warmth of his thumb rubbed its way across her bottom lip in a touch that made her knees wobble.

Good lord, what on earth was making her react to the man like this? Fingernails biting into the leather of the book she held, her mouth went dry as she glimpsed the desire shining in his gray eyes.

Mesmerized by his touch, she didn't move as his head lowered toward her. To her dismay, she simply closed her eyes and allowed him to kiss her. The touch of his mouth against hers was a light touch. She sighed at the pleasure sailing through her. A moment later, his tongue darted into her mouth. It teased and provoked her until she leaned into him of her own accord, seeking to warm herself in his heat. An instant later, she was cold.

"Remind me in the future to elaborate on *The Golden Lotus*," he whispered against her brow as he stepped back from her. There was a strange look in his eyes, as he continued. "What time shall I call for you on Saturday evening?"

Nonplused by his retreat, she shook her head. "I ... I'm having a small party before the dance. You're welcome to join us. Supper is at seven."

"Then I shall be here at seven." Taking her hand, he turned it over so he could study her palm. "Have you ever had your fortune told, Ivy?"

Startled by the odd question, she shook her head. "No, I don't believe in that sort of nonsense."

Although she tugged slightly at his grasp, his firm grip didn't release her. "Then let me read your palm for you. In the not too distant future, you're going to discover a completely new world of pleasure. I intend to be your guide into that world, Ivy. And I promise you, it will be even more stimulating than that book you're holding."

It was impossible to keep from gasping at the innuendo, but it was the way his mouth warmed her palm that made her stomach somersault. Before she could respond, he released her hand and stepped away from her. Bowing slightly, he left the salon before she could gather her wits and respond to his bold statement.

The quiet thud of the salon door closed behind him, and Ivy swallowed hard. She was mad. What had possessed her to agree to the man's proposal? Voltaire papers or no, she had a feeling she would come to regret saying yes to the man, if only because she was becoming too well acquainted with the sensation of the man's lips on her mouth and skin. Even more alarming was how much she liked it.

* * * *

"Ahh, so this is when you fell in love with him." The Grand Dame's lyrical voice warmed the cool white fog surrounding them.

"Yes." Ivy nodded reluctantly. "That's when I fell in love with him. He was impossibly arrogant, but there was something about him that drew me to him. But none of this changes anything. He's no different than Whitby."

"Are you so certain of that? Deep inside you knew Whitby only wanted you for your money. We both know he didn't really love you."

"That's not true! He would have married me if it hadn't been ... if he hadn't been told I was a commoner."

"Sometimes it's convenient to hide from the truth if it makes the pain easier to bear." The gentleness of the Grand Dame's voice brushed over her in a soothing touch. *"But we both know the truth about Whitby."*

It was a sensation she'd not felt since her childhood. The spirit's motherly manner made the memory of her mother acute.

Before her parents died, she'd experienced the joys of love. That had ended with their deaths.

Fostered by her mother's family, scorn and condescension had been the order of the day. Her grief for her parents was only magnified by the way her aunt and uncle treated her. The daughter of an earl, her mother's elopement with a tradesman had been a scandal. In the eyes of her aunt and uncle, Ivy had been a commoner to be scorned and ignored.

"I have no wish to pursue any further discussion on Whitby, and if you *insist* on showing me images from my recent past, then do so or take me back to where I belong."

"You have your mother's temper, I see." Laughter tumbled from the woman's mouth as she shook her white, powdered head. *"Very well, there is still more to see, although I am beginning to see your father's stubborn streak in you."*

Taking her hand, the Grand Dame touched the ruby in the necklace at her neck. Once again the cool mist swirled around them, pulling on her with a gentle, but persistent, tug. Without any other choice, she allowed her ancestor to pull her deeper into the fog.

Chapter Four

Stepping out of his carriage, Simon ordered his driver to return later, then turned to stride up the steps to Ivy's house. He was certain handing over the Voltaire Papers in exchange for Ivy's company this evening would be well worth the expense. When he'd made his proposal to her the other day, it had been a spur of the moment action, but his decision to do so had been the right one.

He'd guessed correctly that Ivy wouldn't be able to resist acquiring the Voltaire Papers for the library, even if it meant spending an entire evening in his company. What she didn't realize was that he had no intention of letting this one occasion be their only time together. Tonight he intended to intrigue and tantalize the woman until she wanted nothing more than to fall into his arms.

With a tug of the doorbell, he waited for the front door to open. The moment it did so, he stepped inside and removed his coat.

As he handed his outerwear to the butler, he noticed the man was eyeing him with a severe expression. He arched an eyebrow at him, causing the retainer's frown to deepen.

Amused by the man's silent disapproval he bit back a grin. It seemed Ivy had another champion besides Anthony seeking to protect and revere her. Quiet voices echoed out of the salon, and the butler moved toward the room's open doorway. Standing just outside the salon, the tall man ushered Simon into the room with a polite sweep of his hand. There were a number of people present he recognized from his literary society, but it was Ivy who captured his immediate attention. She looked magnificent.

She wore a gown the color of an evening sky when the last bit of daylight has faded from view. Covering the material was a thin sheen of netting laced with miniature stones that glittered in the room's soft light. She was radiant.

A laugh parted her soft pink lips, and she fluttered a peacock-feathered fan in front of her in a leisurely movement. There was an elegance and grace to her manner few noblewomen could match. If Anthony had brought her home without revealing her background, no one in the family would have known she was a commoner.

He watched her tip her head to one side as she gave the man standing at her side her complete attention. The sight irritated him. He wanted her to focus solely on him and no one else. No. What he really wanted was to take her away from all of these people. He wanted to spend time alone with her.

Damnation, he'd not been this enthralled with a woman since his eighteenth birthday, the day he learned how fickle and conniving women could be. Shoving the thought aside, he continued to watch her, noting every sensuous movement of her body. He was going to enjoy seducing Ivy Beecham.

The seduction he had in mind was something he'd never tried before. In the past, he'd simply whispered a few sweet nothings into the ear of the woman he wanted and they eagerly acquiesced to his advances. Ivy was different and required a unique strategy.

Seducing her meant he would have to use words that intrigued and excited her. Her intelligence and quick wit would demand nothing less. It was why he'd spent practically all day researching various works of literature to use when the moment presented itself.

Her love of literature was obvious given her work at the library, but it was also clear that her tastes weren't limited in any way.

The memory of seeing a copy of *The Golden Lotus* in her reading chair curved his mouth. The sight of it had stunned yet delighted him. It meant she was adventurous, and that was something he thoroughly enjoyed in a woman.

His gaze roved over her voluptuous body. The gown highlighted the sensuous line of her neck and lovely shoulders. Even more tempting was the way the gown plunged toward the valley of her breasts. They were full and lush, just like the rest of her.

The other day she'd had the look of a siren disguised as bookish spinster. Tonight she was an alluring temptress inviting him to taste her, seduce her. She exuded the aura of a woman who would take pleasure in her lover and give back in equal measure. A sudden hunger to possess her gripped him, and he struggled to control his physical response to her. As if she'd read his thoughts, she suddenly turned her head in his direction.

Immediately he saw the awareness that tightened her body. No matter how much she insisted on denying the fact, Ivy was attracted to him. It was visible in the way her cheeks flushed a soft pink and how she gripped her fan. She smiled graciously at the man she'd been conversing with then moved toward him.

The moment she reached him, she offered him her hand with a wary expression in her eyes. "Good evening, Lord Wycombe."

"My name is Simon. Say it, Ivy."

She hesitated for a moment before obeying his command. "As you wish--Simon."

It was a sweet sound, and taking her hand, he brushed his mouth across her skin. Not ready to release her, he raised his gaze to stare into her lovely sapphire eyes. A slight shudder trembled through her down to her fingertips.

He smiled. "You look enchanting."

The blush in her cheeks darkened. "If you seek to flatter me, my lord, I should warn you that I'm immune to such platitudes."

"Would you have me lie to you?" He released her hand as her lovely mouth tightened into a firm line.

"I prefer blunt honesty to flattery." The tartness of her tone made him laugh.

"Since you prefer honest observations, I can assume you demand nothing less of yourself."

"Of course." She sniffed with indignation.

"Then convince me you weren't thinking about me when you selected your dress for this evening." He grinned as her eyes widened with surprise. An instant later, her surprise turned into glare.

"That doesn't even deserve an answer."

"Evading the issue is far from being honest. Admit it, Ivy, you thought about me when you picked out this dress."

The expression on her face made him smile as he watched consternation, frustration, and irritation slide across her lovely face in quick succession. She was like a cornered cat, ready to hiss and scratch at the first sign of trouble.

"Just because you happened to be on my mind when I pulled this dress out of my wardrobe doesn't mean I chose it as a means of pleasing or enticing you." A serene smile curved her lips as she set her chin at a stubborn angle. The remark was worthy even of Disraeli and he smiled.

"Come, my beautiful liar, I think it's time you introduced me to some of your guests." Cupping her elbow, he guided her forward. "It would seem we're causing quite a stir."

Dismay darkened her eyes as she allowed him to lead her deeper into the room. They stopped at the closest group of guests, where Ivy introduced him to the Countess of Effington. A tall, dour woman, she peered at him through a monocle that hung on a pearl chain around her long neck.

"Lord Wycombe, I knew your father. A devilishly attractive man. You take after him." The woman's deep voice echoed with self-importance. "I understand from Miss Beecham here that you're to be my escort into dinner. I trust you'll have something interesting to say over our meal."

With a sharp glance at Ivy, he saw the flash of mischief that whipped across her face before her smile steadied into polite serenity. The little minx. She knew full well he wanted to spend the entire evening with her. Turning his full attention on the older woman, he directed his most charming smile at her.

"It will be my pleasure to try and entertain you during dinner, my lady." With a quick glance at his hostess, he grinned. "A discussion of famous literary texts, perhaps? If I recall, Miss Beecham had one such text in her possession the other day. Perhaps she could offer up the name of the volume for our discussion."

Ivy sent him a look that would have done serious injury if it had been a weapon. Curiosity gleamed in Lady Effington's sharp gaze, and she pointed her monocle at Ivy.

"Well, Miss Beecham? What's the name of this book Lord Wycombe is referring to?"

"I ... Forgive me, my lady, but I don't recall the name of the book."

"Don't recall the name of the book." The older woman scoffed. "Poppycock, you've never forgotten the title of a book since I've known you."

"Golden something or other, wasn't it, Miss Beecham?"

Cheeks flushed pink with embarrassment, Ivy sent him a furious glare before turning back to the tall lady watching her with a hawk-eyed gaze.

"For the life of me, Lady Effington, I've completely forgotten the title."

"Perhaps you're flustered by the company you're keeping." The noblewoman arched an eyebrow at Ivy then deliberately looked at him. Avoiding the old lady's gaze, he suppressed a grin as he saw Ivy's pink cheeks deepen to a lovely hue.

"If you'll excuse me, I should ensure that supper is on schedule. I'm certain Lord Wycombe will prove adequate company this evening, my lady." Not waiting for a response, Ivy moved away from them with a quiet rustle of her silk dress.

Her back was straight as she walked away, and he knew she was furious with him. A raspy chuckle echoed from the woman next to him. He turned his head and met the woman's amused gaze.

"That woman, my boy, will lead you a merry dance."

"I have no doubt of that. But I'm confident it will a pleasurable one," he said with a smile.

Lady Effington laughed again, her fan tapping playful against his arm as she sent him a broad wink. The woman was right. Seducing Ivy was one thing, taming her was going to be an altogether different matter.

* * * *

Crisp silence filled the carriage as the vehicle rocked forward. Across from him, Ivy stared out the window, her body as rigid as the mutinous twist of her lips. With supper over, she'd had no choice but to submit herself to his presence.

Throughout the meal, whenever he'd managed to catch her eye, she'd done nothing but glare at him. He was certain she regretted pairing him with Lady Effington. Despite her age, the widow had a no-nonsense manner and sharp wit. The woman had persistently tried to coax Ivy into revealing the name of the book she'd been reading. He leaned toward her.

"You're angry with me."

With a hiss of fury, she snapped her head in his direction. "And why shouldn't I be? Lady Effington hounded me all through supper about that blasted book. I'm certain she knows it's something thoroughly wicked."

Before she could protest, Simon quickly changed seats to sit beside her. Keeping his touch light, he trailed the back of his hand along the edge of her jaw. "I doubt Lady Effington thinks any such thing."

His fingers glided down the side of her neck, pausing to caress the rapid throb of her heartbeat. The fragrant aroma of lilies drifted off her skin. Beneath his touch, she stiffened.

"Don't underestimate the woman. She's far more astute than most people give her credit." A breathless note drifted through her words as she trembled against his fingers.

"I'm sure she is, but Lady Effington's literary tastes don't interest me. I'd much rather discuss your personal reading preferences."

"You're absolutely wicked." She gasped.

"True, but in order to be good, I must first be *quite* wicked."

The soft sound of her laughter made him grin. She turned her head to look at him, and the close proximity of her mouth sent tension rocketing through him.

"You're an incorrigible beast."

With a mock growl, he leaned into her and nipped at her ear with his teeth. "Then tame the beast, Ivy."

"What ... I don't know what you mean." The pace of her breathing doubled, and it aroused him in a way that surprised him.

"Oh, I think you do," he whispered.

Staring into her deep blue eyes, he saw the same awareness he'd seen earlier in the evening. With a hesitant move, she leaned toward him. The warmth of her mouth against his, made his cock go rigid in a single heartbeat. God almighty, if she were ever to gain the upper hand in their relationship, he'd be done for.

Desire barreled through him as he pulled her into his arms and deepened the kiss. Her lips parted willingly, and he swept his tongue into the heat of her moist mouth. The peach-brandy cobbler served at supper lingered on her tongue. Smooth and sweet, the taste of her danced in his mouth like the finest of cognacs.

Eager to touch more of her, he unfastened the short evening cape she wore, while moving his lips down the edge of her jaw to the side of her neck. A whimper echoed from her, and in the dim light of the carriage, the tops of her creamy breasts beckoned him with a force that was almost tangible.

Lightly, he slid his finger along the edge of her dress until he reached the cleft between her breasts. He wanted his mouth on her, his tongue dancing in that small hollow in an imitation of what he eventually intended to do with her.

Pressing another kiss to her throat, he lowered his head until his mouth was teasing the plump mounds displayed so delectably. The soft moan escaping her told him she was enjoying his touch. The knowledge pleased him. Ever so slowly, he circled the top of her breasts with his tongue then slowly tasted the valley between the delicious, plump flesh.

"Oh dear lord," she gasped as her body instinctively pushed upward to welcome his wet, hot caress.

With methodical strokes, his tongue slid in and out between her breasts, and she shivered beneath the hedonistic touch. Not even Whitby had ever excited her to this degree. This man's touch stirred a wild and wanton creature inside her. It was a dangerous game she was playing, but at the moment, all she wanted to do was continue playing.

The sudden jerk of the carriage coming to a halt made him raise his head. Dazed by the intensity of his caresses, she could only stare at him as he smiled.

"That's just a taste of what I have planned for you, Ivy Beecham," he murmured in a husky tone.

The sound sent a shiver of pleasure rippling across her skin. Struggling to regain her composure, she swallowed hard. "Even the best of plans often come to naught, my lord."

"But I don't expect to fail, Ivy. In fact, I plan to be quite successful."

Fumbling with the frog loops of her cape, she didn't have a chance to respond as the door to the carriage opened. While she struggled to repair her disheveled appearance, Simon stood outside the vehicle, his hand outstretched to her. The moment her hand slid into his, a wave of heat swelled over her.

Her eyes met his, and her heart skipped a beat. The look in his gray eyes was one of molten steel. Hot and blazing, it held the promise of things she wanted to experience, despite the warnings of her mind. Averting her gaze, she walked up the steps of Clarendon House with Simon next to her.

Inside, the air was already hot and stuffy despite the crisp winter air. As she removed her cape, strong fingers brushed against hers as he lifted the garment off her shoulders. The touch of warm fingers briefly grazing across her skin made her shiver, and she glanced over her shoulder at him.

The look of desire in his eyes made her heart pound against her ribs. The silent offer he extended could not have been clearer. He wanted to be her lover. But was it wise to experience the pleasure he offered her? They were from two different worlds. And his world wasn't one she wanted to become too well acquainted with. Pulling her gaze away from him, she spied Lord Asterly with the Earl of Clarendon.

Without waiting on Simon, she quickly moved in their direction, intent on discussing the Voltaire Papers with Lord Asterly. Both of the distinguished gentlemen welcomed her presence with a smile as she drew near. Offering her hand to first one man and then the other, she smiled back at them.

"My lords, how nice to see you this evening."

"Miss Beecham, Wycombe." Lord Clarendon bowed slightly as the tiny frisson skating over her skin told her Simon had followed close behind her. "Well, Miss Beecham, I understand you're responsible for the Library's most recent acquisition."

"Actually, my lord, it was Lord Wycombe's idea. I was simply the catalyst." Beside her, she caught Simon's soft chuckle.

"A catalyst, indeed, Miss Beecham." Her skin tingled. Despite the formal way he spoke to her, there was a note of intimacy in his voice that teased her senses.

"We're grateful for your contribution, Wycombe." Lord Clarendon's statement was followed by Asterly's own expression of gratitude.

"Quite so, my dear boy. The Voltaire Papers will be the crowning jewel in our collection. Personally, I'm astonished you allowed Miss Beecham to wheedle them out of your possession."

"One wins the victory when one yields to a beautiful woman," Simon said with a smile.

His response pulled a loud laugh out of both men. Lord Asterly nudged the earl and shook his head. "I think Miss Beecham might have found someone to match her knowledge of the classics. I do believe the boy is paraphrasing Sophocles."

She darted a glance in Simon's direction and found him watching her with a spark of devilment in his eyes. The rogue was testing her. Daring her to match him in another battle of words. Well, she wouldn't do it.

Every time she entered into a verbal duel with him, she found herself in his arms. *But then you like being in his arms, don't you, Ivy.* She ignored the voice. No, she didn't like it. She didn't even like the man. *Liar.* With an inward sigh, she shook her head.

"My lords, I confess I am at a loss as to how to respond to such flattery. Now if you'll excuse me, I see Mrs. Simpson and must say hello." Smiling, she nodded in their direction and made ready to retreat. As she turned her head, she caught the gleam of mockery in Simon's eyes, which made her lose her tongue.

"Oh, and I must mention that despite the notion that to the victor belongs the spoils of the enemy, I am far from defeated." Not waiting for a retort, she sailed away from the three of them leaving laughter in her wake.

As she climbed the stairs, a firm hand cupped her elbow. "If you think to escape me, you *must* run faster than that."

"I was not running."

"Walking fast then," he said wryly.

Unable to help herself, she laughed. "You are irredeemable, my lord."

"Simon."

The quiet command made her glance up at him in surprise. "But here? Now? It's not done."

"Now, Ivy." His resolve echoed in his soft voice. Good heavens the man wanted everyone to believe they were far more intimate with each other than was the case.

"Please, if someone heard..." She darted a quick glance at several people standing nearby. Were they close enough to hear their conversation? Her gaze flew back to Simon, whose mouth had become a hard, firm line of determination.

"*Now.*"

"Simon," she hissed. "There. Are you happy with yourself?"

"Quite. I simply want you to get accustomed to the sound of it." He leaned forward to whisper into her ear. "Because in the near future, you're going to cry out my name in a moment of passion."

Although she was certain no one had heard him but her, she still glanced wildly around her, fearing someone had overheard. Satisfied that she was still safe from wild gossip, she lifted her gaze to look at him. Amused complacency curved his mouth upward and she glared at him. Mad. The man was stark raving mad. What made him think she was going to allow him to seduce her? If anything, he'd been the one to propose that she seduce him.

"If you persist in this behavior, people will begin to talk."

"And exactly what will they talk about, Miss Beecham?" The sardonic arch of his eyebrow made her grit her teeth. "I think the only thing they're likely to comment on is the fact that I danced with you quite a bit this evening."

"Well, I've not agreed to dance with you yet, you arrogant beast."

Laughing, he pulled her hand through his arm and guided her up the stairs to the ballroom. "But you will, my sweet Ivy. You will."

The confidence in his voice irritated her, but she refused to say another word, as he was far too quick with his retorts. Despite his arrogance, he was the most intelligent and amusing man she'd ever met. It annoyed her to admit it, because she wanted to dislike him.

She wanted to despise him for the way he'd treated her in the library. She wanted to view him with contempt because he was of the nobility. But she couldn't. As much as she detested the notion of the peerage and what it stood for, she'd seen the love he bore for his nephew in his actions and words. She could hardly fault him for that.

"So deep in thought. I wonder what mischief you're plotting in that quick mind of yours." His voice was husky as he spoke. The teasing note of it grazed over her skin in a sensual caress of sound.

"Emma's Mr. Knightly said that vanity working on a weak head produces every sort of mischief. However, I am far from weak headed or vain."

"True, but you are quite lovely." The sincere note in his voice alarmed her, and her cheeks grew hot as her gaze met his.

She turned her head away from him as they entered the ballroom. Filled to capacity, the dancing had already begun. One of the Library's patrons saw them from several feet away and pushed his way through to greet them.

"Good evening, Miss Beecham, Wycombe. Bit of a crush this evening wouldn't you say?" Oliver Chestertop pulled a handkerchief from his coat pocket and dabbed at his brow. Not waiting for a response, he offered his arm to her. "Now then, Miss Beecham. I believe you promised me your first dance of the evening."

"I'm certain I did so, sir. Shall we?" With a laugh, she accepted Mr. Chestertop's arm. As she pulled away from Simon, she heard his soft growl of displeasure. With a quick glance back at him, his frown of frustration made her smile. Although she knew it shouldn't, it pleased her that he was unhappy about her departure.

More than an hour later, she found herself whirling around the dance floor with another of the Library's patrons. Laughing at something her partner said, she caught a glimpse of Simon standing on the edge of the dance floor. There was a sharp line of determination to his jaw. She watched as he stepped out onto the floor just as her partner whirled her past him. To her amazement, he tapped the older gentleman on the shoulder.

"Excuse me, but may I cut in?" It wasn't a request, more like a command, and her partner blinked with surprise.

"Well, I--"

"Thank you." Without waiting for the man to finish his sentence, Simon pulled her into his arms and left her dance partner standing in the middle of the floor.

"That wasn't very kind of you," she murmured as he skillfully guided her around another dancing couple.

"I'm feeling far from kind at the moment. I agreed to hand over the Voltaire Papers to the Library in exchange for one evening with you, and I've spent less than an hour in your company."

"Very well, I shall spend the rest of the evening with you."

"You're damn right you will."

With another swift turn, he danced her off the floor near a row of French doors that had been opened to provide fresh, cool air to the guests. As she moved out of his arms, he suddenly grasped her hand and tugged her out into the darkness. The shock of the cold air against her skin made her shiver.

"I don't think this is the type of weather where we can take a stroll through the garden," she said with a touch of irony. "It's far too cold for my liking, so may we please go back inside."

Not bothering to answer her, he tightened his grip on her hand and pulled her along the stone balcony toward the wide steps that led down into the gardens. Fallen leaves rustled beneath their feet as they charged deeper into the gardens. Wherever they were going, he seemed certain of their destination. In any other man's company, she'd be alarmed at his outlandish behavior. The truth was, a part of her liked the masterly way he commanded her and others to do his bidding. Stumbling slightly as she struggled to keep up with his long, quick stride, she realized the chill in the air had diminished some due to her exertion.

"Simon, where on earth are we going?"

"Someplace where I won't have to deal with another one of your elderly suitors showing up at your side."

"All right then, but could we at least walk there," she huffed. "I'm having to take two steps for every one you take."

His soft chuckle danced around her ears. "We're almost there."

"*Where?*"

"Here." He tugged her around a tall hedge toward a large hothouse. "This is the one place we can be warm, while ensuring there will be no interruptions."

As they entered the heated building, Simon released her from his grasp. Rubbing her bare arms to ease the chill on her skin, she looked around her. The brightness of the full moon overhead illuminated the hothouse almost to the point of daylight. A profusion of flowers filled the structure, and the scent was intoxicating. From where she stood, a gravel path wound its way deeper into the building.

Enchanted, she followed the path into the heart of the conservatory, stopping every few feet to press her nose into a flower. All the time, she was acutely aware of Simon's presence. Even with a modest space between them, her body ached for the heat of him to embrace her. As she breathed in the fragrance of a rose, she remembered the look in his eyes when they'd arrived at the ball.

The desire in his gaze had excited her. She knew what he wanted of her, and the hunger stirring in her blood urged her to accept his proposal. Her innocence had been lost long ago, and the liaison Simon was offering would involve no commitment, only pleasure.

The soft sound of water splashing against rocks caught her ear, and as the path curved around into the center of the building, she gasped. The path opened up into a small sitting area to reveal two other paths veering off into other parts of the hot house. On her left, a miniature waterfall was nestled in a bed of climbing ivy and tropical plants.

The water tumbled off the handcrafted granite that contained several steps for the water to flow over. Captivated, she stood still and drank in the beauty of it all. She'd never seen anything quite like it. She needed to commission something like this for herself. It would be the perfect place to sit and read. Whoever had designed this building loved their work.

"Do you like it?" The quiet sound of his voice broke the peaceful silence, and she glanced over her shoulder at him.

"Yes, very much. It's beautiful. I was just thinking I'd have to ask Lord Clarendon the name of the architect."

"I'm the architect."

Startled, she jerked her head around to stare at him. "You built this?"

"I designed and oversaw the construction of it. You're surprised."

"No--well, yes."

"It's a hobby of mine." He shrugged his shoulders. "I built one at my family's estate two years ago. Clarendon saw it and immediately demanded that I build one for him."

"It's beautiful," she said as she looked around her.

"Shall I build one for you?" There was something about the question that puzzled her. It sounded almost as if he was asking her something entirely different.

"I would like that very much. I can pay you well for your time."

He walked slowly around her until he stood behind her. The light touch of his fingers across her shoulder made her tremble. The moist heat in the building had settled on her skin, making it slightly damp.

"But will you pay me in the currency I want, Ivy." As he spoke, his warm breath heated her skin.

"I don't understand."

Another tremor shot through her as his tongue swirled a hot circle on her shoulder. The tantalizing caress caused her stomach to lurch erratically as she struggled to remain still. Sweet heaven, she wanted his hands on her, touching her, tempting her with the wanton acts *The Golden Lotus* had described. Her body swiftly took charge as his mouth nibbled at her skin, and she sank back into his chest. She didn't want him to stop.

How long had it been since a man's voice, words or touch had sent her pulse racing or her blood flowing so hot? Never. Simon was the first man to fill her thoughts in such a wicked manner. Tonight, she was more than willing to be seduced. It didn't matter that they came from two different worlds. Nothing mattered except the delicious sensation of his mouth on her skin and the way he made her feel. Tonight she would accept his offer and tomorrow she'd grapple with any repercussions.

Chapter Five

Simon licked the tangy dew off Ivy's shoulder. Drinking in the soft exotic scent of her, he enjoyed the way her back pressed against his chest. Nestled against him like this, he had a pleasant view of her full breasts. The way they rose and fell so quickly convince him that she was excited by his touch. It pleased him.

"You say you don't understand, and yet I think you do." He lightly nipped at her shoulder, one hand stealing around to caress her throat as she turned her head away from his mouth. "Tell me why you were reading *The Golden Lotus*."

Beneath his hands, her shoulders went rigid with tension. "I ... I thought it would be ... I wanted to read it for academic purposes."

"And did you find it academic in nature?" He tried desperately to keep his amusement out of his voice. Despite their short acquaintance, he knew she'd retreat from him if she even thought he was laughing at her.

No ... I mean yes. It was very...very...." The sound of her breathing had become soft pants. He kissed her shoulder once more.

"I think arousing is the word you're searching for, Ivy." His hands slid down toward the low line of her bodice, his fingers warmed by the heat of her skin. "In fact, I'm certain your nipples were quite hard while you were reading the book."

"I ... no ... I...."

"Tell me your nipples aren't hard right now." Slowly, he glided his hands along the edge of her bodice. "Tell me you don't want me to touch you."

This time her gasp was more of a whimper, and her body relaxed into his as he slipped a finger between her corset and her breast. His finger brushed over a hard nipple. Damn, but she was a bewitching siren. Just the sound of her quick breathing had been enough to make him painfully hard. Gently, he eased her breasts upward so her nipples pushed over the edge of her corset. With his thumbs, he brushed over her stiff peaks, then gently circled them, teased them.

"Oh God," she moaned.

"This is only the beginning of pleasure, Ivy. There are more ways than you can imagine to please one another."

With a gentle movement, he caught her wrist and pulled it back behind her to rest on his cock. She jerked slightly, but he wrapped his arm around her waist and pressed her closer to his body. Although she didn't move her hand, she didn't retreat either and the warmth of her touch melted through his trousers. If possible, he grew harder. Without thinking, he rubbed himself against her hand. Christ Jesus, he was more than ready to drive into her hot depths. She was making him so hot, he wasn't sure whether he could continue this slow seduction. He swallowed the desire pounding through him and brushed his mouth over her shoulder before kissing the nape of her neck.

"Do you remember the picture in *The Golden Lotus* of the woman using her hand to please a man?"

As she nodded her head, a tremor shuddered through her. To his delight, her hand stirred against him. They were tentative strokes but without any coaxing from him. The touch of her hand on him felt good. Damn good.

But he wanted her to hold him in the palm of her hand, to pump him until he spewed his cum from the pleasure of her touch. His mouth went dry at the image, and he quickly released his cock from his trousers. The moment her fingers brushed over the tip of him, she jerked her hand away. Turning her around to face him, he guided her hand back to his engorged staff.

"Wrap your hand around me, Ivy. Hold me tight," he rasped as her fingers singed his skin. He was ready to explode this instant. "Now slide up and down. Yes, that's it."

Friction tugged at him, and he groaned from the pleasure of it. She was a natural. Even more than that was her willingness to satisfy his need. His gaze boring into hers, he watched the desire stirring to life in her brilliant sapphire eyes. She was going to be the most delightful creature he'd ever had in his bed.

Her thumb rubbed across the cap of his engorged length, brushing against the sensitive spot beneath it. Closing his eyes, he threw his head back and rocked his hips against the tight grip of her hand. There was a slight rustle of her skirts and she suddenly released him. No. Not now. Why the hell had she stopped? Intense pressure tightened in his groin as he opened his eyes.

The sight of her kneeling in front of him made him go rigid. He swallowed a shout as her tongue flicked out and stroked his erection. Sweet Jesus, where the hell had she learned--the book. She'd gotten more than halfway through the book. The sensation of her tongue swirling around the tip of him, made him jerk. His hands grasped her shoulders in an effort to steady himself.

A moment later, her mouth closed over him. God almighty. It had been a long time since he'd had his cock sucked, and for a novice she was exceedingly adept at pleasuring him. The light scrape of her teeth over his shaft was about to push him over the edge. Base need took over as he shuddered under her delicious caress. He was ready to explode. Barely able to think straight, he tried to remember where his handkerchief was. He didn't want to spill his seed all over her.

Groaning, he tried to pull away from her, but her mouth tightened on him as she increased the pace of her mouth pumping over him. Damn, he needed to pull away, but her mouth on him was incredible. The build up inside him was at the breaking point when her fingernails gently scraped across his ballocks.

"Bloody hell," he cried out as he came inside her mouth. He throbbed beneath the heat of her sweet lips. He couldn't remember the last time he'd experienced such a hot pleasure. She'd actually swallowed his seed. Never in his wildest dreams had he imagined her performing such an erotic act. Slowly, she released him from her arousing lips. The leisurely touch of her tongue laving his skin made him shudder again. Gathering his wits, he stepped away from her. Quickly adjusting his clothing, he looked down into her face. In the moonlight, he could see the blush tingeing her cheeks.

She was the most beautiful, wanton woman he'd ever seen. The moment she turned her head away from him, he caught her chin and forced her to look at him.

"Don't be ashamed, Ivy."

"I'm ... I'm not ashamed." There was just a hint of uncertainty in her voice as she averted her gaze.

Helping her to her feet, he pulled her into his arms. "That had to be the most astounding thing that's happened to me in a very long time."

"I thought you might like it," she whispered against his shoulder.

"I did. Very much." He kissed the tip of her ear. "If you were acting on your academic review of *The Golden Lotus,* I heartily approve."

When she didn't answer, he cupped her chin to tilt her head back. "In your research, did you read about the lotus petals?"

"I don't recall any such phrase in the book." The frown of puzzlement on her brow made him grin.

"Come, sit down on the bench over here, and I'll explain what they are." Taking her hand, he led her toward the hand-carved bench. Once seated, he bent over and lifted her foot into the air.

"What on earth are you doing?"

"Hush, be patient."

He removed her slipper and dropped it onto the walkway. In a leisurely fashion, he stroked the top of her foot then caressed her ankle with a light touch. Resting her foot on his thigh, he pushed back the hem of her gown to reveal her leg.

Black silk stockings encased a lovely calf, providing an erotically tempting picture. She watched him with a mixture of bewilderment and curiosity. Other women would have been affecting a display of arousal at this point. Instead, she quietly watched him with a speculative gaze.

Taking his time, he explored the curve of her knee with his fingers before he slid closer to her, stretching her leg across his lap. The silk layers of her midnight blue gown frothed up past her thigh, giving him a glimpse of what he sought. He glanced up at her face to see anticipation glowing in her eyes. She quivered as he stroked her thigh with one finger.

"Simon?"

He raised his head to see her blushing, and he smiled. "Yes?"

"The lotus petals. Are they what I think they are?"

A fierce blush invaded her cheeks as she darted her gaze away from him. Without hurrying, he moved his hand upward to the slit in her woolen drawers. The curls there were already damp with moisture, and he smiled.

"We both know what the lotus petals are, Ivy. And we both know that I intend to fill those petals with my cock when I can do it properly." Chuckling at her gasp of shock, he leaned toward her and captured her mouth with his. As he slid his tongue into the heat of her mouth, he gently stroked her.

She jumped at the caress, but didn't stop him. He released her lips, and feathered her cheek with kisses as he sought the plump mounds of her breasts. She was hot and wet. Already she was slick with heat from just a few caresses. When the time eventually came for her to wrap her silky core around him, she was going to feel incredible between his legs.

Finding the small bud inside her damp curls, he rubbed his thumb over it. A cry of pleasure flew from her mouth, and she bucked against the touch. As he rubbed the sensitive nub of flesh, he slid a finger up into her.

"Oh, dear lord." The husky sound of her voice barely registered in her ears as she raised her hips up toward Simon's seductive caresses. Not even Whitby's touch had prepared her for something this erotic, pleasure this wicked.

Eyes closed, she gave herself up to Simon's sinful touch. How it happened, she wasn't sure, but seconds later, she was lying on the bench. Startled, she looked up to see him studying her with a gaze of hot steel. It set her blood on fire until it pulsated its way through her body, heating every pore of her skin.

"I like seeing your cunny all hot and slick for me."

The coarse words shocked her, but not because he'd used them. What shocked her was the fact that she liked it. It made her insides tighten as he rubbed that infinitely tender spot between her legs. Even more shocking was the image of him kissing her on that sensitive area. It made her gasp. Staring up at him, she saw his eyes narrow with astute assessment.

"One night very soon, I'm going to enjoy plunging into your sultry, tight core, sweetheart. But for right now, I think what you want is for me to taste you, lick that hot cream off your sweet cunny and suck on you until you explode in my mouth."

"I don't think... Oh God, Simon."

The heat of his mouth singed her as his tongue swirled around the bud of flesh between her nether lips. His teeth gently nipped at it, and her entire body shuddered at the sensation. With long strokes, his tongue teased and tempted her until she craved a release. It was the most sinful act she'd ever encountered, but it was exquisite in its intensity. What she'd experienced with Whitby had been a rushed, clumsy affair.

This was completely different. This was the skilled caress of a master of seduction, and the pleasure he provoked with his tongue was blinding. A moment later, she exploded against his mouth, just as he'd described. With a whimper, she shuddered as wave after wave of delight rolled over her. Unable to move, she remained still, her eyes closed.

The soft rustle of her gown forced her to look up at him as he smiled down at her. When she went to push herself up, a strong hand pulled her upright. With a long, elegant finger, he stroked her cheek. "I take your reaction to mean you enjoyed yourself."

Drowsy and relaxed, she smiled. "Yes, very much."

"No more questions about lotus petals?" His grin was filled with wicked glee, and she laughed.

"No, I think I've experienced quite enough instruction for the time being."

"Come, I imagine our absence has caused some raised eyebrows, and I have the distinct impression that the Library's patrons will prefer that Miss Ivy Beecham maintain her reputation as a starched librarian." Taking her hand, he pulled her to her feet and allowed her a brief moment to shake out her skirts before he led her out of the hothouse.

As they hurried through the garden, she pondered his words. Starched librarian. Is that what everyone thought? That she was a stiff and inflexible bookworm? But then what else were they to think? She'd done everything to cultivate that image. She'd worked hard to build a shell around her to keep people out.

It enabled her to keep fortune hunters and most other men at a distance, but Simon wasn't most men, and already she knew she had a problem. Tonight she had given and experienced true pleasure. The terrifying part was that she wanted more, and that meant allowing Simon to break through her carefully erected barriers. As tempting as that thought was, it wasn't without great risk. For years, she'd avoided all types of risks, but this man made her want to forget all of that, forget everything but the pleasure she knew she would find in his arms.

* * * *

Seated at the secretaire in the salon, Ivy drummed a soft beat against the mahogany desktop. Lost in thought, she stared at the paper in front of her. All her efforts to write thank-you notes to several patrons for their generous donations to the library last night were pointless. She'd been unable to stop thinking about Simon all day. Every carriage that had slowed down in front of the house had made her heart leap with expectation.

She frowned. If she didn't take care, her attraction for the man could quickly spiral out of control. Once before she'd allowed her emotions to control her body. Whitby had taken her virtue in a bumbling fashion, satisfied his own needs, and broken her heart, all in the space of a week. It had taught her a brutal lesson in betrayal. No. Whitby had simply made a fool of her. Carolyn had been the one to betray her. Cramming the past back into its tiny compartment in her head, she sighed.

Last night with Simon had simply been an exercise in temptation, nothing more. But it had been an exquisite one nonetheless. His touch had aroused fires in her of a volatile nature. Never had any man's mere presence sent every inch of her body into a state of arousal. *That* was something Whitby had never done. Simon was unlike any other man she'd ever met.

Whether it was the sound of his voice, the touch of his hand, the way he looked at her or the male scent of him, he set fire to her senses every time they were in the same room. The mere thought of him made her skin tingle. Blast! All of this self-examination was pointless No doubt the man wouldn't even call on her today. It was a disappointing thought.

Irritated by her inability to push the man out of her head, she uttered a sound of exasperation. Why did she persist with this train of thought? The social chasm between them could never be crossed. She'd learned that harsh lesson with Carolyn's betrayal. The last thing she needed was to fall for a man like Simon.

No. Restraint was what she needed. Restoring her life back to its placid gait would help her forget last night. The mere thought of it immediately warmed her blood as her nether region stirred and tightened with the memory of Simon's mouth on her.

With a groan, she buried her face in her hands. She should never have allowed herself to be taken in by the man's intelligence and sharp wit. If only she had listened to her head and not allowed her senses to be captivated by him. She'd even warned herself this would happen. Now she needed to forget him, something that was not going to be an easy task.

Voices suddenly echoed in the foyer, and she lifted her head just as Morris announced Simon's arrival. For a moment, she froze as she watched him cross the room toward her. What did she say to a man with whom she'd been so intimate? Rising to her feet, her heartbeat increased at the sensual smile on his lips as he came to a halt in front of her.

Surprise, followed by delight, swept through her as he didn't even speak, but simply pulled her into his arms and kissed her hard. Resistance was a pointless effort as his lips teased hers. The heat of him enveloped her, drowning any thought of protest. Melting into him, she trembled as his tongue danced with hers. The spicy smell of him caressed her senses, and there was just a hint of sweet wine on the tip of his tongue. His kiss teased and tempted her until an insatiable hunger stirred inside her and settled in every inch of her body.

With her arms wrapped around his neck, she responded to his touch with heated abandon. This was what she'd been craving all day. Now that he was here, all she could think about was touching him and reveling in the pleasure his touch brought her. His mouth left hers to caress her cheek.

"You taste delicious."

"As usual your flattery is an exaggeration," she said with a laugh.

"Well, perhaps you're correct. I have to admit that tasting your sweet cream last night was the sweetest delicacy I've enjoyed in quite some time," he growled softly as he dragged his finger along the edge of her jaw. The intimate words sent heat flooding into her cheeks as she averted her gaze from him. With a chuckle, he released her from his embrace. "I've brought you a present."

Reaching into the inside pocket of his suit jacket, he pulled out a narrow, satin-covered box. He'd had a devilish time finding a jeweler willing to open his shop on a Sunday. It was only his willingness to pay an exorbitant amount of money in addition to the cost of the jewelry that enabled him to secure this particular present.

Women always enjoyed receiving jewelry. Every mistress he'd ever had in his bed had been fanatical in their pursuit of diamonds and other stones. Watching her closely, he handed over the slim case.

Puzzlement arched her eyebrows as she accepted the gift. As the box snapped open, the delight on her face filled him with mixed emotions. He'd been certain that she'd like the bracelet, and the excitement on her face sent a rush of satisfaction through him.

But deep inside, he was disappointed to find that she was no different from any other woman. It had merely been a matter of finding the right currency. From her obvious delight, a jeweled trinket could easily buy Ivy's attention and gain him entrance to her bed.

"Oh, Simon. It's beautiful." Her fingers rubbed over the stones. "I've never seen anything so exquisite."

Disillusioned, his jaw muscle flexed as he took the box from her hand. "Here, let me put it on you."

To his surprise, she took a quick step back and shook her head vehemently. "No. I can't accept it."

"Of course you can. You just said you like it," he said with a frown.

"Well, of course I do. Any woman would, but I can't accept such a generous gift."

He stared at her in amazement. It was a game. She wanted to make him think she didn't want the bracelet, but if he pressured her enough she'd accept it.

"I'm sure I can convince you otherwise. Stop being stubborn and at least try it on."

"No, Simon," she said in a quiet, firm voice. "I'm sorry that you think I'm being stubborn, but I cannot and will not accept such a gift."

"Any other woman would be more than happy to take this present," he said with a frown of frustration. Her features took on a mutinous expression as she glared at him.

"Perhaps, but what happened between us last night was not done with the anticipation of payment in any form, including jewelry. Last night was a pleasant interlude completely devoid of expectations of any sort." Her voice was stiff with injury, while her eyes had deepened to a chaotic, stormy blue.

Stunned, he simply stared at her. She thought he was paying her for last night. And wasn't he? Isn't that what he'd always done with the women he bedded? Those women had expected his gifts. But here was a woman who wanted nothing in return for giving herself to him freely and openly.

The knowledge was humbling as his eyes focused on the diamond and sapphire bracelet dangling from his fingers. With a quick movement, he returned the jewelry to its box, and tucked it back into his coat pocket. The devil take it. He'd insulted her again. This was not going the way he'd planned it. It had been years since he'd bungled his actions with a woman so badly or consistently. Now he had to find a way to ease this tension between them. Clearing his throat, the muscle in his jaw grew taut.

"It would seem that only by folly am I able to acquire any common sense at all," he said through clenched teeth.

For a moment she simply stared at him, her eyes wide with surprise. Then a bright twinkle of amusement filled her gaze as she laughed. "First Catherine Fanshawe, now Melville? I don't think I've ever had anyone continually apologize to me with such panache."

Relief swept through him with the force of a high wind, surprising him with the intensity of the emotion. Damnation, if he didn't take care he'd find this woman leading him around by the nose. He scoffed at himself. Such a possibility seemed quite remote. If things went as he planned this evening, he would be doing the leading. Biting back a smile he pulled her back into his arms and kissed her hard.

She was soft and pliant beneath his touch. An ache wrenched through him as his body reacted to her voluptuous curves. He wanted to undress her and explore every inch of her this minute. All too quickly her eager response made him harder than steel, and he immediately broke away from her. Now wasn't the time, he wanted to woo her with words, and the only place to do that was in the Library.

"No matter how much you resist me, I will see you wearing diamonds. Diamonds and nothing else," he said with a wicked grin. "Now then, I have something special planned for us tonight. I want you to meet me at the Library this evening at eight."

"The Library? What on earth are you up to, Simon?"

He grinned as he captured her chin and gave her a quick kiss. "Come to the Library this evening and find out."

Wheeling away from her, he strode toward the salon door. Behind him, the sound of her disgusted exclamation widened his grin.

"Blast you, Simon."

He chuckled. Tonight, Ivy Beecham was going to cry out his name in a much different tone when he was done with her.

Chapter Six

The cold air made soft clouds of her breath as Ivy stepped out of the hack. Slowly, she climbed the steps up to the door of the Library. There was no light coming from within, and she turned to look up and down the street. Perhaps Simon was late. The only person on the quiet street was a night watchman heading quickly in her direction. Reaching into her bag, she pulled her key out and turned to open the door.

"Good evening, miss, might you be Miss Beecham?" Glancing over her shoulder, she nodded at the watchman. "Well then, miss, the gentleman asked me to give you this. Said you would know what to do."

Accepting the white envelope, she thanked the man and entered the building. As the door closed behind her, she absently flipped the latch as she studied the strong handwriting on the envelope. Simon had written her name boldly across the crisp, white parchment.

Where was he? The man had been far too mysterious this afternoon, and now he was nowhere to be found. Blast the man. Irritated, she tore open the envelope and pulled out the note. Quickly scanning the words, she uttered a small noise of exasperation. The man was testing her again.

Pierre Corneille wrote, "How delicious is pleasure after torment!" If you wish to end our torment and surrender to pleasure, then find the note left for you where Corneille is housed.

He wanted her to find Corneille's works. She tapped the note against her fingertips then shoved it into her purse. Removing her cape, she carried it over her arm as she moved toward the book stacks. She frowned. Where had she last seen Corneille's work? The memory of Lord Lansdowne requesting a book by Corneille triggered a vague recollection of the books being on the second floor of the book stacks.

Draping her cape over the iron banister at the foot of the spiral stairs leading to the second floor, she glanced upward. Was Simon waiting for her upstairs? Eager to find out, she gathered her skirts and hurried up the metal stairs.

Disappointed that Simon wasn't waiting for her, she grimaced. The man was making her throw every caution to the wind. She should be running away as fast as her feet could carry her. Instead, she hurried toward Corneille's books on the end of the second aisle. In seconds, she was scanning the bookshelf for a note. The edge of one barely peeked out from between two of the author's books. Triumphantly, she pulled the envelope out from its hiding place and quickly opened it.

I promised you pleasure, and the Bard himself said pleasure and action make the hours seem short. Tonight, time will fly because I intend to pleasure you in ways you have yet to fathom.

The words on the note card made her inhale a sharp breath. Erotic and sensual, the note shot a bolt of anticipation through her. What was he planning? This game of words was not only intriguing it was almost intoxicating. Shakespeare must be the Bard he referred to in the note. Amused excitement had her running toward the back of the second floor stacks to the classic English literature section. Her fingers trailing across the leather bindings, she saw the white envelope stuck in between two books. Tipping her head to one side, she read the titles and laughed. The Taming of the Shrew and a Midsummer Night's Dream, two of the Shakespeare's comedies. Never had she met a man with such a clever wit. Pulling the envelope from the books, she tore open the envelope and pulled out the note.

"Was this the face that launch'd a thousand ships, And burnt the topless towers of Ilium?"

Helen of Troy. She frowned at the words. Now the game had taken a deliciously wicked step up in difficulty. Homer's poem, the Iliad, was about Helen, but these weren't the words of the Greek storyteller. They were far too modern for the Grecian era. No. These were someone else's words. But who? Closing her eyes, she repeated the words from the card over and over.

The author's name was on the tip of her tongue, but she couldn't quite remember it. It was worse than not knowing what might be in a Christmas present. That was it. Christopher ... Christopher Marlowe. His books were downstairs. Hurrying through the book aisles, she couldn't help but laugh at how amusing the game was.

No one had ever been so creative in their dealings with her before, and she liked it. She liked it very much. Reaching Marlowe's works, she eagerly opened the envelope lying on top of the open shelf beside the books.

"Surely, I said, knowledge is the food of the soul." While this is a true statement, I find it vastly over-rated. Perhaps he should have said the art of pleasure is food for the body, mind and soul.

Smiling she shook her head. For all his rakish charm, he was almost as much of a bookworm as she was. Food for the soul. Was that Plato or Socrates? It didn't matter, they were both in the Greek philosophy reading area, and she only hoped the game was close to ending as his words were seducing her almost as fast his touch.

The note was added to the other clues in her purse as she hurried toward the book aisle where she would find Plato and Socrates. More importantly, she wanted to find Simon. As she turned the corner toward the classical Grecian era, she caught the faint scent of cinnamon and pine. At the end of the row of books, a soft light flickered against the wall. A light that wasn't suppose to be there.

Simon. He must be in the small reading room in the back of the Library. Smiling she hurried past the rows of dusty volumes to the end of the aisle. Light filtered out into the darkened Library from behind the partially open door of the reading room. The door allowed just enough candlelight to shimmer out into the book section. She shivered as she put her hand on the door and pushed it wide open.

The sight in front of her made her suck in a sharp breath. Stretched out on a bed of soft furs, Simon smiled at her. It was a deliciously wicked smile, but it was his nakedness that stunned her. The maleness of him set every nerve ending beneath her skin on fire.

One leg bent, his arm rested nonchalantly on top of his knee. The confidence in his bearing set her pulse skidding out of control. Even if she wanted too, it would be impossible to resist him. The raw, animalistic aura he exuded excited her. She wanted to glide her hands over him. Feel the hardness of the shoulders sloping down to arms that were solid and sinewy with power.

But touching wouldn't be enough. She wanted to taste him. Press her lips against the sculpted muscles of his chest. It wasn't fair that he could affect her this way. She tried to swallow, but her mouth was dry simply from the heat blowing through her. Unable to help herself, her gaze took in the hard muscles of his chest before she followed the thin line of hair that dove toward his phallus.

His hard length was jutting upward to brush against his stomach, and she swallowed. The sudden dampness between her legs told her that she was as aroused as he was. Wild, wanton sensations flooded her senses. The sight of him made her want to do things she'd only contemplated in the privacy of her own mind.

"Are you ready for our evening of pleasure, Ivy?"

She swallowed hard as she nodded and continued to stare at the splendor of him. Tonight would be one she would never forget-- she was certain of it. The real question was whether she would emerge unscathed. At the moment, she didn't care. All she wanted to do right now was to touch him and enjoy his touch in return. She watched his smile deepen into one of skilled seduction.

With a lithe movement, Simon rose to his feet. He reminded her of a jungle cat as he moved toward her with a leisurely stride. Heart pounding, she sucked in a quick breath as he stopped in front of her. The narrow space between them shot a bolt of excitement through her as his hand brushed lightly across her throat then down to the top of her breasts. It was a light touch, but it only increased the desire streaking through her.

She'd never experienced the craving tightening her belly with Whitby. All thought of her past was obliterated as Simon bent his head and ever so lightly feathered her lips with a kiss. Unable to resist him, she leaned forward hoping for more, but he pulled away, his lips curved in a wicked smile.

"Not just yet, sweetheart. Pleasure isn't something to be rushed. It's a whisper that seduces slowly, yet completely."

He circled her, the beautiful strength of his naked body outlined in every step he took. From the sculptured curves of his chest and arms to the sinewy line of his legs, he tempted and teased her senses simply by his mere presence. A shiver trickled down her spine as he stood behind her. The heat of his breath stirred the stray hairs on the back of her neck.

Sweet heaven, she wasn't certain she'd be able to stand this excruciatingly slow pace. She wanted to be in his arms, touching him, enjoying the pleasures of his touch. Even the scent of him intoxicating. It was a tantalizing mix of bergamot and something else. Spicy and male, just like him.

Ever so lightly, his fingers trailed across the nape of her neck before undoing the back of her dress. He didn't say a word, and the silence between them thickened and grew hot. Trembling, she gasped as his mouth nibbled at her back, while slipping her gown off her shoulders until it pooled at her feet. With an experienced hand, he removed her slippers and her stockings.

The tips of his fingers stroked the inside of her thigh as he briefly explored the bareness of her skin. Raising his gaze to meet hers, his fingers slid upward to the opening of her combination garment. The intensity in his gaze shot a thrill through her. Yes, oh please, yes. She wanted him to caress her there. Silently she pleaded with him, her hunger for him holding every nerve ending in her body hostage.

With a small smile, he rose to his feet. Disappointment forced a sigh past her lips and sent need raging through her veins. Dear God, the intensity with which she wanted him had become almost unbearable. No man had ever made her feel this way before.

As he faced her, she stretched out her hand to touch him. The hard flesh beneath her fingertips was hot and solid, intensely arousing. Although he didn't take her into his arms, his lips seared the tops of her breasts, branding her with an intense, unexpected heat. With bated breath, she watched as he unlaced her combination, which was discarded as quickly as her gown.

The garment left her naked except for the thin, fragile chemise covering the upper half of her body. The feathery touch of his hand left a blaze behind as he dragged his fingers down to glide over the top of her chemise. The tips of her breasts were hard and achy. Oh God, she wanted his mouth on her, on her breasts, sucking on her to ease the sensation of longing that was sweeping across her skin with the ferocity of a wild wind. A smile curved his mouth slightly as his eyes locked with hers.

"You remind me of Corinna in Marlowe's translation of Ovid's Elegia 5," he murmured.

With measured movements, he slowly removed the pins in her hair. "Do you know the poem, Ivy?"

The question made her mouth go dry as she nodded. "Yes."

"Then came Corinna in a long loose gown, her white neck hid with tresses hanging down." The seductive note in his voice teased its way through her blood until her heartbeat spiraled completely out of control. "Tell me the next line, sweetheart."

"Resembling fair *Semiramis* going to bed, or *Layis* of a thousand lovers sped," she replied in a husky voice.

"Ah." The weight of her hair tumbled down onto her shoulders. "I snatched her gown, being thin, the harm was small, yet strived she to be covered therewithall."

Steel gray eyes bored into hers as his hand reached out and gently but firmly tore the thin, delicate chemise she wore from her body. Gasping, she instinctively tried to cover herself, but he shook his head.

"*Don't*," he growled. "I want to look at you."

Facing him completely naked, she trembled at the blazing desire in his eyes. It was as if he wanted to devour her. It was in his gaze, the way his erection jutted stiffly out of the dark hair at his thighs. But it was in his voice as well. The raspy sound of it seduced her as he continued to entice her with the sensual words of Marlowe's poetry.

"And striving thus as one that would be cast, betrayed herself, and yielded at the last. Stark naked as she stood before mine eye, not one blemish in her body could I spy." His hand reached out to her, his caress moving in rhythm with the poetry. "What arms and shoulders did I touch and see, how apt her breasts were to be pressed by me."

The rough pad of his thumb grazed her nipple, the touch unleashed a coil of desire inside her, and it whipped through her body with an intensity that was both agonizing and pleasurable in the same instant. She hungered for his touch, but she knew he wanted her too.

"Oh God, Simon, please. I--"

"How smooth a belly under her waist saw I," he said in a voice that was a deep growl of desire as he ignored her plea, his hands touching her as if she were the poem herself. "How large a leg, and what a lusty thigh."

The moment his hand touch her mons, she moaned deeply. The scent of lilies mixed with the musky fragrance of her desire to make him harder than he could ever recall. When he'd started this seduction, he'd never imagined how hot she would make him feel. Eager to feel her honey against his skin, he slowly parted her damp curls.

"To leave the rest, all liked me passing well, I clung to her naked body, down she fell, judge you the rest, being tired she bade me kiss."

Christ Jesus. If mere words had made her this slick with heat, what would she do when she was wrapped around his cock? She clung to his shoulders as he slid a finger into her, stroking her as her head lolled back and her eyes closed. He found the small nub within her folds and caressed it

"What do you desire, sweetheart?"

"You," she breathed with a mewl. "I want you."

Restraint no longer within his means, he tugged her down onto the fur blankets he'd had brought in for this very occasion. The feel of her silky skin against his only fueled his desire as his mouth sought a nipple. A keening cry poured out of her as he tried to hold onto his seed. When had he ever had such a delicious morsel in his arms? She responded to him with wild abandon. Rolling her onto her back, he hovered over her for a moment.

"Tell me what you really want, sweetheart."

"I want you inside me." Her sapphire eyes darkened with a hunger that clenched at his stomach. "I want you to fill me completely. *Now.*"

Without a word, he buried himself inside her slick, velvety core. Instantly, she uttered a cry of intense pleasure, her body arching upward to meet his thrust. Damn, she was tight. Hot and tight around his cock. Slick with heat, her body clung to him as he slowly retreated then pressed into her again. Lowering his head, he flicked his tongue out over a taut nipple. The sweet taste of it danced in his mouth. Another ripple shook through the sultry core of her, gripping him like hot vise.

Quickly the rhythm of her strokes matched his as he plunged in and out of her. With each stroke he pulled her to a higher peak. *This* was what she'd come here for--the pleasure she'd known she would find in his arms. The intensity of it pulled at her, teased her, tempted her. As she clung to him, the tension building up inside her exploded.

Head thrown back she sobbed at the tumultuous waves of pleasure cascading over her. Almost immediately, he drove into her one last time, a guttural cry parting his mouth as he throbbed inside her. Clinging to him, she shuddered beneath him.

The sensations pouring over her skin were like a blazing fire as it cooled to embers. His face buried in the side of her neck, his breathing was as ragged as hers. Eyes closed, she savored the warm, heavy feel of him against her. Bergamot, mixed with the musky scent of his hot skin, teased her senses. He smelled wonderful. Deliciously male. Blind to everything but the feel of him against her fingertips, she traced the line of his shoulders and down a strong arm.

As she reached his wrist, he shifted and caught her hand in his, entwining his fingers with hers. He rolled onto his side, still holding her hand. Propped up on one elbow, he studied her in silence. There was a wicked gleam of amusement in his eye, and she arched an eyebrow at him.

"Is there something that amuses you, my lord?"

"Actually there is. I was thinking about something Oscar Wilde said in the club the other day." He chuckled softly as he released her hand to tuck a lock of hair behind her ear.

"And what was that?"

"He said he could resist everything except temptation, and I have to agree on one point. *You're* the one temptation I couldn't resist, Ivy Beecham."

She wasn't certain what to say. This was new territory to her. Whitby had been a brief encounter, but Simon was her lover. A lover she couldn't afford to lose her heart to. Pushing the thought aside, she rested her hand against his hard chest. Beneath her palm, she could feel the steady beat of his heart.

"Then I suppose we should both adhere to his other comment on the subject." She glanced away from him as she spoke. "The only way to get rid of a temptation is to yield to it. Now that we've given in to temptation, we can free ourselves of its entanglements."

Her gaze flittered back to his, and she watched him narrow his eyes at her. There was an expression of assessment in those steel-gray eyes of his. What was he thinking? It was so difficult to read his thoughts sometimes. And what on earth had provoked her to open up the topic of the short-term status of their relationship? She was insane. He'd think she was trying to secure a commitment from him.

The sudden movement of his head downward caught her by surprise as he captured her mouth in a hard kiss. Breathing in a quick breath, she moaned quietly as his tongue swept into her mouth. The way his tongue mated with hers brought back the memory of what she'd just experienced. His touch made her insides grow hot, as she kissed him back. Slowly the intensity of the kiss eased until he lifted his head.

"If you think this is a way to rid yourself of me, Ivy, think again. Tonight is only the beginning of temptation. Something I intend to make you yield to over and over again."

As his hand slid up to cup her breast, she tugged in a sharp breath as his mouth suckled at her. It was an exquisite sensation and she gave herself up to the pleasure of his touch once more.

* * * *

The soft thunder against her ear was a soothing sound as she lay nestled in Simon's arms. They'd made love several times, each experience new and enticing. Relaxed against him, the warmth of him made her sleepy.

"Sleeping isn't the order of the night, Ivy." His wicked chuckle made her lift her head to look at him.

"I wasn't sleeping."

"Good, because I don't intend on letting you sleep. I've not had my fill of you yet."

She reached over him for a glass of wine next to the picnic basket he'd brought. Stretched across him, her breasts brushed against his lips, and with a flick of his tongue, he made her gasp.

Goblet in hand, she put some distance between them and glowered at him. "Behave."

"I am behaving," he said with a wicked grin.

"You're impossible." She laughed. "If I'd behaved so badly when I was younger, I can't imagine what the consequences would have been."

No, that wasn't true. Whenever she misbehaved, she was sent to her room without anything to eat except a slice of bread and a glass of water. It had not been the worst of punishments though. The worst had been her aunt and uncle's cold rejection of her. They'd punished her for her mother's sin of marrying a commoner. A gentle touch on her arm pulled her out of her reverie.

"You still miss your family."

The quiet statement tore at her heart as she nodded. "Yes, very much."

"Tell me about your childhood."

She jerked her gaze toward him. There was no avid curiosity in his expression, only sincere interest in her response. Despite his expression, she had no intention of discussing her hellish existence at Parkland. With a shake of her head, she avoided the topic. "One can never change the past, so it's best to simply forget."

"And yet our childhood is a part of who we are," he said gently. "And one can never run from one's self."

Turning away, she stared off into space. The words he'd spoken held a ring of truth to them that was difficult to deny. Perhaps it would be cathartic to share some of past, to cleanse the demons from the darkest corners of her soul.

"Carolyn," she whispered before she'd even realized she had spoken, "she was--" With a sharp shake of her head, she turned to look at him.

Reaching out, he captured her chin in a gentle grip. "It's all right, sweetheart. When you're ready, you'll tell me."

Smiling he pulled her to him, enjoying the feel of her soft, fragrant body against his. Whatever had transpired between Ivy and this family member called Carolyn, it had obviously brought her great pain. But there was also the sadness of a woman who wanted nothing more than to see her family again.

He would have to give it further thought, but at the moment, the only thing he could think about was the need to make her his again. There were so many things he wanted to show her, teach her. As he rolled onto his back, he pulled her with him. There was an expression of surprise in her eyes as he made her straddle him.

"I cannot believe you didn't finishing reading *The Golden Lotus,* before you brought it back here, Ivy."

"I ... I did."

"Then I think you know exactly what I want." He paused as he watched desire flare in her eyes. "Ride my cock sweetheart. Make me come inside that creamy hot core of yours."

Her gasp of shock evaporated into a cry of passion as he sheathed himself inside her tight passage. Every time he was buried inside her, the sensations grew infinitely more pleasurable. Deep inside his mind, a small bell of alarm went off, but it was quickly drowned out as she ground her hips down on his. The sensual movement pulled a groan from him. At the moment, the only thing he cared to think about was how damn good it felt to be inside her.

Chapter Seven

Outside, snow was falling lightly to the ground. From her seat at the fireplace, she could see the large flakes sticking against the windowpanes before sliding downward as they melted. With Christmas less than two weeks away, the snowfall only added to the beauty of the season.

For the first time in years, she was excited about Christmas. She knew Simon wouldn't be with her for the entire holiday, but he'd already mentioned coming for supper on Christmas night. Over the past few weeks, they'd been almost inseparable during the nights. These had been glorious moments, each one more exquisite than the last. Her days at the library, once so short now dragged on interminably until she was in Simon's arms. She was certain their relationship would end eventually, but for now, she wanted only to enjoy the pleasure of his caresses.

Simon's attentions seemed far from waning, but they had never discussed the future. Even if they had, she wasn't certain what could be said. He was a peer. His world was completely different from hers. There would always be a gulf between them, a chasm she didn't want to cross.

The bell at the front door rang, and she closed the book she was reading. Laying it on the side table, a little smile twitched at her lips. She'd returned *The Golden Lotus* back to the Library some time ago, but part of her still jumped any time she was reading and a caller rang the bell. Smiling, she turned toward the door as Simon entered the room. The unexpected visit widened her smile.

Crossing the room toward her, he grinned. "I hope whatever you were reading was educational and completely sinful."

"Now how do you know I've been reading?" She asked as he pulled her into his arms.

"Because you're wearing the same guilty expression you did the day I caught you reading *The Golden Lotus*." A strong knuckle lifted her chin so he could capture her lips with his.

A wave of heat cascaded over her as she wrapped her arms around his neck and pressed her body into his. Her lips parted slightly so she could lace her tongue over his mouth. With a growl, he probed the inside of her mouth, their tongues mating with each other in a dance that was so familiar and yet so new and exciting each time they kissed.

The need to feel his skin against hers without any barriers had her fingers quickly removing his tie and unbuttoning his shirt so she could press her mouth against his chest. The tangy male scent of him filled her nostrils as she slid her lips along the side of his jaw then down his throat to where his shirt splayed open.

Playfully, she slid her hand over his groin, noting the way his phallus jumped, before it grew long and hard beneath her fingers.

With her lips pressed to his chest, the low rumble echoing out of him was a certain sign that she was pleasing him. She wanted him. Waiting until tonight would be interminable. All they had to do was lock the salon door. No one would disturb them, and the fire would keep them warm enough afterward.

"Simon, I want you," she murmured against his throat. Her fingers undid one of his trouser buttons and reached inside to caress him through his underclothing. "I want you to please me like you always do, and I want to please you. I want to please you just as I did that night in the hothouse."

His phallus was rigid and solid against her fingers as she spoke. Then with a groan, he released her and put some space between them. Hastily, he repaired his appearance as he stared at her in frustration.

"Damnation, I can't think straight when I get close to you."

The statement and his expression made her heart skip a beat. What did he mean? Was he coming to care for her? A tremor sailed through her. No, that wasn't possible. They both knew their place.

Enjoying the pleasure of each other's company was one thing, but she had no wish to change things between them. He couldn't care for her. It wouldn't do. Uncertain as to how to respond to his words, she pressed a hand to her stomach as she saw the irritation on his face.

"I'm flattered, but I can hardly believe that you're so easily disconcerted by me."

"You underestimate yourself, Ivy." He returned to her side, his hand capturing her chin. "I find you most distracting. So much so that I agreed to my sister's demand that you attend our family gathering this evening."

Turning away from her, he shoved a hand through his hair. It left the dark locks tousled, enhancing the air of danger that always surrounded him. At first, she didn't comprehend his words. He'd mentioned her and a family gathering all in the same breath. The way he'd phrased the statement was as if he'd been forced into agreeing to the suggestion. Inhaling a sharp breath, she stiffened.

He was upset because he didn't want to bring a commoner into his house. It was one thing to be cordial or dally with the lower class, but associating with his family was a completely different matter. She'd known from the start how he felt about commoners marrying up the social ladder. It had not been problematic for her because she didn't want to marry, especially not a member of the nobility.

She didn't want to marry anyone. She was quite happy with her life right now. The first time she'd ever even considered taking a lover was the day Simon had entered her life. But now that she'd made that choice, she recognized the freedom such a relationship offered her.

There had never been any expectations spoken between them that would lead either one of them to consider their arrangement permanent, but declaring her unfit to meet his family rankled. The arrogance of the man to consider himself superior to her simply because he had a title. She had blue blood running in her veins as well. It might not be pure, but it was there all the same.

"Thank you for the invitation, my lord, but I've already made plans for the evening."

"What the hell does that mean?" he snapped.

"It means just what I said. I'm otherwise occupied this evening." She straightened her shoulders and tipped her head at a dignified angle. "If you expected me to be enamored by your social status, you're sadly mistaken."

"My social--" He glared at her. "This isn't about my perspective on class, Ivy. It's yours."

"*Mine*," she gasped. "Don't you dare try to cover up your prejudice by blaming me."

"Damn it, that's not what I'm trying to say." He grasped her by the arms and gave her a slight shake. "I know how you feel about the social circles I come from. I know how uncomfortable you are when you're surrounded by the nobility, and I didn't want to feed you to the lions if I could help it."

"Don't be ridiculous." She tried to tug free of his hold, but she failed. "You don't know me that well. We're lovers, and beyond that you know very little about me."

"Oh, I know you, Ivy. I know you almost as well as you know yourself. I don't fully understand why, but you despise the aristocracy. I've seen it in your eyes every time you've interacted with the nobility, even the patrons at the Library. Your back becomes straight and rigid the moment a peer of the realm speaks to you. Even with me you sometimes have a distant air, and all because of my social rank. It's there in that polite, serene mask you wear whenever you're conversing with one of *us*."

The stark words made her freeze in his grasp. It wasn't possible. She didn't act that way. How could she? It would make her no better than-- The harsh reality of his observation shamed her. She was no better than any peer who'd snubbed her.

Even worse, she realized how much like her aunt and uncle she had become. The only difference between them was the situation was reversed. Horrified by the realization, she flinched and tugged free of his hold. Turning her head away from his probing gaze, she struggled with the shame flooding through her.

"I'm sorry," she whispered. "I didn't realize...."

He moved to stand behind her, his hands resting on her shoulders. "Tell me why you despise us, the peerage, so much."

"I can't....please don't ask it of me," she said with a shake of her head.

Turning her around to face him, his piercing gaze met hers. "As you wish, but understand this. If you think you can distance yourself from me simply because of the differences in our social status, think again. I want you Ivy. I want you more than any woman I've ever known, and I'm not about to give you up anytime in the foreseeable future."

The possessive note in his voice alarmed and thrilled her. They were the words of a man determined to have his own way and damn anyone who tried to stop him. Swallowing hard, she stared up at him. "I have no desire to distance myself from you."

"Excellent, then say you'll come to supper this evening. Once we've satisfied Abigail's curiosity, she'll leave us alone to do as we please."

Unable to offer up any type of excuse she slowly nodded her head. It was insanity. She was certain of it, but she wanted to make him happy. If attending this small event achieved that, then nothing else mattered.

* * * *

Ivy stepped out of the carriage and stood on the sidewalk staring up at the façade of Lady Claiborne's home. Why had she agreed to come this evening? She wanted to turn around and climb back into the carriage.

Beyond that door was the potential for the same type of humiliation she'd endured growing up. She was certain Simon's family would find her sadly lacking just like her aunt and uncle. Inhaling a deep breath, her fingers gripped her purse more tightly. She was no longer a child. She was a grown woman, capable of leaving if the evening became too unbearable.

Avoiding the Marlborough Set was something at which she'd become quite adept. Now, here she was feeling like Daniel about to enter the lion's den. For a moment, she almost did return to the carriage. Instead, squaring her shoulders, she moved up the steps and rang the bell. The door opened to reveal a cadaverous butler, whose gaze skimmed over her with something akin to disdain.

Lifting her chin, she met his gaze steadily. "I'm Miss Beecham. I believe I'm expected."

"Of course, miss. Welcome to Claiborne House." Opening the door wide, he invited her inside with his hand smoothly slicing through the air. "Allow me to take your cape."

Undoing the frog loops of her cloak, she shrugged it off her shoulders and handed it to the servant along with her purse. Without her cape, she felt naked, exposed for any member of the Set to ravage her with insolent barbs and asides.

"The family is in the drawing room, miss. If you'll follow me."

As the butler moved forward, Ivy hesitated, frozen in place. She didn't belong here. It wasn't safe. If she moved quickly, she could grab her things and be gone before the man opened-- The double doors of the salon slid apart as the butler announced her arrival in sonorous tones.

Her mouth went dry with fear as she moved forward and stepped into the salon. The first person she saw was Simon. The familiar tilt of his dark head made her heart skip a beat. Heat coursed through her body at the sight of him.

His gaze locked with hers, his desire tempered by something else. Warm reassurance softened the harsh planes of his features as he silently offered her encouragement. It surprised and pleased her in the same breath. Before he could move forward to greet her, Anthony uttered an exclamation of pleasure and crossed the floor to her side.

"Miss Beecham, how wonderful of you to come this evening. I'm delighted that my uncle was able to convince to you to join us." Taking her hand, he pulled her toward a woman sitting on a scrolled back sofa talking with a young lady. "Come, let me introduce you to my mother."

As they approached, the woman rose to her feet to greet her. Although plain in features, the woman's brown eyes danced with merriment, and when she smiled, it was clear she was Simon's sister.

"Mother, allow me to introduce you to Miss Beecham. Miss Beecham, my mother, Lady Claiborne."

Her hostess clasped her hand warmly. "Miss Beecham, how lovely to finally meet you. Anthony has spoken of you often, as has Simon." Curiosity and assessment hovered in the woman's tone, but there was no hint of disdain.

"It was kind of you to invite me." For the first time since setting foot in the house, she relaxed slightly. Warm and genuine, the woman's welcome put some of her fears to rest.

"We're delighted to have you. Come, let me introduce you to everyone." Lady Claiborne turned toward the young lady beside her who had risen to her feet. "This is Olivia Hunter, Anthony's fiancée."

Startled, Ivy's gaze flew toward Simon. He'd actually given his approval for Anthony to marry a commoner. No, he wouldn't have done such a thing. The man had been so adamant that day in the Library. As if he could read her thoughts, he arched his eyebrow at her in his usual, arrogant manner.

Tugging her gaze away, she struggled to suppress the feelings of inadequacy flowing through her. Why had he asked her to come? It didn't make any sense. Her gaze focused on the young woman in front of her. She was pretty, and there was the bright gleam of intelligence shimmering in her wide hazel eyes.

Shyly, Olivia shook Ivy's hand and smiled at her. "I'm so pleased to meet you Miss Beecham. Anthony has told me so much about you."

"And he's told me a great deal about you. May I offer you best wishes on your engagement?" She squeezed the girl's hand.

With a gentle pat on the Olivia's arm, Lady Claiborne smiled. "I think my Anthony is a very lucky young man. Olivia will provide a steadying influence on him."

Steeling herself to hide her surprise, she averted her gaze from Lady Claiborne's face. Once again her eyes met Simon's from across the room. The quiet assessment in his gaze puzzled her. The man was looking incredibly mysterious this evening, more so than normal. And to find out that he'd agreed to Anthony and Olivia's engagement was astonishing. What had Anthony done to bring about such a miraculous change in his uncle? Perhaps he had come of age and forced his family to accept the girl.

With Simon so adamantly opposed to a commoner marrying into his family, it was only logical to assume that Lady Claiborne had felt the same way. But Anthony's mother seemed quite happy with her son's choice. She frowned as she shot another glance in Simon's direction and saw his stoic expression. She wished she could understand the way his mind worked. It would give her insight as to what was running through his head at this very moment.

Lady Claiborne grasped Ivy's elbow in a light yet firm touch to guide her around the rest of the room. She waved a hand in Simon's direction. "You already know Simon, so we'll move on to the others."

With his sister's cavalier dismissal, she saw his mouth tighten with irritation, and Lady Claiborne winked at her as they moved toward an older couple. Dear lord, did the woman know about her relationship with Simon? The thought sent her stomach churning with embarrassment. The gentle touch at her elbow pulled her attention away from her internal thoughts as Lady Claiborne introduced her to the elderly couple.

"This is Lord and Lady Marston. They're old and dear friends of the family."

As the couple greeted her, Lord Marston kissed her hand and winked at her. "I doubt you remember me, but I met you quite a long time ago when I visited your aunt and uncle at Parkland. You were still a child at the time."

Ivy stared at the man for a long moment, then nodded her head as she laughed. "You managed to sneak me several bon-bon treats after my aunt told me I couldn't have any."

"Ah, so you do remember." He chuckled.

"I never had the chance to say thank you. It was a kind gesture you showed me, and not one I forgot either. So I shall thank you now."

He grinned at her. "It was my pleasure."

Standing beside the older couple was a handsome gentleman. For a fraction of a second, Lady Claiborne's fingers bit into Ivy's elbow. "And this is their son, Viscount Halstead."

Ivy offered her hand to the Viscount, who smiled at her before kissing her hand. "Good evening, Miss Beecham. It's a pleasure to meet you."

Smiling she murmured a greeting, while beside her, Lady Claiborne touched her arm lightly. "I understand from Simon that you are very good at word games."

"I'm sure I'm not nearly as skilled as Lord Wycombe."

"I have a feeling you are as consummate as my brother. He would not have mentioned your abilities otherwise." The twinkle in the woman's brown eyes warmed her plain features as she shot her brother a glance of amusement. "In fact, I insist on you being my partner this evening for a round of The Name Game. I'm certain we will royally trounce Simon--something that rarely happens."

"Although Miss Beecham is most accomplished in many ways, having her for a partner will not save you from defeat, Abigail." The humor in his voice was evident, but it was the look in his eyes as he spoke that told her he was thinking about other things at the moment as far as she was concerned.

"I would be honored to be your partner, Lady Claiborne. The great Bard himself said that pride must have a fall, so we must hope that Lord Wycombe will suffer only a gentle injury should he lose to us this evening."

Laughter lighting up her face, Lady Claiborne wagged her finger at her. "I am certain of it now, Miss Beecham, especially when we team him with Anthony. Lord and Lady Barton have always refused to take part, but Olivia and Lord Halstead can partner with each other."

"Anthony and I shall fare quite well I'm sure," Simon retorted as he scowled at his sister.

"It seems Abigail has been plotting your downfall, Simon." Lord Halstead chuckled. "I would take care, old man, as it seems Miss Beecham is quite knowledgeable. I think she'll make you a most impressive opponent."

"Miss Beecham and I have waged battles with our words before, and in the end I generally emerged the victor." Confidence threaded through his voice, as his steel gray eyes met hers. The wicked desire she saw dancing in his gaze sent a rush of heat to her cheeks. Before she could rebuke him, the butler stepped into the room and announced supper.

Immediately, Lord Halstead presented himself to Ivy. "Allow me to escort you in to supper, Miss Beecham."

The invitation caught her by surprise, and she hesitated as she caught the look of pain on Lady Claiborne's face. Anguish disappeared from the woman's features as she became aware of Ivy's gaze. A brilliant smile on her lips, Ivy's hostess nodded.

"What an excellent idea, Royce, especially since Miss Beecham will be sitting next to you at supper."

It was impossible not to miss the tension in Lady Claiborne's body as the viscount offered his arm to Ivy. Sliding her hand through the crook of Lord Halstead's arm, she met Simon's gaze from across the room. Even from where she stood, she could see the muscle in his jaw flex, and she recognized the flash of anger in his eyes. She recognized that look of possession. It was the same expression he'd had the night of the Library ball when he'd dragged her outside to the hothouse. The memory of that night and the others that had followed made her breath hitch.

The rest of the evening proved to be a lively affair as the conversation ranged from current politics to a discussion on the differences between the philosophies of Friedrich Nietzsche, Plato and Voltaire. Even more amusing was the game the small gathering played after their meal.

Blindly pulling a famous individual's quote from a container, she was required to offer up clues so that her partner could name the renowned person. It had been a challenge, but Simon's sister had proven herself an excellent partner, and they'd soundly beaten everyone at the game.

When the last round had been played, Lady Claiborne smiled triumphantly at her brother. "I do believe you're frowning, Simon."

With a chuckle, he shook his head. "No, but you're most certainly gloating."

"So I am," Lady Claiborne said with a laugh as she patted Ivy's hand. "You were brilliant this evening, Miss Beecham. It gives me great pleasure to beat Simon at this game, something that rarely happens, I might add."

"I confess I am enjoying our victory as well." Ivy smiled at the woman's gleeful triumph.

"We must do this again." Lady Claiborne patted her arm then suddenly stiffened with excitement. "I know. You must come celebrate with us on Christmas Day."

The unexpected invitation startled Ivy, and she bit her lip. Tonight had been such a wonderful experience. So wonderful that she didn't want to leave. But she didn't belong here. She wasn't a part of Simon's world any more than he was of hers. It would have been so much easier if his family hadn't been so nice.

"Thank you for such a lovely invitation, but I'm not certain what my plans for the holiday are at the moment."

"Nonsense." The woman sniffed. "Simon, you must convince Miss Beecham to spend the day with us on Christmas."

"I've learned from experience that Miss Beecham does not like to be coerced," he said with a slight smile. "However, I will do my best to convince her to come."

Unwilling to subject herself to any further persuasion, Ivy rose to her feet. "I can only say, we shall see. For now, I must say good night as it is growing late."

"I'll see you home then," Simon moved to stand at the salon doorway as she said her goodbyes. Linking her arm with Ivy's, Lady Claiborne walked with her out into the hallway.

"Now, you must come for Christmas, Miss Beecham. I really do insist." The woman squeezed Ivy's hands. "If you don't, Simon will make me pay for this evening, so my fate is in your hands."

With a laugh, she shook her head at Lady Claiborne. The woman was every bit as determined as her brother when it came to getting what she wanted. "I promise to give serious weight to the matter."

"Simon?" Arching her brow at her brother, Lady Claiborne's eyes were sparkling with mischief. "Surely, you're not about to tell me that your persuasive powers have evaporated into thin air."

Despite his scowl, Simon refused to take his sister's bait as he snatched Ivy's cloak from the hands of the butler. His movements swift, he crossed the floor and settled the cape on her shoulders. There was something in the look that passed between the siblings that sent her heart racing. Abigail was referring to something completely different than Simon persuading her to visit Claiborne House for Christmas. Whatever it was, he was looking decidedly irritated. Hastily pecking his sister on the cheek she offered him, he grasped Ivy's arm and pulled her toward the door.

"Come, Miss Beecham, before my sister tries to persuade you into doing something else."

Abigail's pleasant laughter trailed after them as Simon pulled her out into the cold night air toward the carriage waiting at the sidewalk.

* * * *

"You didn't expect to like them so much, did you?" The soft words echoed through the mist as the images in front of her faded. The statement chilled her as she turned her head toward her ancestor.

The steady blue gaze so like her own made her quickly look away. The knowledge she saw in the Grand Dame's gentle expression made it difficult to speak. The woman was right. She hadn't expected to like Simon's family so much. She'd gone there expecting them to treat her with condescension simply because she was a commoner. Instead, she'd been greeted with a warmth and kindness that astonished her.

Worse than that, it had made her consider the possibility that she might have a future with Simon, a future that she was afraid to hope for. It had made her realize the inevitable had happened. She squeezed her eyes shut at the thought.

"This was the first time you admitted that you were in love with Simon, wasn't it?" Tenderness hovered in the Grand Dame's voice.

"Yes." Ivy swallowed hard.

"And being with his family made you see how wonderful life could be with him."

Blinking back tears, she nodded. "It was the first time I allowed myself to imagine such a thing. But falling in love with him was the worst thing I could have done."

"You seem so certain of that, and yet I sense something else inside you. Love is really quite simple, dearest. It's when we throw up obstacles in its path that it becomes difficult."

"Why are you doing this? What is the purpose of this examination of my relationship with Simon?" Hands clasped in front of her, she squeezed her fingers together until her knuckles were white. A gentle hand lightly touched her arm.

"You called me here with your wish, Ivy."

"No," she snapped bitterly. "I wished for Simon to love me, and he doesn't. I'm simply a commoner who shares his bed. Nothing more."

A heavy sigh passed the Grand Dame's lips. *"So stubborn and so certain. What if you're wrong? What then?"*

"I'm not wrong." She stared out into the white mist that surrounded them, refusing to look at the woman. What did she know about betrayal? The woman was actually suggesting that she might be wrong about Simon. The Grand Dame was mistaken. He'd betrayed her in the worst sort of way. He'd made her long for a life she could never have. A vise wrapped around her chest, tightening until she didn't think it possible to breathe any longer.

"Sometimes, Ivy, we see things that aren't really there."

"If you're referring to yourself, I understand completely." The irony of the situation threaded her voice with just a hint of humor. Although she could find nothing humorous about her current state of affairs.

"No dearest," the Grand Dame chuckled before her voice softened, *"Sometimes the obstacles we believe are real don't really exist."*

Grasping Ivy's hand, she pulled them back into the mists of time.

Chapter Eight

The silence in the carriage pulled Ivy's nerves taut. What was he thinking? They were almost at her house and he'd not spoken a word to her. Not about to look at him, she kept her eyes focused on the passing scenery.

"I can't imagine that the evening was so miserable that you're refusing to talk to me." The harsh note in his voice made her quickly turn her head toward him.

"I beg your pardon?"

"Or perhaps you're thinking of a certain Viscount with whom you seemed to be enthralled this evening," Simon snapped.

"What on earth are you talking about?"

"Halstead and your coquettish behavior around the man."

Astonished, she simply stared at him. She'd done no such thing. It had been obvious Lady Claiborne was in love with Lord Halstead. It would have been cruel to deliberately flirt with the man while Abigail looked on. Hurting someone like that was the last thing she would ever do, not when she understood so well the pain of loving someone who didn't reciprocate those feelings.

An icy chill rolled over her skin. She was in love with Simon. Dear lord, had she lost her mind? She couldn't be in love with the man. They merely had an arrangement between them. Nothing more. How could she have been such a simpleton to fall in love with a member of the peerage? A man who would never marry below his station.

She inhaled a sharp, ragged breath. Tonight had shown her what life with him would have been like if it weren't for her commoner blood. The thought sent her stomach lurching as the carriage rolled to a stop.

Barely giving her time to gather her skirts, Simon dragged her from the vehicle and up the steps to her front door. As she fumbled in her evening bag for her key, his anger vibrated over her skin. Why was he so furious with her? She'd been polite to Lord Halstead nothing more. The man was acting like she'd committed a mortal sin. The key in her hand, she started to unlock the door, but he tugged the metal from her hand to open the door himself.

Inside the foyer, he barely allowed her time to remove her outerwear, before he pulled her up the staircase toward her bedroom. He'd visited her room many times before, only tonight was different. Tonight he was going to make her understand that she was never going to belong to anyone else but him. She was his and no one was ever going to take her from him. As he dragged her into her bedroom, he closed the door behind them.

Leaning against the barrier, he narrowed his gaze to study the irritation on her lovely features. She'd put several feet between them, and there was defiance in the mutinous twist of her sensual lips. Damnation but she'd bewitched him. What the hell was wrong with him to be this upset by Halstead's attentions to her? Something whispered in the deep recesses of his mind, but he pushed it aside.

"You're mine, Ivy." He saw her blue eyes flicker with an indefinable emotion. With a measured step, he approached her. She didn't retreat, but once more he saw a flash of emotion in her gaze. It irritated him that he couldn't define it.

"You're mine, and I have no intention of surrendering you to Halstead or any other man who thinks they can take you from me."

"I should have said arrogance, not pride, must have a fall. To presume you own me is the height of arrogance," she snapped.

Anger flushed her cheeks, and her lovely breasts rose and fell rapidly as he halted in front of her. With his forefinger, he lightly traced a path from her ear down to her neck, his gaze following the trail he made.

"There's a difference between owning and possessing, Ivy. It's your body I possess." He smiled as she turned her head away from him. Pleasure shot through him as she trembled beneath his fingertips as he ran them across the top of her silky shoulder. "See, sweetheart, your body responds to me at the slightest touch. We both know neither Halstead nor any other man can excite you the way I can."

Lowering his head, he pressed his mouth against her shoulder. Lilies scented her skin, and he breathed in the exotic fragrance of her. She smelled good enough to eat. The thought made him smile. That was exactly what he was going to do to her tonight. He wanted to hear her cry out his name over and over again as he pleasured her throughout the night. Another shudder broke through her, and he straightened to stare down into her vivid blue eyes.

Desire burned and flared in her gaze as she stepped back from him. He watched in delight as she reached behind her and undid her gown in silence. With the dress undone, she slowly eased one short sleeve down her arm. A moment later, the other sleeve followed suit. If she meant to seduce him, she was doing it superbly. Just the expression in her eyes a moment ago had roused his cock to attention. No woman in his memory came close to transfixing him as she was doing right now.

Her pink tongue flicked out to moisten her lips, and his groin tightened with a sharp, arousing tug. Christ Jesus, she knew exactly what she was doing. She *was* seducing him. He swallowed hard as she slowly she began to unlace her combination corset. The laces slid through her fingers like ribbons in the breeze. They fluttered downward until the garment was completely undone.

Not once did her gaze leave his face as she removed the combination and casually tossed it aside. Kicking her slippers off, she lifted the hem of her petticoat to reveal her well-shaped legs encased in silk stockings. The black hose were held in place with a red garter, and his mouth went dry at the sight. He wanted to pick her up and take her to bed where he intended to keep her for the remainder of the night.

With great care she unhooked the garter, then rolled the stocking downward at a pace that was becoming increasingly unbearable for him. Growling, he took a step toward her, but she gestured for him to stop. Firelight from the hearth made the auburn in her brown hair shimmer in the room's dim light. A seductive smile curled her lips as she tossed the stocking aside and proceeded to remove the stocking from her other leg.

Another groan rumbled in his chest, and she smiled as she discarded the second stocking. Need blazed in his gray eyes and triumph surged through her. Although she knew he didn't love her, he was enthralled with her.

"You're right, Simon. There is no other man who excites me like you do." She whispered the words as she undid the front of her chemise and slid it off her body until she stood naked in front of him. "But is there any other woman who can make you feel the way I make you feel?"

The deep growl that erupted from him foreshadowed his swift movement as he eliminated the distance between them. Strong hands grasped her forearms as he tugged her toward him. Even if she'd had the strength to do so, she wouldn't have resisted him. Loving him as she did, she had no desire to be anywhere else but in his arms.

As he swept her into his embrace, the heat of his mouth captured hers in a deep kiss. The rough edge of his tongue swept across her lips to dance wickedly inside her mouth. Cognac and a hint of tobacco tingled across her taste buds as his tongue swirled around hers. Soft wool brushed across her sensitized skin, heightening her need to touch him--to have nothing between them.

He cupped her with his hand and circled her taut nipple with his thumb. The caress pulled a soft mewl from her throat as his lips moved to take the hard bud in his mouth. Sweet heaven, what would she do if she ever lost him? Lost this passion? She shoved the thoughts aside.

The present was all that mattered. The past and future were irrelevant. She wanted nothing more than to love him and relish his seductive touch upon her skin. Already the heat flooding her body had stirred the familiar sensations of desire and need. She wanted to feel his skin next to hers, and she twisted lightly out of his grasp.

Their eyes locked, and she smiled at his ragged breathing. His aroused state was more than evident, and she lightly ran her fingertips across her breast until they circled her hard nipple. Gray eyes glowed with a fire hot enough to burn her as he watched her caress herself.

"Don't you think it's time you undressed?" she asked softly.

Ripping his jacket off his shoulders, he threw the garment aside as his eyes caressed her across the short space between them. She watched his long, elegant fingers tug his silk tie off his neck and hastily unbutton his shirt before tugging it out of his trousers. As his shirt drifted to the floor and he removed the rest of his clothing, she savored the beauty of his muscular torso, the way his sinewy arms flexed.

His clothing pushed aside, he stood in front of her with his erection jutting out from the dark curls at the juncture of his thighs. Powerful muscles rippled in his legs as he stepped toward her and pulled her into his arms. The heat of his skin singed hers as he picked her up and carried her to the bed. Laying her on the coverlet, he hovered over her, his arms braced on either side of her.

"Tonight you're going to forget the name of every man you've ever met, except for one," he murmured. "Mine."

The weight of him settled on top of her as he nibbled at the side of her neck. His possessive words reassured her that he would not tire of her too soon. Perhaps he might come to care for her after all. The rough pad of his thumb brushed over her nipple as his mouth made its way downward until his lips gently clamped down on her.

The keenness of the caress tugged a cry of pleasure from her lips just as his fingers parted her slick folds to stroke the nubbin of sensitive flesh there. With a flick of his tongue, he released her nipple and kissed his way to her belly.

"You have a beautiful body, sweetheart. I don't think I'll ever get enough of it." As his mouth reached the fleshy mound above her curls, he continued to stroke her. Her mouth formed a small "o" as her hips bucked against his touch. "Tell me what you want, Ivy."

She whimpered as his thumb rolled over the small nub inside her nether lips. Dear lord, but she wanted his mouth on her. She craved the sensation of his tongue flicking its way over her most intimate area. The deep notes of his voice scraped across her skin. "Tell me."

"Oh God, please, Simon...." Her hips thrust up against his hand as her body indulged in the sinful delight his touch was evoking. The pressure of his thumb against her increased as he slid a finger inside her. Immediately, her insides clenched around him as spasms shuddered through her. She whimpered at the need for more, to have his mouth teasing her into one climax after another.

"Simon, please...."

"Tell me, Ivy. Tell me how I should pleasure you." Satisfaction lined the deep note of his voice as he brushed his lips against the inside of her thigh.

"I want...." She struggled to speak as her senses pitched to a fevered peak. " ... I want your mouth on me, Simon."

"Like this?" He whispered as his fingers parted her curls. An instant later, his tongue slid across the sensitive nub hidden in her folds. Heat melted her insides as his wicked caress tugged another cry of pleasure from her. Every time he aroused her like this, she was certain she had never experienced anything so sinfully delightful in her entire life. A wave of heat swept through her until her insides shattered under the exquisite sensation of his mouth on her.

Wave after wave of delight cascaded over her, as his mouth moved to feather the inside of her thigh with kisses. Rising up on to his knees, he skimmed his hand over her leg. Gently, he bent her leg and lifted her foot to his mouth. The way he nibbled at the inside of her foot tickled and she uttered a breathy laugh.

Mischief gleamed in his gray eyes as he stared down at her. With one more nip at the sensitive area, he grinned. "It seems I've discovered one of your sensitive spots, which tells me you have more."

Laughing, she trailed her fingers across the top of his hand. "You are far too wicked for your own good, my lord."

"Then join me in sin, because with you I find being wicked immensely satisfying." Desire replaced the devilment in his gaze as he raised her leg higher until it rested on his shoulder. Startled, she shook her head slightly.

"Simon, what are you--" Her words died in her throat as he slid his rigid length into her. The unusual position intensified the way he expanded her, filled her completely. Eyes fluttering closed, her body mated with his in a rhythmic hunger that sent excitement sliding through her veins.

With each thrust, the intensity of their joining grew. Watching her from above, he drove into her at an ever increasing pace. She was slick with heat--and tight. So tight that the friction surrounding his hard rod had him struggling not to come too soon. He had never been so out of control.

Her insides clutched at him like a vise, tightening his ballocks up into his groin as his engorged flesh cried out for more friction. It demanded more heat. Pumping himself into her, he caught the musky scent of her passion as she shattered over his cock. The rippling spasms of her hot insides grew even hotter with the cream she spilled over him as her back arched, thrusting her lovely breasts upward. With one last thrust, he buried himself inside her heat, and a shout of pleasure poured out of his throat as he came inside her.

Time stopped as he throbbed inside her silky depths, content to remain sheathed inside her warmth. He gently lowered her leg, and smiled at the afterglow of passion on her face. Utter contentment curled her mouth upward and his heart skipped a beat.

She was a beautiful, voluptuous siren. And she belonged to him and him alone. No matter what it took, he'd keep her at his side. Ivy was unlike any other woman he'd ever met. She was special. He'd known it from the first time he'd heard her voice. He simply hadn't expected her sensuous body to entangle him so deeply. Clearly, he was heading down a path he'd never walked before, and the knowledge was unsettling in more ways than one.

* * * *

Simon entered the London Library, and picking up the morning daily, he sat down in one of the wide arm chairs occupying the small reading area at the front window. For the better half of the morning he'd spent his time sparring with almost half a dozen partners in an attempt to purge Ivy from his thoughts.

For almost three months, his ability to concentrate on anything other than Ivy had been impossible. Every waking minute was filled with the scent, taste and feel of her. And then there was the sound of that siren voice that always clutched at his groin with such intensity. Even in his dreams she was there, tempting him, caressing and teasing him with her warm, voluptuous curves.

He'd never been so preoccupied with a woman in his entire life. He was so obsessed, one could almost accuse him of being in love. Fingers tightening on the paper he held, Simon's body froze as he struggled to comprehend the thought that had just flashed through his head.

What the devil was he thinking? He couldn't be love with Ivy. It wasn't possible. It was simply a physical arrangement that suited both of them. Stunned he stared at the print in front of him without focusing on the words. The thoughts rushing through his head were far more astonishing than the latest news from Parliament. The incredible had happened. It explained everything.

Ivy had shown him that blood mattered for little if one wasn't happy. It also explained his motivations for the surprise he was planning for her. Why else would he be willing to travel to the country at this time of year if not to please her? She'd once mentioned how much she missed her family, but had never explained how she'd lost touch with them.

Determined to please her, he'd located her cousin Carolyn and after corresponding with the woman, had invited the widow and her family to London for Christmas. The woman had politely refused both of his invitations until he had assured her Ivy would be delighted to see her. Not about to take no for an answer, he'd arranged to fetch the woman from Ipswich.

Despite having already purchased several gifts for Ivy, this present would show her how much her happiness meant to him. Glancing toward the circulation desk, he watched her conversing with a patron over the open book between them. Her head bent as she pointed to a passage in the tome on the counter, she looked up at the man opposite her and smiled.

With a nod, the patron closed the book and retreated back to one of the worktables. The light accentuated the auburn tint of her hair, making it shine. His mouth went dry as he remembered how lovely her nipples were beneath the starched white shirt she wore, the way she always arched upward into his mouth whenever he suckled her. Of all the women he'd ever been with, she was the only one who had ever responded with such abandon, wantonness and heated passion.

What would she do if he asked her to marry him? The fact that he was a peer was a serious disadvantage where Ivy was concerned. Her aversion for the peerage was something he'd never understood, given that her mother had been a member of the nobility. What had happened to make her have such antipathy for those born to a title? The other night at his sister's he'd seen how much Ivy had enjoyed herself. She'd even confessed it to him later when they were lying in her bed.

Well, the fact that he was a peer didn't matter, she was going to marry him whether she liked it or not. He was tired of waking up most mornings without her by his side, and he wasn't about to give her up. The only thing left to do was convince her to marry him. From his seat, he studied her closely until she turned her head to meet his gaze. A surprised look swept across her face. Barely nodding his head in the direction of the book stacks, he rose to his feet. With a slight shake of her head, she silently argued with him. Not about to let her thwart him, he headed toward the circulation desk with a purposeful stride.

As if aware that he wasn't past creating a small altercation, she gathered up a small stack of books and headed for the book stacks at a quick pace. Grinning, he remembered the first time he'd chased her through the aisle of dusty volumes. She disappeared around a corner, and he followed her into the depths of the library. The last time she'd been quick to avoid him, but this time he wasn't about to let her flee so easily.

Lengthening his stride, he walked through the book stacks and peered through the thin space between a row of books and the shelf above them. On the other side of the shelving, he saw her hurrying down the aisle.

They both reached the end of the row at the same time, and as she tried to dart away from him he caught her wrist and pulled her to a halt. The books she held slipped easily from her grip as he took them from her. Setting them aside on an empty shelf, his hand grasped her elbow as he firmly pulled her deeper into the book stacks.

"This way, Miss Beecham. I have a small matter I wish to discuss with you," he said quietly.

"So help me, Simon," her words were a fierce whisper as they moved to one of the more reclusive sections of the building. "If you do something to make the Board ban me from the Library...."

Satisfied that they were safely out of view of anyone browsing the aisles, he tugged her into his arms and captured her mouth in a hard kiss. She whispered protests against his lips as he pressed her close. Desire surged through him as his fingers brushed over her throat and down to her breasts pushing up softly against her white shirt. With a groan, he lifted his head and pressed his forehead against hers.

"You, Miss Beecham, are the most enticing creature I've ever met. You have no idea how tempted I am to lock us in the reading room and pleasure you until you scream out my name."

Blue eyes darkened with need as her fingers brushed against his mouth. With a seductive smile, she shook her head. "There's always tonight. Is it really that long of a wait?"

"Unfortunately, sweetheart, I can't come to you this evening. I'm leaving town on business for a few days." Dismay and perhaps a glimmer of fear passed over her lovely features. The stark expression warmed his heart. She would miss him. Perhaps there was a chance for him yet. "I promise I'll return as soon as I can."

"Will you be gone over Christmas?" There was a forlorn note in her voice.

"I promise you, Ivy. I'll be back in time for the holiday. Do you believe me?" When she hesitated, he cupped her face with his hands. Slowly, she nodded. Satisfied, he kissed her again and brushed his thumb across her bottom lip.

She was so precious to him. He wanted to declare himself now, but he needed time to formulate a plan. If he'd been less of a fool, he would have realized how much she meant to him sooner. Then he would have been able to woo her until she had no other choice but to accept him. Marry him. With one more kiss, he released her and walked away.

* * * *

"Did you doubt him?" The Grand Dame turned to look at her, the ivory brocade swags of her overskirt rustling softly.

"No ... yes ... I don't know. I wanted to believe him, but I didn't dare hope that he cared for me. It was too hard."

"Why?"

The simplicity of the question struck her as preposterous. There were so many reasons why it had been so hard to believe Simon, reasons that were wrapped up in her past as well as the present. She'd willingly chosen to be his lover, expecting nothing more than a pleasurable interlude. Her head had dictated her actions, but it was her heart that demanded more than she was certain he was willing to give.

"I can't give you a simple reason. It's far too complicated."

"Is it possible you've misjudged him ... and Carolyn?" There was just a hint of disappointment in her ancestor's voice.

"Honor among the nobility had always been in short supply. Whitby proved that to me."

"Don't you mean Carolyn?"

"I don't know what you mean." She gritted her teeth at the second mention of her cousin's name.

"She was as dear to you as a sister and yet she betrayed you with a man you didn't love." The gentle note in the Grand Dame's voice made Ivy turn away from the matron.

"Discussing my cousin will not change things. What she did was unforgivable. It doesn't matter that I came to realize Whitby was a pompous ass and that her treachery saved me."

"So it was her breach of trust you could not forgive."

"Yes," she snapped as she clasped her hands tightly in front of her. "Will you please get on with this? I'm beginning to feel like a character from one of Mr. Dickens' serial novels."

She didn't want to be here. She didn't want to discuss Carolyn or Simon with anyone. All she wanted to do was forget.that she ever cared. That she'd ever dared to hope for something more. It was too painful.

"Forgetting can be arranged, but before we do so, there's more I wish to show you," said the Grand Dame.

Stunned at the woman's ability to read her thoughts, Ivy gasped. Whatever the woman's intent was, there was no doubting her intuitive nature. Once more, a warm hand took hers and pulled her across another deep void as the white fog thickened around them like a cocoon.

Chapter Nine

Laughter parting her lips, Ivy stepped out of the milliner's shop as she wished the shopkeeper happy Christmas. People scurried to and fro along the street, their cheerful mood thrumming through the air with an almost tangible force as she crossed Bond Street and walked toward the apothecary. Even though she missed Simon dreadfully, it was difficult not to be affected by the happiness surrounding her if only a small amount.

It had been almost a week since he'd said goodbye to her in the Library. She had tried to believe his impassioned statement that he would return to her, but with each passing day that belief was slowly crumbling to fine dust since she'd yet to hear from him. This provided her mind with plenty of fuel to stoke the fires of trepidation inside her heart.

She'd fought a long, hard battle to stave off the fear, but as Christmas drew nearer, it was becoming more difficult to sustain her belief that he would return. She picked her way across the slippery cobblestones to the sidewalk where she could smell the lemongrass soap from the door of the apothecary.

About to enter the shop, a frisson skated up along her spine and she turned her head. The sight of Simon stepping out of a carriage sent her pulse racing. He was back. Why hadn't he come to see her, sent her word of his return? Puzzled, she took a step in his direction, then stopped as she saw him offer a hand to someone inside the carriage.

Another woman. He was with another woman. The cold December air bit through her clothing as if she were standing naked in the street. Biting her lip, she remembered Abigail. It was probably only his sister with him. Still shaken, she watched as the woman stepped out of the vehicle. Spying the familiar blonde hair and lovely features was akin to being kicked in the stomach.

The pain lashing through her bent her double in the doorway of the apothecary. Oh dear God, he'd done the unthinkable. He'd brought *her* here. Why would he do such a thing? The loud cries from inside the apothecary made her stumble forward into the shop. Commotion. She had to stop the commotion. If they continued making a fuss, Simon and Carolyn might join the small group of onlookers beginning to form around her. Once the two of them discovered it was her, they'd no doubt find her distress amusing.

A strong arm wrapped around her waist and half carried her to the back of the shop. Seconds later a cup of tea was placed in her hands. Grateful for the opportunity to regain what little self-control she still possessed, Ivy shuddered. Tears pressed against her eyelids, but she refused to shed them.

That's exactly what Carolyn would want her to do. The woman would find her distress most amusing. It was something her cousin had missed the last time. Time flew backward and she was sitting in her small room, sobbing her heart out because Carolyn had married Whitby in a quickly arranged ceremony.

From the moment she'd heard the news, she'd retreated to her room. Outside her door, her cousin had pleaded to be given entry, but not even all the hounds in hell could have forced her to do such a thing. Although her aunt and uncle had never made her feel welcome, Carolyn had become her one and only friend. Her champion.

It had always been Carolyn who'd ensured she was included in family events, standing up to her parents at every opportunity. It was why her betrayal had been so devastating. The one person she thought truly loved her had taken the only real piece of happiness she'd possessed since her parents had died.

Instead, her aunt had been the one to gloat. The woman had taken great pleasure in pointing out that Whitby could never marry a commoner. A few days after Carolyn and her new husband left for the Continent, she came of age. When the barrister from London arrived to formally present her with full access to her fortune, she'd left Parkland and never looked back.

A gentle hand touched her shoulder, and she looked up into the worried expression of the apothecary's wife. "Well now, Miss. You've got some right better color in those cheeks of yours. I near thought you were going to faint if it hadn't been for my Lawrence being there at your side."

Wanly, she smiled at the buxom woman hovering over her. "Thank you, Mrs. Bailey. I'm not quite sure what came over me."

"Well, you just stay right here." The woman clucked over her like a worried mother hen. "You need to take better care of yourself seeing as your condition and everything."

About to respond, the sudden sound of Simon's voice filtered into the back of the shop. Oh dear God, she wasn't ready to meet him yet. She needed more time. Time to show he'd not devastated her. Hands trembling, she set the teacup Mrs. Bailey had offered her on the small table in front of her. Quietly, she rose to her feet.

"Mrs. Bailey, if you don't mind, I'd like to leave through your back door."

"Oh, Miss, no." Appalled, the large woman shook her head. "Why it's not fittin' for you to walk through the mews."

"Nonetheless, I prefer that exit. There are ... there are people...." Again the tears welled up against her eyelids as she turned her head away. A gentle hand patted her shoulder.

"There now, Miss. If you've got your heart set on it, of course you can. Come along, now."

With the woman guiding the way, they wove their way through crates and barrels until they reached the shop's back door. As she stepped into the fetid alley, Ivy touched the woman's arm. "Thank you, Mrs. Bailey, and if you would be so kind, would you please send my usual order to the house."

"But of course, Miss, of course I will. Now you take care of yourself. It's not just yourself you have to worry about now you know."

Nodding, she lifted her skirts and hurried along the narrow mews toward Brook Street. Blindly, she stumbled out into the main thoroughfare and into a solid shoulder. Strong hands steadied her as she excused herself and moved away.

"Miss Beecham?"

The deep voice calling her name sounded familiar, but she couldn't quite place it. Glancing over her shoulder, she saw Lord Halstead moving toward her. Dear heaven, if it wasn't bad enough that Simon had brought Carolyn to London, now she had to endure conversing with his friends. She forced a smile to her lips as she turned to face him.

"Lord Halstead, what a pleasant surprise."

"Are you feeling well, Miss Beecham?" The penetrating look he sent her forced her to stiffen slightly.

"But of course. Whatever would make you think otherwise?" She swallowed hard at the stern frown on his face.

"You're quite pale, and most women don't venture off the main streets into the mews alone."

Sweet lord, he'd seen her coming out of the mews. She struggled to come up with an excuse, but her heart was in such turmoil it was impossible to think straight.

"I'm sorry, you see ... I really do have ... Please forgive me, my lord. I must go home."

Not waiting for his reply, she turned to scurry away from him. A strong hand held her back. "Then let me offer you a ride home. I'm sure you'll find it quite comfortable."

The man didn't wait for her agreement as he gently, but firmly, pulled her toward a waiting carriage. Once they were seated inside, the vehicle rocked forward and Ivy kneaded the leather drawstrings of her purse. Staring out the window, she tried to focus on the moment at hand to disguise her true state of anguish.

"Let me help you." They were simple words, but the strength and kindness behind them nearly pushed her over the edge of rational thought. With a shake of her head, she straightened her shoulders as she turned toward him.

"Thank you, but I'm fine, really. I'm simply feeling a bit peckish. I should have eaten before I left home." She forced a smile to her lips, and the muscles in her face ached from doing so.

"I'm not unfamiliar with the circumstances of a woman's delicate condition. I'm an uncle three times over." Again, the kindness in his voice touched her. She shook her head as she met his look of assessment.

"No, really. I--" The image of Mrs. Bailey's rotund figure warning her that she had to worry about others besides herself bolted its way through her mind. Inhaling a sharp breath, her chest tightened as the reality of Lord Halstead's words sank into her consciousness. A woman's delicate condition. Simon's child. She was carrying Simon's child.

Closing her eyes, she shuddered as she frantically counted backward. They'd been lovers for less than three months, and the last time she'd had her monthly cycle was a week or two before Simon had made love to her in the Library. The irony of it all lashed through her with the sting of a whip.

That night at the Library he'd persuaded her to share some of her childhood memories. Memories that stirred the long buried desire for a family of her own to love. Warm fingers closed over her icy hand, and she looked at the man seated opposite her in the carriage. There was no judgment in his dark eyes, only concern.

"I think perhaps I should call a doctor when we reach your house. You're not looking well at all."

The knot in her throat tightened as she shook her head. "No thank you, my lord. I simply need to rest. I think perhaps I should contemplate visiting a warmer climate. I have always found London so cold during the winter."

"Is there nothing I can do ... no one I can--"

"*No.*" She jerked her gaze away from his sympathetic eyes. "I appreciate your kindness, my lord, but I ... there is no need to concern yourself with me. I shall be fine."

As she stared out the window, she heard his sigh of resignation, but she ignored it. This was her problem and hers alone. The thought scraped at her heart, but it eased some of her pain as well. Simon had given her the one thing she'd always wanted. A child of her own, someone to love unconditionally.

The carriage came to a halt, and Lord Halstead immediately stepped out of the vehicle and offered his hand to her. When she was on the sidewalk, he escorted her up to the front door of her house. At the door, he took her hand and raised it to his lips.

"I wish you would allow me to fetch the doctor," he said with a hint of frustration.

"No. Thank you just the same, my lord. I'll be quite all right after I rest."

"I can see why Abigail took to you so quickly." With a shake of his head, he smiled at her with open amusement. "You're as stubborn as she is."

"Thank you again, my lord, for your kindness." Turning away from him, she entered the house and closed the door behind her.

Her back pressed into the wooden barrier as she stood there for a long moment. Eyes closed, she tried to stop her head from spinning as the reality of her situation began to sink into her consciousness. He was gone. She was never going to see him again. First one tear and then another streaked down her cheeks until she was sobbing softly.

The sound of footsteps coming toward her from the kitchen sent her racing up the stairs. She had no wish for anyone to see her like this. The last thing she wanted from anyone, including her staff, was pity.

* * * *

Sunshine streamed through the salon window, warming her cheeks as she read through a set of documents her barrister had sent her earlier. When she'd returned home yesterday, she'd allowed herself the luxury of tears for most of the afternoon. As she drowned in her sorrow yesterday, she'd suddenly realized that Simon might try to win custody of their child.

It was a terrifying thought, and she'd immediately sent word to her attorney that she had decided to leave England for sunnier climates. Now, as she reviewed the arrangements outlined in the paperwork, a sense of calm settled over her. No matter how much her heart and body ached for Simon, she had to focus on the baby's welfare from this point forward. Nothing else could take precedence.

Picking up her pen she signed the documents where marked, then returned them to the stiff envelope for delivery back to the attorney's offices. The scent of fresh greenery teased her senses as she pressed her fingers against her forehead. Christmas Eve. She'd completely forgotten today was Christmas Eve.

The thought made her close her eyes, as she swallowed the sudden onslaught of tears threatening to pour out of her. Fists clenched with determination, she inhaled a deep breath as she concentrated on controlling her emotions. Then the front bell rang, interrupting her focus.

Tension laced through every muscle in her body as she recognized Simon's deep voice in the foyer. Why had he come? She didn't want him here. Springing to her feet, she hurried toward the salon door intent on locking it. Anything to keep him out. She realized she was too late, as the door swung open.

The sight of him took her breath away. His smile was brilliant as he caught her hands in his and kissed her fingertips. Shaken by the strength of her feelings for him, she tugged free of his touch. The frown furrowing his brow forced her to straighten her shoulders as she silently met his steely gaze.

"Something's wrong." Quiet certainty threaded through his words. It was an understatement, and a sharp laugh passed her lips.

"Not at all. I'm simply surprised to see you." The serenity in her voice sent relief coursing through her body. She simply had to withstand being in his presence for just a short time longer. He'd explain the purpose of his visit and they would part company.

Narrowing his eyes, he studied her for a long moment before he shook his head. "No, that elusive air is back. The one that shuts me out."

"Don't be ridiculous," she scoffed with a wave of her hand and turned toward her secretaire, but a firm hand tugged her against his hard, muscular frame.

"Look at me," he snapped. "I've been gone less than a week, and you're acting as if we've just met."

"Has it been that long?"

She heard the slight crack in her voice, but she managed to keep her expression nonchalant as she struggled with the way her body was responding to his presence. Fire raged through her blood at being so close to him, the heat of him burning through her clothing to warm her skin. She wanted it to be the way it had been before he left. Before *she* had come between them.

"Bloody hell," he hissed as he glared down into her eyes. Then in a movement so quick she couldn't escape, he captured her mouth in a searing kiss.

The sweet passion of his touch wilted her willpower to refuse him. Clinging to him, she trembled against the solid strength of him. If only for a few short moments of heaven, she was willing to endure the years of hell without him. The moment of pleasure was all too brief as he broke away from her. A flash of what she thought might be relief sprinted across his features as he smiled at her.

"That response, sweetheart, explains everything. You're angry that I've been gone so long. But there was an excellent reason. I went to find you a Christmas present. One I think you'll like very much."

Her heart fluttered at his words. Was it possible she'd been wrong. Had she maybe imagined she'd seen him with *her*? With

Carolyn. Confused, she shuddered as he moved quickly toward the salon door and gestured for someone to enter.

First one little girl, then another entered the room. They were lovely children, their eyes bright with excitement. Smiles heightened their sweet features, and as they saw her, they offered her a curtsey. Who on earth were they? The poor dears wore clothes that, although neat and clean, were threadbare and worn. Had Simon suddenly taken to fostering orphans? For that was what they looked like.

A moment later, a third child entered the room. Rocked by the young girl's appearance, she swayed on her feet as she stared at the child in front of her. Blond curls framed her angelic features, and the green eyes watching her threw her back into a past she preferred to forget. It was as if the Carolyn she'd known as a child had stepped into the room. She was beautiful. As beautiful as her mother had been at the same age.

Pain clenched every nerve in her body as her stomach churned violently. What had he done? Surely he hadn't thought to bring Carolyn here. He wouldn't be that cruel, that heartless. She saw him glance over his shoulder at her and frown slightly.

Then the moment she feared the most happened. He *had* brought her cousin to her house. As Carolyn entered the room, she immediately crossed the floor toward her.

"*Ivy.*"

Horrified, she shuddered at the smile on her cousin's face. The woman was here to gloat. To rub salt into the open wounds of her heart. To point out that the nobility were far superior to mere commoners. The moment Carolyn took her hands and kissed both her cheeks, Ivy jerked away from her and stumbled toward the window. This was by far the most malevolent thing anyone had ever done to her.

One hand braced against the window jamb, she pressed her other hand against her stomach in an effort to stop the nausea roiling in her belly. Eyes closed she could only stand at the window in silence, desperately trying not to completely lose what little composure she still possessed.

"Go away," she uttered in a hoarse whisper.

"Ivy, please. You never gave me a chance to explain." Carolyn's soft voice scraped across her skin like a branding iron. Each word seared her cousin's betrayal deeper into her soul. She didn't need an explanation that was nothing but lies. Did the woman think she was stupid? Carolyn had married Whitby without any misgivings whatsoever.

"I have no need of any explanations, my lady. The past is dead. There's nothing in it that I care to remember."

"Don't say that," Carolyn exclaimed sharply. "We were like sisters. I loved you. I always have. I wanted to explain, but when I came back to Parkland, you were gone. No one would tell me where you were or allow me to find you."

Wheeling about, Ivy glared at her. "You would have found me no more forgiving then than you do now. If you came here expecting to vindicate yourself, you've wasted your time."

"No, I came because Lord Wycombe told me it would give you pleasure to see me again after all these years."

At Carolyn's response, she quickly turned her head toward Simon. The scowl on his face infuriated her. How dare he act as if she were the one who had committed a sin. Did he expect her reaction to Carolyn's visit to be a giddy one?

She'd only spoken of her childhood that night in the Library after much coaxing, and now he'd betrayed the trust she'd placed in him. He'd said goodbye to her, only to return with a part of her past that was tearing her to shreds. Discovering her innermost secrets, he'd recklessly chosen to bring her face-to-face with demons she had no wish to ever visit again.

"I also came because it was my hope that I could make things right again between us, and I wanted you to meet your namesake."

Carolyn's soft words made her drag her gaze away from Simon's face as she turned to see her cousin coaxing the youngest girl toward them with a wave of her fingers. Hands on her daughter's shoulders, Carolyn introduced the child. "Ivy, darling, this is your Aunt Ivy."

With the impulse of a child, the girl stepped forward and wrapped her arms around her waist. The loving gesture sent a cold chill through her as she remembered the similar manner in which she'd greeted her aunt when she'd arrived at Parkland. The pain of her aunt's rejection was the only thing that prevented her from shoving little Ivy away from her now. Swallowing hard, she gently brushed her hand over the child's head.

"You're quite pretty, Ivy." Her whisper was hoarse as she forced a smile to her lips and looked at the child. Had there been that much trust in her eyes the day she'd arrived at Parkland? The day she experienced her first lesson in rejection and betrayal. And why would Carolyn name her daughter after her? She didn't know the answer, nor did she care to.

With a kind, but firm touch, she urged the child to return to her mother's side. If Carolyn thought to use her children as a means to ingratiate herself back into her good graces, then the woman was sadly mistaken.

"Forgive me, but I would like you to leave now," she said quietly as she turned away and took two unsteady steps to her desk.

"Is there nothing I can say to you that will make you listen," Carolyn pleaded. "You had one of most loving, giving hearts of anyone I've ever known. If you do not have it in your heart to forgive, could you at least not listen to what I have to say?"

"I cannot, Lady Whitby. We both know that noblesse oblige is reserved for peers, not commoners such as me," she said coldly.

Carolyn's gasp of shock emphasized how cruel the words were, but it was the incoherent oath of disgust Simon uttered that made her wince at her insensitive remark. Even now, despite his breach of trust, his opinion of her mattered. Unable to look at him, she remained still as out of the corner of her eye she saw him ushering Carolyn and her daughters out of the room. With the door closed behind them, a wave of nausea rolled over her. Grabbing the back of the desk chair, she fought to remain on her feet. She wanted to crawl into a dark hole and never come out. But she couldn't. She had to remember that she was no longer alone. She had to think of her child.

A soft click jerked her head in the direction of the door, and the sight of Simon leaning against the room's only exit pulled a sharp breath of anger from her. Arms folded across his broad chest he simply stood there watching her. Why was he still here? Hadn't he tortured her enough by bringing her past back to haunt her so vividly? Raw fury swept through her, and she sent him a cold stare. He simply narrowed his gaze.

"I want you to tell me just what the hell happened in here." Despite the calm note in his voice, she heard the suppressed fury beneath the words.

"You were present. What exactly wasn't clear to you?"

With a violent move, he shoved himself away from the door and crossed the space between them in three strides. Caught off guard, a soft cry broke past her lips as he grabbed her by the arms and gave her a sharp shake.

"God damn it, Ivy. That woman is as poor as a church mouse. It took me two weeks to convince her that you would be happy to see her, and what do you do? You humiliated her, in front of her children no less."

"I didn't ask you to bring her here." Twisting out of his grasp, she put several feet between them. "If anyone's to be blamed, it's you."

"Was it so wrong of me to want to please you?"

"What just happened in here was far from pleasure, my lord," she hissed. "Perhaps you should consider pleasuring my cousin. I'm certain you're infinitely suited for one another."

"I have no desire for your cousin or any other woman for that matter. You're the one I want. No one else."

"Then I'm afraid you're about to be disappointed, my lord, because our association is finished."

"Like bloody hell it is," he said through clenched teeth.

"Perhaps I didn't make myself clear. I don't want to see you anymore."

"I want to know why."

Ivy turned her head away from the stark fury on Simon's face. He'd betrayed her, and he still couldn't see it. In his arrogance, he'd betrayed her trust, just as Carolyn had. While their original arrangement hadn't required her trust, she had given it nonetheless. Breaching that confidence, when she had so little to give, was the most brutal of all betrayals.

Even if she tried to explain it to him, how could she possibly make him understand that they came from two different worlds, that it would always be a barrier between them? Her cousin had claimed background accounted for nothing, but her actions had revealed her true feelings. When Carolyn had entered the salon a short time ago, the past had rushed up to assault her senses with the sharpness of a kitchen blade. The rejection, the humiliation, the constant reminders that she was inferior to those of the peerage.

No. The chasm between her and Simon was too wide to cross. It was a barrier that would also hinder their child. The thought etched its way through her with a pang. Deliberately, she focused on the Christmas tree in the corner of the salon and the garland on the window. The sight tugged at her heart.

Underneath the tree was the one thing she'd been certain would ensure her happiness. The one possession she owned that she thought would help her win Simon's love. Oh God, how could she give him up? Wouldn't it be worth the price she'd pay in heartache simply to be in his arms, to love him in spite of his betrayal? Could she forgive him that?

She was capable of forgiving him anything, but this afternoon had proven how far apart the rift was between them. He'd expected her to forgive Carolyn. If he couldn't understand why her cousin's betrayal cut so deep, he would never understand why his actions had devastated her. Sorrow enveloped her like an icy blanket. Swallowing hard, she inhaled a sharp breath before looking at him again.

"Sometimes there isn't a reason why, Simon. I just know I can't see you anymore."

* * * *

White mist obliterated the scene before her, and a tear slid down Ivy's cheek. The Grand Dame had brought her full circle. Relief skimmed through her at not having to relive Simon's cruel words or the look on Morris' face as she'd fled the house to come here--to the library. If that's where she really was.

Reality had slipped away from her the moment the Grand Dame appeared to her in the book aisles and started her on this journey. And even in the company of her ancestor, she'd never felt more alone in her life. Simon had told her he didn't want anyone else, but he'd not mentioned love. And not even love could bridge the gap between them.

"It takes courage to let go of certainties, Ivy. When we become so certain that our beliefs are the only perspective, we can easily miss a real and pertinent truth."

"The only truth you've shown me this night is that the two people I loved the most in the world betrayed me with their actions."

"Did they, or have you betrayed them?"

"Me ... betrayed *them*?"

"My time with you grows short. Watch." There was a stern, but loving note in the Grand Dame's voice as the woman's fingers rubbed across the large ruby resting against her breast.

Like a curtain pulled back to reveal the sun, light spilled into the small area of fog the two of them stood in. The scene in front of her was almost idyllic. On a lawn of green, Simon played with a young boy, while Carolyn's daughters played with a small toddler in the grass. A large house sat graciously on top of a hill to the left of the scene, and it wrenched at her heart. It was a home, just like she'd always imagined in her dreams, a home where love and happiness was in great abundance.

With a laugh, Simon picked up the boy and carried him like a satchel on his hip. Squealing with amusement, the boy kicked his legs, demanding to be put down. A reluctant smile tugged at her lips. Somewhere in the deep recesses of her mind, she'd known Simon would make a good father. No doubt, he would find happiness with Carolyn. The thought squeezed her chest until she had trouble breathing.

"This could be yours, Ivy." The Grand Dame's voice was gentle as she spoke. *"All of this could be yours. Carolyn never betrayed you. You betrayed her by not giving her a chance to explain how Whitby forced himself on her and how her parents hastily arranged to marry her off to the man, despite her protests."*

The words crawled across her skin with insidious repulsion. Could it be true? Had she misjudged Carolyn? No, she couldn't have.

"Open your eyes, Ivy. Have I shown you anything but the truth this night?" Her ancestor's voice had taken on a sharp note of exasperation.

Swallowing hard she struggled to accept the reality of the Grand Dame's words. It was a painful truth, and her heart cried out from the agony of it. How could she have been so wrong? She'd turned her back on Carolyn when she'd needed her most.

The memory of her cousin pounding on her bedroom door forced the air out of her lungs as tears streamed down her face. The Grand Dame was right. The betrayal had been hers for shutting Carolyn out of her heart before she'd heard her cousin's explanation. How could Carolyn ever forgive her, when she'd been so brutal with her words this afternoon?

"And what of Simon, dearest? What of him?" the Grand Dame's voice whispered through her head as the salon came into focus and the smell of evergreen told her she was home. The Christmas tree was still there, the presents lying underneath the green branches. The scents and sounds of home were vivid and real.

Running across the room, she opened the velvet box. The necklace. It was still here. Had she imagined everything? All the memories and images the Grand Dame had shown her flooded through her mind. Frozen, she tried to make a decision. The clock on the mantle ticked the seconds off quietly as she stared at the face of the timepiece. It was almost six o'clock. She gasped. The Grand Dame had brought her back to the moments just after Simon's furious departure.

"Trust him, Ivy. He's already shown you how much he wants to please you. Go to him."

The Grand Dame's soft words echoed in her head and with a loud cry, she called out his name. "Simon."

Racing toward the salon door, she flung the door open wide. Morris was at his usual post, and he gave her a startled look as she charged out into the foyer.

"Morris, did his lordship say where he was going?" she gasped out in a frantic tone.

"Why no, miss. I only heard the slam--"

The butler never finished his sentence as the front door crashed open. Determination etched on the hard planes of his face, Simon strode across the floor and pulled her into a tight embrace. Stubbornness darkened his steel gray eyes as he stared down into her face.

"I don't give a damn that you're a commoner, and I don't care what you think about my title," he bit out between his teeth. "I love you, and I intend to marry you no matter how much you object. And as for your cousin, you're going to apologize. The woman has suffered enough, and once you hear her story, you'll be begging *her* forgiveness."

Hands cupping his face she sighed with happiness. "Yes, Simon."

The harsh expression on his face eased somewhat as relief flared in his gray eyes for an instant. Then, glaring at her, he addressed the butler. "You heard her, didn't you Morris? The woman agreed to everything I just said."

"Yes, my lord. She most certainly did." Neither of them bothered to look at the butler as he coughed slightly.

"And I trust you'll exercise your usual discretion when my nephew sends someone looking for us." Simon stated as he swept her off her feet and climbed the stairs toward her bedroom.

"But of course, my lord. Happy Christmas to both of you." Ivy heard the relief in the old retainer's voice and she glanced over Simon's shoulder and mouthed the words *Happy Christmas*. The smile on Morris' face warmed her almost as much as Simon's declaration of love. As he carried her past the portrait of the Grand Dame, she caught a brief glimpse of a white mist before it disappeared as if blown away. But it was the twinkle she saw in the lively eyes of her ancestor that made her smile.

"You're looking quite pleased with yourself, given the misery you've caused me and others today. Your cousin didn't betray you. Nor did I." The harsh note in his voice tugged at her heart. Beneath it was the raw pain she'd inflicted on him.

"I know that now. I've been a fool."

"Yes you have. A bloody little fool," he snapped. "And why the hell I'm willing to stay and put up with you is beyond my comprehension."

The anger in his voice made her flinch. "I'm sorry, Simon. I acted beastly to both you and Carolyn."

A weary sign eased out of him, as he set her down inside her bedroom. "What I want to know is why."

Stepping away from him, she shook her head. "I'm not sure if I can make you understand."

"Try me."

"When I went to live with my aunt and uncle, I had just lost my parents. I'd known only love, and suddenly I was in a place where I wasn't wanted. Carolyn was the only one who cared about me." Her voice hitched at the memory. Swallowing hard, she averted her gaze from his penetrating look.

"My aunt and uncle constantly reminded me that I was a commoner. I wasn't even good enough to have a decent bedroom." The memory of that cold, barren room made her flinch. "But it was the lack of love I missed most. I longed for my parents and the happiness I'd known. Even Carolyn's love couldn't make up for that."

Not moving, Simon watched her struggle to maintain her composure. Her profile reflected a wounded look of vulnerability that made his heart ache for her. For the first time since they'd met, she was opening herself up to him, and he could see how difficult it was for her to do so.

He wanted to pull her into his arms and keep her there until she understood how much he loved her, would always love her. But she needed to finish. This final barrier between them needed to collapse. He could see that now.

Everything that had confused him before made sense in this moment. If he went to her and held her, she might never have the courage to completely open up to him in the future, so he remained motionless, despite the craving to hold her close.

Hands clenched tightly in front of her, the drawn look to her features made his decision not to touch her that much harder. He watched her biting her lip as she blinked back the tears misting her eyes.

"When Whitby rejected me because I wasn't of the nobility, I was devastated. It only reinforced what my aunt and uncle had been saying for years. And in the end, it made me despise everything the nobility stood for." She inhaled a deep breath.

"But when I learned he was to marry Carolyn, I became convinced she'd been the one to tell him I was a commoner. I believed she'd done so simply so she could have him for herself, because she knew he wouldn't want me as I was. In my eyes, she had stolen the one thing that had brought me happiness."

She paused and finally turned to look at him. The anguish in her face wrenched at his gut with the force of a misplaced blow from a sparring partner. Her mouth trembled as she met his gaze. "But that wasn't what hurt the most. We'd been like sisters, and yet she'd betrayed me. How could she really love me, a commoner, if she was willing to betray ... me?"

The crack of her voice drove him forward. It was impossible not to gather her into his arms and hold her. Absorbing the warmth of her into his body, he held her close, saying nothing as she buried her face in his shoulder and sobbed.

Lilies. The scent brushed his senses as his face pressed into her hair. Her scent. Anywhere he went the fragrance would always bring her into his mind. Tonight she'd opened herself up to him with an honesty that humbled him. It was proof that she loved him.

But he wanted to hear her speak the words, to admit that she loved him and no one else, to know that her heart would always be his. Slowly, her shudders and tears eased into silence. As she lifted her head, she brushed away the dampness on her cheeks and sniffled. "I must look a sight."

"You're beautiful."

A flush of pleasure blossomed across her face, and he swallowed the stirrings of desire that rammed through his body. God, he ached for her. Needed her. Wanted her beneath him as he buried himself inside her. Gently, he cupped the side of her face. "Tell me why you called my name?"

"You heard me?" The look of amazement on her face made him frown. Had he really heard her cry out? As improbable as it was, he knew without a doubt that he'd not been imagining things when he'd heard her call his name.

"I don't know how, but I heard you. I heard you as clearly as if you were right behind me. It's what convinced me to come back. I refused to let you give me up so easily. Now tell why you called out my name."

For a moment, she stared up at him with a look of puzzled incredulity before a sweet smile of seduction curved her tantalizing mouth. "Because I realized how much I loved you. That I didn't want to live without you."

Her hands slid inside his jacket and pressed against his chest. The heat of her barreled through him as he crushed her to him, his mouth seeking hers in a passionate kiss. He quickly pulled the pins from her hair, allowing his fingers to slide their way through her silky tresses. It only made him want to feel more of her.

Need took over as he probed the sweetness of her mouth, tasting her, drinking in the warm, soft flavor of her. Damn but he wanted her. Now. No soft strokes, no sweet caresses, only the tight feel of her wrapped around his cock as he pounded his body against hers until he exploded inside her.

His mouth still locked with hers, he tore his jacket off his back followed by his shirt. Equally eager, she panted her frantic need as she tugged at her own clothing. Helping her remove her dress and then her combination corset, he uttered a groan as her breasts spilled out into his hands. The sight made him hard and stiff with an agonizing ache that was exquisite in its intensity. His thumbs rolled over the stiff peaks, triumph sailing through him at her cry of pleasure.

Swiftly he unbuttoned his trousers, disposing of the rest of his clothing before pulling her silky, fragrant body into his. The tip of him pressed against her wet curls, and he slid his hand between them, seeking her hot, slick folds. Drenched with cream, she shuddered as he stroked the small nub of flesh inside her silky curls.

"Oh God, Simon, please. Love me."

The urgency in her husky voice drove him over the edge. She wanted him as badly as he craved her. Refusing to wait a moment longer, he carried her to the bed. Spread before him in a beautiful display of sensuous and voluptuous curves, he wrapped her legs around his waist and buried himself deep inside her hot, satiny folds.

Tight and slick, her muscles clenched at him with a raw intensity that pulled a cry of desire from his lips. She was his, now and for always. She was his, and no one would take her from him. With each hot stroke, she bucked against him, matching his furious rhythm.

It was wild and passionate, and she loved it. Loved him. He filled her and treasured her with every inch of him. The desire pouring out of him into her body was unlike any lovemaking they'd ever shared. The frenetic pace between them escalated the sensations skimming through her body until with a sharp cry of fulfillment she exploded from the heat of their passion. As her body clenched around him, he cried out her name as he drove into her one last time and throbbed inside her.

Relaxing in the wake of their heated joining, she murmured a protest as he retreated from her. A moment later, he pulled her back into his arms as they curled up on the bed together. The harshness of his breathing eased as they lay quietly in each others arms. Aware that they had one last secret between them, she sighed.

"Simon?" Pushing herself up on one elbow, she brushed her hair out of her face.

"Umm." Eyes closed, he wore a look of contentment. She hesitated upon seeing his expression. Would he be terribly angry with her? Her silence made him open his eyes, and she bit her lip at the curiosity glittering there.

"Do you want children?" For a moment he just stared at her, curiosity giving way to surprise, then wariness.

"Do you?" He asked cautiously.

"Oh yes, very much." She nodded as she tried to read his expression. As a smile curved his lips, he trailed his forefinger down her throat and across her breasts.

"Then I suggest we take all night ensuring your wish is granted."

"Actually," she paused to swallow as he arched an eyebrow at her. "We've already accomplished that."

Amazement, excitement and happiness crossed his features in swift succession. Rolling her over onto her back, he hovered over her. "Do you mean to tell me you're with child?"

"Yes. And I'm certain there will be talk," she murmured in a hesitant voice.

"Not by anyone who matters, sweetheart. But to save you any pain, I'll make you respectable within the next day or so." The love in his eyes warmed the deepest corners of her heart. "My only regret is not having you to myself for much longer. But as for the boy, I'm delighted."

Gently, he kissed her lips. Puzzled, she frowned up at him as he lifted his head. "How do you know the child will be a boy?"

With a shrug, he shook his head. "I'm not sure. Something just tells me you're carrying our son."

A smile tugged at her lips. The Grand Dame. One day she would tell Simon of her experience, but for now she was content to keep her own counsel. *Happy Christmas, dearest Ivy.* The voice whispered through her head with warmth and affection. She was the most fortunate of women. The power of love had brought the Grand Dame to her, and her ancestor had shown her the way to true love and happiness. Perhaps the woman would do the same for one of her own children. Outside, darkness had fallen, and there was the soft sound of carolers making their way from door to door. As the fire in the hearth flickered then died to a soft glow, she burrowed into Simon's arms and sighed with happiness. It truly was a Happy Christmas.

A Kind of Magic

Charlotte Featherstone

Chapter One

The room was dark, except for the bright blinking of an immobile cursor. Downstairs, the radio played Jingle Bell Rock. It was six o'clock in the morning on December the twenty-first and Julia Taylor, a thirty-year-old struggling midlist romance author rested her head on top of her desk. It was utterly useless-- *she,* was utterly useless.

'Just let it come,' Natalie, her agent had advised. 'Just let the characters write it the way they want to write it'. *Right.* Julia snorted as she looked up through a curtain of ash blond hair. Let the characters write the story. Well, hell where *were* the characters? The friggin' cursor was still blinking at her, and there wasn't a damn word on the page, and just to make her vexation more complete, Simon and the Chipmunks were now squeaking out their version of seasonal happiness.

"Forget it," Julia grumbled, jumping off her chair and leaving the study. She needed a drink. A rum and coke to be precise. God, she needed a hell of a lot more than alcohol, she muttered to herself as she strolled into the kitchen, wincing when she saw the dishes that lay scattered on the counter. What she needed was a full time maid, a cook, and one hell of a manuscript. But none of that was going to happen. Not in this lifetime, and most especially not during the Christmas season.

If there was one thing she detested, it was Christmas. She hadn't always hated it. In fact, she used to make herself so excited she would end up spending the night throwing up--all in anticipation for Santa and the carols and her cousins who were expected to arrive the next day, not to mention at least one extra shortbread cookie she hadn't needed.

Julia glanced at the clock on the microwave--6:05 am. Much too early for rum. What the heck, she thought, tossing out the old filter from the coffee pot, she'd have a little Bailey's in her coffee. That ought to get her going. She smiled, remembering how her mom had always indulged in a little 'treat' in her Christmas morning coffee.

Her mom loved Christmas, but it had been a long while since Julia had fond memories of the holiday. Everything was so commercial and fast paced. It was over before it started, and far too much work for its worth. Where was the anticipation? The family and the fellowship of man? Where was the love?

She was a dreamer. A hopeless romantic lost in today's high-tech, fast paced world. Of course, she wouldn't admit that to anyone. The Julia Taylor everyone knew was a modern young woman with a sound head on her shoulders. Only her mom knew her dreams and realized that inside Julia was more than just a desire to dally in fairy tales--she wanted to live one.

"Whatever happened to sleigh rides and kissing beneath the mistletoe?" she muttered, opening the carton of cream and sniffing it to make certain it wasn't past its expiration date. What about balls and soirees and elegant gowns, and men in cravats?

Pouring a liberal amount of cream and Bailey's into her coffee, neither of which she needed, she took a large satisfying sip and groaned when she heard the familiar voice of her fiancé--ex-fiance, she mentally corrected.

"You're listening to 95.1 FM, home of the classics. Well, it's freezing outside and you're waking up to a fresh blanket of snow. Kind of gets you in the spirit, doesn't it?"

Julia levelled the digital display on her stereo with a menacing glare. "Gets me in the spirit, right. I have no spirit. You took it when you said I was frumpy and fat."

But Scott kept on talking, always having to have the last word. "Four days till Christmas," he said merrily. "Here's a little something to get you in the mood."

Judy Garland's *Have Yourself A Merry Little Christmas* came over the airwaves and Julia bit back the tears that immediately sprung to her eyes. "Asshole," she choked, tightening the sash of her old terry cloth robe before reaching for her coffee. "You just had to play that one, didn't you?"

Damn Scott. What had she ever seen in him? Sure he was good looking and funny, but he had always been an unfeeling clod. But, she reminded herself as she trudged up the stairs, once again sitting before her computer screen, the simple truth was, he'd been the only man to pay to her any attention. She'd been a hopeless failure in high school and university, always too plain and a few pounds too heavy.

With a depressed sigh, she raised the cup to her lips and watched as the cursor blinked insolently back at her. Well, she certainly didn't feel like writing now that she'd heard Scott on the radio, all cheery and full of Christmas spirit. The writing was crap anyway. She snorted, hitting the delete key and watching as the cursor ate her words. Now where to start?

Judy had finished and now *O Holy Night* was playing. This one had always been her favorite. Tears sprung to her eyes and she looked about her study in a vain attempt to keep them from spilling. She was *not* going to cry over Scott Marchand or the fact that it was going to be Christmas in four days and she was thirty and unwed and unattached ... and ... and what ... *lonely*?

Her gaze landed on a portrait of a stunning couple that sat proudly above the fireplace in her study. No, she wasn't lonely. She had her family and her friends to keep her company. It wasn't that. It was more. Like a feeling of homesickness, but that didn't make any sense, she was home. Her parents lived ten minutes away for heaven's sake. But still, she couldn't shake the gnawing in her belly. She just didn't feel....complete.

The longer she stared at the portrait the more palpable the feeling became. She wasn't settled. Raising the cup to her mouth once again, she drank deeply and wondered if she'd put too much Bailey's in the coffee or if another tear was threatening to slip the confines of her lashes--for what other reason could there be for the sparkling twinkle she saw in the Grand Dame's blue eyes.

"Nuts," she muttered, shaking her head. The couple in the portrait were her grandparents, several generations removed. They were long since dead, their only reminder a portrait of them in their Georgian costumes and a chandelier styled diamond necklace bequeathed to every daughter down the line. Their story was one of love and passion, and more than a bit of intrigue, for her grandmother, it was said, was an impish young lady, who, once she had something set in her mind, was not wont to give up her hold. And that something had been the man she married.

"A very good making of a romance novel", Julia said, grinning as she saluted the pair with her coffee cup. "I daresay I could make a best seller out of your lives."

She clutched the mug to her chest and looked around the room when she heard *'well, do it,'* whisper past her. Definitely too much Bailey's she thought, staring into her empty cup. But a good idea nonetheless. Who would know that it was alcohol induced?

"Where to start," she said, staring at the screen and cracking her knuckles.

Why not start at the beginning, dearest? the clipped, English voice whispered in her ear with an aristocratic authority

"Yes," Julia grinned. "They're already talking. C'mon, tell me your story, gran." Already her fingers were poised on home-row, waiting to hear the character's voice again. Nothing better than a character that speaks to you.

With a deep breath, she typed the first thing that came to her mind. *She wanted him, and there wasn't a damn thing on earth that was going to stop her from having him.* Hmm, feisty, Julia smiled. Obviously Grandmother Langdon had more than imp's blood coursing through her veins.

Julia sat back and looked at the line. It wasn't the best opening, but it wasn't the worst, either. Could lead somewhere--to the bedroom most likely. But hey, this was her breakout book. This was the manuscript that was going to propel her to the top of the New York Times Best Seller list and launch her out of her midlist blues.

The next sentence was easier, followed by the next. Soon she was lost in a blinding whirl of typing and watching the words on the screen that seemingly came from someone other than her. It was beautiful. It was magic. She didn't even hear the sappy Christmas carols playing on the radio anymore, until that oh-so-familiar sound....*buloop*, shattered her concentration.

Ah, no, not Tanya, Julia groaned, staring at the familiar instant messenger name. Her friend had infallible timing.

Teats: U there?

Julia stared at the line for seconds, debating whether to click it off and ignore it, or admit to being awake this early in the morning. Ah, what the hell. Tanya was her best friend.

J.T.: Yeah, I'm here. Just writing. I'm close to deadline.

Teats: Oh, cool. You got them doing the nasty yet?

Sighing, Julia reminded herself that Tanya was really her very good friend. Although, it wasn't easy being friends with someone as perfect as Tanya. Her IM name said it all. Tanya Teats. She'd earned the nickname from the football team in high school, and of course it had carried through to her adult years. How could it not? Tanya had made the most of her teats, even showing them off in Playboy for an astonishing amount of money. Much more than a midlist romance author earned.

Teats: So, you got them going at it hot and heavy, or what?

J.T.: I may write hot, but I write historicals, Tanya. It takes some time to get them into bed. You know, they had that thing called propriety.

Teats: Well, that sucks. How long does it take for your hero to get his gal in the sack?

Julia gritted her teeth. It didn't matter how many times she explained things to Tanya, she would never get it. Tanya would never understand the fact that it just wasn't heroic for a protagonist to jump his lady in a carriage on page ten. It just wasn't done. *Why ever not? I can remember numerous ladies who were willing to break the rules for love.*

The voice was astonishing real, not to mention utterly superior sounding. Julia looked over her shoulder and around the room. No one was there. She really needed to stop drinking Baileys.

J.T.: Look, Tanya, did you need something? Sorry to be so blunt, but I really have to get to work. I'm way behind, and my deadline is looming. My career is on the line, here. If this book doesn't sell well, Sapphire Publishing is gonna cancel my contract.

Teats: You worry too much. Hey, you're not still stewing over this Scott thing, are you? I hope not. He's an A-1 asshole, you know.

Julia grinned. Leave it to Tanya to be succinct.

J.T.: Nah, I'm ok. He wasn't the right one. I know that now. *At least you've come to your senses in that matter. I was positively certain you would marry the bumbling fool*

Teats: You need to come to New York. You need to get laid. *Sweet Heaven, your friend is so vulgar.*

Okay, this voice in her head was getting very annoying. Ignoring the musing of her character, Julia tried to focus on her virtual conversation.

J.T.: No more men, Tanya, do you hear me? I'm swearing off them for a while....well, at least till I get this book finished.

Besides, it's Christmas, and you're going to Paris for that photo shoot.

Teats: Why don't you come with me, Jules? What are you doing, having turkey with your parents again? C'mon, live a little.

Julia bristled at the thought of spending another Christmas bored silly and depressed. Tanya was right, stuffing herself on turkey and plum pudding had been the extent of her festive plans. Although, she could spring for the money it would cost to her fly to London and attend Sapphire Publishing's yearly Christmas ball. But she would be alone, and she wasn't sure the holidays were the best time of the year to spend in solitude.

Why not visit Harrow Lodge in Kent? It was always one of my favorite places to visit. I am certain that you will find something useful and romantic there for your stay. After all, there is a great deal of family history there, and I think you will find dozens of wickedly amusing stories. Even some about me.

A research trip. The idea had merit.

Teats: Anyway, big news. I'm meeting this totally adorable guy for breakfast and mimosas. He's from England and he speaks with an accent and everything.

J.T.: Yeah, well, most people from England talk with accents.

Teats: No, really, Julia, I think he could be the one. He's so cute, and ripped.....my God is he ripped.

J.T.: Ripped? Don't tell me you've already done him.

Teats: Nah, he's too much of a gentleman. We met in the gym at the Ritz. He was lifting weights. I was on the treadmill. No shirt. Totally ripped.

How many times had she heard similar things come out of Tanya's mouth? Frankly, she was tired of hearing it. Not to mention the fact she was bloody jealous. Tanya always managed a healthy glow whenever she worked out. She, on the other hand, always looked like something the cat dragged in.

Teats: No shirt, totally ripped!

Sighing, Julia typed whatever came to mind.

J.T.: No wonder you caught his attention--no shirt.

Teats: No. HE wasn't wearing a shirt. Julia, are paying attention here? Are you drinking or are you writing while we're chatting?

Writing, no. Drinking, yes. God, just the thought of Tanya working up a sweat on the treadmill made her reach for her cup that was unfortunately empty. Tanya with the big breasts, little waist, and flat stomach. Tanya with her pale blond hair and blue eyes. Tanya, the perfect female specimen.

Julia looked down at the blue pants of her 'sleeping princess' lounging pj's and the ratty white terry robe covering them. Julia of the widening butt and full thighs. Julia who was always a touch too plump. Julia who had never had any success with men. Julia who couldn't hold a candle to Tanya.

Teats: Oh, that's the buzzer. He's here.

J.T.: Cool, she wrote, but her heart wasn't in it. Tanya would be spending the day wining and dining while *she* sat alone in her candlelit study, struggling to conjure up a sex scene between two imaginary people. God, her life was spiralling to nowhere.

J.T: Oh, before you go, what's his name?

Teats: Brock.

Brock. She liked it. Strong. Masculine. A touch old sounding. Good hero's name.

Teats: He's in publishing. Gotta run, girlfriend. Good luck with the book. And please, forget that asshole Scott. You're better off without him.

J.T.: Have fun

Teats: Oh, I intend to. Mr. Publisherman won't know what hit him once he gets a look at Tanya's Ta-Ta's.

Julia stared at the grinning smiley icon flashing back at her. Tanya's Ta-Ta's? And people had the nerve to say romance writers wrote bad prose? With a smirk, she clicked off the IM conversation, and started reading the opening of her book. She had just finished the last line when the phone rang.

"Hello?" she answered, stretching the phone cord from her bookcase to the desk while managing to knock off a few coffee cups and an empty can of coke in the process.

"Jules?"

Scott. Damn. She didn't need this now. "Hi, Scott."

"Hi. Um...." Scott cleared his throat, and Julia pretended to blow some imaginary dust off her keyboard. "You working?"

"Yeah. My deadline is in four weeks."

"How's it going? With the book, I mean."

"All right."

"Yeah?"

"Yeah."

The static on the phone line hummed as the silence stretched on. Mercifully Scott ended it. "So, um, Merry Christmas."

"Yeah, you too."

"Ah, did I leave my golf clubs there?"

"I don't know." Oh, yeah, he'd left them, and she'd promptly taken a little drive out to the lake and deposited them into the waves.

"I can't find them."

"Well, I haven't seen them recently." Last time she'd seen them they'd been sinking their way down to the bottom of Lake Erie.

"Mind if I come over and look?"

Her fingers shook around the phone. Don't come over, don't come over, her mind chanted. "Whatever." So much for listening to her inner voice.

"What do you need them for if you don't mind me asking? There's two feet of snow outside. I hardly think the driving range is open."

"Jules, we need to talk."

"I thought you already said everything you wanted to say."

"I told you I didn't mean to say those things. I was in a bad mood. You know how work gets to me."

"I don't recall you mentioning anything about work. But I do remember you had a plenty to say about me."

"Jules, you know I didn't mean it. Look, I shouldn't have said it, sweetheart. I know it was wrong. It's just that I bought you that membership to the gym and when they told me you hadn't been there yet to set up your program I saw red. I shouldn't have lost it, I know that. Honey, lets start over. I miss you."

And do you miss my fat ass, too, she wanted to shout, but she wouldn't stoop to his level. Come hell or high water, Scott Marchand would never know how much he'd destroyed her fantasies and shattered her fragile self-esteem.

"You know what I need the golf clubs for, Jules? I'm going to the Caribbean for Christmas. You know, to get away. I thought you might want to come."

Oh sure, book a trip to the islands when they were no longer together. She had begged and pleaded with him for over a year to take her on such a trip, but he'd flatly refused. Tanya was right, he was an ass.

"Look Scott. I gotta run. I've got a deadline to meet. Can we talk about this some other time?"

"What about what I need? It's only about you, isn't it Julia?"

"It is now. Bye, Scott."

* * * *

"Hi there."

Brock Maitland stared at the buxom bottle blond behind the door. Inside the apartment he could see a silver Christmas tree decorated with blue and purple balls. A jazz recording of Silent Night played softly in the background . She really wasn't his type, but what the hell, he hadn't had sex in months. And sex was all this chit was good for.

"You want to come in?"

He smiled, trying to ignore the way her leather dress creaked with her every movement. He'd always hated leather on women. What ever happened to chiffon and silks and corsets, for that matter? Good God, he'd give a million pounds to find a woman wearing a corset. And not one of those trashy things found on-line or in a catalogue. But a real one, with expensive French silk and lavish embroidery. Something made by a modiste who outfitted the *ton*. Something that Fiona would have worn.

"Drink?"

He nodded and forced aside thoughts of Fiona. No use dwelling on that particular memory. He'd have many nights to ruminate on his affair with Fiona Montgomery--hell, an endless lifetime of nights.

"Champagne and orange juice?"

He grimaced. One thing he hated about living in the twenty-first century besides the fact the women dressed like Haymarket Whores was the liquor. He hadn't come across a decent brandy or champagne since.....since, well, it must have been 1900, in Russia.

"Well?" his host asked, holding a magnum of champagne and a carton of orange juice. "Or would you rather we skipped drinks and went for the main course?"

"Water," he said, clearing his throat. Jesus, what was he doing here with a creature such as Tanya? He hated women like this. He was the man, he should be the aggressor. In his world the man was the hunter and the lady, if Tanya could be called such, would be the prey. Now the tables were turned and he didn't like it one bit. It certainly didn't make his cock rear to attention. No doubt Tanya thought that a flash of ass and a glimpse of saline enhanced breasts would make him hard as iron.

"So," she said, flopping down beside him on an oversized couch, sending the tree ornaments jingling against one another. "What do you want to do?"

He really shouldn't be here. He hated this, this constant hunger, the impossible search for someone he could never find. Damn his body for having needs.

Tanya tucked her red painted toes beneath her legs and inched closer to him. Her mammoth breasts, which he knew were enhanced, rubbed the shoulder of his sports jacket. He loved breasts--the bigger the better. But he liked them natural. He liked to squeeze and mold them, to feel the heat in his hand. Fake breasts always felt cold. It could be 110 degrees, and Tanya's tits would still be cold as ice.

Clearing his throat he tried to ignore the way Tanya was threading her fingers through his hair. Looking about the room, he tried to find something to remark upon. "Who's this?" he asked, picking up a picture that turned out to be a mini-photo album.

"Oh, that's Trish. She's a friend. Those are pictures of her wedding."

"She had a costume wedding, did she?" He noted the familiar French neckline. It was close, but not an exact replica. He ought to know. He'd had more than his fair share of experience disrobing Regency ladies.

"Trish is totally into that *Pride and Prejudice* thing. Not my bag, but it was fun. That's me," she said, pointing to the first picture in the album.

"I recognize you." How could he not, she had a cleavage to her chin.

"Must be my face."

"Something like that."

"And that's Trish's husband."

"Ghastly knot," he couldn't help saying. "Who tied the poor man's cravat?" He would have dismissed his valet in a heartbeat had the servant sent him out amongst the *ton* wearing such a getup.

"Oh, I don't know who tied it. Some guy, I suppose."

He snorted. How articulate of Tanya. Getting information out of her was going to be as difficult as cheating at cards at White's. But he knew she had the information he needed. Something had drawn him to Tanya. He couldn't deny it. Like a vampire was attracted by blood, he was drawn to something about Tanya. Why, in God's name, he hadn't a clue, but there it was. He *had* to see her today.

Tanya snuggled closer and rested her chin on his shoulder, pushing her breasts into his arm. Ignoring her, he continued to flip through the pages, stopping at a group shot of the wedding party. He skimmed the faces with a detached eye and was about to turn to the next photo when something stopped him.

His heart, which normally beat at sixty a minute, trebled. His blood, which was always slightly lower than the normal 98 degrees instantly heated up. Only one person had ever made him feel this way. His eyes scanned every face until he at last saw her. *Her*. Fiona.

"Who is she?"

Tanya raised her chin and looked at him quizzically before following his finger. "Oh, that's just Julia."

"Just Julia?" he nearly choked, heart beating frighteningly fast. "Tell me about her."

Tanya shrugged and turned the page. He had the almost uncontrollable urge to take the tart by her shoulders and shake her till the information he wanted fell out of her mouth.

"What do you want to know? She lives in a small town in Ontario. That's where I'm from too."

He didn't give a damn where Tanya was from. She could have been spawned in hell for all he cared. He wanted to know about her friend.

"Julia is a romance writer. She's sort of struggling right now."

"How?"

Tanya looked at him again and he fought for control. He couldn't make the chit jealous or else he'd never get any information out of her. But he now knew what drove him to come to Tanya's this morning. He was close, so very close to finding her. His soul mate.

"She's struggling with her career. Her publisher is threatening to revoke her contract if she doesn't sell through on this next book. And then there's Scott."

"She's married?" His heart suddenly stopped and dropped to his stomach. Good God, no, she couldn't be married. Not now, not after he'd just found her again. She wasn't supposed to be married. It wasn't supposed to happen like this. The old gypsy had told him what would happen. When she had placed her magic spell upon him she damn well hadn't mentioned anything about finding his long lost love only to discover she was married.

"Nah, she's not married. She was engaged to him, but he called it off. Said she was getting fat and he was tired of competing with her characters for her time and affection."

Brock blinked then looked down at the picture. "Fat?"

Tanya turned the page to a single photo of Fiona--Julia. "Well, she kind of has put on the pounds. She always was a bit on the plump side, you know," Tanya drawled, "at least compared to me."

"I don't know," he said, staring at the woman smiling back at him. "I find her rather attractive." Her face certainly was, and her breasts most certainly were. All natural there, Brock inwardly smiled.

"Well, Scott was right, but he shouldn't have told her he didn't want to be with her anymore because of her body. He could have at least told her he'd found someone else."

Brock fought the urge to trace Julia's smiling face with his finger. How she must have felt to hear the worthless Scott say such things to her. She was beautiful with a face that was innocent yet sensual. Her body, what he could see of it, was voluptuous and womanly. Her Regency gown looked as though she had walked straight out of Almack's, and her hair, all pulled up and dangling in ringlets, made him ache to run his fingers through the curls, dispelling all the pins.

There were many men who coveted the sort of fake beauty that Tanya ascribed to, but he was not one of them. He wanted his women to look like women. He'd always preferred buxom and voluptuous to straight and skinny. Julia the romance writer was every inch the woman he desired.

"So," Tanya purred, closing the album. "What do you want to do?"

"Why don't you finish getting ready," Brock suggested, bolting from the couch and stepping a precautionary foot away. "Then we'll grab something to eat."

Tanya pouted, then shrugged. "All right then. Is this ok?" she asked as she smoothed her hands down her leather dress.

"I thought we might go somewhere a little less ... formal," he muttered, already thinking of ways to ditch Tanya.

"I'll be in the washroom, getting changed. Help yourself to anything you want."

"Great," he called over his shoulder while he rifled through the photo album and removed the picture of Julia from its protective plastic. With great care he put it in his breast pocket and searched the drawer of the end table beside the couch. Cigarettes, a lighter, pens, scraps of paper, some hair elastics. *Bingo*. Tanya's little black book. Julia....Julia, what, he thought as he thumbed through the pages. Like a mad fool he rushed to the J's and nearly shouted his success when he read Julia Taylor. Tanya was thorough if she was anything. All there in black and white was Julia's vital statistics. Address, phone number, email addy, even her birth date. To him it was like winning like the lottery.

Ripping out the page, he shoved it into his jacket pocket and looked around the room. In a corner sat a small wood desk with a computer, the screen framed in garish gold and silver Christmas garland . An IM square with the conversation still showing, blinked at him. Hearing water turn on in the bathroom and figuring he had a few minutes, Brock sat down and read the screen.

J.T. had to be Julia. He read the line about deadlines and knew it was Julia. He owned his own publishing company, he knew enough about authors and their deadlines. He grinned when he read the bit about historical propriety--boy did Julia have a lot to learn. There wasn't going to be anything remotely resembling propriety when he finally got his hands on her. *This* hero didn't give a bloody farthing about appearances, he only wanted Julia and he'd get her any way he knew how.

He came to the end and was disappointed. She was witty and smart. Hell, he'd even laughed aloud at her crack about his accent. God, he missed her, or at least he missed the person she used to be.

He'd wondered what it would be like to find Fiona, had dreamt of this day. And now he was unsure of how to proceed. Would she know him? Did she--Julia, that is--have any inkling that she belonged to a man who was over two hundred years old?

What if she wanted nothing to do with him?

The water was still running in the bathroom and Brock looked down at the keyboard. With a grin he looked up at the screen and gave into temptation. What would it hurt? He wanted desperately to say something to her. He'd waited for this moment for over two hundreds years.

Hey sweetheart, it's been a long time, but I've finally found you. He poured out his heart in two minutes. When he heard the taps in the bathroom shut off, he hurriedly signed off. *Sweet dreams, baby. We'll be together again soon. Very soon.* Then he clicked off the screen and bolted for the door before Tanya could lay her hands on him. He reached for his keys on the sofa table and noticed a paperback beside them. He picked it up and flipped it over to the front cover. *'Beyond Seduction' by Julia A. Taylor.* Brock smiled slowly while he weighed the book in his hand. Julia A. Taylor had absolutely no idea just how far beyond seduction this was going to turn out to be.

With a low whistle, Brock let himself out of Tanya's apartment, happier than he'd been in over two hundred years.

Chapter Two

Pulling her carry-on luggage from her aching shoulder, Julia sank down in an empty chair and sighed heavily. Outside Pearson International airport, the snow was falling heavily. Today was not a great day to leave for Kent. Today was *not* a great day for flying.

Straightening her sweater, she looked around, searching for a means of distraction. The terminal was busy with people running for connecting flights and the speaker was on constantly updating last calls for boarding and in coming flights. The dizzying pace, not to mention the bleak weather rattled her nerves, and she reached into her bag for one of the little pills that would get her through the flight. She'd made it this far, only another hour and then the seven hour flight to go. She'd made the decision to spend Christmas researching her ancestors at Harrow Lodge in Kent, now was not the time to back out or allow her composure to be consumed by fears.

Swallowing the pill, she took a sip of tea and settled into her chair, listening to the carols that were coming from the book and magazine store beside her. She watched the endless parade of people walk before her, and soon her eyes began to feel heavy and she closed them, just for a second.

She was at a ball, dressed like a Greek goddess in a shell-pink gown of silk, the empire bodice constructed of embroidered velvet. The chapel-length train of pink silk, edged in lace, swished behind her. As her partner, a tall, black-haired rake gathered her in his arms and brought her to his chest, Julia looked around in awe and confusion. It was a scene right out of one of her books, and the guy ... she stole a look up at him and felt her heart hammer uncontrollably, the man was far sexier than any rogue she could have ever conjured up.

"Thank you," he drawled.

She blinked madly, wondering if it was possible that he was

somehow privy to what she was thinking about him.

"Where am I?" she asked as they twirled past a pair of marble and gilt Acanthus columns and a group of gentlemen dressed as dandies, drinking claret out of elaborate crystal goblets.

"My home," her partner whispered, sending a shiver down her spine.

"Who are you?" she asked, finally looking away from the guests who looked as though they had just stepped out of a scene in Pride and Prejudice.

"The Duke of Maitland," he answered while his deep, indigo-blue eyes liberally and lazily scoured her. "You know me," he purred, when she was about to protest that she had never heard of him before. "Search your soul, Julia, you'll find me there."

"But how...." she trailed off, her eyes landing on a young woman who looked oddly familiar to her and who smiled and nodded in her direction as they twirled by.

"That is Mrs. Nightingale, but you may know her as Lady Holly Harrington."

Julia looked at the beautiful young woman and saw the familiar blue eyes, the same hue that both her mother and herself shared. If this man--this duke--was to believed, than she was looking upon her aunt, the same aunt who had been alive nearly two hundred years ago. The aunt that had married the rich Nabob, Andrew Nightingale. The aunt whose love story had inspired her since childhood to believe in Prince Charmings and happily ever afters.

Disbelief made her search her surroundings, looking for a way to escape. But he gripped her fingers tighter and brought her closer to his chest.

"I'll not lose you again, Julia. I'll not let you run from me."

"How did I come to be here ... to be with you?"

He smiled, and his rakish grin melted her insides. Good lord, the man was everything she had ever dreamed of. Every hero she had ever penned was fashioned after this man. And yet she knew she was dreaming, that this was just a fantasy, something her overly romantic nature had created to keep the loneliness away.

"You're here because you let me in. You opened your mind--"

She shook her head. "This is just a dream. You're not real."

"I'm real, Julia," he said darkly, his gaze focused on her mouth. "I'm very much flesh and blood. I'm a man--shall I prove it to you?"

Her fingers trembled, and she felt her stomach knot tightly. She was no virginal heroine. She was a modern woman with needs, and it had been so very long since she had engaged in even the mildest flirtation. She was defenseless against this man and his aura of sensual danger. How could she not be, when it had been so long since a man had looked twice at her?

"I have only looked at you once, Julia, and the reason for that is because I've never been able to look away."

He brought her closer, so that her breasts brushed against his brocade waistcoat. Her breath caught, and she felt a tremor of fear course through her. He could read her thoughts ... he knew her desires ... knew what she secretly yearned for.

"We share the same desires, Julia, and you'll be able to know what I feel in ways I could never express. Soon, you will be able to enter my dreams just as I have come into yours."

"Final boarding call for flight 546 to London."

Julia came awake with a start. Wiping her eyes with the back of her hand, she tried to make out the blurry screen behind the Air Canada counter. A green garland with twinkling lights framed the display. Letters and numbers melded together until the words were nothing but a long, green, digital line.

With an oath, she rifled through her carry-on bag. Finding her glasses, she placed them on her nose. Flight 546--to London? Oh, God, she thought in a panic, that was her flight.

Grabbing her bag, she jumped from her chair and ran to the ticket counter. The man glanced down at her ticket and with a nod he ushered her through the gate and down the ramp to where the stewardess was about to close the plane door.

"Wait," Julia shouted, cursing herself for wearing a skirt and high-heeled boots. What sort of moron wears heels on a plane, she thought belatedly as she struggled for air. *Women have always done desperate things to secure the attentions of a man, dearest.* That damn bothersome voice whispered in her head, but she shut out the sound. Now was not the time to be distracted.

Gasping, she handed her ticket to the stewardess who was trying very hard to keep her smile. "Sleeping?" she asked, her lips appearing frozen as she maintained her strained smile.

"Can you tell?" Julia winced, raising a hand to her cheek and feeling the tell tale ridges left from her fingers.

"Just a bit," the stewardess smirked, glancing down at Julia's wrinkled skirt, before scanning the ticket. "I'm afraid there's a problem with your ticket, Miss Taylor. Unfortunately, this flight has been overbooked."

Great. This was the last thing she needed. Nothing had gone right from the minute she woke up at her desk two mornings ago to find that strange IM message flashing back at her. It had been from Tanya's address, but the writer had most definitely not been Tanya. And the story that she had read on her screen had rekindled something in her mind, not so much a memory but a feeling. A strange feeling that she couldn't seem to put out of her mind. And then there were the dreams....

"Miss?" the stewardess asked.

"Oh, sorry," Julia said. She had to stop thinking about the strange man who had invaded her dreams. Strange, but she sensed him prying into her emotions and thoughts this very minute.

"The overbooking?" the stewardess began, exasperation finally showing in her face.

"Oh, right, right," Julia nodded, hefting her carry-on bag higher on her shoulder and trying to collect her scattered thoughts. She was going to freak if this blonde bimbo told her there wasn't a seat for her. She'd sit in the bloody lavatory if she had to. There was no way she was not getting on this flight, not after the hell she put herself and her family through to get here.

Julia winced at the remembered scene in her mother's kitchen yesterday. First her mother had wept uncontrollably because her only daughter would not be home for Christmas, then Julia had managed to send her mother from tears to brutalizing the shortbread dough when Julia confessed that she had paid for this trip by pawning the family heirloom--the Grand Dame's priceless ruby and diamond necklace, to be exact.

Julia thought she might have given her mother a heart attack when she admitted that, without much thought, she had pawned the invaluable necklace. Well, it wasn't like she had *sold* it, she had merely loaned it to a very reputable pawnbroker in exchange for enough cash for a two week holiday in the English countryside over Christmas. It wasn't like Mr. Hogarth was going to sell it on her. Besides, her advance was due the first of January. She had plenty of time to return home and pay Hogarth, thereby securing the necklace for the next generation of Harrington women--*whoever* they might be.

"Miss, if you'll follow me."

"Oh, of course," she said, trying to smile as she straightened her glasses. When she stepped onto the plane and followed the stewardess, not right, but left, she tapped the woman on the shoulder. "Um, my ticket isn't for first class."

The blonde tossed a smirk over her shapely shoulder. "I am aware of that."

"Well, if you're aware," Julia said, trying to rein in her sarcasm, "why are you taking me there?"

"Overbooking, remember?" she said, as if she were far more intelligent than Julia could ever hope to be.

"Oh, right, because it's normal to put the leftovers in first class when a plane is overbooked," she snapped, hating the stewardess for being beautiful and petite and for making her feel like a bull elephant while she lumbered behind her.

"Here you go," the petite goddess said, pointing to the aisle seat in a row that was approximately halfway between the cockpit and the galley.

"Thanks," Julia mumbled, sinking down into the soft leather chair that reclined all the way back. What luck to be in first class of all places. She hated flying, despised every second of it, but maybe with the attention and niceties afforded to first class patrons the flight might be a heck of a lot more enjoyable. Finally her luck was changing. She sighed, squirming in the seat until she found a comfortable spot.

The stewardess reached for her carry-on and put it in the bulkhead, slamming the door till she heard the latch click. "I'm Jackie, and I'll be your stewardess for the flight. Can I get you a drink before we take off, something to calm your nerves, or"--she winked saucily--"wake you up."

"Ah, no, no thanks," Julia murmured, looking around the cabin. Not even her recliner at home was as comfortable as this chair. And why she wondered, at the height of the Christmas season, was the first class cabin of a supposedly overbooked flight empty with the exception of four customers?

"Ok, then, I won't be able to serve you until we get the all clear from the captain."

"That's ok," Julia whispered, feeling her stomach tighten as the engines began to gear up. Suddenly nothing mattered, only the extremely unsettled feeling in the pit of her stomach. Frankly, she felt nauseous.

"All right then. We'll be taking off in about five minutes."

Julia nodded and watched Jackie saunter up the aisle to the cockpit. Recalling how cumbersome she felt walking behind the svelte Jackie, Julia raked a hand through her short curls and traced what she hoped was a fading handprint on her cheek.

Then she smoothed the creases out from her angora sweater and tried to take comfort in the fact that she had much larger breasts than Jackie. Men adored large breasts, didn't they?

The engines became louder, and any vanity she had left flew out the window. Her nerves were acting up and she was certain she was going to disgrace herself by using the brown paper 'sickness bag'. Where were her drugs, she thought, frantically searching around for her carry-on.

Damn that stewardess, she'd put her valium up in the bulkhead and now she couldn't get to them. She couldn't fly without them. Panic and irrational fear seized her, and she fumbled with the buckle of her belt. She needed the valium. The one she had taken before she fell asleep in the departure lounge would not be enough to sustain her for the entire flight.

"Right this way, sir,"

She heard Jackie's voice, and Julia swiveled in her seat, trying to catch the stewardess' attention. Her mouth dropped open and she pushed her glasses back on her nose when she saw Jackie escorting the most gorgeous man she had ever seen.

Shutting her mouth, she slouched down in her seat. She was acting like a lunatic. She needed to get a hold of herself. She couldn't be acting like some featherbrained twit when they strolled past her. She had to appear in control, together.

"Here you are, sir." Jackie said in a throaty whisper.

Julia darted her eyes to the left and came face to face with a gold zipper on the fly of a very expensive pair of tweed dress trousers. Swallowing hard, she looked up and noticed that above the fly was an oatmeal colored cabled sweater, up higher to a wide chest and broad shoulders, up even further to a chiseled chin and sculpted lips, lips which were parted in a sexy, rakish grin.

"Your flight mate, Miss Taylor," Jackie said gleefully. "Mr. Maitland."

Blinking rapidly, wondering if she hadn't taken too many Valium already, Julia looked up into an eerily familiar face.

"Good afternoon, Julia," he said in his perfectly cultured English accent.

It couldn't be, she thought, gripping the arm of the seat. It couldn't be possible. But when he smiled at her, and his blue eyes danced with mischief and unmistakable sensual promise, she knew it to be true. This was the man of her dreams. This was the Duke of Maitland.

Chapter Three

Julia swallowed hard and looked up into the face that now seemed so familiar to her. This man had haunted her dreams for days. As absurd as it sounded, she had felt him probing her mind, invading her thoughts even in her waking hours. That he should be standing before her, on the same plane, destined for the same city, was beyond comprehension. Had he been able to read her mind after all? Was he reading it now? She bristled and straightened in her chair. She was being silly, thinking such thoughts. Too many paranormal romances, she mumbled to herself, attempting to close her mind off to him. She was being overrun with fanciful, romantic notions that only happened in the make-believe worlds of books. Things like this--like beautiful strangers desiring her, reading her mind and invading her dreams--did not happen. She was overtired and her active imagination had at last run riot over her common sense.

Believing is far from difficult, Julia. If you only allow yourself to believe, embrace the possibilities, dearest. After all, what is there to lose in doing so?

That irritating voice that had been her in head for days suddenly re-appeared, and she closed her ears to it. Perhaps she was going mad after all. Perhaps Scott's betrayal had finally taken its toll on her.

"May I?" Mr. Maitland, or the duke, or whoever he was motioned to the seat beside her.

Reaching for the buckle of her seat belt, she flicked it opened--she was stopped from standing by his hand, soft and warm atop her fingers.

"Please, do not trouble yourself."

Swiveling her knees to the side, she allowed him past and watched as he meticulously placed his folded overcoat on the empty chair beside him. He lowered his tall frame in the seat next to hers. Why wouldn't he have left that empty and taken the one beside the window? He was quite tall, well over six feet with long legs. How could he want to be so near her when he could have more leg room if he took the other seat?

But then I wouldn't be close to you, now would I? I wouldn't be able to smell your scent or feel your warmth, or hold your hand.

His voice, so loud and clear, interrupted her thoughts. It was his voice--that perfectly accented, aristocratic English accent. The sound had the ability to make her knees turn to mush. The duke's voice.

He smiled broadly at her, and she immediately looked away, cursing herself for thinking such things. She didn't know how to explain it, but she was certain the man had the ability to enter her mind.

Nonsense. Utterly impossible.

The plane's engines whirled and the sound of the wheels moving along the tarmac soon made her forget the enigmatic man beside her. Thousands of butterflies were unleashed in her belly, and she gripped the arms of her seat until her knuckles were white and her fingers numb. *Deep breath in, and blow it out.*

She practiced the chant while the plane moved in to position on the runway. She was aware of Mr. Maitland watching her intently but she ignored him. Unable to think of anything other than the impending takeoff and the catastrophic possibilities, she closed her eyes, said a prayer to her maker that everything would go off without a hitch, that her tranquilizers would soon begin to work, and that she would not disgrace herself in front of this man by falling apart and giving in to her fears.

The engines were in the final stages of revving up. Her breathing became heavier, more labored, and she lost the ability to talk herself out of her paralyzing fear of flying.

"It's all right, sweeting," he whispered beside her as the sounds of the wheels squealing propelled them down the runway. "Give me your fear, and I'll keep you safe."

He reached for her hand and peeled her fingers from around the leather armrest. He clasped her shaking hand in his and brought it his mouth, holding her gaze steady, mesmerizing her with his deep, indigo eyes.

She felt her breathing slow, her heart return to an almost normal pace--not the frantic beating that threatened to make her faint. Her fingers stopped trembling and all she could think about was the exotic blueness of his eyes. How wonderfully sculpted his mouth was. And then he brushed her hand against his lips and kissed her fingers.

She closed her eyes, savoring the kiss, the romantic, almost passionate look in his eyes. It was a few seconds before she realized that the floating sensation she was experiencing was not just an illusion brought on his by kiss, but the very real fact that they had left the ground and were heading for the clouds.

Do not panic, Julia. His words entered her head, slicing through the thick fear that was once again enveloped her. *Trust me, Julia. Trust me with your life, your heart, your soul....*

She turned and looked at him, her eyes suddenly heavy. He became slightly blurred, sitting there beside her, and she knew that the tranquilizer she had taken earlier was beginning to work.

Trust me, he said again.

"It is so very hard to trust," she whispered, letting her head droop to the side so that she could rest it against the seat.

"I know," he said. His voice sounded so very close to her ear and she realized as her eyelids closed despite her attempts to prevent it, that he had positioned her so that her head was lying against his shoulder.

"Sleep, sweeting," he whispered against her temple.

"Yes," she sighed, snuggling against him, thinking of how wonderful he smelt, and how delightfully muscled he felt.

"I will come to you, Julia," he murmured before she slid into the darkness of sleep. "Don't shut me out again."

Her last thought was the realization that it was an order not a request.

* * * *

She was dreaming. Brock peered down and studied the way her eyelids flickered. Beneath her lids, her eyes moved rhythmically back and forth, signaling the fact she was deep in REM sleep--the easiest time for him to invade her thoughts.

But he was not quite ready, he realized, watching her face in the dim light of the cabin. He wanted to study her, to sear every inch of her face and body in his mind. This was the first time he had come face to face with his soul mate, and he wanted to enjoy every second.

She was beautiful. He had known she was. He had invaded her dreams and had discovered how lovely and soft she was. But nothing compared to having the flesh and blood Julia in his arms.

He traced his finger along her pink cheek, delighting in the softness of her skin, the light, enticing floral scent of her hair. She was very feminine, he thought, allowing his gaze to travel lower, to the fuzzy angora sweater that was buttoned over her breasts and the delicate lace camisole she wore beneath. She shifted on the chair, and he caught a glimpse of her breast, the milky white swell inching above the lace. Very feminine, indeed, he thought appreciatively.

She stirred again and pressed her cheek tighter against her neck. Her breasts brushed his arm and he grew heavy, aroused, his body searching for release--the release that only Julia could provide.

"Your Grace?" she mumbled sleepily, drawing him in. And he followed her willingly into her deepest fantasy.

They were at a ball again-- the same ball, in fact. They were dancing, and when he wrapped his arm tighter around her waist, she smiled beautifully up at him.

"Where were you?" she asked shyly, looking up from her golden blonde lashes.

"I was waiting till you were ready to receive me."

"Oh." Her cheeks became flushed, and he turned her in a wide arc. They were now before the door that lead to his apartments.

"Where are we going?" she asked, her voice husky and full of sensuality. He smothered a groan as he felt his cock fill with blood, his erection brushing against the silk flap of dress breeches.

Without answering her, he reached for her hand and led her up the stairs to his chamber. Reaching for the latch, he opened the door and led her inside. Her little gasp told him that she was pleased by what she saw.

"This room-" she trailed off, turning around until she had studied every nook, every corner. "This room is just like the one I wrote about in my last book. Right down to the blue brocade coverlet and bed hangings."

"Of course," he said, trailing his fingers down her spine. "It was, after all, your fantasy."

She wheeled around, her eyes wide. "This is a dream. This isn't real. You're not real."

"I am," he said. And then he did something he had ached to do for days. He lowered his lips to hers and kissed her--softly at first, then with increasing hunger before slipping his tongue between her lips and tasting her.

She mewled softly and reached for him, clutching his hair in her fingers, brushing her swelling breasts against his silk waistcoat. He groaned, hardening the kiss, turning it from an elegant dance to carnal need. With an oath, he tore his evening jacket from his shoulders and flung it the ground. She reached for the gold buttons of his waistcoat and opened them with eager, hurried fingers. Thrusting the brocade aside she smoothed her palms along his chest and down his belly, and he felt the heat of her breasts searing him through his thin lawn shirt.

"Oh, God," she whispered as he trailed hot kisses down the column of her throat. "I shall never want to give you up if you continue to make me feel this way."

"What makes you think I'll let you give me up," he growled, cupping her bottom and pressing his hardness against her mound.

"Just a dream," she said again, protesting the reality of what was happening.

"No."

"Yes," she said again, even as she reached for his cravat and pulled at the ends, undoing the elaborate knot. "I don't believe," she whispered, kissing him softly before running her tongue along his lips. "I can't allow myself to believe that this is anything but an erotic dream."

He picked her up and carried her to the bed and lowered his body so that he was partially covering her. "I will make you believe." And then he kissed her hungrily, tearing at the bodice of her gown, freeing her breast so that he could watch his hand cup her exquisite ivory flesh.

"Yes," she moaned. *Yes, I have always dreamed of a man who takes what he wants. A man who takes the decision away from me so that I may be swept away with passion.*

He read her thoughts and gazed into her eyes. "You want to be taken," he said silkily. "You want to know what it is like to be at my mercy." She swallowed hard and shifted her gaze from him. "You always ached for more, for something that *he* couldn't, or wouldn't give you. " She didn't look at him but she nodded in agreement. Her fingers curled into the silk coverlet and he watched as she gripped and twisted it. "You want the elation of being swept away, you want to know what it is like to hold your lover enthralled."

"I don't have that ability," she whispered, her gaze focused on the flickering candle flame.

"Do you not?" he asked, then reached for her hand and uncurled her fingers from the coverlet. "Feel for yourself and see if you do not hold me enthralled. I am at your mercy, Julia."

He brought her hand to his trousers. Beneath the fabric his erection swelled further. She turned her head, meeting his indigo gaze.

"I'm enthralled," he whispered. "I can't stop thinking of you, can't stop wondering what it will be like when I finally get to make love to you. I can't stop hoping that you'll remember me and the past we shared."

Her eyes went round and she studied his face in the candlelight. She searched her memory and felt a faint flicker of reminiscence. Had she known this man before? Had she seen him somewhere, or had he just been part of a fantasy she had once believed in?

"I won't let you get away, Julia. We belong together,"--he murmured against her neck--"forever".

She was looking at him as if she was trying to believe, trying to force her rational mind to believe in fairy tales. Her mind would not be easily swayed. She was nervous and skittish. Even in sleep she doubted what she saw and felt. How would he be able to reach her? How could he make her believe that they belonged together, that he had traveled the world for two centuries, searching for her?

She was stirring restlessly beneath him, rubbing her mound in a slow, undulating rhythm against his silk breeches, building the ache inside him so that he became restless and eager, so eager that he pulled her bodice down, baring both breasts. The fragile silk sheared, the sound sending a gasp from deep in her throat. But it was not a sound of fear, but of desire.

As he buried his mouth between her breasts, she reached for him, clutching him to her.

"I want this," she sighed. "You can have no idea how much."

"I know how much, sweeting, because I want this as much as you do."

Grasping handfuls of her skirt, he raised it to her waist and stole a look at her. Golden curls glistened with desire and he set his palm to her, feeling her heat and the dampness .

"He never pleasured you with his mouth did he?" he murmured, looking up at her. "He never tasted your desire."

She swallowed hard and looked away. He knew the answer, he heard the silent word as it slipped from her weakening resolve.

"And you want it, don't you?" he asked, parting her swollen folds. "You want my mouth on you, tasting you, licking you," He lowered his head and inhaled her arousal before flicking his tongue along the length of her. "Tell me you want this, and I will give it to you."

She shook her head in protest, but her body arched beneath his searching tongue. She could not admit to such a thing.

He looked up at her, a wicked gleam in his eye before he trailed his tongue up her. "You don't have to say the words aloud, sweeting. I can read your thoughts, and I already know that you crave this. I already know that in the end you will submit to me. I already know that you will arch and moan and come in my mouth, and I will watch you and take great pleasure in being the first to taste your passion."

An uncomfortable popping sound echoed in her ears, and Julia watched helplessly as the duke faded into a misty vapor. Reluctantly, she opened her eyes and started. She was no longer sitting up in her chair. Instead, it was reclined all the way back as if she were lying in bed. Someone had removed her glasses and covered her with a wool blanket from her neck to her toes.

She looked to the right and there, peering down at her was Maitland. He was looking at her so intensely that she gripped the blanket tighter to her throat. Good lord she hoped she hadn't been snoring--or worse, talking in her sleep. Oh God, she wanted to groan, what had she said?

"Well, Julia?" he asked, his hand snaking beneath the blanket so that he could skim his hand along her belly.

She licked her lips and tried to ignore the circling of butterflies in her stomach. His touch was burning her, just like it did in her dreams when he was acting the part of the duke.

"Part your legs," he commanded, and she felt his hot hand reach for her skirt, sliding the hem along her thighs.

Her stomach coiled tightly, her panties instantly became wet. She was aching for this--his hands touching her, exploring her. She wanted this so much. She wanted to be awake and to feel everything that she felt in her dreams.

But she didn't do this, her mind protested. She was not the sort of girl who dallied with nameless men or participated in one-night stands. She was not *that* type of woman.

His strong fingers reached for her thighs and, not waiting for her to comply, he parted her legs. He reached between them, cupping her damp mound in his palm. His eyes grew dark and his lashes lowered. She felt his fingers skimming the lace edge, and then she felt his fingers, long and skilled, snake beneath the lace frill to touch her curls.

She gasped, straightening away from his hand and looking fearfully around the cabin. It was dark, and what handful of people were in first class were fast asleep.

His fingers probed deeper, sinking between her sex until two of them were embedded in her. He pressed closer to her, pushing them deeper inside her. His breath caressed her jaw and she heard his growl of appreciation when the humiliating rush of desire seeped out of her.

"What do you think you're doing?" she said on a gasp of outrage and pleasure.

"Fingering you."

Her heart skipped a beat. How arousing his words were. How much she wanted to give in to this beautiful stranger and his magic hands.

"Unbutton your sweater," he commanded, then kissed her jaw so softly she thought she might have dreamed it. For reasons she could not decipher, she did as he asked. His eyes darkened further and she felt him begin to stroke her in a rhythm was that was unhurried and deep.

"Bare your breasts," he whispered against her neck. She did and he trailed his tongue along her neck as he slipped another finger into her. "Now then, slide the blanket so that I can see them." She stiffened and darted her eyes back to the sleeping passengers. "Do it."

She did and she saw that he dropped his eyes to the blanket, watching as she revealed her breast. He smiled slowly then gazed back at her. "I know your every secret desire, Julia. I know what you yearn for, and I'm going to give it to you."

She began to shake her head, but he grinned and chuckled deep in his throat. "Oh yes, Julia," he purred, lowering his head so that he could flick his tongue along her aching nipple. "It is much too late to turn back now. I have you where I want you. Now then," he said before sucking her nipple between his full lips. "Take off your panties and let me feel of all of you. I want you spread wide for me."

She did as he asked, all the time wondering if she truly had lost her mind. "Now then, Julia," he said, looking up from her breast and watching her with his dark, mysterious eyes. "Tell me you want this."

"Please," she whispered. He captured her mouth in his and the last coherent thought that filtered through her mind was that he felt the very same way as he did in her dreams.

She really was going mad....

Chapter Four

She was aroused. He smelt her desire, wafting up to his nostrils from beneath the blanket as he pressed closer to her. He closed his eyes, drugged by the scent of her--the feel of her--wet and silky beneath his fingers. Groaning, he parted her lips and thrust his tongue deep inside her mouth, pushing closer to her, kissing her deeper as she pressed herself into the seat.

Don't be afraid.

She heard him and slowly softened. Softened and relaxed so much that she parted her soft thighs, allowing him to slide his entire hand beneath the silk and lace. What he wouldn't give to see her. To watch the lace slide along her milky skin. To see his large male hands covering her beautiful, feminine panties as he pulled them off.

She whimpered as he probed deeper with his fingers, and she clutched at his sweater before snaking her hands beneath the wool and placing her trembling fingers on his back. He arched, almost as if he had been branded. The electric current that shot up his spine was nothing he'd ever experienced before.

He couldn't understand the depth of feeling that roared through him as she clutched at his shoulder blades and kneaded the taut muscles beneath his skin. She felt the same as she did when he came to her in her dreams, but the passion, the desire that was coursing within him was stronger than anything he had ever felt in his two hundred years. It was consuming, burning. He had never felt this level of lust and passion for Fiona. *Never.*

She whimpered as he slid a third finger into her and he belatedly wondered if he was hurting her. She was stretched full of him, yet he wasn't satisfied. He wanted more. He wanted her to take more of him inside her.

Hungrily he explored her mouth, dueling with her tongue and searching the depths of her mouth. His thumb sought her clitoris--already swollen and erect--and he groaned when she bucked against him when his finger flicked her.

My clit aches for you, he heard her mind whisper. *Give me another finger, fill me....*

He broke off the kiss and peered down into her eyes and slowly inserted another finger, watching through hooded eyes as she arched, taking him in. Her lips parted on a silent pant. Slowly he probed her and her eyes closed, her golden lashes fanning against her flushed cheeks.

So good, she sighed. *Never have I felt this, this uninhibited yearning. Never have I hungered for a man the way I am hungering for you.*

"Take my cock out," he growled against her throat. "Put me inside you."

Suddenly she stiffened and fought to pull her skirt down. She reached for his wrist and tugged.

"Don't fight me," he whispered, trying to lull her into complacency. "I won't hurt you."

"I don't even know you," she gasped as he sought her clitoris. "I don't want this."

"Liar," he murmured in her ear. "Your clit is swollen and slick, it wants it. *You* want it, Julia."

"Get off me," she hissed, shoving him away. *Oh, God what am I doing? I'm acting like a slut. I don't even know this guy.*

"Sssh," he whispered, trying to soothe her.

"Please," she whimpered, looking up at him with her large, fearful eyes.

Reluctantly he removed his hand from her body and straightened her skirt. He allowed himself the liberty of stroking her pert nipple as he pulled her lace camisole down to cover her breasts.

Her face was crimson, and he traced her cheeks with his finger. "There's no need to be embarrassed, love, it's natural this attraction between us."

"I don't even know you," she snapped, buttoning her sweater. "I don't even know your name."

"Brock."

Her head snapped up and her eyes narrowed. *Tanya's Brock? The English guy with the ripped chest and beautiful English accent? Oh, God what he has done with Tanya?*

She tried to get out of her chair, but he reached for her wrist and pulled her towards him so that she was gazing into his eyes. "It was not her I wanted, Julia. I came for you."

Nut case!

Wrenching her hand free, Julia got gracelessly up from the chair and stumbled. High heels and weak knees did not make it easy for her to steady herself as she turned in the direction of the lavatory.

"Julia." He reached for her hand. "You cannot run from me. There is no place for you to go. You might as well just stay in this chair."

"Not on your life," she snapped, tugging her wrist.

"I will not touch you if that is what you want."

He studied her, as if he were trying to decipher her emotions. Damn her sexual needs. She was still on fire for him, could still feel her clitoris throbbing with unrequited yearning. He grinned, his eyes twinkling, and she knew, *knew* that he could read her thoughts.

With a vicious oath she yanked her hand from his and turned on her heel, praying she would not disgrace herself--praying he could not see how her knees shook.

Good Heavens. How is it possible you are a descendent of mine?

Julia raised her chin and refused to listen to the nagging female voice inside her head.

What are you running from? The clipped accent was filled with a note of exasperation and disappointment. *You felt desire for the man, Julia, and he for you.*

Julia ignored the voice and walked down the aisle till she reached the business class section of the plane. There before her were numerous empty seats.

For pity's sake, surely you can see he planned this. He arranged all of this just to be alone with you. He wanted you in his arms. I really can not understand why you find it so hard to let yourself love or feel the desire he provokes in you.

"Leave me alone," she murmured beneath her breath. Straightening her sweater, she strolled down the aisle to a row of empty seats.

Running away will accomplish nothing, Julia. You have needs--needs only he want to fulfill. And at the moment, you seem completely oblivious to the possibilities.

"I do not fool around with men I don't even know," she muttered, mostly to convince herself of that fact. Any longer, and she would have definitely found herself doing more than just fooling around with him.

Finally she reached the empty row. As she glanced down the row she saw that a chair was pushed back and someone was sleeping. Gingerly she lowered herself to the chair and smoothed her skirt down her thighs. Her legs were still trembling she noticed, and her panties, soaked with her desire, felt cool against her heated flesh.

"Jules?"

Her breath froze in her lungs. Her eyes went impossibly wide. It couldn't be.

"It is you." Julia looked to her right and saw Scott push his chair up. His brown hair was mussed and he wiped it from his brow. "My God, I can't believe it. How did...."

"I didn't know you were on this flight," she began, her tongue thick in her mouth.

"Your mother," he said, then swallowed convulsively. "Your mother said you were spending Christmas in London. It's not like you, Jules."

He doesn't understand a bloody thing about you, does he?

Brock's irate voice penetrated her thoughts. Quickly she shut him out. "It's a research trip," she muttered, looking away from Scott's inquisitive brown eyes. "Besides, I thought you were going to the islands."

"Jules," he whispered, reaching out to stroke her cheek. "Baby, I've missed you so much."

Her body stiffened, and she felt Brock trying to reach her. Damn him, what sort of freak was he? What was happening to her?

"Babe?" Scott asked, his voice concerned. "Jules, are you crying, honey?"

These voices, she wanted to scream. These damn voices won't leave me alone. And my dreams ... I can't forget them, or *him*. What is wrong with me? I'm going mad. I'm dreaming of a stranger, of ... of ... what? Of fucking him? Oh God, she had nearly had sex with Brock, right in the middle of the first class cabin. And she had wanted to, still wanted to.

"Come here, baby," Scott said, reaching for her.

Come to me, Julia.

She heard Brock's command and ignored it. Instead, she allowed Scott to take her in his arms and hold her tight.

Do not make the mistake of incurring my anger, Julia. I will not lose you, not when I've just found you.

"It's all right, baby," Scott soothed, rocking her back and forth. "I know this whole thing is a shock. I know you're hurting. And I'm hurting, too. I was on my way to London to find you. I have to tell you. I love you, Jules."

She looked up at Scott through a veil of her hair and a mist of tears. She tried to think of only Scott. Tried to think of what he was telling her, but Brock's voice, dark and dangerous overruled whatever it was Scott was saying.

You're mine.

A shiver snaked down her spine and she looked up from Scott's shoulder to find him standing before her, his eyes dark and unreadable.

He can't worship you the way I will. He can't give you the pleasure that I can. He won't love you the way I love you.

She met his gaze and knew, however strange it might be, that he meant the words.

"Come," he said, his voice a dark whisper. He held out his hand and she pulled away from Scott's embrace as if she were in a trance.

Come to me. She heard the words again, and slowly, as if in a dream, she placed her hand in his.

Chapter Five

The remainder of the flight was excruciating agony. An hour of trying to understand Brock, of trying to get him to enter her mind proved useless. Instead, he sat perfectly straight, his eyes focused on clouds outside the plane, his finger resting pensively on his lip.

She shivered and straightened away from him, trying to put some distance between them, but he reached for her hand and grasped it in his warm one. She did not know what to make of him. His touch was gentle, like that of a lover, but his face was a mask of fury, an anger that clearly radiated from him.

The plane began its descent and Julia stiffened, forgetting the strange circumstances she now found herself in. Fear replaced confusion and she shifted restlessly in the chair.

Let me hold you, Julia, and I will keep you safe.

Her gaze met his and he opened his arms and lifted her onto his lap and tucked her close to his chest so that her face rested against his neck.

She knew that the flight crew would be around, checking to see that everyone was strapped in. It would only be a matter of minutes before she would find herself buckled in her seat, bereft of Brock's arms.

"Ssh," he murmured in her hair while his hand stroked her side. "Nothing--*no one* shall tear you from my arms."

She trembled, and the fear of the descent and the landing subsided, replaced by an aching awareness that settled deep in her chest. He was giving her the succour she had always desired. The caring, the selflessness that she had always wanted from Scott and never got. She so wanted this--his gentleness and loving touch. Her heart ached for it. Her body ached it for it. And suddenly she knew that he was the only man who could give her this. Who could take care of her and love her and cherish her as if she were the most priceless thing in the world.

Who was this beautiful stranger that had the ability to enter her mind and her dreams? That filled her body with such addicting passion that she felt aroused just thinking of what he had done to her? What did this man represent in her life?

"Your past," he whispered, peering down into her face. He traced her lips with the tip of his finger and slowly lowered his head until his lips grazed hers. "Your present." He kissed her softly and trailed his finger along her jaw. "Your future." She blinked, feeling a wave of magic weave itself around her. "I am your dream companion, your friend, your lover, your life."

And then he captured her lips in his and kissed her softly, with drugging intensity, so that she was clinging to him and sliding her tongue in his mouth, and he was cupping her bottom and sliding his hands beneath her skirt and rubbing his fingers along her satin panties.

Mine, he said, over and over. *You're mine*. He repeated it again and again, hypnotizing her with his melodic voice until she was aware of nothing else, only him. Only her in his arms.

* * * *

"Thanks for helping me through the flight." Julia's words came floating back to him and he mentally brought forth the vision of Julia reaching up on her tiptoes and kissing him on the cheek. "See you around," she murmured, reaching for her luggage that sat on the floor beside her.

"You're not leaving me."

She looked up, her eyes narrowing. "I beg your pardon."

"I'm coming with you--to Harrow Lodge." Brock smiled to himself as he remembered Julia's astonished expression.

"What do you mean?" she'd asked, gripping his arm as he maneuvered them through the crowded terminal.

"I own Harrow Lodge," he replied, watching her eyes widen in surprise.

"No," she said shaking her head. "That's impossible. You can't have known about where I'm staying," she said, attempting to pull away from him. "This is nuts. What are you, some kind of stalker?"

He'd seen the fear in her eyes and he felt that fear coursing through her fingers as she tried frantically to peel her fingers off his arm. *He's going to kill me.* He remembered the words as they filtered through her sub consciousness. *He's stalking me and now he's going to kill me. Stupid, so stupid to have fallen for this elaborate hoax.*

"My car is waiting, Julia, and I swear to you, I have no intention of harming you. Trust me. Forget what your brain is telling you, and feel what your heart is saying. Look at me, do I look like I want to hurt you? *Feel*, the answer."

She stared up at him for a long time, and after what felt like a lifetime, she slowly nodded, although he knew that it was rather reluctant. She still did not trust him. It had taken her at least a half hour in the limousine before she could relax. She hadn't said a word, but just stared out the window. She had finally fallen to sleep, and he had brought her close to him as she slept quietly. He did not want Julia to fear him.

The snow was coming down softly, the wipers brushing the flakes from the windshield as quickly as they landed. Brock looked out into the darkness, the white crystals illuminated by the moon and the streetlights. He was home at last. In London, the city of his birth, the city of his life.

Julia snuggled sleepily up against him and he brought his arm around her, folding her closer to him. Good Lord, he didn't think he could stand the torture of driving the remaining twenty minutes it would take to arrive at Harrow Lodge in Kent.

"A good flight, sir?" Roger asked, looking at him in the rearview mirror.

"Indeed," he replied, watching as Roger turned the volume up on the radio.

"Don't mind, do you, sir?" he asked. "It's me favorite carol."

The strains of God Rest Ye Merry Gentlemen filtered through the car, drawing him back to another time. A time when there had been no cars or airplanes, cell phones or the internet.

He closed his eyes and rested his head against the leather seat. He thought of that night, so long ago, nearly two centuries ago now. The yearly Harrington Christmas Eve ball. How he adored Holly. He smiled, thinking of her and how she was such a cheeky, spirited little thing. What a dear friend she had been.

He recalled standing around the fire, his mug of wassail lifted high in the air as he belted out the words to the carol that now played on Roger's radio. He remembered being more than a trifle tipsy and wrapping his arm around Holly and kissing her soundly on the cheek.

"Dance with her," Holly hissed, nudging him in the ribs. "I shall, but only because you asked me so prettily," he had answered back.

Julia stirred against him, sending a frisson of awareness snaking along his skin and ending directly in his already hypersensitive groin. It was the same sort of frisson that he had experienced that night at Holly's.

He waited for the pleasant memory to come floating back. Waited to see Fiona's challenging gaze, her ivory bosom flaunted in the latest style of French gown. But the familiar image did not spring to his mind. Instead he saw *her.*

Stiffening, he recoiled as the image of a woman, her head lowered, her gaze focused on her gloved hands sprang to mind. His body tightened, and his heart sped up. It was that same feeling, the same feeling that had washed over him in Holly's ballroom those two centuries before.

Good God, it couldn't be. He shifted his weight and Julia stirred beside him. The woman in his memory raised her head and focused her eyes on him. His heart felt like it stopped in his chest. Julia's eyes stared back at him, her crooked smile was the exact same as the woman in his vision.

"We're home, sir," Roger said as he turned the car into the lane. Black and gold iron gates opened and the limo passed through them, up the lane to the stone country house that had at one time belonged to Holly Harrington's ancestors--Julia's ancestors, he corrected.

"Sweeting," he murmured, rousing Julia with soft kisses in her hair and cheek. "We're home, love."

"Hmmm," she said, almost incoherent. "Scott?"

He tamped down the urge to yell. How he despised hearing that bastard's name on her lips. What the devil did he mean to her? Did she still love him, is that why she continued to resist him?

"Scott," she said again, pushing herself off of him. "Does he know where I am?"

"Do you want him to know where you are?" he snapped, keeping his gaze averted from her so that she would not see his anger.

"I ... I ..." she swallowed hard and moved away from him. "I don't know."

He made fists of his hands and pressed them into his sides. God help him if she still loved the worthless Scott Marchand. God help *her*, he corrected, for he would not stand by and allow her to go to Scott.

"What is it?" she asked.

He met her gaze and looked deeply into her eyes. *You don't remember what I told you earlier. You're mine and I will not share you.*

She backed away from him and glanced uneasily at Roger.

He can't hear me. Only you can hear me. We're connected, Julia, don't you see that? There is more here than physical desire. We have a bond, a spiritual, magical bond that binds us together. It can't be broken.

She wet her lips and he followed the trail of her tongue as it moistened the pink flesh. His cock throbbed and he reached out and skimmed his hand along the side of her breast.

I want you. I would take you right here if you would allow me. I would have taken you on the plane but you ran from me. I didn't trust myself to take you when I took you out of Scott's arms. I was too angry. Too sexually needy. And I didn't want to hurt you by taking you hard. Her eyes widened and he felt her nipple harden. *Did you want it, Julia? Do you want it now?*

She nodded, her eyes round and knowing. She looked to Roger who met her gaze in the mirror. The driver immediately looked away and focused his eyes on the golden rays of headlight that illuminated the gravel drive.

Raise your skirt for me. Show me what I want to see.

She did, slowly revealing her white thighs, then the shell pink panties with ivory lace. His mouth went dry. Such beautiful, feminine things. He always was a sucker for lingerie.

He reached out and ran his hand down her mound, curving his fingers along the damp fabric that shielded her slit. His finger slid beneath the lace and he ran it down over her soft curls. He watched as his hand inched further beneath the silk. He heard her pant of arousal in the quiet. His gaze lifted to find hers in the darkness.

"'Ere we are, sir," Roger said, coughing discreetly.

"Thank you, Roger." Slowly he slid his gaze down to where his hand lay concealed by Julia's panties.

The car came to a stop and he removed his hand and lowered her skirt. Brock's driver got out of the car and opened her door. Roger reached his hand inside, assisting her out, holding her tightly as her knees shook with unfettered desire. This was madness. What was she doing staying in the home of man who could read her thoughts? A man she knew nothing about? This recklessness was so unlike her.

She sought Brock's gaze as he stood on the opposite side of the car and she shivered. What was he going to do to her?

Fuck you.

Her breasts instantly tightened and he came around the car and lifted her into his arms. Hungrily he kissed her, then he swirled around and stalked up the steps.

A man dressed in a black suit opened the door and nodded. "Welcome home, sir."

"Thank you," Brock replied, stepping over the threshold. "I shall be in my study, Thompson. Not to be disturbed."

"Very good, sir," Thompson said emotionlessly.

Julia looked quickly around the entrance hall and gawked in surprise.

"Later," he growled below her ear. "I'll tell you everything later. Now, I must have you."

He opened a heavy mahogany paneled door and stepped in, walking toward the desk. The door suddenly closed behind them, the clicking of the lock was barely audible over the loud beating of her heart.

"Get this off," he commanded, tearing at her skirt as he lowered her to the desk. In the process, he ripped her skirt, and then stared down between their bodies. His hand reverently brushed her panties, before he captured the lace frill of the leg and pushed it over, exposing her curls and one plump labia.

His mouth parted as he stared down at her. And then he ran his finger along her. "Shall I use four fingers again?" he challenged, watching as he sunk two fingers inside her.

"Yes," she moaned, tearing his overcoat off his shoulders and flinging it to the ground.

"I want to see you in nothing but these panties," he murmured against her throat. "I've never seen anything more arousing in my life."

Jubilation soared through her at his words, and she reached for him and pulled his sweater over his shoulders. Taut muscles glistened back at her from the low light of the candles that flickered in the wall sconces. Never had she seen a more beautiful set of shoulders and chest.

Raking her hands along him, she squeezed at his arms and gasped as he pulled the leg of her panties over more, allowing him access to her.

"Show me your breasts," he rasped as he licked her neck. "I want to see them move as I thrust into you."

Light-headed with desire, she obeyed him and pulled her sweater and camisole up and over her breasts. She moaned as he lowered his head and fastened on to her nipple, suckling hungrily. Throwing the sweater behind her, she reached for him and grasped handfuls of his silky hair.

"Such fabulous breasts," he said before flicking his tongue against her. "Large and full, the way I like them."

He licked at her nipples, hardening them, then greedily suckling until she moaned, until she felt her womb clench and the wetness seep out of her body. He caught it on his fingers and brushed it along her curls before he parted her and stroked her clitoris. He watched as he did it and she saw that his trousers were tented with an enormous erection.

"Take it," he said, sliding a fourth finger into her and pulling a deep, guttural groan from her. "Take it out and touch me."

She unzipped his trousers and reached inside, freeing him. He was long and thick, the vein running the length of his shaft was engorged--pulsating with blood.

He clutched her closer and brought her forward, then he slid inside her, inching in with teasing slowness.

And then she scraped her nails along his shoulders and she bit him softly. "I want it," she panted. "I want it so much."

He sought her mouth and plunged his tongue inside, ruthlessly mating with hers. He clutched her bottom and spread her cheeks before slipping his finger inside her panties and tracing the cleft of her bottom.

"Such perfect breasts," he murmured against her jaw. "Such a perfect ass." He looked down between their bodies and watched as he slid inside her, her silk panties an enticing visual against his cock. "Such a perfect, accommodating pussy."

"Brock," she screamed as he thrust into her hard. She clutched at him and he ground into her, impaling her with his length.

"My God, I can't get enough of you. I want more. Even when I'm taking you like this, even when I'm fucking you hard, I can't get enough."

He reached down and found her clitoris through her now transparent panties. She was so wet, so aroused, that he could easily stimulate her through the silk. And he watched as he did it, and she felt him swell further inside her. It was so wicked to know that he was getting off watching.

Nothing is better than watching my cock slide in and out of your glistening quim, Julia. Nothing.

She met his gaze and he captured her lips hard in his. She stiffened, feeling her body reaching out to his, feeling her climax rushing upon her.

Nothing is better, sweeting, than being inside of you, a part of you.

And then she clutched him close and screamed into his mouth as he stroked her relentlessly until he stiffened and poured his hot seed inside her.

"Oh, God," she moaned as he collapsed atop her.

"That, Julia," he said, smiling down at her. "Is what I wanted to do you to on that plane."

Chapter Six

The log in the hearth snapped, the flickering flame whispered in the quiet. Julia inhaled the delicate scent of pine and cinnamon as she looked around the dining room. Cedar bows were hung along the mantel and along the long double hung sash windows. A large cluster of mistletoe hung from red velvet ribbons in each doorway. The scent of shortbread cookies and spicy wassail wafted from the kitchens.

A sense of nervousness settled over her and she could not help but look down the length of the glistening mahogany table to the man that was busily eating from the most exquisite china she had ever seen.

Reaching for her wine goblet, she brought it to her lips, savoring the rich red wine. She studied Brock from the rim of the priceless crystal and wondered just who he was. And whether or not she was insane to be staying in the house of a man she did not know. She had no experience with this sort of situation. She didn't know what to think, or how to proceed. How did one go about getting to know someone they've only just hours before screwed atop a desk?

Brock suddenly looked up from his plate and found her eye. "You have not eaten very much of your dinner, Julia."

"Everything is delicious," she murmured, looking down at the prime rib on her plate. "It's just that, well, I am not that hungry."

He nodded slowly then reached for his fork. Avoiding her gaze, he began eating again and Julia took that time to study him. Something was wrong. He had been so warm and passionate in his study--Lord, he had been more than warm, he'd been hot for her. Hotter than any man had ever been for her. But like any other male, his emotions had quickly cooled once their fierce sexual encounter was over.

Moments after he had lain gasping against her, he'd straightened and pushed away from her, telling her that she must be in want of a bath. She had tried to refuse, wanting to stay in his arms, but he had rebuffed her and left, allowing his staff to see her to her room. Julia bit her lip and wondered what she had done to bring about this change in him. Not pleased him, more than likely. And why did she care, she didn't know this man, and would likely never see him again.

It was obvious Brock was highly skilled sexually, and she had only ever slept with Scott, who was admittedly not overly adventurous in bed. Her skill was lacking, she knew. She also knew that her body had likely been a huge disappointment to him. She was soft and round, not sleek and toned like the women he most likely took to his bed. His own body was magnificent, leading her to believe that he favored gyms and more than likely preferred ladies who did as well.

Frowning, she shoved her plate away. Scott had been of the same mind. He'd always tried to drop subtle hints that she should think about joining a gym--for health reasons only, but she knew different. She'd been livid with him when he took it upon himself to purchase a membership to the local gym for her. And he'd been bloody furious with her when she had refused to go. And that had started the downward spiral of what remained of their relationship.

Brock reached for his linen napkin and cleared his throat. "If you're finished with your dinner, would you care to see the rest of the house?" he asked, peering up at her.

"I'd love to," she said, resting the crystal glass against the shining table. After all, that was the reason she had pawned her family's priceless heirloom--research. She was not supposed to be spending this time having frantic, passionate sex with complete strangers--strangers, she admitted, that she could easily fall in love with if she allowed herself the liberty.

No, she thought, shoving back her chair and standing, she could not afford to let Brock become a distraction to her. She had research to do, and a book to write. And she could not allow anything to come between that. She had allowed Scott to affect her work, and her career had suffered for it. Now was the time to get back the control of her life and career.

Brock reached for her hand and little currents of electricity tingled up her fingers and arm. With a sigh she allowed him to lead her out of the dining room, knowing that it was going to be far too easy to be distracted by Brock Maitland.

* * * *

Brock followed Julia from room to room, watching as her eyes became bigger and rounder. Appreciative gasps and sighs escaped her parted lips as she took in the furniture and draperies and the object de art.

"I cannot believe this, it's like a living museum. How long have you collected antiques?"

"A while," he murmured, avoiding her gaze and settling his on the window. Outside the snow was gently falling, coating the pine trees in a thick blanket. A classical recording of Christmas hymns played softly in the background. He lifted the cup of wassail to his lips and drank deeply. How could he tell her? She was not ready for the truth--of that he was certain. Hell, not even he was certain of the truth. She would ask too much, he knew that. She was an inquisitive little thing with a sharp mind. She would want to know the events, moment by moment, and he confessed that he remembered little of them.

She glanced at him and he saw that she was nibbling her lips nervously. She thought she hadn't pleased him. He had read her thoughts throughout supper and it nearly crushed him to hear her think of herself in such a way. Lord, he was hard for her again. He could think of nothing through supper but having her on the table before him, feasting on her. She was beautiful and sexy and the way she inflamed his body was like nothing he had ever experienced before. And therein lay the problem. She should feel familiar to him. She was Fiona after all, just in a different casing. But she had not felt like Fiona when she was beneath him. She did not have Fiona's laughing, teasing qualities when he was inside her. No, he had been with an entirely different person altogether this evening and the thought scared the hell out of him.

What if he was wrong? What if this person was not the one he was searching for to lift the gypsy's spell?

He glanced at her again and knew that he should say something. He should be doing something to alleviate the worry in her eyes. Those beautiful blue eyes. Eyes he had once looked into. He'd been filled with such hunger, such need when he'd looked into them, he remembered that now. But the memory didn't make sense, because Fiona's eyes had been a rich brown, like the finest melted chocolate.

"When I researched Harrow Lodge on the internet," she said, her voice a little shaky, "the advert said it was a country house hotel, not a single dwelling."

He lowered his glass and found her studying him from across the room, her fingers trailing along the marble mantel of a huge hearth. They were in the yellow salon, his favorite of all the sitting rooms in the house.

"I occasionally lease it out when I'm abroad."

"So I am the only guest then?" she asked, tossing him a questioning glance.

"You are. My butler sees to the reservations. I am not opposed to having visitors for the Christmas Season."

"Oh, so you do this often?"

He could not help but read her thoughts. *Oh, so he always does this, picks up strange women and takes them to bed. What a fool you are to think that this is anything more.*

"Normally I have little association with the guests," he said, studying her ram-rod straight back as she turned from him. "I certainly do not make a habit of tumbling them in my study."

"Who are you?" she asked suddenly-- nervously.

"Brock Maitland. I am the owner of Crosby Books Publishing in London. I am the owner of this house."

"House?" Julia asked incredulously. "This is not a house, nor is it a lodge. Good God, this is a Georgian mansion. A *mansion,* I might add, that is filled to the rafters with priceless antiques. Not just a few," she said, warming up to her topic, "but *filled.* Everything in this house is an antique."

He shrugged. "I am an avid collector."

She strolled the room studying every nook and cranny. "I have never seen anything so beautiful," she said softly.

"Would you like to see the ballroom?"

"Yes," she said, her eyes lighting with excitement tempered with wariness. "That would be excellent for my research."

He nodded and ushered her through the door. They walked down the long corridor in silence. He saw her flipping through her notepad to an empty page. He wondered what she was writing in that pad of hers. Suddenly he had the mad urge to tear it from her hands, to see if there was anything about him in there.

"Here we are," he said, pushing the door open. She followed him in. She looked about and immediately dropped the notepad.

"I've been here before," she whispered, her voice wavering with emotion. "I've danced here," she said, trancelike, walking slowly about the room, her eyes scouring every inch of the gilded plasters.

He studied her, wondering if she was recalling the ball at Holly's. He had danced numerous times that night with Fiona. He had even stolen a kiss and a grope in the corner by the fireplace.

Julia's head snapped to the fireplace, and her eyes focused on the shadowed corner of the ballroom. Her eyes darkened and shaking fingers reached out to her lips. She was remembering. Soon she would remember everything. Soon she would know that they were meant to be together.

"I've never dreamed of this place," she whispered, almost to herself, "and yet I know that I've been here. I've sat in the corner of this ballroom many times." She shivered and wrapped her arms about her, rubbing her hands along her upper arms. "I've watched from the shadows, watched the dancers, the gentlemen smiling at the ladies as they twirled by. I've watched, desiring the same for myself."

"No," he said, stepping close to her so that he could run his finger along her back. "No, you never had to watch from the periphery. You were always the light of the ball. You always threw yourself into the fray."

She whirled around and he knew that somehow this was not Julia staring back up at him. Nor, he thought, swallowing hard, was it Fiona.

"You're wrong."

Her voice was softer, infused with a haunting sadness that quickly engulfed him, sending the hairs on the nape of his neck rising sharply.

"I was always on the periphery, always alone. Always wanting and never having."

"Julia," he said, gripping her arms. And then her eyes changed and she blinked wildly as she looked about the room.

"Julia, are you all right?"

"Fine," she said through a shiver. "I just had a feeling of déjà vu, that's all. I always hate those."

He was looking at her as if she were mad. And maybe she truly was. For what other reason could there be for her vision? A vision of her sitting alone in a chair watching the dancing and the merrymakers? Watching as he--Brock--danced and smiled at the most beautiful creature she had ever seen.

Maybe she was losing it, imagining he could penetrate her thoughts and read her mind. Imagining that he had wanted her as fiercely as she wanted him.

She was embarrassed by her strange behavior. But really, she could not shake the feeling that she had when she'd entered the room. She had ceased to be Julia, and had suddenly become someone else. Someone just as insignificant and bland as she was. Someone ignored, someone crying out to be loved and cherished.

"Perhaps I should return to my room," she whispered.

"Yes, perhaps you should."

And then she ran from the room and found her way to the winding staircase. Blinded with tears, she ran up the stairs and found her bedroom. Slamming the door, she rested against it, her chest heaving as tears streamed down her eyes.

Good God what was happening to her? She was going mad. She was hearing things that weren't being said, seeing things that weren't real. Oh God, she had never felt more alone.

No, my darling, the voice whispered softly from the recess of her mind. *Never alone.*

"Go away," she cried, covering her ears with her hands. The soft voice no longer echoed in her head. It was in the room with her. "You're not real."

Believing is often a leap of faith, Julia, and in time you will accept the truth that has brought you here. Brought you home.

"No," she shouted, turning so that she was shielding her face against the cold wooden door. "I don't believe. I *won't* believe."

In time you will. In time you will be able to accept the truth.

"I want to go home," Julia whispered through a sob.

You are home, Julia.

Slowly she lowered her hands from her face and turned to look into the empty room. As if in a dream, a form started to take shape out of vapor, and slowly she recognized the figure of the Grand Dame begin to take shape. It wasn't possible. She was going mad. She couldn't actually be seeing her ancestor, her great-grandmother several generations removed.

First it was the white pompadour wig, covered in pearls and emeralds. Then the white powered face and the deep blue eyes that sparkled with laugher and the sweet and gentle expression.

The dress she wore was identical to the one in her portrait. It was rich blue silk with ivory brocade gathered up in a graceful swag on either side of her waist. Pink lace edged her square bodice while a delicate bow of pink nestled at the vee of her gown. The same pink lace trimming on her bodice edged the cuffs of her sleeves that ended just below her elbows.

"You could not see me, Julia if you did not believe at least a little."

Her vision began to swim and slowly she allowed herself to sink to the floor. "This is too much. I've lost it."

"But you will find it, dear," the Grand Dame said, smiling as she floated over to her. "Before the night is through, I shall show you your past and give you a glimpse of your destiny."

"No," she said, her voice sounding almost like a whimper. "No, I won't believe this. I'm overtired. Too much stress. That's all."

"Is that what your heart tells you, Julia?"

"My mind," she screamed at the vision before getting up and running to the phone.

"Whatever are you doing now?"

"Getting the hell out of here."

"Why ever would you want to?"

"Because I'm going insane, don't you see? First of all I'm talking to the ghost of a person that has been dead for two hundred and fifty years. Second, I'm staying in the house of man who lives in a bloody museum and who I think can enter my mind and my dreams."

"He can, and quite well I imagine, considering your reaction," the Grand Dame said with an amused smile.

"Bullshit," Julia snapped, reaching for the phone. She dialed Scott's cell phone number and prayed he had it with him and that it was on. On the fifth ring she despaired that she would be that lucky.

"Hello?"

"Scott?" she cried, falling apart when she heard his voice.

"Jules?" he said, his words almost breathless. "Where are you?"

"Scott," she sobbed into the receiver.

"Are you with him?" Scott asked. "Has he hurt you?"

Yes, the word filtered into her mind. But it was not her voice. It was someone else's.

"Baby, tell me where you are, and I will come and get you."

"Where are you?" she asked through choking sobs.

"Green Park hotel in London. I just got in. I spent four hours searching the airport for you. How did you get through customs so fast?"

"I ... I don't know. I don't remember," she mumbled, rubbing her head and trying to think of the events that had led her to Brock's home.

"Where are you, Julia?" Scott asked, his voice rising in panic.

"Harrow Lodge in Kent."

"I'm coming," Scott said. "Stay there and stay in your room. Don't let him near you. Do you understand me, Jules? Stay away from that guy."

The line clicked off and Julia clutched the phone to her chest. Why had she called Scott? He was going to think she was nuts when he arrived. She didn't want him seeing her this weak and broken and blubbering like an imbecile.

She hung up the receiver and looked about her room. It was empty, save for the movement of the curtain. And then she felt it, a cool draft and the curtain billowed once, then stopped.

She shivered and sat on the bed. Pulling down the bedcovers, she got into the bed and brought the blankets up to her throat.

How long would it take for Scott to get here? And why did she suddenly have the compulsion to call him and tell him not to bother?

* * * *

The brandy infused his veins with warmth, and slowly Brock let himself slide deeper into the chair that sat before the hearth. The log cracked, sending orange flame shooting up the flu. Crossing his legs, he stared into the flames, allowing himself to be transported back in time to the last night of his natural life, Christmas Eve 1805.

He'd been enjoying himself, drinking and singing and making merry. Holly was busy falling in love with Andrew Nightingale and he laughed, recalling how easily the rogue had won her heart.

He also recalled that he had been following Fiona about for most of the night, trying to get her to escape to an empty room so that they could replay the events of the night before, but she was proving difficult. Always a teasing minx, he thought, sipping his brandy and seeing another person in the flickering flames. James MacGregor had been there also, trailing after Fiona. He had seen some very strange looks pass between the two of them. He'd thought very little of it at the time, but now that he was more attuned to his memories he saw that they were strange, intent looks--intimate looks. He saw the image of himself looking over his shoulder, searching for Fiona and his gaze landed on a quiet creature in the corner.

His hand gripped the brandy and he skipped over the memory. The memory of Juliet Hastings, the shy, awkward friend of Holly. The girl Holly had made him take pity upon and dance with. The same dance that Fiona had spent in MacGregor's arms.

His belly knotted and he felt a sharp stab of regret. While he had danced with Juliet, he had been less than a graceful partner. He had ignored her, had disregarded the way her fingers had trembled in his, the way she had trod on his boots in her nervousness. He had not looked at her and instead allowed his attention to be focused on Fiona. He hadn't spoken to Juliet, instead he had kept every one of his senses riveted on Fiona, trying to hear what MacGregor had said to make her smile so brightly.

Mindlessly he turned Juliet about the room, all but ignoring her as his body moved in a practiced, unconscious way. And then for some unknown reason, he allowed his eyes to trail away from Fiona and down to the upturned face of his partner.

Sapphire blue eyes met his and he stared down at her, almost hypnotized by their glistening depths. She said nothing as he scrutinized her, but bore his curiosity well. His gaze slipped down to her red, bow mouth and he felt his heart begin to hammer a mad beat. His head lowered and he felt her warm breath brush his cheek. He studied her lips, feeling them beckoning to him. He forgot everything, Fiona, MacGregor, even the fact that they were in Holly Harrington's ballroom in front of dozens of people.

He was just closing his eyes and giving in to the inevitable, when the music stopped and she stepped out of his arms. She turned from him and he saw himself reach out to her and clasp her hand. She looked shyly up at him and smiled. That smile, that warm, sensual smile was the reason for the heat that had filled his veins.

"Thank you for dancing with me," she had whispered. "I know you would have rathered it was someone else."

"No," he shook his head, clutching her hand tightly in his.

"No lies, Your Grace," she said, her blue eyes turning misty. "Let us just leave it as such."

And then she had left, melting in to the crowd. From the corner of his eye he saw MacGregor usher Fiona from the room and he felt curiously devoid of any proper feeling. The only feeling that he wanted to experience was the warmth and the flush of yearning that infused his veins when Juliet Hastings had stared hopefully up into his face.

He'd followed her--Juliet--onto the terrace. Waited for her. There was something about her, something that warmed him, something that made him want to be a better man and he never felt that way ever before. And then she had appeared and he looked down into her face and felt the ice that had built up around his heart begin to melt and suddenly he knew that this woman was special.

He'd bent his head, his lips so close to hers, her breath mingling with his, and then Fiona had appeared, gasping and crying and she had ruined it all. Both women had run from him, and he'd been torn, literally felt himself being ripped in two, unable to decide his path. He recalled standing on the terrace, a feeling of helplessness churning inside him as he tried to decide which path to take. And then he'd heard it, the crack of a whip and the creaking of carriage wheels down the cobbled drive, and he had run around the house, only to see a red cape billowing out from atop the carriage box.

The carriage recklessly rambled down the drive, and he tasted the fear. Both women had been wearing red capes. Both women had run from him. As he reached for the reins of a horse, he hefted himself into the saddle, not knowing which woman he chased. The only thing he was certain of was that the woman who was driving the carriage that was near to out of control was his destiny.

"Foolish man, she is not for you."

The gypsy's words suddenly floated back to him and he rubbed his hands along the brandy snifter he held in his lap allowing the memory to resurface, the memory he had suppressed for nearly two hundred years.

"Do something," he had begged the gypsy, feeling the burning in his chest. "Everyone knows you're a witch."

"Why would I waste my time on someone like you?"

She had been right of course. Why should she have bothered? He'd never done anything for anyone in his life. He was a selfish aristocrat concerned with his own pursuit of pleasure. He'd never truly cared about anyone except for in those last few minutes of his life.

The gypsy's voice rang in his head and he flinched as the vision of the out of control carriage flashed in his mind. He was back in the past, reliving the last moments of that night. He called to the driver of the carriage, but it only sped faster along the rutted path. He heard the shot ring out, echoing off the leafless tree limbs. He recalled the burning in his chest, the feel of the lead ball that was lodged deep in the muscle, close to his heart. He felt the warmth of his blood pumping through his veins and on to the linen of his shirt.

"You should know better than to be out alone," the gypsy had grunted as she dragged him from the ground into her small cottage. "It is Christmas Eve, every highwayman is out, trying to rob your sort."

"The carriage. It was out of control. I saw it rushing down the lane. Too fast, much too fast."

"And why did you go after it?" She had asked, helping him to lie down atop a table. Then she tore at his shirt and pressed a cloth on to his chest.

"My lover ... "

"Your lover was in the carriage, was she? Are you sure about that?"

"Fiona ... " he remembered murmuring as darkness began to cloud his vision.

"The woman is dead."

"No!" He remembered shouting the word, remembered clutching at the gypsy, begging her to tell him it wasn't so. "Let me see her."

"No."

But he had persisted and she had ignored him, working to save him from his wounds.

"Please," he had begged. "One last look. I know I shall die, and I want only to look upon the face of my beloved one last time."

"Your beloved," she had asked peering into his eyes. "Your

soul mate?"

"Yes, my soul mate. My other half. Please. I know it was her. I felt her, I felt her leave me."

He saw the gypsy reach for the corner of the brown blanket, saw her brown hands slowly pull it back. The blackness engulfed him and he struggled to stay awake long enough to see the woman beneath the blanket. This was where his memory always faltered. Try as he might he had never been able to recall this portion of the night. He could only summon the fear, the impossible gut-wrenching agony that wrenched through him when he realized that Fiona had been lost to him forever. For some reason his mind could not summon up the courage to face what he had seen that night.

"You are not ready," the gypsy announced, releasing her hold the blanket and brushing her thick fingers across his eyes. "Sleep now," she commanded. "When you are ready you will see her. I will make it so you can see her and remember everything of this night."

He had tried for close to two centuries to recall the events after that, but he could not. He saw nothing but blackness, remembering only the next morning, awaking in the gypsy's home to find that she had cursed him with two hundred years of loneliness.

"No," her voice whispered in his head. "Not a curse, but a chance for true love."

"Show me," he murmured aloud, closing his eyes he rested his head against the chair and suddenly he transported back to the gypsy's cottage and that night. He could see the gypsy's weathered hand pulling back the tattered brown blanket.

"Your other half," she said, looking up at him. "Your life, your heart."

"My love," he had said through tears of profound grief. Never had he felt anything as strong as he had in those few minutes, and he wondered if he really was ready to finally see the face of the woman beneath the blanket.

"Fate, what a fickle mistress," the gypsy had murmured sadly. "To show you what you could have had. To give you a glimpse of the joy you might have found in this love you have only just discovered."

"Please, one last look."

And then she had nodded and pulled the blanket back to reveal part of a pale face, dirtied with blood and wet hair that was matted to white, lifeless cheeks.

He saw his shaking hand reach out, his fingers trembling as he brushed the hair from her face. Slowly she was revealed to him, and through blurred eyes he searched her lifeless features.

"Your love. Your soul mate," the gypsy murmured, putting her hand beneath the shoulder of the woman so that he could see her from his position atop the table.

His vision faltered, and his heart stilled as he gripped the snifter in his hands, waiting to see. Waiting to know if what he had believed for two hundred years was the truth.

And then the visions became focused and he saw her, those beautiful sapphire eyes staring unseeing up at him and he had cried out with horror, with rage. Juliet's beautiful eyes were now lifeless. Dead.

He had seen those same dead eyes tonight when Julia had stared at him in the ballroom. He had seen those lifeless eyes come back to haunt him.

"Your love. Your life. Your other half," the gypsy had whispered.

"Yes. My love. My life." And then he had reached his finger out and caressed her cold lips, hating himself for never having paid attention to her. Despising that he had spent so many years in dissipated pleasure while she had been so close to him, so patient, so quiet, waiting to be noticed by him. How he wished he had kissed those lips when they had been pliant and warm and full of life.

"You will meet again," the gypsy said, covering Juliet with the brown blanket. "I have seen it. You will have your love when the time is right. When you can unselfishly come to her. When you can love her for what she is. When you can want her without changing her."

"Yes," he had whispered. "I'll do anything for one more chance with her."

"It will not be easy. You will have to work very diligently. You will have to have her love first before this spell will be lifted."

"Anything for one more chance."

"This will not last forever. If you do not find her, or if you do not make her love you within two centuries, you will no longer exist. You will have gone through many lonely years never knowing love, never feeling warmth."

"Do it," he commanded, thinking of nothing but another chance to right the wrong he had done to Juliet. He wanted love.

He wanted the warmth. He wanted to be whole with Juliet at his side.

And after two centuries of searching of searching, he had finally found his other half. All this time he thought he was searching for Fiona. He, had believed that it had been she he had chased after, leaving a stricken Juliet alone. And yet, despite all the times he had been with Fiona, both carnally and emotionally, he had never felt anything like he did when Juliet looked up at him and smiled. The gypsy had been right to not show him who lay beneath the blanket, for he had not been ready to accept the truth. He would not have believed that one simple dance and a smile could have changed his life forever.

But he had been ready tonight to see her, to remember the rest of events that unfolded in the gypsy's cottage. Juliet had been the one. And she was here now, in Julia. And he wanted her. So desperately. He loved her--loved Julia, but she could not believe. She would not confess her love by tomorrow night. She would not. And now she had summoned Scott. Now he would never know what it was like to be loved. Two hundred years of suffering, of waiting. Of hoping.

"Julia," he whispered, closing his eyes. "Come to me. Let me love you. Let me kiss you and touch you and see you naked beneath me. Julia ... come...."

Chapter Seven

He was calling to her. She sensed him probing her mind, commanding her to come to him, but she blocked out the sound and turned on her side, closing her mind to him.

Don't shut me out.

He was angry, she heard the barely controlled fury in his voice in her mind, but she tried to ignore it, and instead she watched through the window as the snow-laden branches swayed in the frigid wind. Soon, the howling and snapping of the fire in the hearth lulled her into relaxation. The branches, the glistening white crystals that gleamed in the moonlight, entranced her, and her eyelids became heavy. She closed her eyes and fell into a deep sleep.

She was coming to him. Brock felt his body harden in

anticipation. She had tried to block him from her mind, but he had persisted, waiting until he felt her--unguarded and unquestioning--fall into a deep, dream-like state. Soon she would be here, in the deep recess of his mind. She was close, calling for him, her voice, deep and husky, aroused him, but he pushed his eager need aside. This was *his* fantasy, and Julia was here now, ready to fulfill it.

He felt her reaching out for him, felt her insecurity and tasted her fear. He savored it for a moment, relishing the strength he felt course inside him. He was going to rid her of her insecurities if it was the last thing he did. Suddenly, the need to fulfill his yearning for his soul mate mattered little. It didn't matter to him if he was able to make Julia love him, it didn't matter if he would be dead for good come midnight tomorrow night. All he cared about was making Julia forget Scott and Scott's hurtful accusations. All he wanted was for Julia to realize her self-worth, and see herself through someone else's eyes.

He knew, the first time that he had entered her dreams, that this woman he had found was not the woman he had been searching for. The gypsy was right. Fiona was not the woman for him. The woman that was his soul mate, his other half, had been that shy, quiet creature in the corner of Holly's ballroom. The lady he had danced with to appease Holly. The lady who had not been able to look him in the eye while they danced, the one who trod on his boots and whose hand trembled in his.

She was here now, his soul mate. And he was going to do whatever it took to bind her to him. For he was not discarding her as he had that night. He was not going to leave her, with her face tilted in the moonlight, her eyes closed, waiting for his kiss.

Brock?

Yes, my sweet. I am here, he called to her, welcoming her into his mind, and his most arousing fantasy. The one he had harbored for nearly two hundred years. The one he was about to have fulfilled--every thrilling second of it.

It was so cold, Julia thought, opening the door and walking out onto the snow-filled terrace. She pulled the shawl around her shoulders in an attempt to cover her exposed skin. She was in an unfamiliar place, in an unfamiliar gown.

She whirled around, blinking as snowflakes landed on her lashes. Evergreen boughs were hung along the balustrade, and she could see the golden flicker of the candles shining through the glass of the terrace doors. Inside, people danced and clapped, smiling and laughing while they drank their wassail and sang God rest ye merry gentleman with vigor. She sensed that she should be inside with them, not out here, in the cold, alone.

The wind rose up, and she shivered. Something was wrong. She should not be out here; her reputation was at risk. An overriding fear of being caught crept over her, and she looked around before reaching for the door latch and discovering that it was locked. Frantically, she pulled, trying to let herself inside.

She knew it was another dream, another silly fantasy that she was living out, but she could not shake the fear she felt. It was too real. It was as though she was truly someone else, living another life, in another time.

The latch finally came free and she pulled open the door, only to see a hand reach out from behind her and close it.

"Don't leave," said a deep, commanding voice.

She shivered, and not from the cold. She had heard those words before, uttered by the same voice. From somewhere deep in her mind, she heard them, and realized that she had once stood at this very spot, a long, long time before.

His hand left the brass latch and came to rest against her neck. It was warm, despite the cold wind and snow. His fingertips grazed her bounding pulse and she held her breath, just as she had that night so long ago.

"Let me see you."

He turned her to face him and Julia froze. She was staring into the blue eyes of Brock. Her own eyes widened and she stepped back knowing for certain that she was now someone else.

She would be ruined if she were discovered with him. He would never marry her; he could never marry someone like her. What had she been about, following him onto the terrace--for she knew that now, had recalled how she had watched him leave the ballroom. Felt that same familiar tingle down her spine as she had when he glanced over his shoulder and caressed her with his beautiful, intent gaze.

"You remember," he murmured as he lowered his mouth slowly to hers. "You remember that night. The night I first saw you. The night you awakened me to life."

She shook her head, unable to talk. It was a dream. She knew it was. She was Julia Taylor. Not ... she mentally tripped over the realization. It couldn't be possible. She could not ... no, she stopped the thought. It was utterly impossible.

"Yes," he purred taking her lips between his. "You were once

Juliet Hastings. You were alive in 1805. We danced, we looked at each other from across the room. You wanted me."

"No," she protested. "It cannot be." And yet she didn't feel wholly like herself, like Julia Taylor, the modern, sensible woman who concealed her weaknesses and fragile feelings. She felt different, as though a part of her, the part she kept carefully hidden, was suddenly in control.

He clutched her face in his hands and brushed his lips against her mouth. "Look up at me, Julia. Gaze at me with those beautiful eyes. Fill my veins with the same heat you gave me those long years ago."

She looked up at him, the strong, eerie sensation of *déjà vu* assailed her. This was real. She felt it, tasted it--the different world, the difference in him, the difference in her.

He kissed her then, a soft, melting kiss that made her knees weak. It was the type of kiss a man gave to an innocent to lull and weaken. He groaned and clutched her to him, deepening the kiss, sliding his tongue in her mouth and languidly moving it in time with hers. She tasted the claret, rich and piquant, on his tongue. Tasted also the cinnamon and cloves that laced the bread pudding he had eaten. She had watched him eat, delighting in the forbidden sensation she had gotten when he ran his tongue along his lips, licking away the sweet sauce that drenched the pudding.

He gripped her tighter, and she steadied herself by clutching his shoulders. She knew, seconds before it happened, what would occur to tear him from her arms and her heart. She heard the feminine gasp and went rigid. Fiona Montgomery had caught them in the act.

Julia's spine was ramrod straight, waiting to hear Fiona's stinging comments. She waited to be deprived of Brock's warmth as he tore himself out of her arms to run to Fiona's. She steeled herself for the onslaught of humiliation that would come as she watched the man she loved race across the lawn after Fiona Montgomery--the woman who had been betraying him for months. The woman who could never love him as completely as she loved him.

But those moments did not come. Instead he clutched her tighter, kissed her harder and soon Fiona's hurtful accusations faded into the wind. She felt herself being lifted, felt time shift as she struggled to open her eyes from her strange, evocative dream.

When she opened them, she found herself in a strange

bedchamber--one she had never seen before. She was lying upon a brocade chaise, a crimson silk sheet covering her. She was naked beneath. She discovered that as her taut nipples grazed the cool, satiny fabric.

She had never been here before. It was not a scene from a past dream or something she had imagined for one of her novels. There was nothing familiar about it, save for the awareness she keenly felt whenever Brock was near.

"I'm here," he said, entering the chamber through a door at the side of the room.

She looked around, noting how the room was decorated in the masculine style. "I'm in your dream," she whispered. This could not be her own dream, for she preferred more subtle colors to the golds and reds of this room, yet she could not dismiss the erotic tone it set. This had to be Brock's dream, for what other reason could there be for her to be lounging in a seductive pose with only a thin red sheet covering her nakedness? She never appeared in her dreams in such a state. She would never dare be this bold.

He smiled, obviously reading her thoughts. "This isn't just a dream, Julia. This is *my* fantasy."

She had entered his mind. The thought aroused her as much as it frightened her. So much was happening. So many unbelievable things. Things that shook her very thoughts and beliefs. What was real and what was imaginary? She could no longer tell the difference between awake longing and sleeping fantasy.

"Everything is real," he said, as he set his tumbler of brandy on the bedside table. "Everything you are going to hear and feel is real."

"I don't like this," she whispered.

His eyes flashed to hers and narrowed as he studied her. He looked dangerous. She had never seen him looking more virile, more masculine, and she suddenly felt like one of her heroines being brought to a quivering puddle beneath her lover's heated gaze.

"What is it you don't you like, Julia?" he asked, removing his jacket and laying it across an empty chair. He unknotted his cravat and left it dangling around his neck as he proceeded to unbutton his waistcoat. "Do you not like the fact that you are in my thoughts? Do you not like to be trapped in my dream with no way to escape?"

She tried to move, tried to free her hand to pinch herself so she could awaken, but she couldn't. She struggled and the sheet slipped, just enough to reveal her wrists which were tied with perfect red bows to the wooden frame of the chaise. She gasped and moved her legs, finding that her ankles were tied in the same fashion.

"There is no escaping this," he said with a slow smile that made her body liquefy. "I have dreamt of this night for too long to let you slip free."

"I won't have this," she said, but her voice lacked conviction.

"You won't have what?" he asked, his voice a silky purr. "You won't have me, or you won't be a party to bondage?"

"Please," she begged. "Please, I do not like this."

He stood before her. He was shirtless, wearing only his black breeches and shining black books. He looked like a marauding pirate, and the image of her as his captive burned in her brain. There was something about letting him have his way with her that was highly arousing. She had explored this many times in her books, thinking of it as a fantasy she would never indulge in.

"Why do you pretend not to be excited by this?"

Because she shouldn't be, she wanted to scream. She was a modern, independent woman. No woman should want to feel at the mercy of a man. It wasn't right.

"Not at my mercy," he purred, bending his knees so that he was eye level with her. "You will not be at my mercy, but yours--your sexual mercy."

She licked her lips and watched as his gaze fixated on her mouth. He reached out and touched her lips with the pad of his finger. "I know everything about you, Julia. All your thoughts. All your desires." She whimpered, feeling exposed, more vulnerable than if she were lying naked before him. "There is so much that needs to be said between us. So much that you will need to believe before we can move forward. But this night, Julia, this night is just for pleasure. For both our pleasures."

She watched as he trailed his finger down her chin, down the column of her throat to the edge of the silk covering that shielded her body. "Why did you not follow me that night, Julia?" he asked, gripping the sheet and sliding it down to reveal the upper swells of her breast. "You wanted me. I felt it in your kiss. We had a connection, something I had never felt before. Could you not tell that I felt it?" He looked up at her, his eyes blazing with emotions. "Why did you not save me? Why did you let me suffer two centuries of loneliness while I searched for you, fearing with each passing year that I was chasing nothing but dreams and pinning all my hopes in the words of a gypsy?"

"I didn't think I was enough for you."

The words were uttered from somewhere deep in her soul. It was Julia's soul. Not Juliet Hastings, the Regency spinster, not Julia Taylor, the awkward romance novelist, but just Julia.

"I was a fool to believe myself in love with Fiona. I was a fool to have never looked at you all those times you were with Holly. But I am going to look at you now, and the whole night through as well."

He slid the sheet from her body and Julia stiffened as her body was revealed in the firelight. He rested back on his heels and studied her. She bore his scrutiny, wishing she could discern his thoughts. She tried to probe into his mind, but she didn't know how. She couldn't think straight enough to listen for his directions. All she could think about was what was going through his mind. What did he see? And furthermore, did he like what was lying so helplessly before him?

From somewhere deep inside, he felt the stirring of his demons. Passion, hot and scorching, rushed through his veins as his hungry gaze took in the picture of Julia, her pale limbs outlined against the blood-red velvet while shadows cast by the fire danced across her creamy skin.

Swallowing hard, Brock allowed his eyes to rove every inch of her, admiring her lush thighs, the roundness of her hip, the full, heavy breasts that swelled under his perusal.

He wanted her.

It wasn't merely a need to make love to her, or to kiss her senseless. He desired her, craved her, with a possessive passion that frightened him. He had only ever felt this once before, and that was when he had lowered his lips to hers that very first time.

He trailed his finger along the blood-red tie that shackled her wrist before standing. She followed him with her wary gaze as he strolled behind the chaise and rested his thighs against the curved arm. Seeing her sprawled out provocatively, he thought of all the different things he wanted to do to her. All the things that could awaken the budding sensuality he felt within her. She only needed to feel safe, he told himself. Safe and cherished and secure in her ability to arouse him.

Unable to resist temptation, he leaned over the arm of the chaise and stroked the hair from her face. When his fingers trailed down her cheek she instinctively curled into his hand. His fingers continued to trace a path to her neck, where they shook, he was chagrined to admit, as he lightly skimmed his finger over the top of her left breast. A log cracked and sparked in the hearth, sending a flicker of light shadowing along her thighs, illuminating the curls that lay nestled between her legs. He itched to part her and taste her. To arouse her with his mouth. Already he was hard and erect, his cock hungering to be inside her. Seeing how the blood-red velvet brocade evocatively contrasted against her milky skin and outlined her curves making his cock thicken even more.

He was no saint, and waiting patiently for this woman was more than he could bear. His lust was screaming to be fed, and tonight, he promised, he would feed it. He was powerless, both mentally and physically, to control it--and for tonight, he had no wish to.

His gaze once more moved up the length of her legs. How he was going to take great pleasure in feeling them against his waist--soft, welcoming, infinitely feminine. He imagined his fingers pressing into their softness while he plunged into her, her husky moan welcoming him, telling him she needed him as much as he needed her.

He peered down into her upturned face. He traced the wrinkled lines of worry that marred her lovely eyes. She was worried, and he hated it. She took a gulp of air, her breasts bouncing as she did. He reached forward and trailed his hands up her torso before cupping her breasts in his hands. They were full and heavy, the nipples already peeking out from between his fingers. Unable to resist, he pressed her breasts together, kissing each firm bud before circling the areola with his tongue.

She moaned wantonly, arching her back, thrusting her breasts further into his mouth. Suddenly he wanted to feel her touch him, so he released her breasts and freed her bonds. He groaned when he felt her hands steal behind her head, her fingers busy clenching his hair.

"I've been waiting for you for so long," he murmured against her mouth before sliding his tongue inside. Indulging himself, he opened his eyes as he kissed her, watching his hands, the skin much darker than hers, cup and squeeze her breasts. She moaned, angling her hips invitingly. His hand stole down her belly where he kneaded a path to her glistening curls. It was powerful visually to see his large hand stroke her. It gave him a feeling of ownership, of possession. She was his, and he wanted her to want him as fiercely as he wanted her. Damn it, he wanted her to moan and writhe for him. He wanted to hear her beg him for it.

He said not a word as he tore his mouth from hers and walked to the side of the chaise. He captured her wrists in his hands; pressing them together, he held them above her head. "I need you, Julia." Her fingers gripped his hand and her legs clamped tightly together when his finger slid into her. She whimpered as he parted her and slid his finger along the length of her sex. He watched his finger slide along her wet curls, watched the way it disappeared inside her body. "I've gone to bed alone, longing for the taste of you, aching to be inside you. I will not deprive myself of the pleasure any longer."

He lowered his head and kissed her silken belly, drawing a trembling, whispering breath from her pursed lips. He ignored it and skimmed his lips down the length of her until he reached her sex and gently inhaled the scent of her. *Aroused, yearning for it. Nearly begging for it.*

Yes, she cried, and he heard her thoughts in his mind, knowing that they were now sharing everything with each other.

You yearn for my mouth on you.

She whimpered and blocked him out of her mind. Her thighs restlessly parted and he tried again to probe the thoughts she kept from him.

I've read your books, sweeting. I know what you want. All those vivid, erotic details, told with such passion but without the realization of the pleasure it can give a woman. You've never had that pleasure, have you, Julia?

Men don't really like--

They do, Julia, he interrupted her, while he skimmed his fingers along the inner facing of her thigh. *They do want to taste a woman's sex. I want to taste you, Julia. Scott was a fool to never have pleasured you in a such way. But I will be the first to initiate you to this pleasure.*

His tongue was hot as he flicked slowly down the length of her sex. "Oh, God," she cried, clutching him. What sinful pleasure it was to feel him between her thighs. Yes, like that, she started to say, but she stopped, fearing he would hear her and her wanton instructions.

Like this?

His voice penetrated her fears, and she heard his words as he circled her.

Yes, like that.

Circle your clit with my tongue, then flick it, slowly, then build you up. Is that what you want me to do with my mouth? Do you want to hear the sounds of me against you? Do you want to hear and see me between your thighs as I taste you?

Yes. Oh God, yes. I want to see you, your beautiful mouth on me. I have to know you want to do this.

I want to do this, Julia. And a whole lot more.

She was panting now, she could feel her body tightening, coiling. She felt her body clench then become wet. She tried to pull away, but he pinned her with his body, driving her on with his tongue as he pushed two fingers inside her.

Come for me, Julia. You're so close.

She cried out as he flicked his tongue repeatedly against her clitoris. His fingers drove deep inside her, and she felt him stretch her with a third finger. "So sweet," he murmured, as he sucked at her swollen lips. "So damn sweet. I could feast forever like this."

She began to pant and twist beneath him. He loved how she raked her hands through his hair, tightening her grip as he increased the pressure and the rhythm of his tongue. She moaned for him, and this time he couldn't help but look up at her while his mouth loved her. She was beautiful in her passion, writhing beneath him, searching for fulfillment, the fulfillment only he could give her. And then he was watching her as she suddenly jerked and arched in his arms. He had never savored a woman's orgasm the way he was savoring Julia's. He watched her, felt her, tasted her as she shook in his arms, a possessive, almost primal feeling invading him as he watched her fall apart. But then she suddenly stopped, and he heard her thoughts.

Not yet. I don't want to stop now. I don't want this to be over.

"Touch me," he said, placing her hand over his erection. "I want your hand around my cock."

"Show me how you like it. I want to make you feel as good as you make me feel."

"Good?" he choked, kicking off his boots and sliding his breeches down his hips before settling her hand around him. "Is that all you feel? I would have you beg me to fill you, to plead with me to bring you to completion. Yes," he hissed, tossing back his head. "Like that. Faster, Julia. Stroke me."

He knelt before her, his legs straddling hers, her small hand stroking him as her fingers circled the sensitive skin at the tip of his erection. He had never felt anything so exquisite, so enchanting.

Opening his eyes he found her focused on her task, massaging him, gripping him tightly, stroking the whole length of him. He had never seen anything quite as sensual.

God, I can't wait to feel your mouth on me, sucking me, tasting me.

His words filtered in her mind and she looked up at him, knowing that he knew she had heard him. He watched her, his eyes wary, and all she could do was wet her lips and grip him harder in her hand as she fondled the soft sac that rubbed against her hand. And then she brought her mouth to his engorged tip and licked the white drop.

Yes.

The word was a hiss in her head, and he thrust forward, sliding his erection past her lips and into her mouth. She eagerly took him and curled her tongue around his shaft, sucking and licking and stroking her hand along his shaft. He removed her hand and grasped his phallus with his fingers, stroking himself so that he was pumping his erection in his mouth.

I want to feed this to you, Julia.

She looked up and saw the intensity in his eyes, the way he studied her, the way he hungered for her. *Take me, Brock.* She let the words come unimpeded. He received them with a low growl. *Show me what is like. Take control of this and have me any way you'd like.*

He groaned then, unable to hide the thickening of his already swollen shaft and he stroked himself harder, watching as Julia willingly took the length of him in her mouth, sucking him with her lovely reddened lips. Hadn't he dreamed of that? Hadn't he fantasized of Julia giving herself to him and his wicked desires?

"Are you offering yourself to me? To be my slave? To grant me my every desire?"

Her eyes went round, but she stared, unblinkingly, unfailingly into his eyes. "Yes. Show me how to please you."

Oh, God, she shouldn't have done it, shouldn't have offered to service his every whim. But then, this was his fantasy, and he had longed to have her in his bed for so long. He could make it right for her. He could live out his every desire and still make her feel loved and desirable.

Jerking himself away from her mouth, he untied her ankles and picked her up from the chaise and carried her over to the bed. "I will show you what I want."

Her eyes were round saucers as he placed her on her knees before him. The fine flush of sexual arousal glistened on her cheeks, spreading out to cover the flesh of her neck and breasts. His own body responded to the knowledge that he was responsible for her current state.

"Come," he said, his lust at last crashing through the last barrier of his self-control. "Pleasure me."

And then he wrapped his fingers about her neck, guiding his cock into her mouth, drawing her head down, encouraging her to take all of him.

That's it, sweeting, take my cock in your mouth. All of me. Let me see you.

You want to see your cock in my mouth?

God, yes, baby. I want to see it. I want to see it sliding in and out from between your glistening lips. I want to see you want it, crave it.

He refused to give in to the need to toss his head back and close his eyes. Instead he kept them trained on her while he continued to set the pace, commanding her with subtle pressure against her neck.

He told her how to enhance his pleasure by teasing him with licks and flicks of her tongue. He felt like a pasha with a newly bought slave, enjoying the pleasure of her mouth. Yet just as much, something base inside him enjoyed the fact he was guiding her, molding her to meet his needs--to service him as his desire decreed. It was a bold, powerful feeling to be connected by thoughts, telling her what to do, and seeing her on her knees before him, obeying his commands.

She learned quickly what pleased him, what drove him to the brink. Soon, he no longer had to guide her. Instead, he sat back against the pillows and watched her, her clever fingers curled around his rigid length as she sucked and licked him.

How damn sexy you look. How much I want you beneath me. How much I want you to feel me stretching you with my cock.

How much I want to be stretched with it

"Take me inside you. Now," he commanded feeling as though he was going to spill himself any second.

"How?" she asked and he saw a bit of fear creep into her eyes.

On top of me, so I can see every inch of you. So I can look into your eyes while we're reading each other's thoughts.

He pulled her up to straddle his hips, his fingers sinking into her thighs as he slowly lowered her onto him.

Yes, fill me. I want to feel your cock deep inside--and then she stopped the words, blocking him out.

What was she saying? She was talking like a sex-crazed porn star. What was he going to think of her? Scott had always said that bedroom talk made a woman appear cheap and tawdry.

It makes you damn sexy.

She opened her eyes and met his intent gaze. He raised his index finger to her face and traced her lips, which were glistening.

I want to taste every inch of you, hear every little moan and whimper, every little naughty word you would utter. This is our passion, Julia. This is what we have together. Talk to me, tell me what you like, what you don't. Tell me how to be the best damned lover you've ever had. Tell me what you want so that you will never want to leave me.

She was gloriously wanton as she rode him up and down, her nails digging in to his shoulders. He couldn't have imagined a more stunning response to his lovemaking. Her eyes flashed behind her golden lashes as she read his thoughts. Then, without a moment's hesitation, she sunk down onto him, her body arching elegantly so that her breasts bounced evocatively with every one of his thrusts.

"Your breasts," he rasped, "touch them."

She looked at him, her eyes glazed with passion, a smile of womanly superiority furled her lips, driving him to recklessness.

"Cup them. Show me how you dream of me touching you."

He gritted his teeth as he watched her take her breasts in her hands. Watched how her thumb stroked her erect nipple, slowly back and forth. He could only stand the torment so long before he lifted her from him.

Kneeling on the bed, he placed her back against his chest, twining her arms around his neck so that her fingers were grasped his hair. He brought her atop his lap and slid inside her wet sheath, rocking slowly, as he moved his hips in a rhythm that was both slow and seductive. She panted and moaned, and tweaked her nipples until she writhed her voluptuous bottom against him.

His finger stole into her curls and she whimpered in appreciation. "Now," he whispered into her ear as he felt her bottom still and tense as he stroked the nubbin of sensitive flesh.

"Take all of me inside of you."

She sunk further on him, totally impaling herself on his length. "Yes," he breathed into her ear. "You're a dutiful little slave, are you not? So eager to please me."

He heard her suck in her breath, and he nipped at her ear as his finger continued to tease her sensitive flesh. She tightened, then jerked in his arms, her bottom provocatively grazing his thighs. He smiled into her hair as the soft cries of her release splintered the air, and he watched as her face softened into exquisite bliss.

How beautiful you look in my arms, naked and wanton. How I've waited to see you like this.

Still limp in her climax, he pressed her forward till her breasts grazed the bed sheets. He stroked his fingers down the length of her back to her bottom. He repeated the action, this time working up from her buttocks to her neck, his erection stiffening further as she quivered beneath his touch. Supreme satisfaction flooded his veins as he watched the gooseflesh begin along her spine, sweeping along her back and down to the soft globes of her perfect bottom.

Yes, he heard her purr in her mind. *I want to be taken like this.*

"You belong to me," he said, stroking her damp flesh. Bringing her hips back to him, he filled her completely in one thrust. "I belong to you as well. Don't ever forget that, my little angel. No matter what might happen, never forget me or this night. This is real. Never forget that."

She moaned deeply as he pulled out, filling her again, his fingers biting into her hips as he repeated the movement, watching as he slid inside her wet sex. He pulled out and thrust deeply, and she threw her bottom back at him, wanting more of him deeper inside her.

He was mindless now, watching and listening as he made love to her. The bed creaked and groaned under his thrusts, the sound of skin against skin heightened his senses, driving him to the precipice. An almost primal surge of possession engulfed him. This is what he had waited nearly two centuries for--this burning in his chest, this feeling of completeness, this love he had for Julia, a love with no beginning or end.

His seed spilled forth as he continued to rock against her, her warmth enveloping him, caressing and tightening around him.

"I won't ever let you go, Julia," he said against her hair. "No matter what happens, you'll always belong to me."

Chapter Eight

Daylight streamed in from the window and Julia sat up, brushing her hair and the sleep from her eyes. She looked about the room, slightly disoriented and noticed that she was still in her clothes from the night before. Then she remembered what had happened.

The vision of the Grand Dame, her frantic call to Scott. The strange dream she had of being someone else. She flushed and recalled the heated erotic dream she'd had of Brock making love to her.

It had seemed so real, she still felt it, his touch, his lips along her skin, him inside her, loving her deeply and passionately. She had never felt such passion, not even yesterday in his study had she felt such a keen sense of fulfillment and desire.

The sun brightened and filtered into her room, and she got out of bed and padded barefoot over to the window. The snow that had fallen last night blanketed the earth. Today the sunbeams shone on the crystals, sending them dancing and twinkling. The bells of the village church rung in the distance and Julia felt the old familiarity wash over her. The sound was very reminiscent, very dear to her.

"Julia?" She whirled around and found Brock standing in the doorway of her chamber. "May I come in?"

She swallowed hard and smoothed her hand through her hair, trying to do something with her bed head.

"You look beautiful," he murmured, closing the door behind him.

"I look like a mess," she said. "I slept in my clothes last night."

"Did you?" he asked, his brow arching suggestively.

Had it only been a dream, she wondered? Had he shared it with her? Had he come in to her mind and made love with her?

"What do you think?" he asked.

"About what?" she said, flushing.

"Do you think I came into your dream last night and made love with you?"

She looked away from him as she floundered for an answer.

"Or do you recall that you came to me and gave yourself to me in my bed? Can you still feel it, Julia, my hands on you, my mouth on you?"

She blushed furiously but nodded. "How can a dream feel so real?"

"Because it was real," he whispered, walking to her. "Let me show you."

And then he was reaching for her camisole and lifting it away from her body, baring her breasts. He studied her heaving breasts and she felt her body clench as he did so. A soft, loving expression filtered in his eye before he slowly reached out and stroked her distended, reddened nipple. "Do you remember how I suckled you last night?" he asked, stroking her areola as he watched her with his hooded eyes. "Do you remember how I said I was going to mark you?"

"Yes," she whispered.

"Well, look." When she looked down she saw the tiny bruise on her white skin. "Do you recall this? Can you remember what it was like when I was sucking you so fiercely? Do you remember begging for it, for me to suck harder as my fingers plunged deep and fast into you?"

"Yes."

"Do you remember how you could come in to my mind and I told you how much I wanted you?"

"Yes."

"That was real, Julia. This is real." He lowered his mouth to kiss her reverently against her breast. "My feelings are real."

"We hardly know each other--"

"Do you believe that, Julia? Do you honestly believe that?"

"I don't know what to believe anymore."

"Believe *me*, please," he whispered against her lips. "*Please.*"

"I ... I want to. But it's just that ... I don't know."

"Give me a chance. Come with me. One last time." She nodded and raked her hand through his hair as he nuzzled her nipple with his lips. "In an hour, meet me in the stables."

"All right," she whispered, closing her eyes and moaning softly as he cupped her.

"So beautiful," he said against her. "You will remember that, won't you, Julia? Whatever happens you will remember that you were beautiful to me. That you will forever be the most beautiful woman I have ever seen--inside and out."

And then left her. She watched him go and felt a familiar sinking feeling deep inside her. She had once watched him walk away from her. She knew that, but how she did was something she could not understand.

* * * *

"A sleigh ride!" she cried, as she watched the two brown mares emerge through the stable doors. They were harnessed to a beautifully carved wooden sleigh.

"Sound good?" Brock asked.

"Oh, I've always wanted a sleigh ride."

"I know," he grinned.

She shot him a smile and clambered up into the sleigh. He followed her, then covered her lap with a thick plaid blanket.

"Where are we going?" she asked, snuggling beneath the blanket.

"Some place that I hope you will remember." Brock reached for the reins and flicked them against the horse's sides. The sleigh moved forward, the snow crunching beneath the runners. "It's not far, I'm afraid."

"Oh, that's all right," she murmured, watching the scenery pass by her. "I'm just so thrilled to be having an old-fashioned sleigh ride, and on Christmas Eve at that."

"Do you like Christmas?" he asked, watching her from beneath his lashes.

"Actually, no, I don't," she said with a frown.

"I wonder why that is?"

"Well, I haven't always felt this way. It's just been the last few years that I've felt ... well, sort of depressed by the whole thing."

"Depressed? How?"

"Oh, I don't know," she sighed, looking away from him. "It just feels like my life is over. I know that's strange, but I get the blues whenever it's Christmas. I always feel lonely, even when I'm with my family. I don't understand it. It's like it's not supposed to be that way--me at home with my parents."

"Maybe it's not," he said quietly. "Maybe you were meant to be some other place."

"But where?"

"Here," he said, turning his head to look at her. "With me."

She looked away, tamping down the mad beating of her heart.

"I know you said you came here to do research for your book. But have you ever thought why? I mean, why did you decide to write a romance novel about your grandmother?"

"I don't know. I can't explain it. It just happened. It was so real, and her voice--I hear it in my head, like she's directing me."

"Perhaps she is trying to you show you the way."

Julia shrugged. "It's not normal to hear voices and see things."

"What about me being able to enter your thoughts and dreams?"

"Well, that's not normal either." She snorted. "And how, may I ask, do you do it? Do you have ESP or something?"

"No, nothing like that. Julia, what would you say if I were to tell you that a gypsy cast a spell on me a long time ago, and that was how I came by the skill?"

"I'd say you've been editing too many paranormal romances."

He smiled and reached for her hand, bringing it to his lips. He kissed her fingertips and raised his eyes to hers. "What if I told you that two hundred years ago I was living in this very village. That two centuries ago I was the Duke of Maitland and I was friends with your great, great grandmother, Holly. What if I were to tell you that in 1805 you were alive and you were Juliet Hastings, the best friend of Holly Harrington."

Julia felt her eyes begin to blink very rapidly. What was he saying, that he was a ... a ... *ghost*?

"Not a ghost, sweeting. Just a man. A man that has been alive for over two hundred years. A man who has been trapped between life and death for two centuries while searching for the one thing that can lift the spell that the gypsy weaved over me."

"That isn't possible."

"I know it will take some time to believe, but try, Julia, try to not think with your head, but your heart. Search your soul. You know it to be true, you felt it when you were in the ballroom last night."

"I did feel ... something."

"Tell me," he said, slowing the horses so that the sleigh glided smoothly over the snow.

"I don't know how to describe it. It was like *déjà vu* only stronger. More palpable."

"What did you see?"

She looked at him and scoured his face with her blue eyes. "You."

He nodded and halted the horses. "I was afraid of that."

"But you were not you," she said in a rush. "I mean, you looked like you, but you were different somehow, more aloof, more cold."

"Go on," he said, jumping down from the sleigh and walking to her side. He reached for her and plucked her out of the sleigh. Grabbing her hand, he pulled her to a bush to the left of the sleigh.

"I can't explain it. I know it was you, but you ... you didn't seem to see me. I was sitting in the corner and I could feel how much I wanted you to notice me, but you didn't. You were searching the room, as if you were looking for someone else."

"Tell me about the room," he asked quietly as he parted the snow covered branches and guided her into the dark bush.

"It was Christmas time, and everyone was dressed in Regency clothes, as were you."

He closed his eyes for a second. "I was wearing a blue jacket and a dove gray silk waistcoat. It had silver thread through it and diamond buttons. My cravat was knotted in the style of the waterfall and my breeches were black."

She gasped. "Exactly."

"And you were wearing an ivory gown with a gold embroidered bodice. Your hair was upswept into a bun and you had wispy tendrils that framed your face. You were wearing a pretty gold locket in the shape of a heart."

"How did you know?" she asked breathlessly.

"I was there."

They were standing before a tumble-down cottage, and Julia looked between the weathered wood and Brock's intent expression. What madness was this, to be allowing herself to believe in such outlandish stories?

"Please," he murmured, waving her forward.

Swallowing hard, Julia stepped forward and reached for the latch of the door. Pushing hard, she broke the seal of cold and ice and shouldered her way through. Inside it was cold and dark. The smell of sulphur wafted from behind her and she saw that Brock had lit a match and was taking a candlestick out of his overcoat pocket.

The familiar scent of garlic and turmeric washed over her and she looked to her left, sensing the little kitchen was beyond the door. Following her intuition, she reached for the latch and let the door open on a creak. Brock followed silently behind her, observing her, probing her mind, and she shut him out, wanting to assimilate what was happening first, before sharing any of it with him.

"There is something about the kitchen," she said quietly. "I *have* to go there. But I'm afraid. A part of me doesn't want to go."

"I'm here," he said, reaching for her hand.

"You are, I sense you. I know that you are here physically with me now, but you are here in another form, as well. I know that doesn't make sense."

"No, it does. I know what you sense."

Stepping over the threshold, the uneven floorboard creaked and cracked with her weight. She ignored the sound, now drawn like a moth to a flickering flame to the kitchen table that lay beyond the door. Her hand shook in his, and he gripped her fingers tighter, smoothing his thumb along the top of her hand.

It was a long table, three wooden planks wide. It was bare, with the exception of an old brown stain at the left corner. She stood before it and reached out a hand, her fingers trembling as she circled the stain. An image flashed in her mind and she saw white linen awash with crimson. Saw the pale flesh beneath the linen. She closed her eyes and she felt Brock press into her and graze his lips against her ear.

Her body shook and it was not from the cold, but from the memory that came unbidden within her mind.

"I have been here before."

"Yes," he murmured softly, kissing her once more.

"As were you."

"Yes."

Her eyes snapped open and she traced the brown stain with a trembling fingertip. "I was not on this table. You were. I see you now, bleeding. I feel your pain." She covered her mouth and closed her eyes. " I see a brown sack--no," she corrected as the visions became clearer, "it is a blanket."

He breathed heavy against her and squeezed her hand. "Yes," he said, his voice cracking.

Her body shook and he reached for her. "I'm in the blanket, aren't I?" she asked suddenly feeling ill and cold.

"Oh, God," he whispered clutching her to him.

And then she saw the whizzing of naked tree limbs and the whirl of white snow as she closed her eyes to the memories. "I was driving the carriage. I didn't wait for the coachman to assist me. I took it and was off, charging away from the house. I couldn't see for the tears," she said, feeling disembodied and seeing the visions floating before her, but she heard her voice crack with emotion.

"Why?" he asked, his voice hoarse.

"You."

"No," he whispered, pressing his face to her cheek. "No."

"I saw you running after her, that girl in my dream. You were chasing her, calling her name, and I could not bear it. I loved you--I did," she choked suddenly feeling the pain of the person she had once been. "I loved you and you never noticed me. I would have done anything for you, *anything*, but you only had eyes for her. And she didn't care about you, she didn't love you--not the way I loved you. And she had been betraying you with James McGregor for months, and I had been so true, so faithful to you in my heart. Yet you ran to her."

She stared down at the brown stain on the table and then she saw him, his face contorted in pain and she was confused. How had he come to be here, where her lifeless body was hidden in a blanket? How had he known? She remembered that the person she had once been had left immediately, ran to the mews and jumped atop the carriage, not thinking that she had never driven a carriage. She only cared about running, running from her humiliation.

"The horses reared when I pulled on the reins and they went galloping down the lane. The ice was thick and slippery. The carriage began to slide and jostle and I screamed, frightening the horses."

"I heard the scream. I went running after you."

"No," she said emphatically, "Not after me. You thought it was Fiona."

"I don't know," he murmured. "I can only tell you the fear I felt. Like my soul was being wrenched from me. I had never felt that way. I had never felt that way with Fiona."

She ignored him and focused instead on the vision. "I was thrown from the carriage and I landed against the tree. My head," she said, touching her forehead and rubbing her fingers against it. "My head hit the trunk and I saw black."

"I came upon you then, but someone was already there. I wondered if it was your coachman, but then he turned and I saw that he had a pistol in his hand. He had torn the necklace from around your neck and he was stuffing it in his pocket. I realize now that I recognized the necklace, that I knew who was lying before me. My mind knew, but I couldn't make myself believe it.

He told me not to come any closer, but I did not listen to him. All I could hear was my heart beating, my mind crying out that it could not be you lying limp against the tree. It couldn't be you, you couldn't be gone after I had only just found you."

"He shot you."

"Yes."

"And the gypsy, she came out and dragged you in. She dragged me in, too. And I saw you."

He went rigid against her and he turned her in his arms. "Are you telling me you are seeing what happened or are you actually remembering?"

She frowned and looked up at him. "Remembering."

"Impossible. You were gone. When I brushed your hair back from your face you were already gone."

"No," she whispered, clutching his face, "I was not. I saw you, saw the way your face contorted with rage and pain. I saw one tear escape from your eye. And then I smiled. I know I smiled. Maybe it was inside, I don't know. I just know that I was going to die looking at the man I loved."

"Oh, Julia," he cried, clutching her to him.

"I *was* someone else," she whispered, feeling awed and overwhelmed. "And all this time I was searching for you. That was why I was always unfilled, always hungering for something that no man could give me."

"I have travelled through every country, sailed every ocean searching for you."

"And the Grand Dame?" she asked. "What role does she play in our story?"

"I don't know," he laughed, kissing the top of her head. "I only knew her for a few months before she died. All I know is, I bought Harrow Lodge from your mother's mother because I could not stand to see it fall into another's hands. Somehow I knew it was connected to my soul mate, and I feared that if I let it go I might never find you. It was the only shared connection I had with you."

"Perhaps she was steering me towards my destiny," she whispered, nuzzling her face against his chest, trying to accept all of these new feelings and memories.

"Perhaps. Maybe there were other forces at work here than just a gypsy's old curse."

Julia lifted her head and smiled up at him. "And Tanya?"

"Oh," he groaned. "Well, she was a link to you. I couldn't deny that there was a pull there, but it was not a sexual pull, it was more curiosity."

"Hmm," she muttered. "Curious just how big her ta ta's really were?"

"No," he laughed. "Actually I found her rather gauche. I so hoped that she was not the one I was searching for. But then I saw a picture of you wearing a Regency gown and looking like you stepped out of Almack's."

"Trish's wedding," she groaned.

"And then I knew I had found you. I sent Tanya to the bathroom to freshen up and I rifled through her apartment looking for anything about you. I found her black book and discovered everything I needed. Then, I saw your IM conversation on the computer screen and I couldn't resist writing to you."

"And my thoughts? How did you do that?"

"I don't know," he shrugged. "I could just feel you, and the more I thought of you the closer I felt. Soon I was hearing you, and I so wanted to be with you that I started entering your dreams."

"I still can't believe this. I'm not sure that I ever can."

"It's a kind of magic, Julia. Don't question it, just accept it."

"Kind of like your love?" she asked, peering up at him uneasily.

"Exactly like my love," he growled, capturing her lips. "Never question it. Just accept it. Just accept that I love you body and soul. That I think you're the sexiest woman I've ever met and the most beautiful. Just accept that I want no one else."

"I think you've managed to make me fall in love with you, Brock."

"Ah, Julia, I love you."

* * * *

"Well, that was very strange, wasn't it?" Julia said, searching through the box that lay at her feet. "I'm certain that Scott will waste no time in informing my mother that I require the assistance of a shrink."

"I did not appreciate being called a Mr. Darcy clone," he grunted. "I look nothing like Colin Firth and his infernal Darcy portrayal."

Julia smiled as she studied him. "Well, you do have a bit of his arrogance."

"Nonsense," he scoffed. "Darcy was a gentleman, I am a rake."

"True," she demurred. "No one will deny that. But really, Scott did it rather well, didn't he all things considered." Julia asked, hanging a red sparkling ball on the tree.

"I have no wish to talk about your old lover, Julia. I am the only man in your life now."

"Are you jealous?" she asked, feeling an absurd rush of elation at the notion.

"Insanely," he said with a grin. "Come here, sweeting. I have a surprise for you."

"What?" Julia asked, draping the velvet ribbon on the tree.

He motioned to the seat beside him and patted the cushion. "Come here and see." Dropping the ribbon, she walked to the settee and giggled when he reached for her and sat her on his lap. "This is for you."

"Oh," she whispered, looking at the beautifully packaged box he was holding out to her. "It's too beautiful to open. Besides, it's only Christmas Eve."

"Open it," he whispered against her temple.

Pulling the ribbon she let it slide through her fingers. Carefully she lifted the lid and parted the crimson velvet that lay inside the box.

"Oh my God," she cried, looking between the necklace and Brock.

He smiled and kissed her hard. "Merry Christmas."

"The Grand Dame's necklace," she cried, pulling the diamond and ruby necklace from the box. "How did you, where did you...."

"I read your mind," he said with a smile. "Now, let me see you in it."

He placed it around her neck and clicked the clasp closed. "Tonight, I want to see you in nothing but this," he whispered huskily against her neck.

And maybe the corset, too, so I can unlace it slowly, teasing you, watching you pant with yearning.

"Corset?" she cried, twisting on his lap.

"I can see I'm going to have to be very careful around you now."

"You want to see me in a corset?"

"Oh yes, a lovely silk and lace one. And I want to undo it and kiss each patch of skin as it peeks through the lacings."

"Oh, you really are wicked."

"I know."

"The ballroom is ready, sir," the butler called from the hall.

"What's in the ballroom?" she asked.

"Another surprise. Now close your eyes."

And then she felt herself being lifted in his arms and carried against his chest.

"What in the world are you doing?" she giggled.

Shocking, a familiar voice gasped. *How utterly base.*

Her eyes flew open and she saw that the ballroom was packed full of people. But not just ordinary people, people from the ton. She looked down and saw that she was wearing a beautiful red gown and that Brock was dressed in a cravat and frock coat. He arched his brow and smiled rakishly at her.

"A Regency Christmas," he said. "The way it should have been."

"Put her down, Maitland. You are causing a scene," someone said behind her.

Julia looked over her shoulder and saw the Grand Dame striding toward her--smiling.

"Julia," she smiled before flicking open her fan. "Has no one ever told you how terribly unladylike it is to be carried into a ballroom in the arms of a most notorious libertine?"

"Yes," she smiled, gazing up at Brock, "but illicit pleasure is frequently the most enjoyable, is it not?"

The Grand Dame's eyes sparkled before she glanced over her shoulder at a tall man who was looking at her with love in his eyes. She had seen him before, in the portrait hanging in her study. He was the love of the Grand Dame's life.

"Indeed, my darling," she whispered with wicked amusement. "Illicit pleasures are *always* the most enjoyable."

With a wink she sailed on past them.

"I cannot believe that I am in a room full of ghosts," Julia whispered.

"About bloody time, Maitland," a soft feminine voice whispered past her.

"Holly," Brock smiled, and Julia looked to her right to see Holly Harrington staring brightly back at her.

"I've found her, Holly, and I'm never giving her up."

"You made it too easy on him," she winked at her. "He deserved to suffer another couple hundred years."

"Where is Andrew?" he asked Holly.

"Waiting beneath the mistletoe, of course," she said saucily. And Julia saw a handsome young man motioning with his finger for Holly to come to him.

"We shall catch up on old times later," she said with a smile. Julia watched as Holly weaved her way through the crowd.

"Always was a saucy a minx," Brock growled.

"Who is that couple over there?" Julia asked.

Brock scanned the room and followed her gaze. "The Viscount and Viscountess Wycombe. Simon and Ivy, if I recall correctly. They're your great, great grandparents. They make a handsome couple, don't you think? I always enjoyed being their guest when they entertained. The dinner conversations were quite amusing and both of them were exceptionally gifted in their knowledge of literature. Perhaps, my love, that is where you inherited the talent from."

Julia watched the couple as they glided to the dance floor. "I look forward to meeting them."

"Well, then," Brock said while nuzzling her ear, "shall we dance?"

"Well," Julia said shyly, staring up at him as he held her in his arms. "I rather hoped you might wish to steal some shameless liberties with me in that shadowed alcove."

"You did, did you?"

"Well, I often wondered as I sat watching you in all the ballrooms what it would be like to be taken advantage of by you in a dark corner."

"My dear, you shock me," he teased, but he strolled through the ballroom with her in his arms and only let her slide down his body when they were hidden in the alcove.

"Now, Julia, what would you have me do?" he asked as he caressed her throat with his lips.

"Show me what it's like to be with a rake," she whispered back.

"Reformed rake."

"Oh, very well," she sighed as he skimmed his hands down her body.

"But reformed rakes can act very rakishly," he murmured in her ear.

"Oh, show me," she purred, reaching for his cravat.

"There's nothing like firsthand research, is there, sweeting?"

"Absolutely," she said between kisses. "How can I write a convincing scene of seduction in an alcove if I've never experienced it?"

"Indeed," he said, reaching around and unfastening the tapes of her gown. "Now, Lady Julia, watch and learn how a rake works his magic."

"It's already working," she moaned as he palmed her breast and sought her mouth with his.

"Oh, good," he whispered back, "I'd hate to think the magic was reformed right out of me. I'd like to think that I've got a few more good tumbles left in me."

"Me too," she said. "Now then, have your wicked way with me, my love."

And then he was showing her just how uplifting an experience it was to be thoroughly in love with a Regency scoundrel.

The End

Printed in the United States
67034LVS00001B/63